S0-DJM-742

THEIR KIND OF TOWN

RICHARD WHITTINGHAM

AVON BOOKS ◆ NEW YORK

If you purchased this book without a cover, you should be aware that this book is stolen property. It was reported as "unsold and destroyed" to the publisher, and neither the author nor the publisher has received any payment for this "stripped book."

This novel is a work of fiction. Names, characters, places and incidents are either the product of the author's imagination or are used fictitiously. Any resemblance to actual events, locales, organizations or persons, living or dead, is entirely coincidental and beyond the intent of either the author or publisher.

AVON BOOKS
A division of
The Hearst Corporation
1350 Avenue of the Americas
New York, New York 10019

Copyright © 1994 by Richard Whittingham
Published by arrangement with Donald I. Fine, Inc.
Library of Congress Catalog Card Number: 92-54979
ISBN: 0-380-72502-9

All rights reserved, which includes the right to reproduce this book or portions thereof in any form whatsoever except as provided by the U.S. Copyright Law. For information address Donald I. Fine, Inc., 19 West 21st Street, New York, New York 10010.

First Avon Books Printing: February 1996

AVON TRADEMARK REG. U.S. PAT. OFF. AND IN OTHER COUNTRIES, MARCA REGISTRADA, HECHO EN U.S.A.

Printed in the U.S.A.

RA 10 9 8 7 6 5 4 3 2 1

*For Knox
and his varied virtues
of faith, guidance, goading,
cajoling and sense of humor*

I had Ambition, by which sin
The angels fell;
I climbed and, step by step, O Lord,
Ascended into Hell.

WILLIAM HENRY DAVIES,
Ambition

✦1

PHILADELPHIA INTERNATIONAL WAS SWARMING WITH PEOPLE at eight-thirty in the morning: business types with their carry-on luggage and attaché cases, the upscale families with assorted-size kids and enough money to afford to fly to their summer vacations, tour groups moving in chattering clusters, the porters pushing old people or the otherwise infirm in wheelchairs and giving them the rides of their lives. The aisle that accommodated the United Airlines gates was a mass of darting, dodging people, all in a hurry and trying not to bump into each other as they rushed to or from their airplanes.

All except Danny Pack. He was leaning with elbows planted on a stand-up table outside one of the concourse bars, in front of him sat a half-empty Bloody Mary with a yellowish celery stalk and a wedge of lime lying next to it. He stood there contemplating the two-hour ordeal facing him, his passionless, pale brown, almost tan eyes gazing idly down to where his hands, perhaps responding to some subconscious urge, were metronomically inserting an arrowhead toothpick into a hollow plastic swizzle stick, then withdrawing it, inserting it, withdrawing it.

The click-clack of high heels on the marble floor of the aisle drew his eyes over to three approaching flight attendants pulling their luggage carts behind them. Then his eyes hit on the man in the double-breasted linen sportcoat walking swiftly along on the far side of the broad aisle. He yelled, "Roy," but the call was lost in the crowd noise and the man hurried on past without looking over. Danny shrugged, looked at his watch and then picked up the Bloody Mary, finished it in two abrupt swigs and walked back into the bar.

"Bloody Mary," he said to the bartender. "Hold the garbage this time." When he got it, he walked back out to the

1

table, the bartender watching him go thinking what a cheap pecker he was not leaving a tip while Danny was thinking what a rip-off it was charging $3.75 for an ounce of vodka and some spicy tomato juice in a fucking plastic glass.

When he finished it he looked at his watch again, then picked up the overnight bag next to him and started down the aisle. He handed his ticket with the boarding pass to the agent at the gate with the sign: Flight 141 Chicago 8:55, saying to himself, my kind of town Chicago is, and then hearing it in his head in the lilt of Frank Sinatra's voice. There was no line at the gate because it was already 8:52.

Danny Pack, with his blondish hair pulled back in a pony-tail, in his white sportcoat with gold buttons and huge, pointy lapels, black shirt with a mandarin collar buttoned to the neck, black pants, black shoes and white silk socks, did not look like he was a member of one of those upscale vacationing families from some suburb of Philadelphia. Nor did he appear to be someone flying to Chicago for, say, a financial seminar at the Continental Illinois Bank or perhaps to present a pro-posal to the advertising department of Kraft Foods. But he was making a business trip, which was why he had gotten all dressed up.

Danny Pack was from Camden, across the river from Phil-adelphia in New Jersey, born and raised there, and it was gen-erally conceded he was the toughest kid, pound for pound, ever to come out of the Camden County Youth Correctional Center. That was twelve years ago, when he was seventeen and 165 sinewy pounds.

Danny Pack was about twenty pounds heavier now, but it was still solid on his six-foot-one frame. He was not what you would call regularly employed although he was listed on the payroll as an "account representative" of the Jersey Cartage Company, a trucking firm with a warehouse/garage down near the docks of the Delaware River in Camden, which was where Danny hung out during the time when he was not on the street cooking up something. Jersey Cartage, besides occasionally renting trucks to people or businesses who were moving them-selves from one place to another, also had a thriving division that specialized in warehousing and moving hijacked or otherwise stolen goods from one location to another.

"Please take your seat, sir," the flight attendant said as Danny stepped into the plane. "We're preparing for departure."

"Sure, sure, honey." He figured she probably hated to be called honey by someone ten years younger, which was why he did it.

Halfway down the airplane he stopped at an aisle seat occupied by the man he had called out to in the terminal, Roy, who had his face buried in the sports pages of the Philadelphia *Inquirer*. "How about movin' over," Danny said as he stuffed his suitcase in the overhead compartment. "I hate sitting by the window."

Roy looked up. "Cut it kind of close," he said.

Danny shook his head. "I been here more'n a half hour. I yelled at you when you were headed to the gate but you didn't hear me."

"Where was that?"

"Just outside the bar."

"I should've figured."

"Well, seeing as there was no chapel handy I didn't have much choice. I hate to fly, you know. Scares the shit out of me. That's why I don't want to sit by the window—looking down."

"I didn't think you were afraid of anything."

"I'm afraid of flying. I get on one of these things and all I can think about is shooting along up there and the next thing I know the plane's going straight down."

Roy was a couple of years older than Danny, a couple of inches shorter and had a body that lacked Danny's sharp edges. Roy had a circular bald spot the size of a baseball on the back of his head that resembled a flesh-colored yarmulke. Roy was another sometime but longtime employee of Jersey Cartage. It was he, in fact, who had gotten Danny the job there two years earlier. Dressed more conservatively than Danny but not upstairs from Filene's Basement, Roy could maybe pass for someone going to Chicago to try to sell a Sears Roebuck buyer on cataloging his company's new improved toilet paper dispensers.

Roy went back to the article on the Phillies he'd been reading; the team had just won its fourth straight game, which didn't thrill him even though he had been a fan of theirs since he was a little kid because he'd had a fifty down against them, taking the Mets and the odds. The Mets failed to oblige by losing to Philadelphia 5-2.

Danny Pack switched to screwdrivers on the plane. He got the first as they were passing over Harrisburg, Pennsylvania, his second somewhere above Canton, Ohio, and the third with Fort Wayne, Indiana, spread out below and the plane just beginning its descent into the Chicago area.

It was 9:30 Chicago time when the 737 touched down at O'Hare Airport.

"This is something, isn't it?" Danny Pack said as they walked along the moving sidewalk in the new United Airlines terminal with its long line of brightly colored veins of neon tubing overhead, which pulsed in concert with the electronically induced music that was about as far away from elevator music as you could get. "I think maybe the guy made a mistake and landed us in Vegas," Danny Pack said. "They were just finishing this thing up when I moved out of here. Three years. Don't seem that long."

At the end of the concourse, they took the escalator down to the tunnel that connected the airport to the O'Hare Hilton Hotel and then the elevator directly up to the tenth floor, knowing just where they were going. They saw the Do Not Disturb sign hanging from the doorknob of room 1012, but Roy ignored it and rapped on the door. The man who opened it looked at them.

"Carmen?" Roy asked. The man nodded and they stepped into the room. "Roy Echols. This here's Danny Pack." They did not shake hands.

Carmen closed the door after them. "The room's registered to John Dominick from Cincinnati," Carmen said, spelling the last name for them. "Checked in yesterday, be out by Monday. Do I look like a John Dominick?"

No, you look like that fat bald guy who was Mary Tyler Moore's boss on television, Danny Pack thought as he took off his sportcoat and hung it on the back of a chair.

Carmen stared at Danny standing there all in black now except for the white peeking out between the cuffs of his pants and his shoes. "You know, you're not supposed to draw attention to yourself. Jesus, look at you."

"Whaddya mean?"

"Just look at yourself. Dressed like that. Whatta you think, you're going to a Puerto Rican pimp convention?"

Danny glanced down at himself, then at Carmen. "Say, why don't you just go fuck yourself?"

Carmen started to say something, pointing his finger at Danny's chest. Carmen just naturally did not like anyone who was not born and raised in Chicago, preferably in the Patch around Taylor Street or maybe over on Grand Avenue or out around Twenty-fourth and Oakley, Little Italy—and he definitely did not like anyone of the male persuasion who wore his hair in a ponytail.

"C'mon, you guys," Roy said. "Let's say we take it easy. You don't like his clothes, Carmen, he'll make an adjustment." Then to Danny: "They pay, we play. You understand? They cut the rules."

Carmen thought Roy might not be an altogether bad person. "It should go down tonight," Carmen said. "Both of you should be outa here first thing in the morning, the latest." Carmen picked up a white shopping bag with a Bloomingdale's imprint on it and took out a box festooned with a navy blue ribbon. "Something from the Welcome Wagon." He started for the door. "I got a few things to finish off. I'll be back in a couple of hours."

"The particulars?" Roy asked.

"That's when you get them, when I get back." He looked at Danny Pack. "In the meantime, you got something else with you to wear, put it on. If not, find something."

Before Danny could say anything, Roy said, "He does, he will," and sent an eye message to Danny to keep his mouth shut.

"Just sit tight," Carmen said, "don't go wandering around the hotel. You guys were never in Chicago. *Capiche*? If you gotta eat, don't go downstairs, go back over to the airport, and . . ." the finger shaking at Danny again, "don't draw attention to yourself." Carmen started for the door and mumbled, "I'll be in touch."

"Have a nice day," Danny said.

Carmen looked back over his shoulder, shook his head. "A goddamn ponytail on top of it," he said to no one in particular.

After Carmen left, Roy untied the ribbon to the box. It was no big surprise. Inside were a pair of .9-mm Ruger Speed Sixes with two cylindrical silencers to be screwed onto the barrels and two boxes of cartridges. He handed the box to Danny. "Welcome Wagon in Chicago's very thoughtful."

Danny took one of the guns out of the box, felt the heft, aimed it at the lamp across the room, said "Kapow!" Then he put it back in the box. "Feels okay to me." He walked over and dropped the box onto one of the beds and pulled the thick Chicago telephone directory from the shelf under the night table.

"What're you doing?" Roy asked.

"Lookin' up, seein' if some of my old pals are still around." Danny thumbed through the book, writing down a few telephone numbers.

"You aren't going to call anybody?"

"Would I do something like that? When Fat Ass wants us to be the invisible men? C'mon, Roy."

Danny got up and snatched his white sportcoat off the back of the chair and put it on, buttoning the middle button with a flourish and stuffing the sheet of paper on which he had jotted down the telephone numbers into a side pocket. "Gonna go downstairs and get a sandwich, Roy. See you in a bit."

Danny Pack did not take to authority real well.

✦2

CARMEN STOPPED IN THE LOBBY, LOOKING FOR A PAY TELE-phone, and found a bank of them on the other side between the gift shop and the bar. He went to the one on the end, dropped in a quarter and dialed.

"You home, Mr. Manny Peters?" he said to the voice that answered. "Wait a minute, you must be, otherwise you wouldn't be answering your telephone. So, Mr. Manny Peters, I am an agent with the Loop Life Insurance Company, and *how* are you today?"

"I can tell your voice, Carmie. Cut the crap."

"A little joke, Manny."

"Jay Leno you're not."

"Listen, Manny, I know it's Friday but I need to come by today." Monday was the day Carmen ordinarily visited Manny and the other street taxpayers. "I got something I need to talk to you about. You gonna be there for a while?"

"It's a deal that can't wait till Monday?" Manny paused. "I won't have this week's tax till Monday."

"That's okay."

"What time?"

"About an hour from now. Say about eleven."

"Why not."

Carmen dialed another number. "Amalfi Club," he heard on the other end.

"Yeah, Aldo Forte there?" He waited. Aldo came to the telephone in the Amalfi only on rare occasions and this was not one of them. The voice came back on the line: "Not here."

"You sure?" There was no answer to that. "You there?"

"Um-hum."

"Well, Joe Alessi told me to be sure to let him know when

7

his guests got to town. So I am letting him know.''

The voice at the other end did not say goodbye before hanging up.

MANNY PETERS WAS A born thief. After one of his many trips to Area One headquarters for questioning about some burglary or other, one of the Property Crime detectives told a reporter who happened to be there that he had heard that when Manny's mother popped him out forty-some years ago and after the doctor gave him the pat on the butt Manny tried to steal the afterbirth.

Manny had been a first-class shoplifter as a child, moving on to burglary and an occasional robbery as he got older and eventually graduating to be a kind of criminal executive overseeing the work of the band of young thieves he had organized. Much safer, more lucrative, who could ask for anything more, was the way he thought of it. This did not deter him from keeping his own hand in the profession. Manny was portly, no cat-burglar type, but he got in and out of places just the same.

The way it ordinarily worked was that Manny would set up a job, plan the heist, then send out some of his trusted workers to carry it off. He would pay them for their efforts, then fence the merchandise at a good profit. At other times he might just work solo. At still other times he would take in things copped by friends working on their own which needed to be fenced. Manny was a swift mover of material goods. He worked under the sanction and protection of the Outfit because he dutifully passed on twenty-five percent of his financial take to them each week. Street tax. And Manny was on call to the Outfit to carry off special jobs for them. It was, he believed, a good way to keep them on his side or at least off his back.

Manny lived in a two-flat he owned on Morgan Street on Chicago's near South Side not far from Maxwell Street, the open-air market, a landmark in the city since the 1800s that also happened to be one of the locales where he had a variety of his goods peddled on Sundays, the big market day there.

In times past the Maxwell Street neighborhood, besides being a famous Jewish marketplace where one could buy anything at cut rate, was home to many kids who would grow up to make something of themselves, like King of Swing Benny Goodman, the actor Paul Muni, Supreme Court Justice Arthur Goldberg, author Meyer Levin. Now the kids growing up there were poor and mean and if they survived their teens, which was no cinch in the neighborhood, usually made their livings drug dealing, boosting, robbing people or stores. Most of the survivors would end up having their necessities provided by one penitentiary or another.

Manny lived on the first floor with two Rottweilers and a woman he had cohabited with for ten years. She was about as friendly as the Rottweilers to everyone except Manny, because he took care of her. Manny used the second floor and the basement as storage areas. He kept a couple of cots in the second-floor apartment, too, to accommodate some of his proteges when they needed to stay off the street for a while. In this mostly black, high-crime area, nobody ever bothered the forty-six-year-old white Manny Peters—he provided an essential service in the neighborhood.

"Carmie the collector," he said when Carmen arrived. "How's business?"

"Your tax is down lately."

"Is that what you came all the way over here to tell me?" Manny gave his lady, who was sitting on the couch drinking a glass of beer, a flip of the hand and she got up and left the room. She was not a large woman but looked like she could beat the hell out of Manny if she wanted to. The dogs stayed, their black, watery eyes on Carmen.

"No, Manny. Your friend Mr. Alessi wants to have you meet with a friend of his tonight, Aldo Forte, who I believe you know."

"Sure, I know him. What's he want to meet with little me about?"

"He wants to talk to you about a deal's what I been told, a little expansion, something to do with something down in Hammond, Gary, Whiting, I don't know what. But he thinks maybe he can use your special skills in this new venture. He would like you to come talk with him tonight at Malcolm's."

"Malcolm's?"

"It's a restaurant, on Taylor Street."

"Doesn't sound dago. I thought all of them on Taylor were dago."

"It serves good Italian food, Manny."

"Fancy?"

"Not too fancy, but you don't want to go dressed like a bum. He said seven-thirty."

"The *capo* calls, the soldier marches. Right?"

"Good. Mr. Forte will appreciate your cooperation."

"You going to join us, Carmen?"

"Nope, I'm going up to my place in Wisconsin later this afternoon. Can't beat it, Manny. Just sit out there on the pontoon boat, a good cigar, some good dago red, fry up some sausage and peppers on the grill right there on the boat. Maybe I'll bring you along sometime."

"That would be something. Manny Peters out on a boat. The only water you'd ever catch me on or in is the kind that fills my bathtub." Manny shot him a grin. "I didn't think they let Italians into Wisconsin, Carmie."

"They do. I'm not so sure about mutts like you, though." Carmen got up and slapped Manny on the shoulder. "I gotta go. Have a good time tonight, Manny."

DANNY PACK HAD THE white sportcoat slung over his shoulder and his black shirt open three buttons down when he got back from the sandwich he had never ordered. "I thought Philly was bad," he said. "Outside it's like you could sweat off ten pounds just picking your nose."

It was truly one of those dog-day afternoons in Chicago, humid, the air stale, not a breeze in the town known as the Windy City. From their room on the tenth floor of the Hilton Roy and Danny would normally have been able to look out over the airport terminal and see the skyline of Chicago rising twelve miles to the southeast, but today the Sears Tower and the John Hancock and the Standard Oil buildings and the other monoliths downtown were enshrouded in a dense, salmon-colored haze that hung over most of Chicago. For three days in a row there had been an ozone alert.

"What the hell were you doing outside anyway?"

"When I got downstairs I saw Lardass on the telephone in the lobby. I was gonna look around there, see what was going on, you know, but I figured you wouldn't want me to be seen by the man so I went out the front door and walked over to the terminal. Made a couple of phone calls. Talked to a couple of old buddies, and would you believe it, one of 'em told me my old girlfriend's still hanging around. She used to be married to some asshole who drove a bulldozer. Worked like twelve hours a day in the summer. She worked check-out at a K-mart, two-to-ten shift. She used to check me out every which way in the morning while he was out bulldozing. She dumped him, she told me, got a new job and an apartment of her own."

Roy was shaking his head. "Why the hell you do that? We aren't *in* this city. You heard the man."

"I heard him. He'll never know. Besides, it's good to keep up old friendships. Let 'em know you still care, let 'em know you're still on the outside."

Danny and Roy spent most of the afternoon watching the Cubs game and drinking some vodka Danny had ordered from room service over Roy's objections. A fifth of Smirnoff, some tonic water, a bottle of Rose's Lime Juice, peanuts, potato chips, pretzels and Cheez-puffs—$62.50, plus a $5.00 tip. Danny said he would like to be around when the fat man checked John Dominick out of the hotel on Monday and found that on his bill.

With the Cubs proving they were as inept as the Mets, losing to the Cardinals 6-0 in the ninth inning and Danny talking about maybe ordering some dinner from room service, the telephone rang.

"I'm in the lobby," Carmen said. "The car's parked out in front. C'mon down, I'm gonna give you a quick tour of the city. And the particulars. And bring your toys."

3

THE HEAT DID NOT BOTHER JIMMY PAGNANO BECAUSE HIS bungalow in Bridgeport on the city's near southwest side was air-conditioned. He stood naked before the full-length mirror which hung slightly off center from the back of the bathroom door, the water from the shower he had just stepped out of trickling down his body, and gave his reflection one of those "you still got it, kid" grins. Then the same eyes dropped down to his wang and he said, "How you doin' down there, old pal?" He reached down and gave it a gentle squeeze. "You won't be lonesome tonight, Elvis," and then finished toweling off.

At thirty-six Jimmy Pagnano was still in good shape. If he tightened up the stomach muscles and dropped maybe ten pounds he could pass for Jake LaMotta in his prime, he thought. Unlike LaMotta, though, who had to fight by the rules of the ring, Jimmy had never in his life fought fair, which was why he had never lost one on the street or in some barroom. LaMotta was one of Pagnano's few true sports heroes. The only others were Marciano, Graziano, Basilio—white, *I*talian champions. Not that he didn't like sports other than boxing; he followed all the big ones: baseball, football, basketball, hockey. It was just that he didn't like any team in particular or any of the players—overpaid all of them, a thought he hated, monkeys most of them. Actually he did care in a way about the major players, overpaid or not, black or white or in between, because if any one of them got hurt it upset him in terms of how it might affect the odds or the point spread of a given game.

He wrapped a robe around the body that pleased him so much and walked into his bedroom. There were four bedrooms in the bungalow: his, his wife Toni's, and one for each of his two kids, the girl Patti, who was thirteen and shy, and the boy Sonny, who was eleven and withdrawn. It was hard to believe they had inherited a single gene from Jimmy Pagnano. Jimmy's bedroom was the one with the extra-large closet to hold all the shiny silk suits and sportcoats and sportshirts whose top buttons he never buttoned above his nipple line.

When he stepped into the living room he was resplendent in pearl gray Italian silk trousers with what looked like poppy seeds stuck all over them, a pale blue shirt, royal blue tie and matching suspenders. He glanced at the two kids, who were watching television while their mother was fixing dinner in the kitchen.

"Smells good," he said, sticking his head in the kitchen door.

"Lasagna."

"I couldn't tell? Whaddya think, you married a Polack?"

"Sometimes it's hard to tell," she said. Toni, even though there was never any question that she was the junior partner in their Italian marriage, had lip and a sense of humor and was not afraid to use either of them—around the house, that is, *never* in front of any of Jimmy's friends on the rare occasions she had the opportunity to be with them.

Toni was the same age as her husband. They had grown up in the same neighborhood in Chicago but went to different schools, she to the Catholic one, he to the public school. She had finished high school, he dropped out during his junior year to pursue a street career. They started dating around her twenty-first birthday and got married a year later.

"Whaddya mean, it's hard to tell?"

The side of her mouth curled into a little smile. "Nothing. Just gettin' your goat, goomba. You wouldn't by any chance be staying around for dinner tonight, would you?"

"No, I got a couple meets downtown tonight."

"You gonna pay the bills before you go. It's the end of the month and the first half of their tuition's due by next Monday," she said, pointing to the living room with the ladle she held.

"Jesus Christ, bills? I thought I just paid 'em."

"Last month you did. New ones come every month."

"You spend too goddamn much money," he said as he started back into the living room.

"Hey, goomba, if you were home for dinner more than a night or two a week I couldn't make it on the pittance you drop me each month."

He walked over to the cabinet in the corner of the room where the household bills she collected for him were kept. He picked up the large business-size checkbook alongside them. These were the *only* things Jimmy Pagnano ever paid by check. The handful of bills and checkbook made a loud splat when he threw them down on the dining room table. He sat down, saying, "Jesus, I hate this, paying all these assholes."

A few moments later the sound of his voice drilled through the house. "What the fuck is this? Two grand each for tuition! Jesus H. That's four big ones. St. Anthony's a goddamn grammar school. What do they think they are, a goddamn college?" The two children in the living room turned their attention warily toward the dining room behind them. His rages always scared them although he had never laid a hand on either one of them. Toni walked into the room, wiping her hands on her apron.

He was on his feet now, his face flushed, a bill and an envelope in one hand that he was wielding as if he were directing traffic. "This is crazy. When I went to grammar school it was like two hundred a *year.*" He stomped one foot so hard it rattled the glasses on the shelves of the built-in dining room cabinet. He stomped it again and threw the bill and the envelope back onto the table. "I can't believe this. St. Anthony's wants two Gs each? Two Gs! Are they trying to fuck me or what?"

"What's the matter, Jimmy, you want your kids to go to that Booker T. What's-his-name school?"

"Yeah, great kids there. I'd have to get each one a gun. That'd be great. You know? You understand? No, you don't. This city's for shit. You can't even send your kids to a public school here. What the fuck am I paying taxes for?"

"Are you paying taxes, Jimmy?"

He looked at her. "You don't ever ask a question like that."
A beat, then: "No, I don't."

IN HIS CADILLAC ELDORADO, driving down Thirty-fifth Street
on his way to the Dan Ryan Expressway, Jimmy Pagnano was
still fuming about the check he had written to the good priests
at St. Anthony's and the others to the telephone company and
the utility companies and to other assorted annoyances, but
when thoughts of his impending meets slipped in he had a
mood swing. He was suddenly happy, with the air condition-
ing kicked in, Johnny Cash on the radio singing a song about
the Starkville City Jail, thinking about the fun night that lay
ahead. Pagnano liked country-and-western almost as much as
he liked the Vegas singers, as he called them: Sinatra, Da-
mone, Bennett, Martin, Tom Jones, even Sammy Davis before
he died. He wouldn't mind getting back out there one of these
days. It was just that he never seemed to have the time, all
the things going on in his life these days.

His mood, a pendulum, swung back when a convertible with
its top down swerved out from behind, raced past on his left
and then cut back in front of him, causing him to hit the brakes
and the horn at the same time. Neither of the two young men
in the convertible bothered to turn around but did raise their
right hands and gave him the finger.

The *sto cacco* gesture, at least the American version of it,
the insult of it. Jimmy Pagnano pounded on the steering wheel,
screaming. He stayed on their tail, glancing at the eighteen-
inch length of lead pipe secured next to him on the car door
which he still on occasion used to command someone's attention. *No one* does it to Jimmy Pagnano, he said to himself as
he tailgated the convertible. *No one* insults Jimmy Pagnano.
Two fucking punks. Couldn't be more than twenty years old.
Suddenly his heart was thundering in his chest. That was when
he heard the siren behind him, then saw the police car pulling
alongside him, the cop on the passenger side motioning him
to pull over. The rage increased, compounded now by the in-
justice of it all. Jimmy Pagnano being pulled over. For what?

Those dirty little kids were the ones who caused this. *They* gave *him* the *sto cacco*.

He didn't pull over, just sort of double-parked there in the middle of 35th Street. The convertible stopped maybe thirty feet ahead now at a red light, the two in it already having forgotten the guy who had been blaring his horn at them.

Jimmy was out of the car so fast he surprised the two cops getting out of their patrol car. Before they could say anything he said, "Jimmy Pagnano. You guys from the Ninth, right?" Calm now. "What's the problem?"

From the cop who was riding shotgun there seemed recognition of the name. The other one said, "You were following that car awfully close," pointing at the convertible still stopped at the red light. "You ran a red light back there."

"Yellow. Never run a red. You know Tommy McMahon, don't you?"

"Captain McMahon," the shotgun rider said, referring to the Ninth District's commander.

"That's him. He and I've been good buddies for a long time. Real good buddies for a long, long time. You ever hear him mention Jimmy Pagnano?"

"Maybe."

"I'd like to see your driver's license," the other cop said.

"That's okay," the shotgun rider said. Then to Jimmy: "Mr. Pagnano, be careful. They're a lot of people starting up on yellow lights these days. One of them might broadside you the next time. Better to drive defensively." He reached up and tipped his cap.

"Thanks, Officer . . ."

"Bobrowski."

"Officer Bobrowski. You been in nine a while now, I take it."

"Four, five years."

Pagnano watched as the light turned green and the convertible ahead started up. "You see that red car, the two punks in it?"

They looked and Bobrowski nodded.

"You, Officer Bobrowski, should want to look into my car

on the passenger side. You may find something there that I shouldn't have. It may be your duty to confiscate it."

Pagnano turned and got back into his car. He punched the button to lower the window on the passenger side. By the time Officer Bobrowski stuck his head inside there was a fifty-dollar bill on the seat. "And do me a favor," Pagnano said. "Hassle those assholes."

The light was red again and Jimmy Pagnano sat waiting for it to turn green and watched as the police car ran it. Four blocks down 35th Street, two blocks from the Dan Ryan Expressway, he passed the convertible, the two kids outside of it, their hands on it like they were doing push-ups, the cops feeling them up and down. Pagnano slowed to a stop. "Hey, punks," he shouted through the still-open passenger-side window. When they turned their heads, still propped against the car, he gave them the finger and a wide smile.

As he circled down the ramp to the Dan Ryan, still smiling, the memory came back to him. He was about the punks' age then, a mere raw street soldier, just a dogface trying to make a name for himself. That night, it was also a summer one, he and Tony Rice were riding around out in Oak Park, looking at the big houses and the sweep of front lawns, trying to find one that was ripe for breaking into. Another finger. And it was a girl who gave it to them. From a car, a white Ford Mustang, driving her boyfriend somewhere, a meatloaf of a guy, looked like a football player. Can you imagine that, Jimmy thought when it happened, a girl, a smart-ass little liberated cunt, giving them the bird just because they'd blown their horn at her and shouted something that some might have taken as obscene. No, he couldn't. Neither could Tony Rice.

He remembered Tony, who was driving, looked over at him and said, "Did you see that, Jimmy? Did you see what that little broad did?" He remembered Tony smiling now, pulling out fast into the oncoming traffic lane to pass, then curbing the Mustang.

The football player was bigger than they thought when he lurched out of the Mustang, looking like he could do some real battling in the trenches with blockers and tacklers. But on the line of scrimmage they didn't kick you in the balls, which was what Tony did when they came face to face. And the opposing players weren't armed with a softball bat, which was what Jimmy had in his hand. It took maybe a minute, maybe two at most, the girl screaming the whole time, to reduce the football player to a battered lump lying there semiconscious on the grass of the parkway.

Jimmy smiled now, thinking about what Tony did then, saw him in his mind as plain as if it was happening right there again. Tony, shaking his hands that hurt from all the punches he had thrown, walking over to the girl, grabbing her wrist, pulling her out of the car, then wrenching her middle finger back until it pointed straight at her elbow. Jimmy could still hear the snap of bone tearing away from the bone at the joint and the scream she let out.

Wonder if she ever gave anyone the finger again, Jimmy thought as he made his way through the rush-hour traffic on the Dan Ryan. He remembered saying to Tony Rice afterward, "That was a nice touch, the finger thing," and then: "You know, I shoulda done the bird on her other hand." And Tony saying, "Well, hell, nobody's perfect."

Jimmy smiled again. Tony was a helluva guy, one of the good buddies. Too bad he got himself killed. Never should have tried to hold up that Korean grocery store by himself, those gooks could be nuts you try to take their money from them. Mom-and-pop store, pop was in the front, mom came out from the back and put six bullets in Tony, that was the way Jimmy had heard it later. Poor Tony was only like twenty-two.

The Dan Ryan had become the Kennedy Expressway after Jimmy passed downtown, moving into the city's north side. He pulled off at the North Avenue exit and headed east for Old Town, once the area of struggling artists and writers and philosophers and now a glitzy strip along Wells Street for tourists but surrounded by pricey apartments and townhouses inhabited mostly by yuppies. He pulled up in front of one of the newer ones on Larrabee Street for the first meet of the evening.

*   *   *

SHE OPENED THE DOOR to the fifth-floor apartment, a small comfortable one: living room with a dining area separated from the small kitchen by a counter, one bedroom, one bath.

"You want a drink, Jimmy?" she asked as he took off his coat, loosened his tie.

"Quick one. I only got a half hour or so, gotta be somewhere else around six-fifteen, six-thirty. Little Wild Turkey on the rocks."

She was about twenty-four and went by the name of Doe Davenport, the name she chose when she was dancing in the topless bar out in Cicero, figuring her real name of Dorothy Abramowicz did not play real well on the marquee.

Jimmy Pagnano walked over behind her as she was putting the ice in the glass for him and reached around her to cup both of her breasts in his hands, also giving her a little kiss on the side of the neck. She was one of the most popular dancers ever to perform at the Surf & Turf Lounge, which happened to be owned by Jimmy's boss, Joe Alessi, known to his paisanos as Joe-sep. Most thought it was because his first name was Giuseppe, but it wasn't. It was because his full name was Joseph September Alessi. His father had this thing about honoring the month of his children's birth. That's why Joe-sep's brother had been named Dominic January Alessi and his sister, who was married and lived in Phoenix, had been baptized Patricia July Alessi.

Joe Alessi had not wanted to see Doe Davenport leave the world of entertainment, but Jimmy Pagnano did a great sell job and Jimmy was the most trusted employee in Joe Alessi's street crew, so Joe allowed her to take early retirement. Now Doe was a homemaker, she liked to say, making it at home for Jimmy Pagnano, at least in the home away from home he provided for her.

Jimmy had more than a full half-hour, maybe forty-five minutes, with his Doe, and she tried to talk him into staying a little longer.

But he couldn't. "You are a sweetheart," he said to her as he was flipping his tie into a windsor knot. He noticed in the mirror that he was sweating but he did not have time to shower, just time to wash the wang. He was so damn busy these days.

After he put on the silky gray poppy-seeded suitcoat, he reached into his pocket and dug out a wad of bills from which he peeled off ten one-hundreds. "Take care of the rent." Then another two. "Here, get yourself something real nice to wear. Call you over the weekend," he said as he walked out the door.

4

BY SIX-FIFTEEN THE HAZE THAT HAD ENSHROUDED CHICAGO all afternoon had moved east and dissipated over Lake Michigan, raining invisible particles of its pollution into the calm, blue-gray water. It was still hot and humid and breezeless, the kind of summer evening when everyone wished the sun would go down in hopes that the darkness would bring some kind of relief from the muggy heat, everyone except the cops on the street and in the stationhouses who knew too well this kind of night in Chicago brought with it too many other things—people would be outside to escape the steamy projects or dank apartments, tempers would be short, things would happen out there on the streets, in the alleys, the parks.

Inside D'Amico's Ristorante on Taylor Street it was pleasantly cool, despite the open-faced kitchen in the back where several chefs were at work amid the scents of oregano and basil and tarragon and the rich, creamy sauces being prepared for the pastas. It was not crowded when Jimmy Pagnano walked in and headed for the large banquette in one corner that was already occupied by Joe Alessi and his daughter and her new boyfriend, Angelo Franconi, who Jimmy knew to be a well-thought-of, on-the-rise soldier in Aldo Forte's street crew.

As he sat down with them, Jimmy first paid his respects to Joe Alessi's daughter. "Very pleasant," he said to Alessi, "your beautiful daughter being with us. Where's Dominic?"

"Dominic's late for his own party," Alessi said, referring to his brother, who was not there yet but whose birthday they were celebrating. "We'll be moving over there," he pointed to a long table at the back of the room already set for ten people, "when the rest arrive. You know Angelo here?"

"Sure, sure." Jimmy reached out to shake hands with Franconi. "And I hear good things about you."

"That's nice to know," Angelo said. He was a handsome young man with a full head of black curly hair and a strong-featured face who had just turned twenty-eight himself two weeks earlier. They made quite a couple. Anita Alessi was a beautiful girl with hair more glistening than her boyfriend's falling below her shoulders, onyx eyes and an unblemished caramel skin.

Jimmy turned back to his boss. "Incidentally, I got a guy coming here for a meet, but not till eight o'clock. I told him I'd see him in the bar, a guy from Detroit, recommended by Lenny Sasso there. Wants something but I don't know what."

Joe Alessi nodded. "Fine. Now let's get you a drink, or a glass if you'd like some of this wine," he said pointing to the bottles of Chianti Classico and Pinot Grigio on the table and then waving at a waiter.

IT WAS EVEN HOTTER where Danny Pack was standing, sweating out the vodka of the day, now wearing an olive green sport shirt and a tan jacket that Roy had lent him, forced him to wear, for the occasion. He and Roy were waiting in a narrow gangway Carmen had driven them by earlier during their short tour of Chicago, before he dropped them off and left for his weekend in Wisconsin. They were looking out across a rubbish-strewn alley, watching the two-car garage, waiting for the man to show as Carmen had told them he would.

"What a neighborhood," Danny said. "Smells awful."

"We're in the alley. What do you expect?"

Danny wiped the sweat from his forehead on the arm of the

jacket Roy had given him. "They could at least pick up the garbage."

A little before seven-fifteen they heard a door slam shut across the alley, then footsteps coming down the backstairs. A moment later they saw the man dressed in a pale blue sport-coat and a tie coming down the walkway to the garage.

Just as Manny Peters got the side door to the garage un-locked, they moved. He heard them coming and turned to hear Roy Echols say as they approached him, "Manny Peters, the site of your meeting with Mr. Forte has been changed. We've been told to take you to it."

"What's this?" Manny said. "I don't know you guys." And he tried to push past Roy Echols, who had circled to the other side and was between him and the two-flat apartment building. Danny Pack put his hand on Peters's shoulder and turned him back so they were face to face. Danny gave him a sympathetic smile. "He told us to bring you. We're just obeying orders." He tightened his grip on the shoulder and pulled Peters through the doorway into the garage. "I'll drive," Roy said, and took the keys from Peters.

Sitting with Danny Pack in the backseat of his Lincoln Town Car, Peters asked with street bravado, "Just what the hell is going on?" Then: "This is my car, for chrissake. You're taking over my car."

"Don't worry," Danny Pack told him. "Nothing's going to happen to it. Roy here's a helluva driver. Used to drive a taxi for a living. Relax."

Manny was noticeably uneasy when Roy pulled his car in behind the Prime House Meat Market, a neighborly storefront place that handled only the best of veal and beef, not to men-tion its array of homemade sausages in the area known as Little Italy on Chicago's southwest side. The shop was only a small part of a larger operation in the building that accom-modated the orders they purveyed to restaurants and hotels and other specialty meat markets. Roy stopped the car there. "We're here. Mr. Forte's waiting for you downstairs." The three got out and went to the door next to the loading dock.

But Aldo Forte was not waiting for Manny downstairs. No

one was. Manny Peters's stomach began to feel like it was a bowl with fish in a feeding frenzy.

In the basement Danny Pack pushed Manny up against a large butcher's table, scrubbed so clean after the day's chopping and carving and slicing you could see the fine, dark lines between the blocks of wood. An odor of raw meat hung in the air, and it was actually chilly down there next to the walk-in coolers. Danny Pack held one hand around Manny's throat, the other clutching Manny's tie and shirt, Manny's back pressed against the edge of the butcher-block table. Roy, looking over Danny's shoulder at Manny Peters, said, "You have something in your possession which belongs to Mr. Forte, we understand. He wants it back."

"I don't have anything of his. I don't know what you're talking about."

"We were told you lifted something of substantial value, that's what we were told."

"Lifted something? Are you crazy? I wouldn't do anything like that. For chrissake, I pay my tax every week. I been doin' it for years, every week."

Danny Pack let go of him and walked around behind the table.

Roy Echols shook his head. "We have it on very good authority, Manny, that you broke into a home over in Pilsen occupied by one Ramon Sanchez and took ten kilos of coke, which were intended for Mr. Forte and an associate of his. Mr. Forte was expecting them to be delivered to him but they weren't because you lifted them. Those are the particulars that we have been told."

"You guys are crazy—" was all Manny Peters managed to get out before the heavy butcher-knife sharpener, eighteen inches of forged steel with a thick handle and large foil, smashed into his chest, taking his breath away and leaving him with a stunned, deer-eyed look on his face. The second whack from Danny Pack was lower, in the stomach, the force of which doubled Manny over and turned him around so that he flopped forward across the butcher table. Danny Pack grabbed him by the hair and pulled his head back. "We're not here to play games."

"Mr. Forte knows you have been trying to pass the dope," Roy Echols said. "He knows it for a fact. So he knows you are the one who lifted it or had it lifted."

"Let's get straight," Danny Pack said. "Mr. Forte wants the dope. That leaves you two choices. One, you give it to us. Two, you don't and the fun goes on." He crashed the knife sharpener into Manny Peters's ribcage.

Manny squealed in pain.

"Maybe you'd rather talk to us hanging with the carcasses in there," Danny Pack said, nodding toward one of the coolers. "Hanging from a meathook has been known to loosen a lot of lips."

Manny could only talk slowly. "I didn't know it was for Aldo Forte. Honest to God. I thought it was just the fucking Mexican's. I never knew it was for Forte. I wouldn't steal from you guys."

"Where is it, Manny?"

"I buried it."

"Buried it! What are you, a fucking mole?" Danny Pack said.

"Where?" Roy Echols asked again.

"I'll have to take you there."

"I'll go make the call, see how they want to handle this," Echols said to Danny Pack. "Keep him entertained."

THE PASTA COURSE, RIGATONI under a simmering sauce of butter and Parmesan cheese flecked with shavings of Parma ham, had just been served when the maitre d' approached Joe Alessi's table. "Mr. Franconi," he said, "you have a telephone call."

When Angelo Franconi returned he did not sit down but said to Joe Alessi, "That was Aldo. There seems to be some sort of problem come up." Then to Anita Alessi, "I'm sorry, but I'm gonna have to go."

"Aldo, a problem." Joe-sep appeared concerned but then

broke into a big smile. "Always one to break up a nice party, that Aldo. Well, what can you do?"

Angelo nodded. "He said it was urgent. He wants me at the Amalfi . . . now."

"What about me?" Anita Alessi said.

Joe Alessi reached across the table and patted his daughter on the arm. "If Aldo Forte says it's urgent, honey, it's urgent."

She didn't answer, just glanced down at her platter of rigatoni.

✦5

THE AMALFI, A SOCIAL CLUB ON RACINE AVENUE, JUST north of Grand Avenue, has a select membership list: only men from that long-standing Italian neighborhood on Chicago's near northwest side who gathered there to talk, play cards, drink, watch television—a little bonding among the wiseguys. On the first floor there are chairs and tables and a few sofas, a big-screen television on one wall, a bathroom across from it. In one corner at the back is a small kitchen with a refrigerator and a microwave oven and some cabinets, in the other corner was a table with a large coffeemaker. On the second floor there are rooms where big-money card games and craps games are held. There are buzzers all over the first floor that can be pushed to ring upstairs if, by some odd chance, the law decides to enforce the gambling statutes and raid the club. That had happened only three times in the last ten years and no one was ever arrested; by the time the police got to the club the members had been informed that they were on their way.

In his younger days, Tony "Big Tuna" Accardo, who later rose to become *capo di tutti capi*, boss of bosses of the Chicago Outfit, used to hang out at the Amalfi. And Sam "Mooney" Giancana spent some time chatting with his colleagues there before he became really big-time too and started hanging around, it was said, with the likes of Ol' Blue Eyes and Phyllis McGuire and Peter Lawford. But Accardo and Giancana were gone, along with most of the others from the old school. Now it was *capo* Aldo Forte who sat as the big mozzarella at the Amalfi.

Aldo Forte was forty-eight years old, a large man, six-foot-two, maybe two hundred forty soft pounds, who had worked his way up to where he now controlled all the gambling, juice loan operations, prostitution, hijacking and street taxation on the city's near northwest side; he also dabbled in a little extortion now and then, a little drug trafficking, a little this and that. He was the president of Swan Real Estate and Insurance Company and owner of Beacon Distributors, a company that purveyed Italian cheeses and prosciutto and olive oil, among other things, to Chicago area grocery stores. Such legit positions looked good on his income-tax forms.

Aldo Forte was also a registered paranoid, his papers going all the way back to high school, which he never managed to finish. He trusted no one, not his own soldiers, his own accountant and lawyer, nor even his own wife, whom he occasionally had tailed by one or another of his soldiers. Ordinarily they ended up standing out on a street in front of a beauty parlor or a drug store or a bakery wondering what the hell they were doing there.

Angelo Franconi found him now at his favorite table in the back corner by the counter that held the coffee urn and the rolls and cookies and pastries from Lucia's Bakery around the corner on Grand. There were two other men with Forte at the table, one of them was playing gin rummy with him and the other was just watching.

"You made good time, Angelo," Forte said, and motioned for him to sit down. "When I finish this hand we'll go for a little walk."

Angelo sat down, watched until Aldo Forte called with four and won the hand.

Outside, they walked down Racine toward a little park two blocks away. Aldo Forte never talked business in the Amalfi.

He knew how clever and sophisticated the G had gotten in tapping, bugging, even videotaping conversations. He liked to tell the old story about how they had gotten into the Celano Tailor Shop on Michigan Avenue in the back of which Accardo and Giancana and Paul "the Waiter" Ricca and Murray "the Camel" Humphreys and assorted other Outfit chieftains met for fittings of Italian silk suits and conversations that the FBI was always keenly interested in. The G could, it seemed, get in anywhere. Forte was obsessed with this. He did not even trust his own car, often remarking if they could get in Celano's backroom they could get inside his Cadillac. So he conducted all his business outside or from different pay phones or in public places like McDonald's or Walgreen's or a supermarket.

"Angelo, I got a little job for you tonight. Sorry to have to pull you away from your little party."

"No problem."

"You see, what's happened is Joe Alessi and I were given the chance to buy some kilos of very good stuff from Mexico at a very good price. We made the arrangements and one of their people went down and brought the stuff up here last Tuesday. We were to have a meet on Wednesday to finalize the purchase. Only the night before we were to meet, somebody broke into the Mexican's house and shagged the stuff."

Angelo waited.

"That's why I need to have you do something for me tonight. Because I know who lifted it. You know of him, too. Manny Peters."

"Manny? The burglar?"

"He says he didn't know it was intended for me. But I think otherwise, so does my friend Joe-sep. Why would he try to peddle it in St. Louis? Which is what we heard. Why wouldn't he come to Joe-sep, the man he does business with, the man who protects his operation?"

"Manny is maybe doing a little stupid these days."

"More than a little. Anyway, to make a long story short, on behalf of Joe-sep and myself I brought two guys in town to talk to Manny. They have done that tonight. And Manny has agreed to return the merchandise to us. It seems he buried it for safekeeping. Said it was the kind of thing you don't keep around the house." Aldo showed one of his rare smiles. "Anybody should know that, he should, eh?"

Angelo smiled back.

"Anyway that's where you come in. Now that we know where it is, we go into phase two. These two guys are going to escort him to where he buried it. They're going to have to wait till later, maybe eleven or so, when it's nice and dark, nobody around. But see, I don't trust them. What if they get some idea of their own? Who knows? So I am trusting you to represent my interests."

"You want me to go along, get it from them?"

"You got brains, Angelo." Aldo Forte pointed at his temple. "What I want is for you to do back-up. They'll be going in Manny's car. The two guys have been told there's going to be a back-up. They don't know your name, and you don't tell them. You don't want to know their names either. I've got a safe car for you. They've been told to give you the stuff after they dig it up. Then you take the two of them back out to the airport and they're out of here." Aldo took two airline tickets out of his inside coat pocket. "These are open-end. The name of the hotel for the guy who goes to Lauderdale is written down on a piece of paper inside, the same for the guy going to New Orleans. Give 'em the tickets and tell 'em to move. They'll be contacted down there later."

"There ain't any flights that hour of the night."

"I know. They'll have to wait till morning but they got a place at the hotel out there. Just tell 'em to be gone quick as they can."

Angelo did not need to ask but he did anyway. "What about Manny?"

"Manny's a lesson." Aldo looked over at Angelo. "Sometimes, to keep things straight, we have to teach lessons. Right?"

"I imagine so."

When they got to the park, Aldo walked toward one of the

few remaining benches. Most of the others had been stolen or vandalized and left unrepaired, and the two men sat down facing out to the street. Behind them there was a flurry of activity from the kids of the neighborhood, mostly on the small basketball court with the netless rims and rusting half-moon backboards and potholed asphalt paving. The neighborhood this far off Grand Avenue was almost all black by now, and therefore the park's condition was not one of the Chicago Park District's chief priorities.

"Now I'm going to give you a name and address where you drop the goods. The car is fine, you don't have to worry about that. Just leave it at the Amalfi tomorrow and I'll see that it gets returned." Aldo reached in his pocket and pulled out a set of car keys. "Here, the car's already there at the meat market on Blue Island, where I'm going to drop you, which is where they're waiting for you." He clapped Angelo on the shoulder. "You know, Angelo, this is an important thing. The stuff is worth maybe two hundred grand on the street. We were going to pay a hundred for it. Now we don't have to do that. So that ups it to like three hundred for us, the two we're gonna get for it and the one we don't have to pay. The Mexicans lost it, we found it. Sometimes, Angelo, things that don't look so good turn out better than you expect, eh."

"Apparently. Things always seem to come up roses for you, Aldo."

"You got that right. 'Cause I make them happen that way. A little advice. Fuck anybody you can. But don't ever fuck anybody in the crew, not unless you got specific instructions to do such a thing and the only one'd give you such instructions is me."

"I know that, Aldo. I ever let you down yet?"

"No, you been good, Angelo. I got a lot of hope for you. That's why I'm throwing some bigger things to you . . . like tonight. This is a step for you. The whole thing is steps." Aldo stopped as two black teenagers approached, their baseball caps tilted at a forty-five-degree angle, indicating a gang affiliation, but they hurried past under the stares they got from Aldo Forte and Angelo, who the two gangbangers sensed immediately were not tourists from Des Moines. Pass them by was street wisdom.

"I know about your seeing Joe Alessi's little girl. She's something." Aldo Forte smiled at Angelo. "You treat her real nice, with respect, Joe tells me."

"She's a very nice person."

"About a month ago, Joe-sep was asking me about you." Angelo nodded, not surprised. "She's family. Girls that are family are different. I know you understand that."

"I know that very well, Aldo."

"I told him you were a stand-up guy, Angelo. I told him you understood the rules. Respect in the crew, you give it without a question. To the family, the same way. You been with me about three years now and you done very well, very well." Aldo reached over and put his hand on Angelo's shoulder again. "You got a good shot at being made, Angelo."

"That's what I would like."

"You become made, nobody cheats you, not without paying a big price. Nobody whacks you without permission. You make a lot more money than you do now. You are in on just about everything, you get a piece of most things going down. You, *you* are a member of the family."

"It would be an honor, you sponsoring me."

Aldo Forte never committed himself until he was absolutely certain about what he was going to do. "You need *two* sponsors, Angelo. Just remember, like I said—steps. You are coming along. Tonight's a step, Angelo." Aldo stood up. "Let's start back." As they walked toward the Amalfi, he added, "Joe Alessi likes you, you never want to do anything that might change that."

BY EIGHT-THIRTY JIMMY Pagnano had just about given up on his meet from Detroit, whom he knew to be a man named Vaughn Swayze. He knew nothing else about him other than he came recommended, which was enough.

A Sambuca later, however, the maitre d' was there telling him someone was asking for him. In the bar area the maitre d' pointed out a rotund little man about five-foot-six with curly, prematurely gray hair crowning a round, cherubic face. He looked sort of ridiculous, Pagnano thought, a guy with his bulgy form, maybe in his late thirties, maybe forty, wearing baggy stonewashed blue jeans and a madras sportcoat.

Pagnano walked over to him. "Vaughn Swayze, right?" he said as he looked him up and down like he was sizing up something he was thinking of buying.

A boyish smile. "That's me."

"Jimmy Pagnano. Let's go sit at the table in the corner over there."

"Great, great." Swayze had a tendency to repeat himself when he was excited, which was most of the time. He stuck out a plump hand to shake, Pagnano ignored it and started walking toward the table. Swayze grabbed his rum and coke and hurried after him.

When they sat down, Pagnano called out, "Suzie," to the waitress who was talking to a customer a couple of tables away. She turned, seeing who it was, and quickly came over.

"Hi, Jimmy. I didn't see you come in."

"I been in the dining room. How about a Sambuca?"

"Sure, hon."

Pagnano looked over at Swayze. "You always this late when you're meetin' somebody? Like forty-five minutes?"

Swayze's smile faded. "Jeez, I had a helluva mess downtown, and the traffic. You know, Friday night, Friday night traffic. And I got lost coming out here. Just a helluva mess. I'm really sorry about it. I hope I didn't screw you up or anything."

"If I wasn't with a party in there," Pagnano said indicating the dining room, "I wouldn't be here. Jimmy Pagnano doesn't wait for anybody."

"Yeah, yeah. I can understand that. Lenny Sasso says you're a very busy guy, very busy."

The waitress came back with a stemmed cordial glass holding the crystal-clear Sambuca. When she put it down in front of Pagnano he picked it up by the stem with just his thumb and index finger, a dainty motion out of character for the man holding it. He held it up toward her as if to propose a toast.

"Just like you, Suzie," he said. "Great curves."

She smiled. "You sure know how to treat a lady, Jimmy."

"That guy over there you were talkin' to, was he hittin' on you?"

"A little, I guess."

"He got good taste." Jimmy put his hand on her backside, rubbing it gently. She didn't move. His hand slid down and rested on the back of her net-stockinged thigh, squeezing it a little. "Now do me a favor, kid. Don't put anybody at the table next to us. We got some business to talk."

"No problem, Jimmy." He gave her thigh a pat and she turned and walked away.

"She is one great lay," Jimmy said.

"Yeah, I'd bet. She's a knockout."

"She got more tricks and treats than a year of Halloweens." He turned back to Swayze. "Now what's this business you got that brings you over here from Detroit?"

"I come over once a month. I'm a salesman. Chicago's part of my territory. I sell office furniture. You know, desks, file cabinets, things like that. It's a big company. I got all of South Michigan outside of Detroit, that's a house account, and all of Northern Indiana and Chicago."

"So you wanna sell me office furniture?"

"No, no."

"Well, what's the business?"

Vaughn Swayze leaned over and said in a near-whisper, "I want to buy a dead body."

"You want to buy what? You mean whack somebody for you?"

"No, no. Buy a dead body, dead body."

"What are you, some kind of fucking ghoul or something?"

"No, no, I mean like buy one from somebody at the morgue. You know, they always end up with bodies that nobody claims and that don't have any identification. See, I got a scam I know I can work. I talked with Lenny Sasso about this, but he says no way in Detroit. They had some big scandal in the morgue not too long ago and everything's tight as an old maid's twat." Pagnano was thinking he hadn't heard the term *twat* in maybe twenty years. And *old maid*? "So he says maybe I should try Chicago. You can buy anything in Chicago, he says, if you got a connection, that is. So he gives me your name and says you got more connections around town than they got laid-off auto workers in Detroit. If anybody could swing a deal, it would be you, he tells me, and for a little something he might talk to you, you know, about you seeing me."

"Lenny and I go back a long time. That's the only reason I'm listening to you." Jimmy Pagnano seemed to be feeling a little more comfortable now. "I done him one very big favor over there once. Very big. Did he tell you about it?"

"No."

"Ask him some time. Just mention Teamsters. Maybe he'll tell you, maybe he won't." Jimmy called for Suzie again. "Give me another," he said, holding up the empty glass with the nice curves. "You want another," he said to Swayze, "whatever the hell it is you're drinking."

"Ron Rico and Coke, tall glass," Swayze said to the waitress, giving her the biggest Munchkin grin he could summon.

"You want a straw with that?" Pagnano said. "Hey, or maybe one of those little paper umbrellas. You still got those, Suzie? Give him one of each."

"I'll see what I can come up with," she said.

Vaughn Swayze was nervous again, Jimmy Pagnano had that effect on people. "So you think you got a connection might get me a body?" Swayze asked after Suzie left.

"Connections are not my problem. But I got to know what this thing is all about. Every fucking detail."

"You got 'em, Jimmy. Here it is. As I told you, I got this job that brings me over here. What if I—pardon the term— pass away over here? That's what I'm talking about. You see, I got a hundred-thousand-dollar life insurance policy with the company, comes as part of the perks. So I also took out another one on my own, another hundred, term policy. You see what I'm getting at. Now we're talking two major vehicles. If I'm dead . . ."

"Sounds like an asshole idea," Jimmy Pagnano said.

"No, no, listen. The morgue has this body nobody claims, so I get it from them, dress it in my clothes, put my identification on it, stash it somewhere, say in a motel room, where it will be found. The body goes back to the morgue as Vaughn Swayze. Then my wife comes over and I.D.'s it. My wife— hey, you like that Suzie over there, you'll love Felice. She's a knockout, too, and she's apeshit for me." *Apeshit*—Pagnano figured he hadn't heard that one in twenty years either. "Anyway, my wife'll do it. She'll do anything for me, I tell you, you gotta believe." Swayze could feel the salesman's momentum building inside him. "So she gets it released and sends it to a funeral home here and they cremate it, cremate it, burn the bugger. She collects on the two insurance policies and we take off with me having a new I.D., a new life, and two hundred Gs. So what do you think?"

"I still think it's an asshole idea."

"It can work, I know it can."

"I don't know if it can work or not. What I do know is I do got a connection at the morgue. I think I could probably get you a stiff. What you do after that, you're on your own. But the stiff is gonna cost you big bucks."

"Like how much?"

Jimmy Pagnano looked at the ceiling. "Twenty grand. Half up front, half when you get your body."

Swayze looked like he suddenly needed to have the Heimlich maneuver administered. "Twenty! Lenny Sasso said he thought it might cost ten, ten tops, tops."

"Chicago's more expensive than Detroit. That's the price."

"Hey, can't we discuss this. Twenty is a big nut. Lenny Sasso said—"

"I don't give a shit what Lenny Sasso said. Go on back to Detroit. Let Lenny Sasso dig up a stiff for you."

"Look, Jimmy, I can raise ten. I got a little stash. I can probably get the ten. Could we like make a deal, say I give you the second ten after Felice collects the insurance dough? Soon as she gets it you get the second ten. The same day, same day."

"What do I look like, you think I got a loaf of bread for a

brain? I told you I think it's an asshole idea. All kinds of things could go wrong after you get your corpse. For one, maybe you don't get your two hundred Gs. You don't, I don't get my ten. Maybe you get caught, you're lookin' at ten to twenty for insurance fraud. Am I gonna get my ten if you're entertaining the buggerboys in the penitentiary? You got the deal, ten now, ten with the body, that's it."

Swayze sighed. "Okay. I guess I got no choice."

"Don't look like it."

"I'll be back with the ten next week."

"Cash. Nothing higher than a fifty."

"Sure, that's the way you want it, that's the way you get it, Jimmy."

"You know where to reach me." Pagnano waved Suzie over. "Give this guy the check. I gotta get back to my party." Then to Swayze, "Tip her good, she's a buddy," and got up and left.

In the dining room Jimmy Pagnano put his arm around his boss and whispered, "Joe-sep, I think I just made us eighteen big ones. You gotta see this guy to believe it." Joe Alessi nodded, "He wants a stiff from the morgue. A throwaway. I figure I can get one from Hawkins, a guy I know over there, for two grand. This Swayze guy says he can come up with twenty. So we pocket eighteen. Not bad for a night's work."

Joe Alessi nodded. "Sit down, have yourself a nice drink, Jimmy."

✤6

THE EXPRESSWAY, SURPRISINGLY NAMED FOR A REPUBLICAN, Dwight David Eisenhower, in democrat-entrenched Chicago, connects the western suburbs with the city's downtown area. It ends abruptly at Grand Park just west of the shore of Lake Michigan. The Eisenhower Expressway, in fact, links up with other interstates so that one can drive all the way from New

Orleans, passing through Memphis, St. Louis and across the seemingly endless farmfields of Mississippi, Arkansas, Missouri and Illinois to the heart of Chicago without once encountering a traffic light.

As the Eisenhower courses through the west side of Chicago it passes through some of the city's most dangerous neighborhoods. At one juncture, a little more than three miles west of downtown, it slides beneath a large railroad trestle. In the dark recess beneath the railroad bridge on the south side of the expressway lies a vacant, dead area of impacted earth shrouded forever from the sun by a concrete bed and strewn with humankind's detritus—trash, used condoms, hypodermic needles, broken glass, hunks of human and animal feces. Mostly bad things happen here.

But on this summery, moonless night it was a place for young love, at least for Rayfield Tees and his twelve-year-old girlfriend, Latrona Meek, who had wandered over together just after eleven o'clock. They settled in because it was one of the only private places in the otherwise overpopulated area. For two blocks either way along the expressway there was nothing that had not been leveled or burned to the ground except for a single two-story ramshackle house patched with asphalt siding a block up the street from where Rayfield and Latrona had squirreled themselves away.

The house was occupied by a Mexican landscape laborer who worked six months of the year and collected welfare the other six, along with his wife, seven kids, brother-in-law, and an ever-changing flow of relatives and friends.

Rayfield and Latrona moved far back up under the bridge, sitting now on a large, flattened-out corrugated box that Rayfield had found among the other stuff that littered the ground there.

There were no lights on the alleylike street that ran parallel to the Eisenhower. The only light was a kind of dreamy, goldish glow that washed over from the sodium-vapor lights of the expressway. Back where Rayfield and his girlfriend were it was very dark except for the glow flickering upward from the pipe that held the crack cocaine they were smoking.

"We gonna juice tonight, Latrona," he said, free hand sliding up and down her thigh just below the ragged hem of her cutoff jeans. "This stuff's makin' me horny."

She didn't say anything, just stared absently out at the emptiness, across the rubble-strewn vacant lot on the other side of the street. She had been on crack for about four months now, ever since she met Rayfield. He had a seemingly endless supply of it because he delivered it around the projects where they both lived on the other side of the expressway for some of the older members of the Western Vice Lords, a gang he was considered a junior member of, being too young at thirteen to be accepted as a full member.

Rayfield was tall for his age and skinny, probably did not weigh more than one hundred thirty pounds. Latrona was little but her body had already begun taking on the shape of a woman's, and Rayfield was exploring it now. The crack gone, she lay there looking up at the underbelly of the bridge feeling warm inside her body, fuzzy inside her head. She liked the way she felt, it was the only time she felt good, after smoking dope.

She took her blouse off. She held the stand-up breasts with the nipples in her hands, squeezing them. Rayfield was busy working at getting her shorts and panties off, his hand now fondling her pubic hairs that had only begun to grow about a half year earlier. Latrona was breathing heavily. Rayfield's pants were down around his ankles and he guided her hand to where he wanted it and she stroked him slowly. "Some bone," he said. "Some bone," she said back.

"Juice time," Rayfield said, and rolled over on top of her. He had just begun when they heard the cars coming down the rubble-littered street, heard the cars drive past them and stop some fifty feet beyond. Rayfield looked over his shoulder and saw the headlights of both cars go out.

He rolled off quickly. In the eerie bronze glow from the expressway lights he saw the back door of the first car open and a man get out, pulling another man behind him. Rayfield squinted, trying to see what was happening, seeing only dark, human forms. Now another man got out of the driver's door of the first car. He had a shovel in his hand.

The second car backed into what once had been a driveway so that it faced perpendicularly to the expressway and could pull out into the street and take off in either direction if there was a reason to get out of there quickly.

"Stay here," Rayfield whispered, hitching his pants back up. "I gotta see what's goin' on." Hunched over, he quietly made his way closer until he was not more than thirty feet from the two men by the side of the car. He was hidden from them by one of the bridge's massive concrete support columns. The man who had been dragged out was leaning against the car, supported by it. The one with the shovel was now standing next to the other two. Rayfield could see that the man leaning against the car was pointing to an electrical power box about twenty feet away from them and was saying something, but Rayfield could not make out the words.

Roy Echols, shovel in hand, walked over to the box and began digging behind it, the sounds the shovel made lost in the drone of expressway traffic.

Danny Pack stood there, his gaze going back and forth between Roy's digging and Manny Peters, who was breathing erratically now and thinking that maybe one of his ribs might have punctured a lung. The pain was piercing and he thought he was going to faint. Finally he said so softly that Danny Pack had to bend toward him to hear, "You take me to a hospital when he's through, okay? I'm badly hurt."

"Yeah, those things they sharpen knives with pack a real wallop."

"You didn't have to do it." Manny start to cough and then shouted out from the pain.

"Be quiet," Danny Pack said. "You'll be okay."

"I need medical help."

"Don't worry, you'll get it."

"I'll tell them it was a hit-and-run. I was hit by a car."

"Yeah, good story."

Roy emerged from the darkness carrying the shovel in one hand and an oversized attaché case in the other. He put it on the hood of the car. "It's locked. You got a key to this?"

Manny fumbled in his pocket and brought out a key ring. He found the little key and held the ring by it. Roy took it, opened the case. Inside were ten cloth bags looking like miniature sandbags. Roy took out one of them, hefted it. "Feels like a kilo to me." He undid the top, put a finger in, dabbed at the white powder, tasted it. "Guess you came through just like you said you would, Manny old buddy."

" 'Course, I did. Soon as I know who it belonged to I give it back."

Roy closed up the attaché case and walked over to the car, where Angelo Franconi was sitting behind the wheel. He dropped it in through the open window onto the passenger seat next to Angelo. "It's good. Ten kilos," and turned and walked back.

"The hospital now," Manny was saying to Danny Pack when Roy came up to them.

"Sure, sure." Then to Roy: "Manny the Mole wants to go to a hospital. I think his ribs are bothering him."

Roy picked up the shovel that was leaning against the front of the car. "Probably gonna want to get those suckers x-rayed. They don't do much for ribs, though. Maybe tape 'em up, give you a little pain killer, that's about it." And then he swung the shovel, catching Manny Peters square in the face, sending a clang into the night and a kaleidoscope of images through Manny's mind just before he crumpled unconscious to the ground.

Rayfield Tees's eyes widened. *Holy shit*, he said to himself.

Danny Pack stood over Manny now and took out the gun with the cylindrical silencer from under his shirt. He pointed it at Manny's head. The sound was a muffled *phtoot*. Altogether there were three *phtoots*. "So long, Manny the Mole," Danny Pack said.

Holy, holy shit, Rayfield thought.

Roy opened the trunk of the car and he and Danny hoisted Manny's body into it, being careful not to get any of his blood on themselves. Then Roy slammed it shut and Danny wiped the car of prints, inside and out, and Roy said, "Let's get the hell out of here."

Angelo Franconi watched the scene from the car, a drama played out in silhouette before him. When he saw the two appear to start back toward the car, he turned on the ignition and flipped the switch for the headlights. In their glare he saw Roy, the shovel in his hand, and Danny, the gun still in his. And then he did a double-take, spotting the other figure behind them, pressed against a bridge support column.

It all happened so fast, Rayfield felt as if an electric shock had gone through him when the headlights came on and he knew he was spotlighted in them. He saw the man in the second car getting out . . . now shouting and pointing. Rayfield bolted.

Roy and Danny turned to see what Angelo Franconi was pointing at. What they saw was a figure dart from the column. Danny's first shot stopped him in midstep, as if the figure were in a movie whose reel had suddenly froze. Rayfield caught in the stop-frame, Rayfield motionless there for a split second, turned by the force of the bullet that entered his lower back and exited his lower abdomen, facing them now. The second shot sent him backward until he pitched to the ground at the foot of another support column.

Roy Echols and Danny Pack went over to him. Angelo Franconi, his face a mask, watched them, every step, the two captured in the bronze glow of the expressway lights. They stared down at Rayfield. "Jesus, Danny, he's just a kid," Roy said.

"How was I supposed to know he was a kid?"

They heard the noise from down the block where some of the Mexicans were coming out of the house, moving their party into the yard, words ringing out in Spanish, some laughter, the sound of a beer bottle breaking after it was tossed into the street, voices garbled in the night. Roy and Danny ran for the car.

Angelo Franconi was still standing outside the car. He, too, heard the noise from up the street and saw the people. The party-goers could easily see the cars, his with the headlights illuminating the Lincoln. It looked to Angelo like they were moving now toward the cars, toward him. He moved back in behind the wheel as Echols and Pack got in from the other side.

As they drove off, away from the sounds of the party, Angelo said, "Don't tell me that that was what I think it was."

"Just somebody who was under the bridge," Danny, sitting next to Angelo in the front seat, said. "Just somebody. In the wrong place, the wrong time."

From the backseat, from Roy: "He was a kid."

Angelo looked into the backseat, then at Danny Pack. It was what he thought it was.

"He looked like maybe twelve or thirteen," Roy said.

"Dead?" Angelo knew the answer.

"Dead." Danny Pack said.

"This is going to bring heat," Angelo was shaking his head. "You gotta believe it." He bounced his fist off the steering wheel. "Why the hell did you shoot him?"

"He saw us."

"He probably didn't see you good enough to I.D. you," Angelo said. "And even if he did, he's a street kid, he's not going running to the cops."

"I just reacted, okay? I saw the guy and I reacted. What the fuck."

"It happened," Roy said, "nothing we can do about it now. It's over. Nobody can tie us to it. It's history."

Nobody except Latrona Meek, who had been huddled in a catcher's crouch behind the broad concrete pillar looking up through wide, horror-filled eyes at the two white men standing over her boyfriend not more than five feet away, expecting them to kill her next, only to see them turn and run toward the car whose headlights had held them in their glow.

Angelo took the guns from Danny Pack and Roy Echols and put them under the front seat of the car. He gave Echols one of the airplane tickets, the one to Fort Lauderdale, and the one to New Orleans to Danny Pack. It was midnight when he dropped them at the O'Hare Hilton.

                    *   *   *

ANGELO STOPPED AT AN all-night Denny's restaurant on Mannheim Road, ordered a cup of coffee at the counter and got change for the telephone.

"Aldo, it's Angelo," he said when a sleepy voice answered the call. "I need to talk to you. Can I come over?"

There was a long moment of silence.

"You will want to hear what I have to say."

"Okay," was all Aldo Forte said.

✦7

ROLL CALL FOR THE MIDNIGHT-TO-EIGHT SHIFT IN AREA Four, Violent Crimes was a relatively casual affair, so much so it almost didn't take place. The twelve detectives on duty in the department for that shift just sort of wandered into the sergeant's office right off the sprawling squad room on the second floor over at Harrison and Kedzie so that the sergeant knew they were there.

Johnny Nolan, who had been in VC at Four for just over eight years now, arrived a little before midnight and found his partner, César Nabasco, already there talking with the sergeant, who was known around Four as Sergeant Bilko because he was bald, wore heavy-rimmed glasses and did look like the late Phil Silvers. His name was Luther Gerherdt.

"Who's the woman out there at the table with Wilson and McCabe?" Nolan asked.

"That's your ridealong. You didn't forget you got a ride-along tonight?"

"No, I didn't forget. You said it was a reporter. I guess I thought it would be a guy."

"Well, Nolan, you always seem to luck out."

"She supposed to be with us all night?" Nabasco asked.

"I hope so," Nolan said.

Sergeant Gerherdt took off his glasses and began to clean

them with his tie, something he did every fifteen or twenty minutes. "It depends on how much stomach she's got."

"So, do we give her a dog-and-pony show?"

Sergeant Gerherdt shook his head. "Remember, Nolan, she's a reporter. Reporters write stories which appear in newspapers. The big whizzes down at 11th and State read those newspapers. They read them every day scared of what they might find in them regarding us and our colleagues. Remember that."

"You got anything for us, Bilko? Otherwise I'll go out and make the young lady's acquaintance, seeing as I have to spend the night with her."

"Go on. I'll fill in Nabasco."

She was talking with Frank Wilson, another VC detective, when Nolan walked out into the squad room. Eddie McCabe, Wilson's partner, was engrossed in the Chicago *Sun-Times.*

"I understand you're going to ride along with us tonight. I'm Johnny Nolan."

"Better be careful," Wilson said, "his partner drives like the streets of Four are staging areas for a demolition derby." Wilson was handsome, with a thin black mustache and a build that could qualify him for a slot in the backfield of the Chicago Bears. He had an attractive wife, two kids and lived in a middle-class, racially integrated neighborhood on the city's far south side. But Frank Wilson was a pessimist. His glass was not only half empty, all he could think of was how grimy the empty half was.

"Don't pay any attention to him," Nolan said. "He's what we call a chronic alarmist."

"How can you not be? Nabasco's half-Hispanic and half-Greek. You give a guy like that a driver's license you might as well give the gangbangers napalm."

"C'mon," Nolan said to her, "I'll introduce you to César. You'll see he's a real mild-mannered type."

"Hey, wait a minute, you guys," Eddie McCabe said, pointing at an article in the newspaper. "Listen to this. This is really great. Any of you ever hear of a Yuk? Y-u-k."

No one had.

"It's a toad. Look at the headline." He held it up.

POISONOUS TOAD HORRIFIES AUSTRALIANS

"You gotta hear this." McCabe began reading from the newspaper. "The Yuk is a plump, slimy and poisonous cane toad found in Queensland and now in New South Wales. It has taken over backyards. It infests the forests and parks. Birds and animals—even snakes—die before they can swallow the Yuk, killed by a lethal dose of poison squirted from the glands on its back. People hate the toad with a passion, mainly for poisoning their pets."

"That's really something, Eddie," Nolan said. "C'mon, Ms. Stryker."

"It's Holly, okay?" She started to get up.

"No, no, wait. I haven't even gotten to the good part yet," McCabe said. "Here. The female produces as many as thirty thousand tadpoles a year, and astonished scientists describe the Australianized male as probably the world's most sex-crazed species. The lasciviousness of Yuks is legendary. Now get this. The male claws himself with powerful forearms onto the back of the female and can't be dislodged. Male toads have been photographed mounting dead females even after they have been flattened by trucks, and Queensland goldfish farmers complain of randy toads leaping into their ponds and catching fish in a fatal embrace. Great, huh?"

"Sounds like some cops I know," Wilson said.

Nolan motioned for the reporter, Holly Stryker, to get up.

"Hey, Johnny, hold it. I'm not finished. You gotta hear the rest. Listen. People sit on verandas with air rifles and spotlights and pop off at the toads all night—bang, bang, bang—but in the morning most of the toads they shot have vanished. And real toad haters often run their cars into ditches and telephone poles while zigzagging after Yuks on the road. When the toads are run over, their intestines pop out of their mouths."

"For chrissake," Nolan said.

"Hey, it gets better. Toads have phenomenal recuperative powers. The ones that are shot often recover and hop away. The ones on the road are often only stunned. After a few minutes they simply swallow their own digestive tracts and limp off into the bushes. Is that *great*, or what?"

NOLAN INTRODUCED HOLLY STRYKER to César Nabasco, a hulking fellow whose dark, penetrating eyes unnerved most people. César always turned quiet in the company of anyone other than cops or criminals. He did not like the idea of a ridealong but there was nothing he could do about it. She had gotten the okay from 11th and State, signed the waiver and Sergeant Gerherdt had assigned them to take her along on their early morning odyssey through Chicago's mean west side.

The midnight shift, also known as the first shift, was different than the other two shifts for the detectives in Violent Crimes. During those hours one did not go around ringing doorbells to ask questions, the dogwork. Instead they were out on the street or in Area Four headquarters doing the shitwork, the paperwork.

"So why is it you want to ride along with us?" Nolan asked.

"The paper's doing a series on homicides in Chicago, seeing as how the city seems to be headed for a record high this year, over eight hundred and August isn't even over yet."

"Well, you came to the right place. The boys and girls out there"—he pointed out the window—"should accommodate you, being a Friday night, heat spell and all. It kind of gets folks revved up."

"So when do we go out?"

"Ten, fifteen minutes. César's making some calls. We got a couple of people we need to talk to tonight. You want to look through some of the uncleared homicides while you're waiting, they're in the wire basket on top of the file cabinet."

HOLLY STRYKER WAS APPROACHING thirty warily and at times with angst. After getting a master's degree from Northwestern's Medill School of Journalism in Evanston, Chicago's first suburb to the north, she was hired by the Chicago *Tribune*, apprenticed writing obituaries and then society items. But after two years she left and landed a job writing political news features for the *Metro News*, a much smaller, burgeoning enterprise trying to make it as an afternoon newspaper, something Chicago had not had in years. Tonight was her first venture into the dark corridors of crime, and she could not have had a more picaresque pair of tour guides.

She was sitting in the backseat of the unmarked car cruising slowly through the gang-ruled neighborhood of projects and other slums west of the Loop.

"We'll be out on the street all night," Johnny Nolan said. "A homicide comes up, Sergeant Bilko says we'll get it for you, even though it's not our turn."

Talking over the sound of the radio crackling with police calls, Nolan asked, "You ever see somebody who's been offed?"

"What? Oh," Holly did a double-take, "no."

"Can be ugly. Especially the stabbings. We had one a couple months ago, this guy was gutted. I mean his guts were all over the apartment."

Holly was making notes, feeling queasy.

"And they cut off his whatsis. It was over a drug deal. Most of them are these days, at least out around here. We cleared that one in two days. Santana Peoples was his name, the killer, I mean. Now all you good taxpayers are going to be footing the bill for Santana's room and board for probably the next thirty years. Unless somebody kills him in the penitentiary." Nolan looked at his watch. "It's twelve-thirty, César."

César did not say anything, just kept heading west on Warren Boulevard. He drove into Garfield Park and then turned onto the narrow road that runs between the lagoons deep in the park.

"You ever been in Garfield Park before?" Nolan asked her.

"Never."

"Prettier in the daytime, but not safe then either. Got a big conservatory, used to be all kinds of nice people came to look at all the pretty flowers, picnic on the grass. Now you wouldn't want to be here alone day or night.''

Alongside one of the lagoons on a little hillock, César pulled to a stop.

"We gotta go down there," Nolan said pointing to what appeared in the darkness to be a bench by the edge of the lagoon. "Business. You can stay in the car if you want. Just be sure you keep it locked and the lights out.''

"I think maybe I'd rather come with you.''

"Sure. Just watch your step, these paths are full of holes.''

They walked down to the rim of the lagoon and stopped by what indeed was a bench, the two detectives looking around, waiting, not saying anything, the silence unreal here in this pocket of the inner city; only an occasional automobile horn sounding somewhere outside the park. Holly wanted to ask what was up but felt she ought to stay part of the silence. The detectives were looking out in different directions.

Holly just stared out across the lagoon, black and rippled on this moonless night. When she heard the soft rustle from the bushes behind her she turned quickly just as a young black man stepped out from them. "What . . . ?''

"Easy, easy," Johnny Nolan said to her. "This is Ambrose. He's a friend.''

"What's happenin', Ambrose?" Nolan said. Ambrose sidled back toward the bushes. Ambrose seemed as surprised to see Holly as she had been startled to see him. Ambrose looked to be about eighteen, a skinny kid with darting eyes.

"What's goin' on here?" Ambrose said, his head moving from side to side as if he expected an attack to come from either flank. "Who this?''

"Hey, not to worry, Ambrose," Nolan said. "We just got a trainee with us tonight. Soon to be a major policewoman, just getting a taste tonight. Didn't know we were teachers as well as policemen, did you?''

"I didn't know somebody else be here.''

"Well, it's a surprise, Ambrose. Now we don't got a lot of time, so let's talk about what you do know. What's going on?''

Ambrose looked at Holly, then back at Nolan. Nolan nodded to him. "Couple of things," Ambrose said. "Dokey's back, got out couple of days ago."

"I thought they were holding him without bail?"

"Got it changed. Down to two hundred thou. Came up with the twenty grand and he's back on the street. Saw him yesterday."

To Holly, Nolan said, "Dokey is Dokey Stokes, one of the biggest dealers on the west side. Narcotics finally busted him about a week ago."

"Where's he hanging out?" César asked.

"His sister's, over on Wolcott, near Harrison Park. You wanna drive over there, I show you the place."

"Okay. What else?"

"Somebody's supposed to walk the line tonight. Don't know where."

"Hope he has fun," César said. "You got a lot of really dumb fucks in this neighborhood."

"Walk the line?" Holly asked.

"Gang initiation," Nolan said. "New member, he's gonna walk through two rows of gangbangers and get to the other end and they beat the shit out of him while he's trying to get there. You don't make it, you don't get in the gang and you gotta try again some time, if you're still able to. It's not something to do too often."

"Any special guns?" César asked.

"Don't know any in particular except for one thing. I heard Topper is carryin' but you gonna have a tough time catchin' him, that little kid's so smart and quick. They had a drive-by about a week ago, the way I heard it, down around Skinner Park. They got Topper down there waitin' and the car comes up and Topper tosses the piece in the window and takes off. They shoot it up, hit somebody, don't know whether they killed anybody or not, and around the corner at the alley there's Topper a-waitin'. They pitch the gun back to him and he's gone."

"That it, Ambrose?"

"Guess so."

"Okay, show us where Dokey's sister's living and we'll call it a night." Holly saw Nolan pass Ambrose a bill.

In the car Holly sat with Ambrose in the backseat. He kept looking over at her, looking away, looking back. She could not figure out whether he was afraid of her or was getting ready to start grabbing her.

César took off out of the park like an ambulance driver on the way to a major disaster, without the flashing lights and siren.

"We got some more talking to do," César said, his arm draped over the backrest of the front seat, looking alternately over his shoulder at Ambrose and then at the street he was racing down. "I'm not sure you're always giving us a fair deal. And if I ever find out you're not, I personally am going to beat you so your mother wouldn't recognize you. But you know that, right? Right. Now, any names for us, Ambrose?"

"New ones over on Maypole, you know the house."

"Little Rock," Nolan said, a well-known drug house.

"Yep. Tonight it's Milwaukee Joe for horse, Lucky Strike for snow, Cold Fudge for the cheap stuff, crack." Code names if you wanted to purchase heroin or cocaine that night from this particular candy store.

"Anything else?" Nolan asked.

"You got it all."

As they drove down Wolcott Street, Ambrose pointed out the first-floor apartment in the three-story building where Dokey Stokes and his sister were hanging out. César swerved into an alley and to a sudden stop, and Ambrose was out of the car as quickly as he had appeared from the bushes back in Garfield Park. He disappeared into the darkness of a gangway.

"Did you do that on purpose?" Holly asked. "Try to scare the living crap out of me?"

"No. Just business as usual. Thought you wanted the tour."

"Just who the hell is Ambrose?"

"Ambrose is a snitch and a junkie and a booster. We turned him about six months ago. Got him off a possession charge. He gives us some decent stuff. You try to turn as many of these guys as you can. Most of the time you can't, but you keep trying.''

"Where does the money come from?''

"What money?''

"I saw you give him money in the park.''

"That we don't need in your article, Ms. Stryker. So let's go see what else's happening.''

They went for a drive through the neighborhood, Nolan giving a running commentary of what he interpreted was going down on the street as they drove by. Of course everybody on the street knew who they were in that car, or what they were—nobody else wore shirts and ties and drove around in a drab four-door sedan on a steamy summer night in the hours after midnight, especially two white guys in a black high-crime neighborhood. People here could smell the Man coming.

"Run her down Madison or Lake,'' Nolan said. "Maybe she can squeeze something from there into her article.''

The hookers were there, standing around or pacing back and forth. Nolan said, "You'd be surprised how many cars we see drifting by with stickers on their windshields from Winnetka, Glenview, Naperville, all your fine fancy suburbs around this time of the morning. I always wonder what the hell they tell their wives. Actually we caught a *wife* down here, from Hinsdale, caught her trying to hook up with another broad. Said she always wanted to do something *outrageous*, plus she plain liked women.''

"What did you do?''

"We gave her a lot of shit. Just screwing her around. Hell, what are we gonna do with her? We got enough serious stuff to worry about. The guys are different. They're usually scared shitless, you glom onto them. But they still keep coming. It's crazy. You know, with AIDS and herpes and all that stuff, but they still keep coming down here to get their rocks off. Keeps the fish and the gumps in business.''

"Fish and gumps?''

"Fish are the regular whores, the girls. Gumps, those are the guys dressed up like girls.''

They were driving east on Madison. "That one of the cars

from the suburbs?'' Holly asked as they slowed next to an
Olds 88 whose driver was leaning out the window talking to
a hooker. When the hooker saw them she backed away from
the Olds.

"She's a gump," Nolan said.

"How can you tell?"

"They dress better," Nolan said.

César said, "Cute." Then: "Anybody like to eat besides
me?"

Nolan did. Holly had no appetite. "How about we go to
Estavo's," he asked, César's favorite twenty-four-hour place,
over in the Little Village, Chicago's largest Mexican *barrio.*

 8

INSIDE ESTAVO'S THERE WAS AN OVERPOWERING AROMA OF
grease mixed with the cloying scent of old hamburger meat.
You could feel the thick aspic in the air.

There were about fifteen people in the place at this hour of
the morning, not counting the two detectives and their ridealong. Two of them were detectives from Area Four, who gave
casual waves when Nolan and Nabasco walked in and curious
stares at the woman with them. The rest were from the neighborhood, closing the night out at the only *bodega* still open.

César ordered the combination platter: enchiladas, tacos,
tortillas, Spanish rice and refried beans. Nolan decided on the
Eggs Rancheros and a side of refried beans. Holly Stryker
went to the salad bar, whose contents were wilted, having
probably sat beneath the track lights and the alleged germ-
protecting plastic canopy since dinner hour the night before.
She put a small sampling of greenery on her plate, covered it
with croutons which looked like some of the dried food she
fed her cat and covered it with a clear dressing.

Halfway through the meal Nolan's beeper went off. He went to the telephone and was back moments later.

"Well, we got you your homicide, Ms. Stryker. Get the car, César, I'll get you a doggy bag."

"You take care of the check, Johnny," César said as he got up. "I'll even us up later."

When the waitress handed the check to Nolan, Holly said, "No, let me take care of it."

Nolan, a cop for eighteen years, had no problem with that.

"Bilko says it's by the Eisenhower, in the twenty-eight-hundred block west," Nolan said to César as he and Holly piled into the car, which started to pull away even before she got her door closed, leaving in its wake the sound of tires squealing. "Take the expressway and get off at Western, I guess."

"I know the city, Johnny. What do you think, I just got off the boat from Kokomo?" César flipped the switch to activate the flashing headlights of their unmarked squad car as he ran a red light and swerved so as not to hit the truck loaded with vegetables on its way to the South Water Street Market that had already entered the intersection and whose horn left a blaring, angry echo in the night's stillness.

"According to Bilko they got a corpse in the trunk of a car," Nolan said to Holly Stryker. "Still warm." He was enjoying this.

When they came off the expressway they could see the squad cars two blocks away. There were two of them, their Mars lights hurling vibrant blue, red and yellow hues into the night, their spotlights focused on the white Lincoln Town Car with the open trunk. César made the two blocks in less than ten seconds, although speed was hardly of the essence, the victim already dead.

The field lieutenant had given the uniformed officers the yellow crime-scene tape to ribbon off the area around the car and was back in his own car on the radio. One of the patrol cops was standing by the trunk of the car, another was rooting about in the backseat. Two others were wandering around, their flashlight circles scouring the ground.

The two patrol officers at the car knew Nolan and Nabasco. "Strange one, Johnny," the one standing by the trunk, Nick Dyckman, said when the two detectives approached with Holly Stryker a step behind. Dyckman looked at her, notebook and pen in hand, then back at Nolan. "You guys got secretaries these days?"

"A ridealong," Nolan said straight-faced.

Suddenly Holly Stryker was confronted with the open coffin, the bloody, perforated head, the death-mask with eyes wide open and milky-glazed, the body squeezed into the trunk in a fetal position.

"What's so strange?" Nolan said.

"Not more than five minutes ago we found another one up there." He pointed into the darkness under the expressway. "And that one's a kid. The loot's calling it in right now."

They hurried into the darkness, their flashlights leading the way to the spot where Rayfield Tees lay on blood-soaked earth. "Holy Christ," Nolan said.

"He's warm, too," Dyckman said.

"Gunshot wound," César said, kneeling over the body. "Looks like at least two." He stood back up. "This doesn't make a whole helluva lot of sense," nodding down toward the Lincoln, "and a kid," he said to Nolan.

"I just radioed this one in," the lieutenant said. He had just come up behind them. "We should have a lot of company in a few minutes." He turned to Dyckman. "Get some lights on this and ribbon it off." He started back downhill toward the cars.

Nolan and Nabasco followed and watched the lieutenant continue on to his own car and his own radio. Nolan said, "I'll write, you look, okay, César?" César flipped his basher back on and started walking slowly around the Lincoln Town Car.

"So tell me the story, Nick."

"We spotted the car from over there," Dyckman said, pointing to the street on the other side of the vacant lot. "Strange place for a car to be at this hour so we came over to have a look." Nolan began scribbling in his notebook.

Holly was doing the same in hers. "The door on the passenger side was open and the radio was pulled half out. Miller—my partner—" he added for Holly's sake, "found the trunk had been sprung and when he opened it, *voilà*, there was the trunk music. The way I figure it, the car was left here because someone wanted it found with its little package in the trunk, but then I'm not the detective. Just a patrolman, but maybe someday I'll get to wear a suit and tie on the job." Nolan gave him a look suggesting he get on with the story. "Anyway, some of the little neighborhood darlings probably found the car and started to strip it, then when they popped the trunk and found the body they figured they better get the hell out of there and abandoned their dismantling project. That's my thought. Say, maybe the guys who were strippin' it are the ones that shot the kid up there."

Nolan ignored that. "You didn't see anybody, any other car around?"

"No. But when we got here the lights in the house down the block there were on. When we pulled up, they went out. Don't know whether that means anything or not."

"You run a check on the car?"

"Not yet."

"Well, what the hell are you waiting for?" Then to Holly: "If I were to wager, I'd bet my house that the car belongs to the man residing in its trunk."

"Speaking of trunks, you talked about trunk music. What's that supposed to mean?"

"An old Outfit saying. A guy who's going to get hit, they say he's trunk music. It means in the not-too-distant future you will be able to hear his flesh decomposing in the trunk of a car. Trunk music."

Holly did not laugh.

Nick Dyckman came back. "The car's registered to a Thurman R. Peters, 1421 South Morgan. They're running a check on him for you."

"Thanks, Nick. Wanna bet a day's pay they find a sheet on him?"

"Hardly."

* * *

THE CRIME LAB VAN was the first to arrive on the scene after Nolan and his squad-car party. The evidence technicians went about their duties taking Polaroids of the corpses and the surrounding area, dusting the car for fingerprints, looking in all the recesses of the car, chalking off where the body of the kid lay up there under the expressway.

"You paparazzi about done?" Nolan asked when it appeared the picture-taking was over.

"He's all yours," one of the technicians said.

Nolan went looking for a wallet or some kind of identification on the body of the man in the trunk, but there was nothing. César did the same on the boy. He found a school I.D. card with a name and an address on it and $386 with a rubber band wrapped around the roll. Not bad for a kid, César thought.

César also had found three shell casings near the car, which he had bagged for the Crime Lab, and handed them over to one of the evidence technicians. There were no shells near the boy's body. He figured as long as this was their case he would come back and go over the area later in the morning when the sun was up.

Four more VC detectives had arrived by now, including Wilson and McCabe, along with Gerherdt; some bigwigs who generally hung out at 11th and State would be joining them because there was something definitely strange about finding a fifty-year-old white man dead of bullet wounds to the head, execution-style, in the trunk of a car, and the body of a thirteen-, maybe fourteen-year-old black kid about forty feet away also dead of gunshot wounds.

Which had prompted Nolan to say to Holly Stryker, "You know, if these two are victims of the same shooter, you might have yourself a story."

She had already figured that out for herself.

César gave the boy's I.D. and the money to Gerherdt. The sergeant would have the job of notifying the next of kin. On the midnight-to-eight shift in Four he'd had a lot of practice making such calls.

Gerherdt also took the call from Area Four headquarters on Dyckman's car radio and learned that Thurman R. Peters was better known as Manny Peters, was forty-six years old, had a sheet on him that went back to when Eisenhower was president and not just an expressway, had served time in the Audy Youth Correctional Home, Cook County Jail and Stateville Penitentiary out in Joliet. He was reputed to have links with organized crime. *Have had* might be a better way to put it, Gerherdt suggested.

Gerherdt got on the radio again. He wanted Organized Crime down at 11th and State to run Manny Peters through their computer.

Eddie McCabe came over to where Holly was standing. "They got you a good one tonight," he said, nodding rapidly. "Double-header. Say, by the way, you know that toad story I was talking about in the squad room . . ."

"How could I forget it?"

"Yes. Well, there was another thing to it I didn't get a chance to tell you because you all left. Get this. Dopeheads over there in Australia love the damned things. It said that among the delicatessen of toxic substances on the skin is something like LSD. They lick the skin, they get hallucinations and the high from the LSD stuff but they also get sick from the other stuff. Not enough to kill you, though. Can you believe that, licking the skin of a toad? Jeez, I hope they don't hear about that in this neighborhood. They'll be smuggling 'em in next week and dealing 'em on the street."

Johnny Nolan came up to them. "Your colleague was just giving me an update on the poisonous toads of Australia," Holly said to him.

"Can't you find something to do around here, Eddie?" Nolan asked. Then to Holly: "C'mon, me and César are gonna go wake up whoever it is lives in that dump down the street."

"You all done here?"

"For the time being. Nothing more we can do right now."

Things were in fact running down at the scene. The ambulance from the morgue had arrived. One evidence technician was wrapping the two victims' hands in plastic bags, which

Holly inquired about and Nolan explained that at the morgue, before they fingerprinted the victims, they would examine them to see if there were any hairs or specks of skin under the nails or on the fingers that might later become evidence. The body bags were already out, ready for the corpses. The whole thing seemed to have happened so fast, she thought, from the time they got the call to the carting away of the bodies. Just like that.

They drove the block to the house and César parked in front of it facing the wrong way. There was no visible doorbell and no one seemed to want to answer their pounding on the door, but finally it cracked about three inches, the length of the chain latch that secured it. A face looked out.

"Police," Nolan said, holding up his star and I.D. to the face. "We'd like to talk to you."

"*No comprendo.*"

"César, talk to this man."

César told him in Spanish that he had better quit the bullshit and open the door. If he really couldn't speak English they would speak in Spanish, but if he found out the man could speak English there was going to be a problem later, which would be resolved in the stationhouse. "*Comprendo?* I think you do." The man nodded back.

César, playing the good cop, told the man there was no problem, they just had a few questions to ask. If his approach didn't work, Nolan could be bad cop.

The door closed and then opened without the chain latch. Behind the man there had to be at least fifteen faces, about eight adults, the rest little kids in the dimly lit room looking out at them. "I do speak little English," the man said. César and Nolan figured him to be maybe forty, acting patriarch of the mixed group staring out at them.

"Your name?"

It was Jaime, he told them, which came out "Hy-mie."

"Hy-mie what?"

"Hy-mie Contagua."

"What do you or any of those people know about the car

down the street, Hy-mie?'' César pointed back to the Lincoln
still illuminated by the squad cars' spotlights.

The man stuck his head out the door and craned to look
down toward it. A puzzled look. "*Nada.*" He shrugged, held
out his hands palms up and turned to the others in the room
behind him. "Car," he asked in Spanish, "down the road,
anybody know anything about it?" They shook their heads.

"Did you hear or see anything earlier tonight going on
down there?"

The man put his hands together as if in prayer and then
rested his cheek on them. "No, we sleep."

Nolan turned to Holly. "Folks talk a lot with their bodies
and hands when they're lying."

"You wouldn't try to be hiding something from us, Hy-
mie?" César asked, still the good cop. "How long has that
car been sitting there?"

"Not see it before now." Turning to the faces again, re-
verting to Spanish. "Anyone know when that car got there?"
Again the heads moved back and forth, a few saying no, no;
a lot of shrugging and looking at each other, expressions of
wariness.

"Okay, I'm gonna need from you, Hy-mie, some identification. And I want the names of everyone else in this room
and their addresses if they live someplace else."

The prayerful hands were clasped together again, now pointing heavenward and pressed against the man's chest. "If I
could only help, that any one of us could, but we know nothing." He took a wallet from his pants pocket and took out a
driver's license. César looked at it, saw Jaime Contagua's face
staring back at him, jotted down the name and number and
logged in the names and addresses that Jaime spieled off of
what constituted the night's household.

When he finished, César said okay and looked at Nolan.
"We're not going to get anything here, at least now."

"We are going to be back, Mr. Contagua," Nolan said.
"We are going to want to talk to you some more. There was
a dead body found in that car. We are going to want to talk
to you *seriously* about it. Talk it over with your friends here.

We want to know who was fooling around down there. They're getting lots of fingerprints down there. Keep that in mind. Withholding evidence in a homicide's heavy duty, Mr. Contagua.''

César handed the man his card. "Now, Hy-mie, if you can think of anything that might help us, you call me. We'll appreciate it . . . and maybe sometime we can be of a little help to you. You *comprendo* that?''

Back in the car Nolan said, "You know, I wouldn't be surprised if they do find a lot of fingerprints on that car that belonged to the fingers of some of those people in there.''

"Tell me," César said.

"You think any of them had something to do with this, the killings?" Holly asked.

"Doubt it, but I bet they were trying to get pieces of that Lincoln.''

Speeding along now, the car weaving sharply this way and that, Holly knew it would be impossible to write anything more in her notebook. She tried to focus, memorize what she needed to put down later. She leaned up toward the front seat. "I need to call this in. How do I get to a telephone?''

"Back at Four we'll get you one. We gotta go back there and write this up. We're off the street for the night.''

She looked at her watch, then out the window. The sun was coming up, yesterday's haze had melted away and the fiery gold disc edging upward to the east off to the side of them had just slipped above Lake Michigan, ushering the city into another day. It was six-thirty in the morning. She remembered when it was three o'clock in the morning back at the Mexican restaurant. It seemed like only a half-hour ago.

"So when do you think this'll be in the paper?" Nolan asked her.

"It'll be in this afternoon, the edition that hits the stand about four.''

"You know you only got a little piece of the story so far. We're gonna find out a lot more after we get the crime lab reports and do some more digging ourselves.''

"I know. We'll go with what we got for now.''

"You gonna mention us in the story, the guys who took you around, Johnny Nolan and César Nabasco?" He spelled the names for her. "See our names in the paper . . . Nolan and Nabasco. Sounds like kind of a damn law firm." He had to smile.

They pulled up in front of Area Four headquarters. "You can get out here, with Johnny. I gotta check the car in."

As Holly was sliding across the seat to get out she said, "Thanks for the ride, César. You ought to try out for the Indy 500." She was careful to smile when she said it and started toward the entrance doors to Area Four.

Nolan looked back into the car and said to César, "She is one fine-looking piece of ass." César nodded back. "I think I may make *the* move," Nolan added.

From a desk in the squad room, all but empty at this hour, Holly called in to her city editor. "I think I might have a helluva story for you."

ANGELO FRANCONI WAS MORE NERVOUS THAN TIRED, STANDING on the corner of Grand and Damen avenues at eight-thirty in the morning waiting to be picked up, knowing where he and his boss were going.

He had good reason to be tired, having gotten home about two that morning after talking with Aldo Forte and getting little sleep after. It had not been a happy chat because Aldo had not been a happy man when Angelo told him about the kid. Aldo had, in fact, as they stood there in his backyard, actually on the concrete patio just back of the house, delivered a raspy tirade in his red flannel bathrobe.

Angelo had not told him that it was he who spotted the kid and pointed him out. Of course, he didn't know it was a kid at the time. All he said was that he had stayed in the car and watched the whole thing go down from there and that after he saw the body had been trunked he started the car and turned on his headlights and this person, back in the shadows, suddenly appeared and started to run, and the guy with the ponytail turned around and shot him.

They got out of there immediately after, with no problem, he told Aldo. Angelo also explained that he had gotten the guns back from the two, got rid of the one the guy with the ponytail had used; the other that had not been used and the two silencers he had stashed and would deliver them to whomever or wherever Aldo said. Aldo did not seem to put any of the blame on him, Angelo thought, but one never knew. Not in the world he was now living in . . .

Saturday morning was a surprisingly beautiful one for Chicago in August, the temperature in the mid-seventies, the pollution gone somewhere else and the sun strong, exploding against a royal blue sky with just some random puffs of clouds floating by . . . but Angelo Franconi did not see it that way. He kept seeing the scene, the boy suddenly there under the expressway, the boy running, the boy going down, the two running up to the boy, the two running toward him and the car. It kept flooding back into his mind, just like it had hours earlier when he was trying to get some sleep. He was thinking: *if* he had not jumped out of the car and fingered the kid, the two hitters would probably never have seen the kid, much less shoot him, and the kid would be alive and they would not have this awful mess that was going to bring major heat from all over the place. And he would not be going out to Oak Brook to the mansion where Aldo Forte's boss, everybody's boss, Gus Tuscano, lived. To tell the story again.

Angelo had gotten to the corner a half-hour before nine, the appointed time. You did not keep Aldo Forte waiting, and the *capo* felt he was being kept waiting even if he was fifteen minutes early and found you weren't there yet. So Angelo just stood there, his hands dug into the pockets of his tan poplin slacks, the short sleeves of his polo shirt pushed up to reveal strong, muscular arms. He looked like he did weights, although he didn't. He diverted his thoughts to the street scene playing out around him—the wizened old black man with the bloodshot eyes and the shoe with an unattached sole that made a flip-flap sound with each step as he moved slowly pushing his grocery cart of plastic bags filled with aluminum cans . . . the police car that cruised by, its occupants eyeing each side of the street probably more in search of an air-conditioned place to have a doughnut and coffee than to find some street offense in progress . . . the little old lady with vein-mottled legs, thick blue ridges pressing out from a rubbery landscape of old skin, her purse clutched tightly to her side, a plastic bag with a few groceries hanging from the other hand . . . the garbage in the street along the gutter, newspaper pages dancing in a gentle wind down the sidewalk, the graffiti on the walls that had their own special meanings to the Hispanic gangs in the neighborhood . . . across the street a young man from Friday night and Saturday morning sweating and breathing heavily, leaning up against the wall of the old red-brick building that once housed the North Chicago Bank but now was boarded up and looking, in its own way, like the little lady with the varicose veins . . . the smell of the buses' exhaust mixed with the scents of garbage that would not be collected until the following Tuesday, the sound of the trucks' airbrakes as they skidded up to the stoplights, and the auto horns, and the scuffle of the street . . . the signs extending out over the sidewalk:

CURRENCY EXCHANGE
CHECKS CASHED
MONEY ORDERS

JACK'S JUMBO HOT DOGS

GOOD'S DISCOUNT LIQUORS

LA PREFERIDA MEXICAN FOODS
& GROCERY STORE

CASA LINDO LOUNGE

and the shabby building in front of which he was standing that bore handmade signs on the wall identifying it as a Medical Center and Pharmacy. Angelo was thinking he'd need to get a tetanus shot *before* going in there. Under the sign, amid the gang symbols and drawings of daggers and guns and other inner-city art objects, was the chalked message: 'JULIO LOVES RITA S.'

At night these streets were mean, during the day they were just sad.

The car pulled up a few minutes after nine and the backdoor swung open. Aldo Forte was in the back, his driver and bodyguard, one and the same, Danny Isso, was alone in the front. Aldo handed Angelo a note as soon as he got in the car. In labored script was written: "You remember in the car we don't talk business." Angelo nodded. Aldo took the note back, stuck it in an ashtray and put a match to it.

"So how's it going this morning, pal?" Aldo said as if he were talking for someone else's benefit. "You look a little, you know, tired."

"It was a long night. I didn't sleep too well. Tossed and turned a lot."

"Yeah, it was awful hot. You got air-conditioning?"

"Hey, of course. It wasn't the heat. I don't know, maybe I just got the jitters. I think maybe I might be falling in love."

"In love? Why you wanna do that for? In this day and age, I mean. A good lookin' young guy like you can get cooze anytime he wants. It's all out there for the taking. But remember the advice I gave you last night—be careful, this love stuff can be *very* serious."

"I know, Aldo." He knew Aldo was talking about Joe Alessi's daughter. Telling him to be careful with her.

"You shouldn't lose sleep over it, though. Let's change the subject. Whatta you think about the Bears this year? You can't tell shit from these preseason games. You can't even tell who the hell the players are on the field after the first quarter, all those new guys, you know, the rookies. I mean isn't that for shit you gotta pay thirty bucks a seat to watch these kids try out? They gotcha though you wanna go out to Soldier Field. Me I wouldn't even bother no more, just watch it on TV. So what do you think anyway, they gonna win their division?''

"I don't know. *The Sporting News* got them to win it. So does that guy in the *Sun-Times*. But I don't think so. Half the guys they got are old, like pretty much over the hill. And the young guys I don't think are anywhere's near as good as the old guys when they were good. Personally I like the Vikings. But don't bet on it just because I said so."

"I wouldn't think of it."

They talked about the Bears and other sports and a new nightclub Aldo was touting these days, then lapsed into silence as they made their way out to Oak Brook and the home of Gus Tuscano.

NOLAN AND NABASCO WERE earning a little overtime the same morning. It was their case just unfolding, and therefore they would stay with it and work with the new shift coming on at eight. Earlier Nolan had walked Holly Stryker back to her car, where she gave him her card and asked him if anything at all came up on the homicides to give her a call. She would be *the* first to know, he said. Looking at her as she slumped into her car, the look on her face, the weariness, he thought that maybe this might not be the time to put *the* move on her. He just tucked the card in his shirt pocket and said goodbye and that he would be in touch.

WHEN HOLLY GOT TO her apartment in Wrigleyville, a trendy neighborhood on the north side near the Cubs ballpark, it was a little before eight. She had not worked the full shift with VC. She felt there was little to be gained sitting around over at Four watching Nolan and Nabasco write up their reports after she had already phoned in the bare bones of her story with a promise to the city editor to get back with details before noon. She was bone-tired, exhausted. She had never worked the late shift on the paper, never spent an entire night taking white-knuckled, whiplash rides around the city or meeting with a drug addict in a slaughterhouse park or looking at bloodied corpses. She took off the Nikes and the tennis socks and the jeans and the short-sleeve shirt and sat there in her bra and panties trying to write down the things swirling in her head. It wasn't working well, so she set the clock radio alarm for ten, unhooked the bra, threw it on a chair and lay down on her side on the couch. Maybe sleep could wash the night away, but she doubted it.

THE DAILY TEN O'CLOCK meeting at 11th and State began, as usual, ten minutes late. Since it was a Saturday, most of the top brass would not ordinarily have been there. Since it was this Saturday, with a double homicide on the sheet that included an Afro-American child, as the report was written, several of the top brass were there: Tom Flanagan, the deputy superintendent of Investigative Services; James Harkness, the deputy superintendent for Community Affairs; and David Coan, the deputy chief of detectives (the chief of detectives was attending what was dubbed an Administrative Inspectors Seminar being conducted at a mountain resort in the Adirondacks in upstate New York). Several others were also invited for this special occasion, including Lt. Ted Goldman and Sgt. Joe Morrison from Organized Crime; Arnie Troy, the lieutenant in charge of public relations; representatives from the Crime Lab and the Medical Examiner's office; the field lieutenant and the watch commander from Area Four, and Sergeant Gerherdt. All told there were eleven sitting at the long table in the conference room just down the hall from the superintendent's office on the sixth floor. None of them looked happy.

There were two basic types of homicide in Chicago. First, the routine, the majority—domestic troubles, a gangbanger shooting a rival gangbanger, a drug deal gone bad, a streetfight that got out of hand, a shopkeeper reluctant to turn over his day's earnings to an armed robber; common killings. Then there were those that caught the eyes of the police and the politicians and the imagination of the public—a child killed in a gang crossfire or murdered inside a school building; a celebrity or society murder, whether domestic or not; a multiple murder; the execution of a big-time hoodlum; any killing in a "good" neighborhood; a cop getting it; a racially motivated murder. The Friday night double-slaying was falling into category two: it had already caught the eye of the police, they knew instinctively it would not be long before it would catch the eye of the pols and the imagination of the public.

"Everybody got a copy of Sergeant Gerherdt's report?" Deputy Superintendent Flanagan asked. Nobody at 11th and State referred to him as Sergeant Bilko. There was a garble of yesses and uh-huhs. "I've also got the preliminary reports from the Medical Examiner's office. The victim found in the trunk of the car, one Thurman Peters, died of multiple gunshot wounds to the head, three to be exact. The other victim, one Rayfield Tees, died as a result of two gunshot wounds, one of which passed through his heart." Flanagan nodded at Deputy Superintendent Harkness. "Bullets were recovered from both bodies. Ballistics will have a report on them by noon, or so I'm told. And we've got a file made up by O.C. on Thurman Peters, according to Lieutenant Goldman here."

Goldman was the new chief of the Organized Crime division, having been appointed to the post six months earlier in one of the routine administrative shake-ups at 11th and State that the mayor directed his police superintendent to make just to keep everybody on their toes and the public aware that Hizzoner was on top of the job, doing his best to keep the city safe, which translated into something like he would prefer to have a newly certified loyalist in a specific position or to have someone who, for some reason or other, had drawn disfavor from City Hall removed from a specific position.

Goldman was pissed because he had had to cancel an appointment with his hair stylist in order to attend the Saturday morning meeting, to which Deputy Superintendent Flanagan had personally called him. He said to Flanagan, "Morrison's got it. Morrison, who was good enough to get out of his bed early this morning and drive down here to 11th and State to fetch the proper files and study them and put something together for us, will read for your benefit."

Joe Morrison looked over at his boss, for whom he had little affection, noticed the fingers with the manicured, clear-polished nails prancing on the table. His boss . . . the dandy. Goldman dressed to impress. He dressed like someone the Con

Squad up on the eighth floor should be investigating, someone whose life's work was talking the less advantaged into investing their life savings in some deal that was sure to double their money in three years or in some worthless real estate in Florida or some other swamp property, Morrison thought. Morrison himself spent more money than he should on clothes, despite his new, severely limited budget, what with child support payments since the divorce a year earlier, the apartment rent and all the other financial burdens faced by victims of recent marital disengagements. The only person Morrison dressed to impress, however, was himself, and he cut his own nails about once every two weeks and got his hair cut for eight dollars at a barbershop worked by two brothers who had been at the same little two-chair place up in Rogers Park for the past twenty-five years.

Morrison's eyes moved up from the tapping fingers to Goldman's pale blue eyes, the blueness of which Morrison thought was probably the result of contact lenses. They held there for just a moment as Morrison thought the sonofabitch called me at seven and told me to get down to 11th and State, me who is living in Rogers Park ten miles north of headquarters while Goldman lives in one of those yuppie apartments over on Printers Row about four blocks from 11th and State. At first meeting his new boss six months earlier, Morrison had wondered how Goldman ended up in charge of Organized Crime. But then it did not take long to learn that Goldman had some very good connections at City Hall, where his lack of knowledge of organized crime, much less the one with the capital *O* and the capital *C* and the word *division* after it, did not seem to matter.

Goldman was not a street cop. After a year on patrol when he first came on the job twenty-one years ago, he put on plainclothes and worked in administrative capacities in various area headquarters and eventually at 11th and State. Morrison was a street cop from the time he joined the force fifteen years ago, became one of the city's most effective homicide cops until he had burned out two years earlier. His heart, though, was still on the street, even if his mind had run from it. What was it they said about some cops, you can take them off the street but you can't take the street out of them. Which was another reason he was not especially fond of his new boss.

Sergeant Gerherdt had his hand in the air. Deputy Superintendent Flanagan said, "You want to add something, Gerherdt?"

"Just before this meeting got under way I got a call from Four. The two VC officers under my command who got this case have been back over to the scene in daylight and found two shell casings in addition to the three that were found earlier. The two casings, I am told, are identical to the other three."

Flanagan, looking over at Deputy Superintendent Harkness again, said, "This, I have the very uncomfortable feeling, is going to be one of the messier ones."

It sure as hell is, the other ten thought.

Harkness nodded. "You know, of course, the alderman over there."

"His Honor and Reverence Lorenz Hunter," Flanagan said. "How could any of us not know of his magisterial self?"

"He hasn't had a good crusade to roll with in several months," Harkness said. Deputy Superintendent Harkness, a black man himself, in his dealings with community relations in the city, had had many uncomfortable encounters over the past few years with Alderman Hunter, who was also known as Reverend Hunter because he was an ordained minister of the Avalon Tabernacle Church on west Madison Street although it was a lingering mystery as to who, if anyone, had actually ordained him. It was common knowledge, however, that he had a major financial interest in the church and it was from the pulpit, actually a dais, that he delivered some of his most inflammatory speeches. It was from that very dais that he had at different times referred to Jews as "malignant money-grubbers"; the mayor as a white racist and the Grand Dragon of Chicago; City Hall in general as a "pus-bubbling nest" filled with "keester-kissers" who mollycoddled all factions except those black; the police department as the Windy City Gestapo; and whites collectively as "genetic genocidists" or "generic genocidists," depending on which adjective first jumped into his nimble mind.

"Well, we don't have to release anything that might imply there's a link between the two murders," Lieutenant Troy of Public Relations put in. "Let's wait and see what the ballistics report has to say. Maybe the bullets won't match."

You've got to be kidding, Morrison thought.

"They're due in in two hours," Flanagan said.

Troy said, "I know, but first they"—referring to the beat reporters and the media—"do not know of the link between the shell casings and we don't have to tell them yet and we do not really have to release anything on the ballistics report until Monday. We're still waiting, okay? We can stonewall it, keep it out of the Sunday papers, which everybody reads, and off the tube until Monday. Maybe by then we'll have somebody in custody."

Morrison wanted to laugh but restrained himself. God, 11th and State was a planet away from the area squadrooms, the district stationhouses, the street, he thought. Does this guy know our record in bringing someone down on a mob hit?

Gerherdt had his hand in the air again. "You may not yet have been informed of this but we had an authorized ridealong last night with the two responding VC officers. She was a reporter for the *Metro News*, a feature writer by the name of Holly Stryker."

Dead silence.

ABOUT A HALF-HOUR BEFORE the meeting began down on State Street, the same Holly Stryker, sleepy-eyed, got up from the couch, awakened by a ringing telephone. When she answered it she heard: "Bet I woke you up. Must've been pretty tired, all the excitement last night."

"What? Who's this?"

"This is Johnny Nolan. Remember, I told you, anything new you'd be the first to know."

"Oh, right." She grabbed a pencil from a Toby jug on the table.

"Well, the guy in the trunk, according to Organized Crime

downtown, was definitely connected and from all appearances was executed right where we found him. And second, my partner and I went back over there and we found two more shells we think might be from the gun that killed the kid. They match with the other three we found. We won't know for sure though until Ballistics gives us a report. We also found a crack pipe near where the kid went down. Don't know if that has any relevance, but it went to the crime lab. In that neighborhood, finding one of those is like finding an empty diet-pop can in yours. But who knows, right?''

"Do you have anything at all on the connection between the two?"

"Not yet, maybe soon. We got a lot coming in," he exaggerated. Nolan paused, got no immediate response. "This one is gonna be a burning bush as we call it, one gets everybody's ass on fire. It's our case, César and me, that's why the overtime. Ballistics should be coming in soon. More info from O.C. too.'' He paused again. "Say, I got an idea, whyn't you meet me for a bite of lunch, around twelve maybe, and I can give you an update?"

Holly suddenly felt aware of her nakedness. The tone of his voice prompted that, she had heard that tone often enough since she was sixteen. She wanted to say aren't you tired, you've been up all night, but there was the story, after all. "Sure, why not."

"Let's see, you got a four-oh-four prefix," referring to the first part of her telephone number, "that's northside, mid-northside.''

"Wrigleyville.''

"Oh, yeah, whyn't you give me the address and I'll shoot by about noon and pick you up.''

"I'm going to be out running some errands. Why don't you name a place and I'll just meet you there.''

Goddamn. "Well, I could pick you up somewhere else. No sense taking two cars, with the parking and all around there.''

"No, really, just tell me where and I'll be there.''

"Okay. How about Little Mo's, it's kind of a sports bar on Clark up around Addison, west side of the street.''

"I'll be there at twelve."

"Great, between now and then I hope I can come up with something juicy for you. See ya."

Juicy—as she hung up the telephone, Holly Stryker suddenly remembered Detective McCabe's poisonous toads.

She quickly punched the button on her touch-tone telephone and heard the tinkling of beeps that would automatically dial her through to the *Metro* city desk.

✣10

ALDO FORTE AND ANGELO LEFT THE CAR AND ITS DRIVER IN the circular driveway in front of Gus Tuscano's twelve-room Tudor-style home that sat on four acres of neatly trimmed lawns lush with bushes and hedges and shade trees. The estate had been professionally landscaped by the previous owner, a mercantile exchange broker who got caught up in illegal trading and had to sell it to pay his fines and lawyers' fees.

A young man with a nose that pointed somewhat in the general direction of his right ear and with small, slightly crossed bullet-hole eyes that seemed to change positions when he was looking at you led them through the house, and across the lannon-stone patio to where Gus Tuscano was propped up on a tufted chaise lounge looking out across a large kidney-shaped swimming pool that glimmered under the rays of the morning sun. The lord of the manor was wearing the next smallest bathing suit to a bikini, a so-called crotch-popper. A towel was draped shawl-like around his shoulders. On the table next to him was a glass of lemonade with a straw, and a plate that held a remnant of an English muffin and pieces of fruit. Music resounded from wall speakers, someone singing an aria from an Italian opera, Pavarotti maybe, or Domingo. Gussy, as most who knew him well enough called him, was a lover of Italian music. Gussy was softly mouthing the words along with the tenor, perhaps seeing himself on the grand stage at La Scala. In his brief bathing suit Gussy actually looked rather ridiculous, with his spindly hairless legs sticking out below and sagging breasts that settled downward on his chest like packets of gelatin. Gussy was seventy-eight years old. He motioned them now to sit down at the umbrella table next to where he was lounging.

"Send Emma out, Cockeye. They may want some breakfast, or maybe a beverage," he said to the man with the bullet-hole eyes. "That's my name for him," Tuscano said to Angelo. "I can call him that. You can't. You call him Mario."

THE MEETING AT 11TH and State ended just after eleven, the ballistics report having arrived earlier than they expected. The bullets recovered from both bodies had been fired from the same gun. Everybody agreed with Lieutenant Troy of Public Relations. Stonewall was in. Let the fan wait awhile for the feces to hit it. See just how hard it would hit. See how big a spray it would send out once it did. Monday was soon enough. As Lieutenant Troy put it, "We are all in agreement, then. We are awaiting the results of the autopsies and the ballistics reports, which we should have by, say, Monday." He looked at the investigator from the M.E.'s office who had brought over their report and who nodded back, then to the technician from Ballistics. "Make sure they understand that upstairs, okay?" The technician nodded his understanding. Troy gathered his copies of the reports and his notes and stuffed them into a blond filing folder, slid it into a leather carrying case and zipped it shut. "That about it for now?"

"That should do it," Deputy Superintendent Flanagan said. "We'll meet here on Monday morning, ten o'clock sharp."

As he headed for the press room downstairs, Troy knew what the questions would be . . . *Lieutenant Troy, is there any relationship between the two murders in Area Four last night . . . Was the time of death approximately the same for both victims . . . Have you any leads so far in either murder . . . ?* And so forth. His answers were equally routine and always evasive, ending with: *Time's up, sorry, but that's all we have for you now.*You didn't win popularity contests in his job, but then again, popularity wasn't his job.

JOE MORRISON WALKED TO the elevator bank with Deputy Superintendent Harkness, thought by many to be next in line for the superintendency. He was a respected administrator now who while on the street working Property Crimes and later Gang Crimes was considered both a fearsome presence and a fair and honest detective. When he wasn't on the street in those earlier days he was in the classrooms of several local colleges, from one of which he eventually earned a bachelor's degree and from another a master's degree in criminology. It helped in his climb up the department's administrative ladder. James Harkness was also the first to admit his color had been a definite asset in his ascension, what with the newfound political awareness at City Hall that black and Hispanic groups could no longer be treated as simple minorities but instead had become sizable and fraternal voting blocks who needed to be taken seriously . . . and then some. Morrison had known Jim Harkness for about ten years and was the first to say that the deputy super deserved the lofty position in the Chicago police department he had attained whether he was black, white, purple or emerald green.

"You need a ride anywhere, Joe? I got the car downstairs. No driver, being Saturday, but I could drop you."

"No, thanks. I'm going upstairs, make a couple of calls. Long as they got me out of bed and down here." He looked at Harkness as they reached the elevator. "I think you're gonna earn your stripes on this one, Jim. Just a gut feeling."

Harkness smiled at him. "I think you may be right, Joe. Think Monday might be a real pisser."

The door to an elevator opened, the arrow pointing down illuminated in red now. But Harkness made no movement toward it. "You got another gut feeling, Joe, on maybe how the two of them managed to get themselves shot together? Something from out of that old homicide mind of yours, the one you've let languish of late."

Morrison shook his head at the fancy talk. "Top of my head, it looks like they were into something together. We know Peters was a full-time thief and fence. And not just petty stuff. From the files in O.C., as I told you in there, he's been tied to hijackings, warehouse heists, stuff like that. We've several things that tie him to different street crews in the city. He wasn't a made guy, obviously, his name being Peters. Not a member of any crew specifically. Just a freelance guy out there who dealt with them and paid his dues. From what we know, he had a pretty good-size operation. Maybe he and the kid had something going that went sour. Maybe it was from the kid's side, you know, gang stuff, some banger from over there was ticked enough to blow both of them away. It doesn't take much these days for them to start shooting. Then again maybe it was somebody from Peters's side and the kid just happened to be with him at the time. Nobody's got anything on the kid yet, but my hunch is he's not a member of any altar boy society or Four-H club."

"You know what I think, Joe? Things aren't all that clear at the moment, like you say. But one thing I think is that two different forces have just had a real nasty collision that's left a representative of each dead with consequences that are yet to show themselves."

"A lot of questions still out there, Jim." The understatement of the year, Morrison thought.

JOHNNY NOLAN BURST INTO Little Mo's like a cowboy through the swinging doors to Miss Kitty's saloon desperate to find Marshall Dillon in some old take of "Gunsmoke." In Nolan's case he was desperate to find Miss Holly, who he was afraid might not be there, him being a half-hour late. He was relieved to see her sitting at a tiny table along the wall under a montage of framed photographs of Ernie Banks, Bill Veeck, Michael Jordan, Gale Sayers, Stan Mikita, Leo Durocher, Dick Butkus, Jimmy Piersall, Walter Payton, all surrounding a slightly blurry blown-up color print of former coach Mike Ditka in a Bears sweater walking across the snow-covered ground of Soldier Field, giving a postgame finger to some photographer who was fortunate to have been in the right place at the right frame of Coach Ditka's mind to capture the moment. She had half a glass of draft beer in front of her, her leg crossed like a man's, ankle resting on thigh. She was wearing tan stretch pants with stirrups, a pair of flat-heeled shoes the same color and a patterned cotton blouse the predominant colors of which were navy blue and forest green. Nolan thought she filled out the outfit real fine.

"Sorry, I'm late. Hope I didn't mess you up."

"No."

"Not a bad place, though. A lot of cops come here. If you gotta wait, better than a street corner, this weather, you'd wilt." He put on a smile. "A good sports bar, what do you think?" He waved his arm around to direct her attention to the ambience—the walls filled with photographs of sports personalities, pennants and other pieces of memorabilia. There were large-screen television sets in three different corners of the room, each tuned to a different channel but with no audio on any one of them so as not to disturb the various conversations and arguments going on at the bar and most of the tables. At the moment, if talk was not the option, Little Mo's customers had the choice of watching a silent major league baseball game, silent golf match or silent stock car race, thanks to the all-inclusive coverage provided by cable TV.

"No problem," she said.

Nolan let out a deep breath. "Well, I'm sure glad you're still here. You'll be glad, too, I got something for you." The move was on. Nolan leaned back on the two rear legs of his chair, his eyes on Holly Stryker but at the same time giving a hand-sign to Little Mo's only waitress, who was schmoozing with the bartender. "You like beer?" he said, nodding toward the glass sitting in front of her. "How about another? Give the lady another beer," he told the waitress. "I'll have a Special Export." Held up his hand. "Bottle." Then to Holly: "You got some rest, huh."

"A little."

"I'm runnin' on adrenalin. It's always that way when you first get into a case like this. It's the most important time in any homicide investigation, just after the killing. You got your best chance of nailin' whoever did it in the first couple of days. After that it gets a lot tougher. In the beginning, you get your evidence right up front, your leads, later there usually isn't any more new evidence and the leads that come in aren't nearly as good as the earlier ones.'' Was she appreciating his insights into homicide investigation? "You can quote me on that if you want."

"Thanks." She wasn't writing anything down in the steno pad that lay open on the table in front of her.

The waitress arrived and set another beer in front of Holly, who hadn't finished her first. She put down an empty glass in front of Nolan, then with a flourish a bottle. "Special Export, in a bottle. Want me to pour it for you?"

"I got two hands with working thumbs." He tapped both against opposing fingers to show her. "I think I can handle it." He gave her a big smile. She slapped the check down next to the beer bottle and went back to the end of the bar where the bartender was looking up at the cars without roaring motors and screeching tires that careened phantomlike around the track.

"So listen," he said, his elbows on the table now, leaning across toward her, "this is something you did not get from *me*. Right?"

"Right." She picked up the ballpoint next to her pad.

"I mean you've got that thing where you don't have to reveal your sources. Because I really shouldn't be telling you this."

"I can attribute it to 'a source at police headquarters.' "

"Well, as I said, I was hopin' to have something juicy for you. And I got that something. That's why I was late." He was talking just above a whisper. "Between you and me, right?"

"Right."

"Sergeant Bilko, you remember him."

"Sergeant Gerherdt, the sergeant on duty last night."

"You got it."

"He caught us over at Four, just after he got back from a

meeting at 11th and State. Things are getting ready to start popping. The ballistics report is in. The bullets that killed the guy in the trunk and the bullets found in the kid—fired from the same gun, nine millimeter. Not announced, though. Not yet.''

"When?"

"Probably Monday."

"Nobody else knows about this?"

"Not outside the department, and not too many in the department. This is quiet time."

"You saw the ballistics report."

"No. Bilko did downtown. They're holding it there. He told us because we got the case. I mean, let's face it, it gives us a direction."

"What *did* they give the press this morning?"

"Nothing. I wasn't there, but according to Bilko they were just told we were working on it and that there was nothing yet that seemed to tie the two killings together. Downplay it for now. They got their reasons, the big guys down at 11th and State, that is."

"Is there anything about what the link might be?"

"Nothing. We don't even know anything about the kid yet, except a name, an address and a mother who told us he wasn't a bad boy. We talked to her a couple of hours ago. She said Rayfield had some troubles, like at school because he didn't show up there very often. A few other things with the cops from time to time, but most of those were mistakes, according to mama. An old story. By the way, he was thirteen, in the seventh grade when he did show up for school. His father was killed five years ago. Beaten to death with a hammer by his cousin. All in the family." He waited for a reaction, got none.

"What was the boy doing there, under the bridge?"

"Don't know . . ."

"Why are they covering this up?"

"Not covering up, maybe stalling. Could be a little dicey, the kid getting whacked too. They're worried about that rabblerouser out there, the alderman."

"Hunter," she said, thinking they probably had good reason to worry.

"Maybe by Monday we'll have more answers. Make it a lot simpler if we do. I'm just giving it to you so that you got a little leg up, you know? But remember, you didn't get it from me."

"Anything else?"

"We got the initial report from O.C. Manny Peters wasn't just some juice loan deadbeat. He didn't *belong* to the Outfit—he was protected, though. He did deals, they say, with street bosses. Looks like the last deal was a bad one, for Manny anyway . . . and the kid, whatever part he had in it."

Holly was scribbling away now.

"So you got yourself a double murder. A kid, and the Outfit, too. So how's that for juicy . . . so far?"

"Juicy, right." She got up, grabbing her purse. "I've got to make a phone call." She gave him a smile. "Be right back," and headed for the pay phone just between the washroom cubicles, *Jocks* and *Jockettes*, in the back of Little Mo's.

Johnny Nolan, feeling pretty good, things seeming to be going in the direction he wanted, ordered himself another bottle of Special Export.

The bar was full now, the regulars and the weekenders and a few casuals, standing room only.

Holly Stryker almost collided with the waitress, delivering Nolan's second beer as she swept back into the room. "Here," she said, pausing for just a moment to drop a five-dollar bill on the table. "I hope this takes care of the beers. Got to get downtown. They're holding the story for me. We'll have to do the lunch part another time. And thank you, Detective Nolan. You are a helluva guy."

"Hey." He started to say something else but she was already on her way to the door. *Helluva guy*, he said to himself. *Terrific.*

✦11

JOE MORRISON HAD BEEN OUT OF HOMICIDE ALMOST TWO
years now. The once freestanding division had been incorpo-
rated into what was now known as Violent Crimes while he
was still in it, but even after the change he had continued to
be known as a homicide detective because that was his specialty and he had built a reputation in that role, until he burned
out.

It had been his choice to get out. He had been involved with
too many murders, seen too many corpses. He had worked the
cases for just over ten years, put in the overtime, the legwork,
the questioning, dealing with the lies and liars—day in, day
out. Unlike some others he kept the scenes and details inside
his head—Joe Morrison's private vault of horrors to which,
unfortunately, only he had the combination. If he could just
forget the left-right numbers, leave the vault shut and sealed,
but he could not. Put together—the hours, the isolation—it
was probably what finally ruined his marriage, but that was as
dead an issue now as the homicide cases he used to investi-
gate. Which was why he was sitting alone in the one-bedroom
apartment on Chicago's far north side at six o'clock on this
summer Saturday evening, sipping a vodka-and-grapefruit
juice, thinking about what his kids, the two little girls not yet
out of grammar school, might be doing on this nonvisit weekend.

Homicide still followed him, though. Why else had he been
sitting down at 11th and State all morning? But it was different
now, or supposed to be. He was there only to provide information on Manny Peters and his connection to the Outfit, to
gather anything O.C. might have about the man that might
help the VC detectives who were doing what he used to do.
Better this way. Five days a week. Overtime pay for today

would come in handy. Tomorrow, Sunday, was his.

So he thought.

The telephone rang. It was Jim Harkness. "You see the *Metro?*"

"No."

"Better go out and get it, Joe. And cancel any fun and games you had for tomorrow."

"What's going on?"

"Get the paper. *The front page.* Where the hell's your boss, anyway? We've been beeping Goldman for a half hour now."

"Maybe he's got the beeper stuffed under some mattress with satin sheets. It's Saturday night. America's date night. And Goldman tends to spend most of his off-duty time with one bimbo or another. Or maybe he's at temple." Morrison paused, added, "And maybe I'm the pope's man from the Vatican."

"Somebody leaked the story, Joe. That woman, the ride-along, she got it from somebody. 'Boy's Murder Tied to Gangland Slaying.' She goes on to say that the ballistics report shows that both got it from bullets fired from the same gun— a reputed mobster and a kid. You read the article and you think that schmuck Peters was Machine Gun Kelly and the kid was an altar boy.

"She also says police officials refused to comment on the ballistics report, that we said we were waiting for final test results on Monday. But according to her, a source inside police headquarters revealed that the tests had *already been made*— that last is in italics—and that the results were positive, the bullets taken from each body came from the same gun. It was corroborated, she says, by a technician in Ballistics who said the results had been delivered to Deputy Superintendent for Investigative Services Tom Flanagan at approximately eleven o'clock this morning. Deputy Superintendent Flanagan could not be reached for comment. How's *that*?"

"That should send a gerbil up Williams's ass." Morrison was referring to Alton Williams, Chicago's Superintendent of Police.

"A porcupine, I'd say. And speaking of Williams, he badly

wants to know where the leak came from. The woman was apparently calling everybody she could get through to downtown. Everybody stonewalled, from what I'm told—everybody but one, that is. And then she got through to some technician in Ballistics, a guy name of Mendenhall who it seems didn't know he was supposed to keep his mouth shut. It does not make us look very good, Joe.''

"You got any idea who the loose lips belong to?''

"No. There were a lot of people downtown and over at Four who knew about it. It could be anybody. You know, at this point I don't think it really matters. It's done. I just can't convince Alton of that. He hates the look of it. Incidentally, you said when we were leaving this morning you were going upstairs to make some calls . . .''

"You think *I* did it?''

"Hell, no, Joe. I've known you long enough. I was just wondering if somebody you talked to might have—''

"I talked to two people. One was my contact with the Bureau, Tim Doyle. I asked him to give me anything the FBI had on Manny Peters and his relationship with the Outfit. He said he'd see what he could find first thing Monday. And I talked with my former partner down in Florida, Norbert Castor. You remember him, got shot on a case with me about a year ago, paralyzed, he's on full disability now down in Sarasota. He knows about everything there is to know about the Outfit. Said he'd think about it—Peters didn't ring a bell but he'd look through his own files that he's got down there and buzz me Monday.''

"Well, Joe, Alton's already heard from the mayor, who is as annoyed as he is. The rest of the press and our friends on the tube and the radio are also pissed at being scooped and they're all over everywhere trying to get something. Troy was with the super when I talked to him. So was Flanagan. So was the P.R. lady from the mayor's office. They're working on something for the press. Troy's going to give a department statement later tonight, I'm told. But the mayor and the super are still real pissed.''

"You know, we shouldn't listen to Troy and all that

bullshit, all the maneuvering. It works for the mayor and his crowd, but we do it and everything gets fucked up. We're not politicians.''

"I know, Joe. Anyway, go get yourself a paper and watch the ten o'clock news. And be downtown at nine. The super wants everybody there who was at our meeting today, and some others of his choice. He says he'll chair it himself.''

"Great. When you finally get hold of Goldman, tell him you already talked to me and I'll be at the meeting in the morning and that I'm out for the night at an unknown saloon, which I may or may not be. You've ruined my Sunday, I don't need my Saturday night fucked up talking to him.''

ANGELO FRANCONI WAS TAKING advantage of America's date night sitting in the front room of the Alessi's sprawling ranch house in suburban Elmwood Park waiting for Anita. He was going to make up for the previous night, take her out for something to eat, some nice place, then a little socializing and dancing down at the Club Chelsea on Chicago's near north-side, *the* place to be these nights, the in place for the wiseguys with their girlfriends. It was not a private club, although there were two guys at the entrance greeting all the potential customers, checking out the young, swinging moneyed guest members who had no idea with whom they were mingling. The Club Chelsea was filled to capacity every night except Sunday, when it was closed. The club did not take reservations, but Angelo had called earlier, dropped a name, a big name. He and Anita would not wait in the line that snaked down Rush Street and around the corner onto Elm Street on a Saturday night. There was another entrance, he was told, and a table would be available when he got there at ten.

It wasn't that Anita was not ready. She was. Dressed, sitting back there in her room listening to an Eric Clapton CD. She was just waiting. Waiting because her father told her he wanted to talk a little with her boyfriend before she went out with him that night. She had no idea what about, but she hoped he wasn't going to give Angelo all of the stuff about how to treat her, respect her, the reminder that his first and only daughter deserved nothing but the finest treatment. She knew her father doted on her, and she loved him for it even though he could be a royal pain at times. He treated her like a goddess, and it was her father—his power, his self-confidence and the respect (she never saw it as fear) that everybody seemed to give him—by whom she judged other men.

Well, he didn't need to worry about Angelo, she thought as she sat in the flowery brocaded chair in the corner next to her dressing table, staring across the comforter on the queen-size bed, which had the same flowered pattern as the chair, at the menagerie of stuffed animals that sat on the pillows and on the shelves above it, all of whom were staring back at her with their agate eyes. It was a large bedroom with a television/ VCR/CD and tape player console housed in a white floor-to-ceiling cabinet, a white-with-gold-trim antique telephone on the bedside table, furniture from Marshall Field's top-of-the-line collection, framed posters of rock stars on the walls, some dolls sitting on a child's rocking chair in another corner. The room had a special mix—the amenities of a starlet and of a little girl.

No, her father did not need to give Angelo an Italian lecture. Angelo had been nothing but a real good guy since they started going together a couple of months earlier. He was warm, considerate, passionate—yes, definitely, but not pushy. He was good-looking, tough-looking—maybe a little too self-conscious sometimes, but if there was ever a problem she would be safe with him, she was certain of that. From the start she had daydreamed about doing things with Angelo that would knock her father out of his Cole-Haans if he ever knew about them. It did not take long for the erotic thoughts floating through her mind to come to life. So her father was wasting his time at the moment while she had to sit here and wait.

Joe-sep Alessi, however, had different matters on his mind. He brought Angelo into the sprawling family room he had had built onto the rear of the house and filled with enough bamboo furniture to have depleted several rattan showrooms. There was also a pool table and a wet bar and large straw-colored mats on the floor that Joe had appropriated from the Singapore

Sling, a nightclub on the strip on Archer Avenue in which he had had a major but silent interest a few years back, just before it burned down.

"Angelo, we should have a little talk," Alessi said as he leaned against the bar. "And I don't want you to get nervous about this. You want something to drink?" shaking the over-sized snifter filled nearly to the brim with Stolichnaya and ice cubes.

"No, thanks, we're going to a couple places tonight. I'll be having something then. The Chelsea, remember."

"Oh, yeah. I hear it's nice." He took a swig of the vodka. "That's good, Angelo, pacing yourself. That's what I like about you. You got responsibility. A good head. You want a soda pop or anything? Pepsi, Coke, Seven-Up, the diet stuff? Anita likes that, keeps her slim and beautiful."

"No, really, I'm fine, Joe-sep."

"Good, Angelo." Joe Alessi was still standing. He paused for just a moment, then settled on one of the barstools. "You know, Angelo, you guys messed up last night." It came out a statement of fact, no threat. No anger. "I been talking with Aldo and both he and me been talking with Gussy most of the day. It is an unhappy situation."

"You're telling me." In more ways than Joe-sep knew, Angelo added to himself.

"You want to know why it's such an unhappy situation?" He did not wait for an answer. "Now don't get me wrong, it is not so much for you to worry about. According to Aldo you did right. The assholes he brought in from out of town, they did stupid. It's things like that that screw up all kinds of things in the business. Gussy is hoping it'll all blow over. Aldo and me, we think it will. The cops, they been around shaking some cages. It don't take no Einstein downtown to figure who did Manny Peters. So they show up and hassle. A little shit for a couple of days, maybe a week or so, then back to normal. Meantime, Angelo, we gotta shut some things down. That's gonna cost us. That's why I say it isn't good for the business."

"Hey, if I'd had my way, it would *not* have turned out the

way it did, believe me. But I couldn't do anything, it just happened—''

"No, no, Angelo, I know that. I just want to have a, you know, friendly chat. Now, you know Jimmy Pagnano was with us last night till you had to go.''

"Just to say hello to, that's about all. I know he works for you.''

"Jimmy's one of the best. Been with me a long time now.'' Alessi tapped the one foot that was on the floor. "He's made.''

"I figured. From what I heard about him, anyway.''

"What did you hear about him?'' Alessi was pouring himself a little water on top of the vodka, giving Angelo a kind of look over his shoulder.

"Aldo's mentioned him. Some others, too. He's got a reputation.''

"He does, Angelo. And that can be good and it can be bad. For example, Jimmy's mean. He loves the stuff, I tell you. Since he was a kid he'd as soon break your arm as shake your hand.'' Alessi held his free hand in the air. "But he's *devoted*, Angelo. I brought him off the sidewalk, a fighter, always in some kind of trouble. But I saw something in him so I got him doing some things for money instead of just the satisfaction of breaking somebody's bones or cuttin' somebody up. Now he's one of my top soldiers. He earned the faith I got in him. That's why I stood for him to Gussy. That's why I got him the other vote. That's why he got made. But I'm getting off the point.''

"You are making a point, Joe.''

"Yeah, but back to the reputation thing. Everybody we deal with knows him, knows what can happen they don't do right with us. That's good. A little fear never hurts. They know Jimmy might kill a guy cause he got too cute, that's all, too cute or too annoying. On the other hand, that kind of rep gets to the wrong people, too. They're gonna be on his ass for every little thing that happens. Maybe even this thing last night. The blue balls downtown start thinking, who might've done this? Hey, Jimmy Pagnano, he likes to kill people so he comes to mind. Well, we know he didn't have anything to do with it and he's got a shakeproof alibi . . . this time. I keep telling him, Jimmy, you gotta quit *liking* this. You like it too much. One of these days it's gonna get you in trouble.''

Alessi got up and went over and sat in one of the bamboo chairs across from Angelo. ''That's one of the things I just wanted to tell you, Angelo. Sometimes you gotta do what you gotta do. We all do it . . . and in a way we still do, in our own way, not ourselves as such, you know what I mean. Just don't get to like it too much.''

''I know that, Joe. I appreciate the advice.''

''Jimmy's got other points too. You know he's got connections all over the city. He's got one of those, what do you call it, double personalities. I mean he can do things to somebody you wouldn't believe if he got reason to, and on the other hand he can be one of the smoothest strokers you ever saw if he wants to get something outa somebody or make a friend at City Hall or wherever for something he might wanna get later.'' There was a silence, and Angelo thought maybe he should say something but he could not think what.

''What I'm saying, Angelo, look at Jimmy's good points. Keep your eyes open and your balls protected.''

Then the point: ''On one other thing, you're getting kind of close, you and Anita. She talks to me. My one and only, Angelo.'' He seemed to drift off for a moment. ''And Aldo Forte and I go way back. We were on the street together the same time. We ran together. And Aldo tells me he's got a lot of faith in you, your future. That's good to hear. And so far I like you, too, Angelo.''

''I appreciate that.''

''But in the business, fuck-ups are not tolerated. We still don't know where this thing from last night will go. We got some newspaper crap tonight. You see that?'' Angelo nodded. ''Nothing too bad that I could tell. Nobody has anything to connect this to us. They can think it, the cops, the papers, and they do, but they don't have a thing. We got out of there clean from what I'm told. But you never know, Angelo. Right now it looks like the cops are taking most of the heat. So far. Gussy's got some people dropping the word in the right places that Peters got himself wrapped up in a drug deal, importing. A solo shot. That's what got him in trouble. Tried to slip one by the Pedros. Gussy'd like it if we can lay it off on someone like the Herrinos or one of them other spic families. Let them take the heat. Hell, drugs is their world. Drugs is *not* our business.'' He looked almost apologetic. ''Sometimes, maybe, Angelo. A deal comes along, well, you gotta take it. But it's only a slop of gravy. Remember that, Angelo. It's too risky. We got meat and potatoes and salad and dessert and good wine on the table—the gravy, if it's okay we might take some. But it's not on the menu. Got me?'' He raised the glass again and drained it. ''You get caught up in something big with drugs, they're gonna take everything you got—the house, the cars, anything they can get their hands on.'' He shook his head. ''The money I got socked away for Anita, number one and only daughter . . . if they can find it, that is.''

''Joe-sep, I'm really sorry about last night—''

''Don't keep swimming in it, Angelo. Let's see what happens. Something comes to somebody who waits, somebody important said that once, or something like it. We're waiting, we'll see. *Wait*, that's the word. Just like my little daughter's doing back there, waiting for you.''

''I understand.'' Angelo was looking at his feet, then back up. ''Joe-sep,'' he said, ''I been getting a lot of advice these days. Aldo . . . you understand, he tells me things, like a father maybe. I told him and I want to tell you, Joe-sep, I really like Anita. I respect her. You know, I really feel for her. Maybe you think I'm out of line, getting involved this way.''

''It's not common, Angelo.''

''But—''

''That doesn't mean it can't happen. Angelo, you watch your ass. That's the best advice I can give you. You behave yourself. Have a good time tonight.'' He shook a finger at Angelo and smiled. ''Not too good.''

He walked to the double doors that led out of the family room. ''Hey, Anita, your guy's here. What're you doing back there? Taking so long. Keeping this nice boy waiting.'' He gave Angelo a conspiratorial smile. ''Come on out, honey.''

When she did, Joe Alessi threw an arm around her. "The guy looks pretty good," nodding at Angelo, "but he needs better ties. That thing he's wearing, it looks like a pizza."

"That's the style, daddy."

"Hey, Angelo, there are styles and there are lousy styles. That's, ah, I hate to say it, a lousy style. Looks like a pizza. Do me a favor, go to Danolo's downtown on Michigan Avenue. Ask for Mr. Danolo. Tell him you need a couple of nice Italian silk ties, tell him Joe Alessi sent you. He'll take care of you."

"Okay, Joe-sep."

"And tell him to put 'em on my account. A little something." Joe Alessi raised both arms like a referee signaling a touchdown. "You kids have a good time."

Angelo Franconi felt like he'd been split in half.

THE REVEREND LORENZ HUNTER, on the other hand, had postponed his planned Saturday night festivities. With the front section of the *Metro* tucked under his arm, and a small group of his clerical staff, he had instead gone to visit Roberta Tees, Rayfield's mother. Even though she wasn't a member of his church, she was a constituent of his aldermanic district and he felt she was now indeed in need of his spiritual consolation.

"I would like you at services tomorrow, Miss Roberta." He had been told she was not married, intelligence from the quick check made earlier by his deputies. The political associates, as they preferred to be called, had also found out that she was a working woman, cleaned the washrooms and kept the paper-towel racks filled in a shopping mall west of the city; two in the afternoon to ten at night every day of the week. She took a bus to the Congress Street rapid transit train every day, rode it west to the end of the line, then took another bus to the mall. The reverse route usually got her home a little after eleven at night. A stand-tall lady, according to the Reverend Hunter, if you don't count the sojourns out into the neighborhood with her boyfriend after eleven o'clock most nights. But with the minimum wage she made at the mall and the stolen food stamps she was able to buy from some of the junkies on the street she managed to get by. Rayfield had been her only child.

"I am going to hold a special service for your son, another tragic victim of the violence of our unprotected streets," the reverend told her. "I would like very much for you to be there. I know you will be making funeral arrangements on your own, but please, tomorrow let the community and our ministry share your grief and offer our sympathies in the embrace of God."

"Rayfield was not a bad boy."

"I know he wasn't, Miss Roberta. He was just a child, one denied the opportunity to grow to adulthood. That's the terrible sorrow."

"A little wild, way he ran around. But I workin' most of the time. And he always come home, never give me no sass. Why somebody have to go and kill Rayfield?"

"Well, Miss Roberta, no one knows why or who yet. No one will answer us about why the streets are so dangerous in this neighborhood and so safe in other neighborhoods where the people are of a different skin color. It is something I have been working to have changed for a long time in the chambers of government at City Hall and in our church assembly. Let's honor your son's short life and grieve his untimely death tomorrow together."

"I don't even have money to give my boy a proper burial."

"Perhaps the congregation can help with that, perhaps a fund. The service is scheduled for eleven o'clock. Will you please come?"

When he reached over and patted her on the shoulder, she nodded tearfully. "Thank you, Miss Roberta, and may the Lord bless you."

Alderman Hunter and his entourage then repaired to the street, where the black Buick Park Avenue, with driver, was waiting for them.

✦12

SUNDAY MORNING BROKE LATE WITH NO SUN TO BE SEEN behind a heavy cloud cover that had moved in some time during the night. Sunrise was supposed to have been at 6:13 that morning but instead the darkness had only turned a charcoal gray at the appointed time. Rain was expected, at least according to the weatherman on the ten o'clock news Saturday night. It looked for once like he might be right.

By seven o'clock the city was taking on a lighter shade of gray, though it was still slaty and oppressive. Now a thin drizzle began dampening the streets, not cooling them, just adding to the humidity. In one section of the city Johnny Nolan was busy on top of his wife. He was home in bed at that hour having been switched from midnights to days because of the Friday night murders and told to be at Four for the eight A.M. roll call. His wife, eyes closed, gave an occasional moan and tried to breathe heavily, hoping it would end soon. It did.

"Sorry I gotta get out of here so quick," Johnny said after rolling back to one side of the bed. He reached over, rubbed her belly. "The way I feel I could break records today . . . if I just had the time."

She looked over at him. "You were wonderful, Johnny." She watched him step out of bed, then take deep breaths, doing a few stretching exercises.

"Don't do anything too strenuous today, kiddo," he said. "Keep your strength, the guy's gonna be back six or so tonight." And off her hero strode into the bathroom.

IN ROGERS PARK, JOE Morrison was reading the newspapers, the early Sunday morning editions of the *Sun-Times* and the *Tribune*. Neither had anything except what the reporters had gotten from the police report and from Lieutenant Troy's restrained press conference the night before.

JIM HARKNESS WAS SITTING at the breakfast table with his wife in their red brick Georgian home on the far south side of the city. He was already dressed but she was still wearing a pink terrycloth robe over her nightgown. There were scrambled eggs on a platter, bacon on a side plate; she was waiting for the toast to pop up. She no longer asked him why he had to work such crazy hours. He had been downtown half a day on Saturday and now it looked like all day Sunday. After being married for twenty-five years to an ambitious cop and now a top police administrator, she had more or less gotten used to it.

LIEUTENANT GOLDMAN WAS BUFFING his tasseled loafers on a Self-Shoe-Shiner that he operated from the handle of a canelike chrome tube, staring down at the furry thing that spun across the top and along the sides of his shoe. He was not happy. This Sunday he had had a date for brunch at a north side bistro with Julie Epstein, recently divorced and, he felt, a woman who was interested in him. It had been her idea and she had even insisted on paying for the brunch. He had had to call and cancel out. Goddamn job, he kept repeating to himself.

JIM FLANAGAN WAS UP by himself making the coffee. He could hear his wife snoring in their bedroom. He was thinking she was always complaining about *his* snoring. *She* sounded like a jackhammer. What the hell, they were getting old, he thought as he poured the coffee and added some milk to it and half a banana to his bran cereal, looked at his watch and figured he better hurry if he was going to get downtown before nine. He was tired, he had been with the superintendent and other administrators until eleven last night. Didn't get home until almost midnight and couldn't get to sleep for at least another hour. Two more years until mandatory retirement.

Was he really only two years away from sixty-three? It was a chilling thought.

GUSSY TUSCANO WAS SITTING inside the Florida room of his house, looking out through the sliding glass doors at his pool and the landscaped grounds. Music was pouring out from the speakers. Pavarotti singing "Piscatore 'e Pusilleco," one of his favorites. Not as special as "Torna a Surriento," nothing was, but it was still up there. He had been to Sorrento and stayed up in a villa on the hillside looking out over the Bay of Naples. There was no more beautiful sight in the world to Gus Tuscano than that.

He was already in his skimpy swimsuit, covered by a thigh-length beach coat, drinking fresh-squeezed grapefruit juice from a balloon wine goblet. Grapefruit, his doctor told him, would get the old ketones going and burn off fat, even though Gussy had no visible fat.

Gussy was thinking that Aldo sure as hell had gotten their Manny Peters message out, but not in the way either of them had wanted. It was a message intended for *certain* people, not the whole goddamn city of Chicago. Still, there was nothing to trace it back to the Outfit. No witnesses. The two creeps from Camden were gone a thousand miles from Chicago. It should all blow over in a few days, he told himself, took a sip of the grapefruit juice and clanked the empty wine glass down on the glass-top table, which made an eerie ring, and said to nobody except himself, "Let's just see what happens. Right . . ."

He slid one of the large doors open and walked to the edge of the deep end of the pool. It was gloomy and sticky outside but it was not raining this far west of the city. He stood there a moment, looked at the water and stretched his arms heavenward, hands touching at the sides of his thumbs, fingers stiff, pointing to the sky. Then he closed his eyes, saw the blue-green water of the Mediterranean stretching from Sorrento out to Capri, and pushed off, arcing his aged body as he plunged into the placid water of his pool.

THE CONFERENCE ROOM AT 11th and State was set up well before nine. The superintendent had called this morning and he was presiding.

Everyone was there by nine. Joe Morrison went over to Franco Norelli. They had been friends at Belmont, Area Six in those days before it was renumbered Area Three for some arcane bureaucratic reason back when Morrison was still in Homicide. Norelli was one of the most successful and publicized homicide cops in the city. Half-black, half-Italian, tall and in good shape for his forty-eight years, he looked like someone you would have to be a little loony to mess with, although his finest quality was his shrewd and calculating mind. If the gray hadn't surpassed the jet black in his full head of slicked-back hair and the crows hadn't left footprints alongside his eyes, he could easily have passed for mid-thirties. His real name was Francis, but everyone called him Franco after Franco Harris, the Pittsburgh Steelers all-pro running back of the 1960s who was also half-black and half-Italian.

"Bringing in the A-team," Morrison said to him now.

Norelli shrugged. "I got the call last night. The way I figure it, this being the kind of case it is, they wanted a good black dick and a good dago dick and what with personnel cutbacks and all they could only afford one, so naturally they settled on me. A two-fer."

"How much do you know about this thing?" Morrison asked.

"Just what I read in the paper, and the brief I got from the watch commander at Three who called to tell me Flanagan wanted me here this morning."

"I was down here yesterday but I don't know much more about it than you do." Morrison clapped Norelli on the shoulder. "So what's new in your life? It's been a while."

"Everybody's okay. Carol's still working for the telephone company. The kids are costing me a fortune but we still sock a little away and get out now and then. I took the little lady to a movie last night, then ravaged her on the living room floor before the kids got home. Amazing the effect today's movies can have on you. Not like when I was a kid." Norelli was a pillar of stability in an occupation known for its marital shakiness. He had been married to Carol for twenty-six years and they had five kids ranging in age from twenty-one to fourteen. "It was a good evening, all things considered. And you?"

"I watched 'Saturday Night Live,' " Morrison said.

"I used to love that show when they had Belushi and Ackroyd and Gilda Radner . . . Roseanna Roseanna Danna. Don't really watch it anymore. Was it any good?"

"Can't say, Franco, because I don't remember. I made a brief visit earlier to the Black Angus to treat myself to a steak and a few pops, which I felt I deserved having worked most of yesterday and facing having to come down here today. I dined alone. As you know, I no longer have a wife to look after my basic necessities."

"I heard. Too bad." Norelli meant it. He hated to see marriages and families break up, something he had seen too often among his friends on the force. He also felt uncomfortable talking about it. Sort of there but for the grace of God . . . "So you going to tell me about 'Saturday Night Live?' "

"I fell asleep during the first part. Maybe it was the schnapps after the steak. When I woke up there was a Charlie Chan movie on which at three in the morning I had trouble getting into. Schnapps, incidentally, is not a summer night's drink. So how's everything over in Belmont these days?"

"Nothing changes, Joe. You know that. The gangs are the worst these days, the drugs and all the guns on the street, worse than when you were there. We get an interesting one every now and then. I suspect this one's going to be one of those."

"Could be," Morrison said.

At 9:10 the large oak door swung open, a uniformed cop handling the doorknob, and Superintendent Alton Williams entered the room sporting a huge smile. Behind him was the woman who handled his personal press relations (as opposed to Lieutenant Troy, whose responsibilities were departmental). She was an appointed member of the department, a slot Williams had created shortly after being appointed as Chicago's top cop.

"Please sit down. We got one snaky problem here. I spoke with Mayor Taylor last night . . . *twice* . . . and again this morning before coming over here." He sat down in the big brass-studded leather chair at the head of the table. "So let's get down to it and get this shit-pickin' piece of trash out of the way. Okay?"

Grumbles, nods.

"We have damn little so far on Friday night's fiasco, as I have been informed," the superintendent said. He picked up the pencil in front of him, twirled it through his fingers like a miniature baton. "Things aren't going to stay that way."

Harkness nudged Morrison, who was sitting next to him at the far end of the conference table. "The preacher gwan hold a service this morning."

"The preacher?"

"Reverend Alderman Hunter." Harkness raised his eyebrows.

"The mayor would like to have something positive to report to the public as soon as possible," Superintendent Williams went on. "It appears this Friday night piece of street shit could become, as they say in your better parts of town, a *cause célèbre*. Alderman Hunter, we have learned, is deeply concerned by the wanton slaying of one of his"—pausing, then pointing at his chest—"*our* own—namely a black child whose name you are already familiar with.

"It is the mayor's understanding that Alderman Hunter is going to assume his religious role and hold a service for the boy this morning at eleven o'clock. The boy's mother will be in attendance. The reason the mayor knows all this is because Alderman Hunter has invited to his hardware-store-turned church over on west Madison Street crews from all four television stations and every radio station that has more than twelve listeners, plus reporters from the *Tribune*, the *Sun-Times*, the *Southtown*, the *Daily Defender*, the *Metro News*. He has not had a lot of time to put his act together, but we all know the alderman can get things done around this city, and his colleagues are already out at this early hour canvassing the congregation and the neighborhood to be sure there's an overflow crowd, plus contributions. The mayor has a problem in the black community as it is.'' He didn't add what they all also knew . . . that some of the mayor's problem was self-inflicted. Some of it courtesy of the alderman-man-of-God, but a lot of it legitimate grievances of the blacks of the city. ''This kind of thing turns his lily-white skin even paler than usual, causes his stomach to churn and makes him an all-around unpleasant fellow.

''We took the hit last night in the *Metro*. We're going to take a bigger one tomorrow. We've got to fight back, come up with something *positive*. Now, along with the help of deputy superintendents Flanagan and Harkness I have come up with an initial plan that will be implemented immediately.'' His eyes roved down one side of the table and back up the other.

Harkness said quietly to Morrison, ''You want to go with me to the service. It's at eleven. I've been told to attend, even though I'm a Methodist.'' Harkness smiled slightly. ''The sacrifices we must make, Joe.''

OVER AT AREA FOUR there were some new faces on the second shift, the eight-to-four. Nolan and Nabasco, the two who had drawn the case, had been switched from midnights. So had Eddie McCabe and the morose Frank Wilson, the only one who seemed unhappy about being moved from the graveyard shift to daytime duty. There was also a young detective from downtown whom nobody recognized and therefore all were immediately wary of. Presiding was Lieutenant Grantham, the day-shift watch commander.

The lieutenant and the other shift bosses were feeling a lot of heat from the Area Four commander and various voices from 11th and State who had been keeping the direct telephone line to the Area Four VC watch commander very busy. Grantham, a thirty-year veteran on the force, took it pretty much in stride, but it caused the more apprehensive Sergeant Gerherdt to clean his glasses every few minutes and at regular intervals stroke his bald head as if there were hair up there that needed to be brushed back.

Grantham's roll call had gone off more formally than usual because of the interloper from downtown. Those not on the Peters/Tees case had then gone on about their duties. The others just wandered out into the squad room, got coffee and sat around, everyone except the detective from downtown, whom Lieutenant Grantham had introduced as Ken Frost. He was, Grantham explained, permanently assigned to Deputy Superintendent Flanagan's office downtown and had been sent over on special assignment to serve as a district liaison in this case—which meant he was there to be sure that Flanagan got *all* the details of the investigation as they came in and as soon as they arrived. Grantham was also waiting for a call reporting on the meeting downtown before letting his men hit the street.

In the squadroom Johnny Nolan sat at a desk with the case file in front of him, but his mind was elsewhere. He was hoping to God they would not trace the leak to him, this case suddenly becoming a big thing. Who the hell knew? He thought he'd just been giving the reporter a little jump on the others with the news, that's all . . . so he might finagle a little jump of his own. Instead all he got was two free beers at Little Mo's and now a stomach courting a peptic ulcer. He got up and went over to one of the desks away from the other detectives, picked up a telephone and dialed Holly Stryker's number. He got her answering machine, thought about hanging up, but then said: "Don't forget your promise at Little Mo's yesterday. *Very* important you don't forget it."

Nabasco had appropriated the chair at the desk Nolan had left to make his call and was talking with Eddie McCabe and Sergeant Gerherdt. "Sergeant Bilko," he was saying when Nolan joined them, "I get the feeling a lot of eyes are on us. You think they think *we* screwed it up some way?"

This time both of Gerherdt's hands went up to stroke the banks of hair above his temples. "No, it's just politics, is all. But just remember, if this gets really hot they're going to be looking for some bodies to nail to the stake. Just remember that." He shook his head. "I should've takin' my old man's advice and joined the union. He was a pipefitter. All he had to do was put some pipes together and go on home. Instead I gotta worry about you guys and the hotshots down at 11th and State, not to mention the types crawling around the streets out there. And things like *this*.''

"You got any idea how that broad got all the stuff on the ballistics report and the other crap?" Nolan asked.

They all shook their heads. "Downtown they'd sure like to know," Gerherdt said.

"Well, it obviously came out of there, 11th and State is the biggest sieve in the world," Nolan said, sitting on the edge of the desk now. "I can't believe she wrote it up like she did. She seemed like such a nice, you know, naive kid Friday night, impressed by all the shit. Then she turns out to be a ballbuster.''

"Nolan," Gerherdt said, "she's a very smart woman. I talked to her for a half-hour before you guys went out with her. If you didn't think of every female in terms of sex you just might have noticed that. If she's busting anybody's balls it's because they deserve it. Hey, she didn't put anything in that article that wasn't true, anything that all of us and half of downtown doesn't already know. Don't blame her, blame the guy with the big mouth. *Person* with the big mouth," he said as Donna Polenski, a uniformed policewoman assigned to the detective front desk, approached with folders in hand. Polenski liked "the guys," liked to shoot the shit with them, but she also had a knack for bringing up the feminist stuff. Still they liked her a lot. She lived with another woman and her sexual persuasion was taken for granted; she took few pains to disguise it. No one cared.

"Sermon over, Sergeant Bilko?" Nolan asked.

"Why don't you go down the hall, Nolan, and leave your scent in front of the door to the women's john. It'll give you something to do."

At the desk that butted up against the one where they were gathered, Frank Wilson was ignoring the conversation, deep into the Sunday *Tribune's* crossword puzzle. Suddenly he looked up. "Anybody know a five-letter word for a boring tool?"

Donna Polenski dropped the folders into the metal rack on the desk. She couldn't resist. "Penis."

"Real funny, Polenski," Wilson said, unamused. The others thought it was funny.

"I don't think it's a boring tool," Nabasco said, looking over at her. "And Johnny sure as hell don't. And Sergeant Bilko, he got six kids with it."

Donna Polenski put on a smile. "You guys forget sometimes it hangs only an inch in front of the doorway to your brains."

"Speaking of tools," Eddie McCabe said, "I read this thing in the paper yesterday about what can happen if you take Valium. I got it here somewhere," he said, his hands flitting from pocket to pocket. "I save these things. Maybe I'll put 'em all together in a book someday. Ah, here it is." He unfolded the newspaper clipping. "Says that in some persons who take Valium or this other drug, Versed—never heard of it—they can have hallucinations, one of which is, and I quote, 'that the person taking the drug believes that his or her sexual organs are being fondled.' "

"So what's so bad?" Nolan said.

"And there's another." McCabe tried to pronounce clomipramine but got tongue-tied so he spelled it. "The paper says it's from the Canadian Journal of Psychiatry. Now, this clomo-whatever-it-is is given to patients who have obsessive-compulsive disorders and some of them, and I quote again, 'experience an orgasm when they yawn.' "

César Nabasco turned toward the front desk. "You hear that, Polenski? It might solve all your problems." Yawn.

She gave them a sudden shocked look and threw her head back, breathing fast and loud, then moaning and shuddering.

"It don't say anything about women here," McCabe said. "Just men. It says one guy yawned so much he had to wear a condom all day long so he wouldn't embarrass himself. Another guy said the orgasms tired him out so much he had to lie down and rest after a yawning spell."

Nolan yawned, looked around the group, shrugged. "No luck."

McCabe said, "I think I gotta subscribe to that Canadian magazine."

Nabasco scratched his head. "I guess I gotta start reading more'n the sports section and death notices."

"Who needs to," Sergeant Gerherdt said, "when we got McCabe around?"

Lieutenant Grantham stuck his head out of the watch commander's office. "All right, you guys, everybody in here."

They stood around Grantham's desk, an unkempt crew—the only one whose tie was not hanging untied was Sergeant Gerherdt's, which, in fact, couldn't hang loose because it was a windsor knot clip-on, one of five he owned and rotated on a daily basis. The bottom tip of the tie rested on the top of his protrusive belly about five inches above his belt buckle. Dress-for-success was not one of Gerherdt's major priorities. Gerherdt was also the only one who wore a shoulder holster, all the rest carried their guns on belts. Some thought Sergeant Bilko had watched too many cop shows on television.

Grantham sat down in the oak swivel chair with the slatted back and the arm rests worn down to bare wood; it was one of the few relics that had made it from the dilapidated old Area Four headquarters on Filmore Street to the sterile new building on Harrison, where everything was Formica and vinyl and chrome and plastic. The old chair had a threadbare mashed cushion on the seat that had accommodated the rear ends of countless watch commanders over the years. It creaked when someone swiveled to one side or another and let out a groan when the person leaned back in it. Grantham did neither, just looked at the notes on his desk that he had taken while on the phone with the folks at 11th and State. When he looked up his eyes moved from left to right across the small squad gathered in front of him, who had assumed their own versions of at ease. "I talked with Deputy Superintendent Flanagan directly on this. The mayor and everybody else are real jumpy. I think you know what that means. We're going to get help here but the bottom line is results, quick ones. The super and

Flanagan decided to set up what they're calling a special investigative team on this one. Its purpose is not only to enhance our field efforts but also, as you've guessed, to show the media and the citizenry that we are taking this case most seriously and are doing our darndest to catch the bad guy or guys who kill kids in our less fortunate neighborhoods.

"So this unit, we're going to call it the PT unit, like in PT boat, like the one JFK got sunk in during World War Two. In this case, the PT stands for Peters-Tees, our victims, in case some of you have been living on Mars the last day or two. It's going to be headquartered downtown and headed by Joe Morrison and Franco Norelli. Some of you guys may remember Morrison from his Homicide days, now he's with Organized Crime downtown. He's an okay guy. And everybody knows Norelli, Chicago's very own Kojak, who makes headlines out of Belmont." It was not said sarcastically because Grantham, along with just about every other cop who ever had dealings with Norelli, liked and respected the man.

"There's a direct-line number being set up, to be monitored, from what I'm told, twenty-four hours a day." He gave them the number. "Should be installed by ten this morning. You can call it the hotline if you want."

"Everybody goes direct to the line?" Gerherdt asked. "Not back here first?"

"I think that would be the thing to do. Or go direct to Morrison or Norelli, who by the way are on their way over here now and will probably be in and out on a regular basis as the thing goes on. Downtown has also authorized some temp duty for PT: two VC detectives from One, four Tac officers from here, an undercover from Narcotics and two officers from Gang Crimes. They're being called in right now. Morrison and Norelli want a meeting with all of us here at twelve-thirty, so eat an early lunch."

Gerherdt said, "I suppose they want me here too. I've only been here since eleven last night."

"I think they probably do. Go take a nap somewhere and leave a wake-up call at the front desk."

To the rest of them he said: "You guys get going now. Let

'em see we're already hard on the job. Pull up any files we've got on Peters' arrests in Four, if they haven't been pulled already. See if there're any security guys in those factories south of the Eisenhower, maybe there was a night watchman Friday. Talk to everyone who was in that adobe hacienda down the street. Round up the gang kids or snitches in the neighborhood, see if you can get anything out of them about the Tees kid. But leave the mother of the kid alone. We talked to her yesterday, got nothing. From what I'm told she's under Alderman Hunter's tent, so it's very touchy, as you can see. Morrison and Norelli want to speak with her themselves. Talk to Peters's live-in again, she wasn't cooperative yesterday. She's a dog. See what you can do with her. Be careful but not too careful. You follow? I understand Peters was sort of a loner, but he must have had a place or two that would be worth checking.

"What the hell am I telling you all this for. You guys know what to do. So get out there and do it and be back here by twelve-thirty."

✧13

JOE MORRISON WAS NOT PARTICULARLY ENTHUSED WITH THE assignment. Homicides, why do they keep finding their way back to me, he was thinking. They were like the recurring bad dreams that haunted too many of his nights. He had managed to live with them and just be thankful when each one ended. The alternative was never to sleep at all.

He knew why he had been chosen. He was in Organized Crime and this particular crime appeared to have every indication of a direct Outfit connection. And, figuring his Homicide background, he was a natural to represent O.C. No one at 11th and State, Slick Goldman especially, gave a rat's ass about what his state of mind was these days about homicide work.

Norelli was also a logical choice; he was currently regarded as one of the most imaginative homicide detectives on the force, his folder filled with commendations and his name not unknown to the press and the media. And there was no question that these two deaths by gunshot in this incongruous case could use the mind of a homicide investigator like Franco Norelli.

Lieutenant Troy was pleased with the selections. The two were experienced detectives with clean reputations, intelligent and, above all, able to handle the newsmongers out there who would be crawling all over them—and him. He foresaw nothing, only a positive reaction when he presented their names as the leaders of Superintendent Williams's especially appointed fourteen-man investigative team at the press conference he had hastily scheduled for one o'clock that afternoon.

AT PRECISELY SEVEN MINUTES after eleven Alderman Hunter took his seat next to the podium on a raised platform in the corner at the far end of his church. The platform, now used as a stage, served in its earlier True-Value days to showcase the hardware store's array of sophisticated power tools, not commercially relevant to the present neighborhood. Hunter had once heard that it was theater tradition that the curtain of a show did not go up until seven minutes after the scheduled showtime in order to be sure everyone was seated. At 11:07 in the Avalon Tabernacle Church the congregation was seated, their hushed conversations blending into a kind of low-pitched drone as the people awaited, in effect, the curtain rising.

In a row about two-thirds of the way toward the back sat Deputy Superintendent Harkness with a young couple in their late twenties who could pass for his son and daughter but who were in fact two Tac officers he had gotten out of the first district to accompany him. People in the media knew him on sight, so did, of course, Alderman Hunter and the members of his political coterie. As he sat there trying to be as inconspicuous as possible, it brought back memories of the early days when he worked undercover.

He was there to hear firsthand just what the alderman had

in mind, the things he would inevitably be confronting later. Community relations with the police in this neighborhood were strained under the best of circumstances, and Harkness had the feeling they were soon to be jump-started into something a lot worse.

Hunter was dressed in a double-breasted black business suit with large pointed lapels, white shirt and black tie with pastel polka dots. He wore a flat silk stole about four inches wide, purple with black fringes, draped over his shoulders which crisscrossed midway down his body, where it was held in place by a large pearl stickpin. It was to signify his state of mourning. He sat with arms folded across his chest, gazing out at his flock. Every one of the three hundred or so folding chairs facing him were occupied and another fifty or sixty people stood along the back wall. The hardware store's air-conditioning still worked if weakly, but Hunter had also arranged for mounted floor fans to be placed all around. After all, they were having a variety of guests visiting this Sunday's service. A section of seats up front had been cordoned off (in a dark purple that matched the color of Hunter's stole) and was full of members of the working press. Among them were the only white faces in the audience, and one of those faces belonged to Holly Stryker. The men with the TV minicams and the primping on-the-scene broadcast reporters who accompanied them and the still photographers were free to roam about.

On the stage with Hunter were his trusted ward committeemen: Jesse Brown, whose job was basically to listen to and smooth over as best he could the gripes of the ward's constituency and, rather importantly, get out the vote on Election Day; Brother Leonard, the church's pastoral deacon, the title given him by Hunter, who also was on the payroll of the city's Streets and Sanitation department downtown under the name of Leonard Haynes; Alderwoman Cora Lee Monroe from the predominantly black ward just south of Alderman Hunter's, an activist who once called herself ''the most dedicated, determined detoxifier of discrimination and defender of the defenseless in the city of Chicago''—the slogan she had successfully campaigned with in the last four aldermanic elections despite the difficulty of squeezing it on a poster, much less a handbill—she was also a wonderfully fiery speaker and had been quickly willing to accept the offer to introduce her good friend and aldermanic colleague, the Reverend Hunter, on this Sunday morning. And, of course, there was Roberta Tees, mother of the slain Rayfield, who in a black ruffled dress and black gloves was sitting next to the reverend.

Hunter whispered something to Roberta Tees and she nodded slowly as she listened. He then looked at the Rolex Oyster on his wrist and gave a hand sign to the other side of the podium. Brother Leonard arose and walked to the microphone.

"The Reverend Hunter, the bereaved mother of young Rayfield Tees and I welcome you all to the Avalon Tabernacle of God on this most special Sunday."

He read a brief prayer, then led the congregation in the hymn "Can't Nobody Do Me Like Jesus," after which he sat back down and Alderwoman Monroe stepped to the podium. Alderman Hunter knew what he was doing when he chose her to serve, so to speak, as warm-up to the main act. The congregation applauded spontaneously before she said a word. She was allowed ten minutes for her introduction and given a roster of subject matter not to be touched upon in it, from Hunter. She delivered it well, rich in her praise for the man she was introducing and subdued in her references to the tragedy that had befallen a boy and his family in their community.

Reverend Hunter got right to the point. "Dear friends, fellow worshippers of our God, citizens of our community, you know why we are gathered in this divine sanctuary. It is the Lord's day. Sunday. A regretful Sunday. A sad, oh Lord, a sad, sad Sunday. Sad because we are here this morning with a grieving neighbor, the mother of young Rayfield Tees. Roberta Tees, sitting here next to me''—he turned and held out his hand toward her, palm up, bowing as he did, and then swiveled back to face the audience—"a victim just as much as the son she raised from a baby. The son whose *very* life she saw torn from him *out* of his childhood, the boy *denied* the fullness and joy of life that God has intended for all of us.

"Yes, Roberta Tees is as tragic a victim as her son who was wrenched from her by the violence and hatred that scar the unprotected streets of *our* neighborhood. *Our* children are not safe. We are not safe. We are not the subject of the city's compassion, not the subject of the police department's care or even their dutiful protection. We are black. We are a black island surrounded by hostile waters . . ."

The sermon lasted a little over an hour, ending with, "Brothers and sisters, this is not over. Not over by any stretch of the imagination. I guarantee it."

"No," Jim Harkness whispered to the two sitting next to him, "it's just the beginning."

Outside it was gloomy and stifling. The early morning drizzle had left the sidewalks wet and the air heavy. Harkness and his two companions amid the worshippers walked east on Madison. His car and driver, who had been called in for overtime, waited for them three blocks away on a side street next to the Chicago Stadium.

Ahead, a jagged flash of lightning knifed through the mottled sky far to the east out over Lake Michigan, followed a few seconds later by a shattering thunderclap that broke into rippling echoes that rumbled toward them. Another stab of lightning, this one with fiery tentacles, struck to the northeast, turning the distant full sky suddenly phosphorescent.

"The Alderman or Reverend, I should say, does know how to add a grand finale to his show," Harkness said.

In the car, Harkness gave the hotline number downtown to the driver and told him to see if Morrison or Norelli were there. Neither was, according to the detective on duty at the phone. Both were at Area Four headquarters.

"Drop me over there," Harkness said. "Then take these two downtown and come back for me." He looked out the window. "We could sure use a good rain."

JIMMY PAGNANO WAS SITTING out the smothering afternoon in the air-conditioned comfort of one of the card rooms at the Greycroft Country Club, a guest of Joe Alessi, playing pinochle with his boss and two others whom Alessi had invited to make up a golf foursome. They had gotten in four holes before the rain started and Alessi said to hell with it and turned his cart back toward the clubhouse.

After a few drinks and lunch Alessi had suggested a little gaming, reminding them with a laugh that pinochle had been Al Capone's favorite game, just like Dentyne gum and Sen Sen were his favorite things to chew on and Ipana his favorite toothpaste and Vitalis the only thing he would put on the little hair he had. Alessi's mentor had been an underling in the old Capone clan and used to regale the then young Joe-sep with stories of the good old days and intimate stuff about the ultimate goodfella.

The other two in the foursome were Joe Fontana, president of Blackthorn Construction Works, an Outfit-controlled company, and Ronald Schackstraw, Alessi's attorney. Both were mediocre golfers, not quite as good as Alessi but better than Pagnano. Pagnano had the tendency to hit the ball like he was pounding a harp seal to death but was timid with the putter, invariably coming up short of the hole. Nobody, including himself, could explain it. And if they thought it, nobody was about to make a joke about not being able to get it in the hole, ha-ha.

Fontana and Schakstraw had class, Jimmy Pagnano thought, and he liked being included in such company. Deep down he really loved the game of golf, whacking that little white ball, hearing the club whip the air and the sharp, chilling crack when the contact was good. He liked the camaraderie on the course, too. But when he golfed with his boss, it was ordinarily just a twosome drummed up on the *capo*'s whim. Today Jimmy was dressed in one of his four golf outfits, this one a yellow mesh golf shirt, green pants and matching green golf shoes. He also had white golf shoes to go with his white golfing pants and yellow shoes to go with pants of the same color and a matching set in scarlet red. He bought them all in the Pro Shop at Greycroft, along with golfballs and an occasional new wood or iron, which made Joe Alessi happy, Jimmy patronizing Joe's club that way. The Greycroft was as opulent as any other country club in the suburbs of Chicago—$35,000 initiation fee. It was restricted to males only (wives or female friends could enjoy the restaurant and adjoining cocktail lounge after six at night if they were accompanied by a member). It was dear to Joe's heart, partly because it was one of the only clubs in the county that had no problem about accepting ranking members of Organized Crime. Joe was one of twelve on the two-hundred-member roll.

Jimmy Pagnano had received two messages earlier, one at the lunch table and the other delivered in the card room, both of which said: "Call Vernon," and both of which he acknowledged to Joe Alessi and then stuffed into his pants pocket. Vernon was the owner of Vernon's restaurant, one of those that opened at seven in the morning and did not close until midnight and attracted everybody from full families who sat for meals at Formica tables to lonely coffee drinkers at the counter. It was also a place where Jimmy Pagnano often hung out to do business and where he got many of his telephone messages. Vernon, a longtime friend and protectee of Pagnano, opened the place in the morning and worked the cash register and kept the employees hustling until four in the afternoon seven days a week. Two other guys Vernon trusted split up managing the night shifts.

When the third message was delivered to the card table, Alessi said, "Whyn't you go call the bum, Jimmy, so we don't keep getting interrupted here." Joe-sep was down about fifty dollars and the only thing he hated worse than losing was being interrupted when he was launching his expected comeback.

"This guy's been callin' here all day," Vernon said when Jimmy called back. "First time about ten this morning. Keeps saying it's very important he talk with you. So I finally figured maybe it really is important and I better call. They keep telling me out there they don't know whether you're there or not but they'll take a message. I tell them I *know* you're there—you told me you would be—but they say just gimme the message. Hope I ain't bothering you."

"You did right, Vernon. Don't worry about it. Who is this guy, did he say?"

"Oh, yeah. Vaughn Swayze's the name he gave me. Says you know him. Real chummy on the phone."

A pause, then Pagnano said, "Oh, yeah, Vaughn, the wacko from Detroit. What's he want?"

"The first coupla times he didn't say. The last time he called, about two-thirty I guess it was, he said he'd be out till about seven tonight his time, that's six ours. Said he'd call back then but if I talked to you in the meantime to tell you that he was coming over tomorrow and he was bringing the thing. I asked him what thing. He wouldn't tell me, said just to tell you that and you'd know what it was, the thing."

Pagnano smiled at the telephone mouthpiece. "Maybe this creep's for real after all," he said.

"Huh?"

"Never mind. Tell him when he calls back to ring you when he gets in tomorrow and leave a telephone number where I can get to him."

"Okay. He said he was driving. Would probably get here about noonish our time."

"I'll be around. Talk to you, pal."

Jimmy Pagnano still had on the smile when he walked back into the card room.

✥14

THE NEXT MORNING MORRISON AND NORELLI WERE SITTING around the PT Task Force headquarters, a windowless one-desk office on the third floor at 11th and State where a two-line telephone had been installed—one for the PT direct line and the other for routine calls. It was adjacent to Organized Crime, in fact just down the corridor from the cubicle that Morrison ordinarily inhabited in O.C. The room had served as the office for a special liaison from the Cook County sheriff's office, a plum of a patronage job, until the liaison and his

chinaman in county politics had been indicted on counts of
accepting bribes, fraud and income-tax evasion. It had remained vacant ever since the Illinois attorney general's office
and a grand jury had nailed the two, although it did not really
matter since the liaison never really liaised with anyone at
police headquarters anyway and spent about as much time in
that office as, say, an ordinary grizzly bear spends stalking the
forest in the dead of winter. That was about eight months ago,
and with all the publicity surrounding the two indictments and
the public revelation of the phantomlike nature of the liaison's
position, the sheriff's office deemed it prudent not to bring in
a replacement.

A desk, long worktable, file cabinet and several chairs remained from the days when the sheriff's appointee claimed
residence there. Morrison and Norelli had already sifted
through the reports of what had come in from Sunday's street-
work, the forms and other scribblings strewn across the desk.
The worktable, where they were sitting, had already begun to
grow piles of its own. The room had been converted from a
barren cell to a hive of activity in less than twenty-four hours.

The only thing in the reports they considered noteworthy
was from one of the Gang Crimes' detectives, Lloyd Ware,
who had learned that Rayfield Tees was a junior member of
the Western Lords, a neighborhood branch of one of the city's
largest and toughest gangs, and that the bangers in that gang
were looking on the slaying of the youngster as a serious matter worthy of their direct attention.

Norelli, after talking with Ware earlier that morning before
the gang cop again hit the streets, had learned that the Western
Lords were trying as hard as the Chicago Police Department
to find out who had shot Rayfield. And they probably had a
better shot at success, Ware added, the way word of such
things passed through the corridors and courtyards of the
Rockwell Gardens housing project where they held court.

The Westerns wanted to find out if the bullet that downed
their cadet had come from the gun of a rival gang member.
The wouldbes or wannabes were covered under the cloak of
the gang's code of protection and retribution just as much as

a full member, Ware explained. After all, they were important, being juveniles and not subject to the harsher penalties for wrongdoing as adults and, of course, being less conspicuous, they served well in their roles as carriers or holders for guns, drugs and other contraband.

According to Ware, who had already been in contact with other GC officers familiar with the particular hood, as the Western Lords called their staked territory, Rayfield was not doing any business for the gang on the night he was murdered.

Morrison had called his main contact at the FBI, Timothy Doyle, who had played fullback at Vanderbilt in the mid-1960s, served a tour of duty afterward with an infantry company as a second lieutenant in Vietnam and managed to return to the States in one piece. He then earned a law degree at George Washington University before signing on with the Bureau. Doyle was not expected in the field office until afternoon, Morrison was told.

The morning papers were on the table. The murders were relegated to the metropolitan sections. Alderman Hunter's call for action and protection and swift justice were duly carried in the same sections. His concerns had also been aired on the four television stations on Sunday night, with on-the-site coverage from the Avalon Tabernacle Church. The minicams had missed the electrical sky and belches of thunder that nature had added for the grand climax.

There had been three calls from the press room down on the first floor, the news-affairs director on duty telling them that Holly Stryker of *Metro News* was there and wanted to speak with either one of them. The third call Norelli was now responding to: "I don't give a shit if she's been there since nineteen sixty-eight. Tell her we're busy working on a homicide and we have nothing whatsoever we can give to the press, especially our fucking valuable time." He slammed down the telephone.

"Antsy, they said downstairs. She's getting antsy waiting," Norelli said to Morrison, shaking his head. "Why don't they just tell her to take a walk?"

"She's doing her job, being a pest. They pay them for that."

"Piss on her."

"I knew a guy who was into golden showers," Morrison said as he got up. "I thought it was sort of disgusting."

"Tell me."

Morrison started for the door of the office. "I have to take a leak, which won't interest you. After that I want to stop in my office, see what's going on there. You can hold the fort."

VERNON GOT THROUGH TO Jimmy Pagnano before noon and told him, "Your buddy, this Vaughn guy's in town. Said he made it from Detroit in five hours, said that was really good time, especially considering stops for coffee and a roll and his wife's pee in Battle Creek. They also had to stop in St. Joe so she could pee again. Says riding in cars jiggles her bladder or something. Ever since she had the hysterectomy, it's been a problem, he said. This guy's a real wing-ding, Jimmy. I think he was about to tell me if she was a good screw before I cut him off. I got a restaurant to run, I told him."

"So where's he at?"

"At the McCormick Inn, that hotel down by McCormick Place. Said it's great, low rates cause there's no conventions across the street in the hall. But try it when the auto show's in town, he tells me, or one of those other big conventions, then it's out of sight. I tell you, Jimmy, this guy can talk for fucking ever. Anyway, he's in room four twenty-two and said he'd wait there till you called." Vernon gave him the telephone number of the McCormick Inn.

Pagnano put the receiver back in the cradle and yelled toward the bedroom, "You got any more of that coffee left, Doe-baby?" He was sitting on the couch in his jockey shorts and undershirt, his bare feet propped on the coffee table.

"Sure, honey," she said as she came into the living room. Doe Davenport could have been back at work out in Cicero the way she was dressed. She was wearing black nylons and lace panties, open-toed backless high heels and a narrow gold chain around her neck, the crucifix hanging from it nestled in cleavage. Her breasts were tanned like the rest of her body to a tone she had acquired at a salon in the yuppie area of north Halsted Street. With her rhythmic sway as she walked across the room it was little wonder she had been a hit at the Surf and Turf Lounge. She disappeared into the little kitchen and reappeared moments later carrying a black ceramic mug with steam rising from it. She curled up next to Jimmy, tucking her legs under her on the couch, her forearm resting on his shoulder and the slender fingers toying with the hair on the back of his neck. "So we got an agenda for the rest of the day? This morning was a helluva start." Her tongue did a hopscotch on his ear.

"I got an agenda. Somebody's gotta work, make the money for all this shit." He smiled and then nuzzled his face in her breasts, his nose touching the gold cross. The coldness of it made him pull back. He looked at it uneasily. "You gotta wear that thing?"

"I like it. My aunt gave it to me when I graduated high school. It's supposed to be a charm for a bracelet, I think, but it's real gold, gold-plated anyway. Jimmy, it's the only thing I got that's real gold that didn't come from you."

He took the cross and flipped it so that it hung behind her and moved back into the cleavage. He tasted the topping of each breast, giving the nipples a playful wag with his tongue, then straightened up and reached for the telephone. She stood up and went back to the bedroom.

Swayze answered on the first ring.

"I understand you been tryin' to get hold of me," Pagnano said.

"Yeah, sure have, yesterday, this morning. We got here at ten, your time, only took five hours from downtown Detroit."

"I heard."

"And I got the—"

"I heard that, too."

"It's right here in—"

"Shut up. The place we met the other night, you remember it?"

"Sure."

"Be there." Pagnano looked at his watch. It was a little after twelve. "One-thirty. And this time don't be late. You know I don't like people being late."

"Yeah, you told me. I understand, understand. One-thirty." Jimmy had hung up and was on his way to the bedroom before Swayze realized the conversation had ended and finally stopped talking.

WHEN SWAYZE ARRIVED AT D'Amico's on Taylor Street a little before one-thirty, Pagnano was already there, sitting at a table in the back corner, eating his way through a green salad that was laced with bits of anchovy, rounds of black olives, hunks of gorgonzola cheese, all smothered in a thick Italian dressing. In front of him were an oversized old-fashioned glass with about an inch of Stolichnaya vodka and three crushed wedges of lime and a wicker basket containing a loaf of warm homemade Italian bread surrounded by thin slices of toast slathered in garlic butter.

Voices up front near the entrance distracted him from the food and vodka and he looked up to see Mama D'Amico, who ran the place during the day, pull to the side the beaded-and-baubled strands that hung to the floor from the Moorish arch that led into the bar area and which seemed more appropriate to a restaurant named the Casbah than D'Amico's. Vaughn Swayze stepped through it, saying something through an ingratiating grin to Mama D'Amico and patting her on the arm as he did so. The woman in the short skirt coming in with him was carrying a cordovan briefcase and walking with a guy in a cherry-red crewneck sweater who also had a sea of red hair combed back like Ronald Reagan's. The redhead, about five-foot-six, had his hands in his pockets and ambled rather than walked, casual and confident.

Pagnano continued to fork the salad into his mouth as he watched them approach.

Swayze said, "Hey, Jimmy," when he reached the table, a boyish smile on his face. "Right on time. Right?" But he was looking a little uneasily at the lunch Pagnano had already started. Was his watch wrong?

"Who the hell are they?" Pagnano asked, nodding toward the couple standing behind Swayze.

"This is my wife, Jimmy, Felice. Remember, I told you about her." Swayze turned to look back at her. "This here's Jimmy, Felice." Then, putting his hand on the shoulder of the short man standing alongside her, "And this is Red, an old buddy." Swayze turned back to Pagnano. "We go back a long ways, Red and me. Red just got in town here about a week ago."

Pagnano, his elbow resting on the table, his mouth clamped on the salad fork, just stared up at the trio. He slid the fork from his mouth and let it drop straight down onto the plate. "What is this, a fucking committee? You bring a fucking committee to talk to me? What are you, some kind of fucking nutball?"

"It's not a committee, Jimmy, not a committee . . . Just my wife and a buddy. Thought you might wanna meet Felice, she, you know, working with us on this thing. And Red, he wanted to meet you. Wants to make some connections in town here. I thought maybe you . . ." He tried to bring the boyish smile back but it came out fractured. "Well, Red's got some ideas maybe you'd be interested in, maybe . . . I thought . . ."

Pagnano was staring hard at Swayze. "Get them out of here, you wanna talk with me."

"But—"

"You don't hear? You don't understand? Which? I said get them outa here you wanna talk with me."

Swayze turned back to the two with a hey-what-can-I-do-about-it look, but there was a trace of pleading in it, too. "Jimmy, ah, calls the shots here. Maybe you guys could just wait in the car, maybe. Just for a while. While we do the business. It'll be quick, quick." He managed to bring the smile back because he was looking at them, not Jimmy Pagnano.

Felice appeared annoyed, pouty-faced, and seemed to be about to say something.

"C'mon, Felice, be a good kid, do it for old Vaughn." He reached up and placed the palm of his hand on her cheek. "For Vaughn-Boy."

The redhead just shrugged and took her by the arm. "We can wait outside. No big deal." They started to leave. "Would like to talk to you sometime, though," the redhead said to Pagnano. "At your convenience, of course."

"Maybe you better leave that," Swayze said to his wife, pointing to the briefcase she was carrying.

She glanced down at it, as though surprised to see it was still there in her hand. "Oh, sure, honey," she said, and handed it to Swayze. "And *real* nice to have made your acquaintance," she added to Pagnano before the redhead, his hand still on her arm, turned her in the direction of the door.

"She's got a lot of spunk," Swayze said as he put the briefcase down on the chair next to Pagnano. "She's a real knockout, right? Like I told you. Best thing that ever happened to me, best thing." He started to slide into the empty booth seat but was almost knocked over as Pagnano got up suddenly, pushing the table away from him and then pushing Swayze. He kept shoving until both of them were out from behind the table, then he grabbed Swayze by the tie and shirt and pulled him along after him, Swayze bumping into unoccupied tables as they went, past the far end of the bar and through a door that opened onto a corridor leading back to the liquor storeroom.

The bartender watched but didn't move. The three men at the bar turned and one of them said, "What the hell's that all about?" The bartender said nothing and went back to the wine glasses he had washed and was now sliding upside-down into the panel of slotted rows above the bar. The three stared at him until he turned back to them.

"Nothing," he said.

Inside the storeroom Pagnano slammed Swayze against a wall of liquor bins, sending bottles smashing into other bottles.

"Hey, Jimmy, what's goin' on?" Swayze's eyes were wide, his hands up in the air as if he were being robbed on the street. "What's the beef?"

Pagnano, still with a handful of Swayze's tie and shirt, pulled him away from the bins, then shoved him back against it. "You expect me to do business in front of people I don't even know? You think I'm some kind of moron, somebody just wandered in off the street? That what you think?''

"No, jeez, Jimmy, no. That's . . ." The pain of Pagnano's knuckles digging into his chest made him gasp for breath.

"You tryin' to set me up for something?"

"No! Honest to God, Jimmy. I didn't think you'd mind, bein' who they are, you know, who they are, my wife, my buddy—"

"I don't even know *you*." Pagnano was breathing heavily himself now. "You come naming a name of somebody who's a friend of mine one day and you're back the next with a couple of people I know even less than you."

"Jimmy, for Jesus sake, take it easy . . . please. I sent 'em away like you wanted. Call Lenny Sasso right now. He'll up for me."

Pagnano's forehead was beaded with perspiration. He had not loosened his grip, fist still plunged into Swayze's chest, and was breathing through his nose in rapid spurts.

"I brought the ten grand, like you said. All I want's the deal, like we talked about. C'mon, Jimmy . . . Jimmy."

Pagnano relaxed his grip, his breathing slowed. He was about to say something when Swayze's eyes opened even wider. "Holy shit," Swayze said, "the ten grand's out there in the restaurant. Sittin' on the chair, Jimmy, on the chair. In the briefcase." There was true panic now in those widened eyes.

Pagnano let go and Swayze slumped forward, catching himself before he slid all the way to the floor. Pagnano had his hands on his hips now. "You think anybody's gonna touch anything at the table *I'm* sitting at in *this* restaurant?"

"No, no . . ." Swayze tried to laugh it off but the effort came out like a cough. "But you see, Jimmy, I'm not used to carryin' around ten grand in cash, ten grand. You maybe are but . . ."

Pagnano grabbed Swayze again. "You keep sayin' it. Why do you keep *sayin'* it?"

"Saying what?"

"The figure. Ten grand. You keep sayin' it." Pagnano was

back to heavy breathing. "Are you wired, you little fucker?"
And both of his hands began moving up and down the front
of Swayze's body.

"Jesus, no, why would I—"

"Wired. If you are fucking wired . . ." Pagnano pulled
Swayze's sportcoat down his back, pinning his arms, then
yanked his tie loose and began pulling open the buttons of the
shirt. He threw it open after the last button and stared at Swayze's hairless chest and flat belly. He felt around behind him,
his hand stroking nothing but bare back. He felt the armpits
and then up and down each arm.

Swayze stood there frozen, no longer thinking of the ten
grand out there on the chair all by itself, his mind as frozen
as his body as Pagnano fumbled with Swayze's belt, then unzipped the fly and pulled the pants and boxer shorts down
around his ankles. He took hold of Swayze's genitals and felt
around them, on the sides, behind the balls, then turned him
around so that he was suddenly face to face with the label of
a liter bottle of Myers' Dark Rum. Swayze felt his cheeks
being spread, then was yanked around to face Pagnano again.
"Gimme your shoes," Pagnano said.

"What?"

"Your *shoes*, goddammit."

Swayze kicked off his tasseled loafers, bent over and picked
them up and handed them to Pagnano, who felt inside them,
looked at their bottoms, shook each one next to his ear.
"Gimme your foot." Swayze tried to raise his foot but
couldn't because his pants were down around his ankles. Pagnano reached down and grabbed him by the ankle and jerked
it upward and Swayze's body slid down the wall of liquor
bins until his tailbone landed hard on the floor. Pagnano felt
around each foot. Then staring down at a stunned Swayze,
sitting there naked as a jaybird, said, "Okay, you're not
wired." Pagnano pulled a handkerchief from his pants pocket
and began wiping the sweat from his forehead. "Get yourself
dressed and we'll go out and have some lunch."

Swayze did as he was told.

*   *   *

NOLAN FINALLY GOT THROUGH to Holly Stryker. He was relieved when she reassured him that his name remained a secret wild horses couldn't drag out of her. He told her how touchy the situation had become, how everybody now wanted to know where she had gotten her information, even the mayor's office was beefing about it.

"Don't worry," she said. "Will it help if I called you Deep Throat?"

"What do you mean by that?" Nolan was thinking of the porno of Linda Lovelace.

"Watergate . . . Deep Throat . . . the source, the one nobody ever found out who he was."

"Oh, yeah, yeah. Well, listen, there really isn't anything more I can give you. We gotta break this off. This isn't my case anymore anyway."

"I know."

"It's gone downtown."

"Joe Morrison and Franco Norelli, I know that. But I can't get through to either one of them. All I get is the pressroom. I tried Organized Crime for Morrison, Area Three for Norelli. They won't call me back." Her voice softened. "How do I get to them? They have a direct line?"

"That's privileged. Inside only, they're touchy as hell about that."

"Johnny, just one more favor and I won't bother you anymore, except for that hamburger you still owe me."

Nolan gave her the number.

"What about these two, what are they like?"

Nolan told her whatever he knew.

THE THREE MEN WERE still at the bar when Pagnano and Swayze walked through the door and back to their table, but they were wrapped up in some kind of story of their own and didn't notice them. Or pretended not to. The briefcase was sitting on the chair just where it had been left.

Swayze reached for the briefcase and handed it to Pagnano, who flipped the snaplocks and opened it a crack, saw the greenery inside and closed it.

"Just like you said, Jimmy. Different bills, tens, twen—"

Pagnano brought a finger to his lips. "Okay, Vaughn. I'm sure you did right." He even had what for him was a pleasant smile as he said it, then he yelled over to the bartender, "Harry, come on over here a minute."

The three at the bar turned, apparently surprised to see the corner table occupied once again by the two who had left it so abruptly and in such an unfriendly manner a while ago. One of them said, "Looks like they patched up their little difference," the remark carrying across the empty room to Pagnano's table.

"Who're those jerks?" Pagnano asked Harry when he arrived at the table.

"Two of 'em are printing salesmen, come in here from time to time. Good drinkers, good tippers. Don't know who the third guy is, probably somebody they sell the stuff to."

Pagnano held up the cordovan briefcase. "Have this taken care of for me, will you, Harry," and handed it to him.

Harry turned and headed off toward the dining room. Pagnano called after him. "And Harry, see if one of the girls are still back there. We wanna order something." Harry nodded and hurried on to the back and through the swinging doors with the portholes to the kitchen.

"You didn't even count it?" Swayze asked.

"You think I need to?"

"No, no, Jimmy, I just thought maybe—"

"If it ain't all there, Vaughn, we don't got a deal."

"Yeah, I guess that's right, right, that's right." His smile was coming back. "Well, it is, Jimmy, all there, certainly is. We got a deal." By the time he finished saying that the money was already out of the building in a large brown paper bag in the hands of Harry's kid brother, who kind of looked after the kitchen help and ran errands for the D'Amicos and certain of their preferred customers.

"Thought the kitchen closed at two," one of the printing salesmen said to Harry.

"Sometimes it does, sometimes it doesn't. Sometimes the bar stays open, sometimes it doesn't."

"Hey, Harry, just kidding around. Total us up."

"You can bring me the veal now," Pagnano said to the waitress, who had followed Harry into the bar.

"I held it like Harry told me, but I don't know if it's any good anymore, sittin' around out there."

"Then have 'em cook another. They got another veal chop in the house, I hope."

"Oh, sure. I'll have them make you a new one."

"And another Stoli." He handed her the glass. "So order up," Jimmy said to Swayze. "I got things to do this afternoon."

Swayze squirmed a little in his seat. "You think, Jimmy, my wife and Red, you know, could come back inside. I mean, the business thing is over. I hate to see them sitting out there in the car, the heat and all."

Pagnano looked at him for a few beats, then said, "All right, go out and get 'em. But no business talk."

"Absolutely, you got my word on it, Jimmy," Swayze said as he scrambled to get out from behind the table. "You got my word, absolutely . . ."

✛15

VAUGHN SWAYZE WAS RIGHT ABOUT HIS WIFE. WHEN JIMMY Pagnano finally paid close attention to her after she and the redhead walked back into the restaurant with Swayze, he decided she could hold her own with just about anybody working out at the Surf and Turf, Doe Davenport excluded.

There were a couple of things that bothered him about Felice Swayze, though. The little sass she threw out just before she left for the parking lot was one. The other was all the cooing and petting and bullshit talk she dumped on Swayze now while they were eating lunch. Pagnano thought that kind of crap was not for public display, not the sappy way she came across. But she did have a pair of legs. He couldn't keep his eyes off them, she sitting there at the table kittycorner and the legs never under the table, the knees always pointing toward him—the skirt covering only about a third of her thighs and she had on those shiny nylons, the kind that make that sliding noise when she crossed or uncrossed her leg, which she did often. Veebee was her nickname for him, Swayze explained somewhere along the line, short for Vaughn-Boy, whose origin he also tried to explain but Pagnano had tuned him out. "Veebee, you are a once-in-a-lifetime guy," she would say, then nibble on his fingers. Too much, Pagnano thought.

When Felice went to the ladies' room Swayze said, "See what I mean, she's something. Right? I tell you, she's all over me all the time. Never, ever I had somebody who went for me like she does. Crazy for me. You can tell, I can tell you can tell."

"Yeah, you're one lucky guy, Vaughn-Boy." Pagnano watched her stroll back from the washroom, wondering what a broad like that could see in a guy whose main ambition in life was to steal a dead body.

The redhead was something else, a man who was expert at the confidence game, Swayze said by way of introduction, but Pagnano had sensed it from the time the guy sat down. Red Ryan was his name, and he had green eyes that were almost pretty, the kind that could worm out trust in little old ladies whose husbands had recently died and left them money they did not know where to invest. But he also had the bluff-walk and the wariness of somebody who had been inside, the aura of someone who had learned to watch his ass.

A little more than a week earlier Red Ryan had, in fact, been released from the federal penitentiary in Terre Haute, where he was on a four-year stay for a scam that Pagnano thought was a good one when Swayze explained it to him.

The scam had also earned Ryan the nickname Little Red Riding Hood, which actually had nothing to do with the thatch of wavy red hair sitting on his head. Red spent four years at Terre Haute for bilking a series of investors in nine states from Illinois to California. What he did was simple, which was the beauty of it. Red, who was mechanically inclined, bought himself a top-of-the-line Schwinn mountain bike, filed off the serial number, engraved a new one, etched in the identification of a Czechoslovakian bicycle manufacturing company, made some welding adjustments here, added some flashy nuances there, and then had the bike painted a shiny fire-engine red. Its new name: the Red Rider.

He had a glossy four-color brochure made up illustrating the bike in all its cerise splendor and extolling the quality and precision that had gone into the manufacture of this high-tech two-wheeler. There was a loose-leaf binder filled with assembly instruction, parts lists and the results of comparative tests of performance, durability and maintenance frequency between the Red Rider and the Schwinn as well as comparable models from western Europe and Japan. The Red Rider mountain bike beat them all hands down in every category.

And then the corker—it would retail in the United States for $269.50, whereas the comparable Schwinn was priced at $389.95, and those imports from such bicycle citadels as France, England, Germany, Denmark and Japan carried stickers anywhere from $450 to as much as $900.

According to Red Ryan's pitch, the Czech company could produce these gems for sale at prices that would easily annihilate the old-line competition because of cheap labor, reduced overhead and a much lower cost for domestic materials.

Then Red Riding Hood set out across the country with his lone Red Rider to sell franchises for exclusive distribution dealerships of the Czech-made bike. He figured he could be through California and out of sight and touch before investors in Peoria, Kansas City, Omaha, Wichita, Tulsa, Colorado Springs, Provo, Santa Fe, Tucson and others realized all they had for their $10,000 earnest money was a handful of papers and a certified bill of lading for the delivery of their own showcase sample Red Rider. He was wrong. Red Riding Hood had just started working his way up the coast from San Diego when the Department of Justice finally caught up with him. Ironically it was in Orange County where a couple of U.S. marshalls put the cuffs on him.

Red had new plans now, worked out during four years of study in Indiana when he wasn't working on the license-plate assembly line there. No more interstate scams. He would work within a single state per scam and keep the feds out of the picture. Illinois was a natural for a start. Chicago the hub. And in the penitentiary down there, which had a fair share of Chicago goodfellas, he also learned that if he was to survive in his chosen profession in that city he would need certain blessings, certain protective arms wrapped around him. That was what he told Swayze, who decided his old pal Red Riding Hood should make the acquaintance of his new pal Jimmy Pagnano.

Over cannoli for dessert, Pagnano said he was not against helping an ex-con get a new start in life. Everybody deserved a second chance, after all.

When they finished, Swayze asked Jimmy Pagnano the best way to get out to Deerfield, a suburb about twenty miles northwest of where they were sitting. "Me and Red want to look at a little business opportunity out there," he said. "I know where the town is but the traffic around this city I don't know. So what's the best way to get out there?"

The check came, delivered in a fake leather folder and placed between Swayze and Red Riding Hood. Pagnano gave it a glance. "Don't take the Kennedy, it's a mess, all the construction going on. The best way, when you leave here get on the Eisenhower and go west to the Tri-State Tollway, 294, then north takes you right to Deerfield, cost you a buck or so in tolls but you can afford it, Vaughn-Boy, all the money you're coming into."

Pagnano looked over at Felice Swayze, giving her a little smile. "Now if you'll excuse me, doll, I got to go tend to some business of my own," he said, making a move to get up. She and her chair had him hemmed into the booth.

"Okay, thanks a lot, Jimmy," Swayze said. Then to Red: "We better hit the road, too." And to Felice: "We'll drop you at the hotel, hon."

Pagnano, both hands on the table as he was pushing himself to a standing position, was staring down at Felice's long legs and heard the sexy sound of the nylons when she uncrossed them to stand up. His eyes traveled up her body and then went over to Swayze. "That's the opposite direction. I can drop her off for you. Save you goin' into downtown traffic."

Swayze said, "Well . . . that okay with you, hon?"

She looked at Pagnano, who was standing now, his eyes on her. "Sure. Be just fine. But you hurry your little self back, Veebee. Your hon's gonna get lonesome in that big room."

"Couple of hours, be back by six, seven latest." Then to Pagnano: "Thanks again, Jimmy."

"No problem." As he was walking toward the Moorish archway, Pagnano could hear Swayze in the background: "I can't help it, Red. So we split it down the middle. Okay? With tip, it comes to seventy each. You gotta tip good here, it's Jimmy's place. Jesus, a hundred and forty bucks for lunch, for lunch."

In the car driving east toward the McCormick Inn, she seemed like a very different lady, Pagnano thought. No batting of the fake eyelashes like she laid on Swayze, no cutesy words—in fact a bit of an edge to her voice, talking as she applied another coat of lipstick as red as Red Ryan's Red Rider. And below, the skirt riding up—an inch or two more and he would be able to see what she had on underneath the suntan-shade pantyhose.

"Big rooms, huh?" Pagnano said as they pulled into the driveway of the McCormick Inn.

"You never been in here?"

"The bar. Not in any of the rooms."

"Yeah, they're big. No suite or nothin'."

He pulled to a stop in front of the hotel entrance. She said, "Thanks." He nodded, looking over at her, wearing a little smile now. She smiled back. "You wanna . . . you wanna see how big they are?"

SOME WERE SITTING, SOME standing around in the watch commander's office at Four: Morrison, Norelli, Nolan and Nabasco, McCabe and Wilson, Lloyd Ware from Gang Crimes, the undercover from Narcotics, and Flanagan's man Frost. The room was not built and furnished to accommodate such a crowd, and despite the open window and the big floor fan whirring away as it swept back and forth across the room in its unvarying arc, everybody was uncomfortable in the stifling August heat. They were going over where they were at, which was basically nowhere beyond where they had been that morning, which did not help in terms of the discomfort index.

Lieutenant Grantham was still sitting behind the commander's desk, even though it was past four o'clock and the end of his watch. His relief, Lieutenant Rivera, ever aware of Grantham's seniority fixation, was sharing butt space with Norelli on the edge of the other desk in the room, listening as ideas and theories were kicked around. Morrison was leaning against one of the door-jambs, Johnny Nolan was holding up the other.

Talk at Four was about the murders and the investigation. Nothing was brought up about the coverage the case was getting from the media. That was downtown business. Morrison and Norelli had met with Deputy Superintendent Harkness before heading over to Four earlier that afternoon, now they were trying to put together something to give to Deputy Superintendent Flanagan when he arrived at 11th and State the next morning.

Harkness's big concern was still Alderman Hunter. Morrison and Norelli had said they thought the alderman's Sunday service had not really chimed a whole helluva lot of bells around town. That didn't matter, Harkness told them, in fact it would probably cause more of a problem—the alderman usually responded to what he considered a slight with special vigor. To prove his point Harkness tossed a copy of the Monday *Metro* across the desk to them.

Under the byline of Holly Stryker, the story was back on the front page after a one-day hiatus, and that only because the afternoon *Metro* did not publish on Sunday. It claimed to be an exclusive interview with Alderman Lorenz Hunter but Harkness noted that the alderman was scheduled to appear live on the NBC six o'clock news and ABC's ten o'clock news that night. CBS, which had the lowest rating of the big three in terms of local news broadcasting, got the Hunter snub but was responding with a special "Dateline" editorial entitled "Savage Streets," focusing on the Peters/Tees case as an example of rampant crime in the city and to be featured on their six o'clock and ten o'clock news shows. Harkness did not know what the *Tribune* and the *Sun-Times* had in the works, the newspapers always being more closed-mouthed than the electronic media, but it had to be something. *Everybody* was out there looking for the story that Hunter was telling them existed in the dark and sinister halls of 11th and State.

No one wanted to find the story more than Morrison and Norelli, they reminded the deputy superintendent.

JUST BEFORE FIVE, MORRISON got a call on the watch commander's line. It was from Tim Doyle at the FBI, calling from a pay phone in the Intercontinental Hotel lobby. He said he was sorry he hadn't gotten back to Morrison earlier, he'd been in the field all day. Funny, Morrison thought, when the G are out they're in the field, when the cops are out they're on the street. Was there a class distinction there? Doyle suggested they meet somewhere. He had had the Bureau office pull a print-out on anything relating to Morrison's case. They hadn't come up with much but it might not hurt to talk, he said.

Morrison looked at his watch, saw it was a little after five, "Yeah, I'd like to talk. We're about done here. Where?"

"Why not Miller's, say, quarter of six." Miller's was a pub where they occasionally met when they did not want to do business in either man's office.

"Fine."

"Might be a few minutes late," Doyle said. "Save me a seat at the bar."

Norelli dropped Morrison at Michigan Avenue and Adams and then went back to 11th and State to drop off the day's report and turn in the car they had been using. Morrison bought a copy of the *Metro* at a corner newsstand and walked a block west to Miller's. It was ten after six and Doyle was still not there. A couple of stools were open at the end of the bar and he took one, ordered a Jack Daniels on the rocks and asked Rodney, the bartender he had a vague acquaintance with, to put a glass of water in front of the stool next to him because he was expecting somebody. Rodney, knowing Morrison was a detective, obliged. Morrison sipped his drink and started to read Stryker's article. He was through with both the drink and the article when Doyle slapped him on the shoulder.

Morrison liked Doyle, the only one in the Chicago Bureau office he could say that about. Doyle was a down-to-earth guy, a good family man, good drinker and storyteller in the Irish tradion. His wife had money of her own and they lived with their four kids—two of them in college, one at Michigan and the other out east at Boston College, a major chunk of change—in a rambling old five-bedroom Victorian house out in Oak Park, none of which they could have come close to affording if they had to live on his agent's salary. The others Morrison dealt with in the Chicago Bureau office were too officious, offering the CPD a sort of weary tolerance most of the time and an undisguised annoyance the rest of it. They were, in Morrison's opinion, a little like the White House detail of the Secret Service when they swooped into town, imperious and gift-wrapped in themselves. Morrison believed that the FBI guys, Doyle excepted, still tended to believe the stuff that J. Edgar Hoover had told them about themselves a couple of decades earlier.

"An Old Fitz Manhattan on the rocks," Doyle said to Rodney the bartender, pushing the glass of water away, "light on the vermouth."

Morrison ordered another Jack Daniels.

"I do it for the maraschino cherries," Doyle said to Morrison. "Recharges my blood sugar level. What's your excuse?"

"I don't have one."

"What do you mean? You're a drinker. A drinker has to have an excuse." He held his glass aloft.

"Well, okay . . . I drink for the demons. The demons, they're like cholesterol, there's good ones and bad ones. I drink to drive out the bad ones and drink to replace them with the good ones. It doesn't, obviously, always work that way.

Mostly it doesn't.'' Morrison lifted his glass and touched it with a clink to Doyle's. ''Here's to law and order, old buddy.''

''I'll drink to that.''

Doyle looked at the folded newspaper lying between them on the bar. He jabbed a finger at the article by Holly Stryker staring up at them and headlined:

WEST SIDE STORY: KILLING OUR CHILDREN

The story began:

> A Metro News *exclusive interview with Alderman Lorenz Hunter. Alderman Hunter announced today he is launching his own investigation into the wanton slaying of 14-year-old Rayfield Tees on Chicago's crime-ridden west side, along with a citywide probe "into the lack of police protection and the second-class-citizen attention given to criminal investigations in the city's black communities."*

''You want something on this, I know, but I haven't got much for you.'' Tim Doyle shrugged. ''This Thurman Peters, or Manny Peters, we have his vital statistics and maybe a four-sentence paragraph on him in the computer. And the only reason we've got even that is because he got nailed on an interstate hijacking about ten years ago. And I'm sure you've got that yourselves. He went away for three years.''

''It's on his sheet. What I want to know is who he offended so badly he ends up in the trunk of his car last Friday night.''

''No idea.'' Doyle took a gulp rather than a sip of his Manhattan. ''He's small-time, at least as far as we're concerned, which means he isn't a concern of ours. Unless, of course, we could've got him to turn a corner for us. We tried when he was on his way to Leavenworth but we couldn't—that was sentence three and four in the computer's capsule bio on him. That's it.''

''You or your computer have any idea who protects him these days?''

''No. One of our people had heard of Peters, that he was a

loner, independent, did jobs from time to time for different *caporegimes* in the city, the county for that matter. But he pretty much ran his own operation. Kind of a free spirit moving in and out of the otherwise orderly world of organized crime.''

''Well, he didn't operate without somebody's sanction. Not for as long as he's been around doing what he does. Or did. He's got to be paying tax to someone.''

''I'm sure. But we don't know who. And the computer doesn't either.'' Doyle gave him a palms-up gesture, then ordered another round.

''You got any way of finding out?''

Doyle shook his head. ''Joe, this is not our kind of thing. That's why I wanted to talk to you. The Bureau's only after the big guys, you know, the guys who make Time and Newsweek and the New York *Times*. A Gotti, who we got. An Accardo, who departed before we could get him. *Capos* of any size or shape, those kinds of guys. This Peters is a little prick. So, I'd say, is whoever carried out the contract.''

''Tim, I want to know if you can help me find out who got tired of protecting him. And maybe why. Or maybe if somebody ignored the protection or just didn't know Peters was being protected. You think your sources could come up with something like that?''

''Joe, what do I have to do to make you understand? The Bureau is happy to share with you what they have, what the computer comes up with. But they don't want to mess with the small-time stuff.''

''But this isn't small-time to us. The mayor's very upset, the superintendent is wetting his pants. It may be all out of proportion from your perspective—''

''The Bureau's perspective. I didn't say mine.''

''Okay, the Bureau's. But my Bureau, City Hall, is very sensitive these days. Remember, three years ago the mayor got only eight percent of the black vote. He even came up short on the Lake Shore liberal vote. He's courting them these days, trying to appease them, not upset them.''

''I know all that, but there's not a whole helluva lot I can do, Joe.'' He took a sip of the Manhattan and held the glass out in front of him. ''Lord, these things are good.'' He looked at Morrison. ''But I don't have to tell you that, do I?'' he remarked, nodding toward the glass in front of Morrison, which now contained only a few melting ice cubes.

''No, and I think I'm going to have another. You?''

''I'll pass. Have one with Judy when I get home.''

''Back to Manny Peters.''

''There's nothing to go back to, Joe. Look, let me take this a step further. This afternoon I got a message to call in to the SAC,'' referring not to the Strategic Air Command but to the regional office's Special Agent in Charge, ''which I did and he wanted to know why the hell I and some of the others in the office were spending time and the taxpayers' money on something that had no significance as far as the Federal Bureau of Investigation was concerned.''

''We're not taxpayers? Chicagoans don't pay federal taxes?''

''You know what I mean. You know him too. He's by the book. At any rate, the SAC said to drop it. He does not want, and I quote him, 'our resources misdirected nor our sources jeopardized.' He said he wished you the best of luck in solving your murders but it was a local matter and we were not to spend any more time on it. Case closed.''

Rodney put a fresh Jack Daniels in front of Morrison, shoved it a little and nodded, meaning he was not going to ring it up.

Doyle drained off the residue of his Manhattan. ''I'll hang around until you finish that, but let's change the subject.''

''Sure . . . tell me, Tim, do you think on gala occasions J. Edgar really did wear a dress and high heels?''

''Can't say, Joe, I wasn't there. But I did hear tell Frederick's of Hollywood catalog arrived regularly marked For the Director's Eyes Only.'' Doyle shrugged and picked up the check, looked at it and put down a twenty to cover it. ''Your turn next time, pal.''

Joe nodded. ''I might hang in and have another Tennessee smoother and something to eat.''

Doyle got up from the stool. "Well, good luck, Joe, and if *I* happen to run across anything all by myself, I'll give you a call."

✥16

MORRISON DECIDED NOT TO HAVE ANOTHER OR SOMETHING to eat at Miller's and to walk a mile back to police headquarters, where he had left his car early that morning. He walked over to State Street. Here in the southern part of the Loop these days it looked like Beirut, so many of the old landmark buildings in the process of being torn down. He remembered when he was a kid that it had, indeed, been a great street, like in the song. It was the merchandising capital of the Midwest, all the magnificent department stores and first-run movie theaters. Every Christmas his parents took him down to see the elaborately decorated windows of Marshall Field's and the other stores on the street. It was always awash with shoppers and Salvation Army Santas with their bells and buckets and it was always snowy and windy but no one seemed to care, especially the kids. It was special in those days to come downtown. Field's was still there, up at the north end, so was the venerable old Chicago Theater, but the street's day had come and gone.

He passed under the El tracks at Van Buren Street, leaving the Loop behind. South State Street had changed too. Once it had been the epitome of tawdriness, a strip filled with penny arcades, strip shows, pawnshops and home to an ever-changing community of derelicts and low-lifes. Now for the most part it was a stretch of parking lots to serve the people who drove the expressways to their jobs in the Loop and the burgeoning areas to the west of it. Even some upscale high-rise apartment buildings had bloomed, but *south* State Street was never going to be a sought-after address. And still a touch of the past lingered. On the corner of Seventh Street and State stood the Pacific Garden Mission, which had fed and put up for the night down-and-outers over the past five decades. Kittycorner across the street was the old Carver Hotel, a flophouse that had somehow escaped the wrecker's ball and sported a new name, the Seventh Street Hotel, and a gin mill on the ground floor named the South Loop Inn.

The stretch here was more populated at this hour on a warm summer night than that area just inside the Loop. And most were street people. As he walked along the east side of the street, just past the South Loop Inn, a woman with a W. C. Fields face approached him. She was wearing two different tennis shoes, one blue and one white, both missing laces. He gave her a dollar. Three black teenagers were standing in front of a hotdog joint on the next corner. They were talking but their eyes roved the street. They took in Morrison from a distance, but as he neared and they saw him staring back they sized him up for what he was and dropped eye contact. He walked past them into the place and ordered two dogs to go with everything, including peppers, and a bag of Jay's potato chips. His eating habits weren't the most nutritionally correct since the divorce. When he stepped back out onto State Street, the skulkers were gone.

He carried his dinner to 11th Street and the twelve-story building with the three flags dangling limply in the windless night above the State Street entrance—U.S., city of Chicago and CPD. He took the elevator to the third floor, where a uniformed female cop was manning the telephone outside PT Task Force headquarters. She knew him but he didn't know her and had to look at the plastic bar above her left breast which said Hennessy.

"You keep long hours, sarge," she said. She had a round Irish face, freckles under the eyes and across her nose. He would bet her father had been on the job.

"Not by choice," he said, although he wasn't sure he meant it, things being the way they were in his life these days.

"I'm sitting in for Steiner," the detective who was assigned to handle the direct line on the third shift. "He went to get something to eat. I'm beginning to think maybe Milwaukee for bratwurst." She had a smile straight from Kildare.

"Been exciting, I bet. Anybody try to steal the phone?"

"No."

"Use it . . . without permission?"

"No. Your partner came in, Norelli. You guys had a couple of messages. He took 'em. Gave me back these two and said to save them for you." She handed him the two while-you-were-out slips. "Said it must be your girlfriend because she had the hotline number."

Both messages were from Holly Stryker with her number and extension at *Metro News,* one logged in a little after four-thirty and the other at five-twenty. Only his name was on the slips, he noticed. He wondered how she had gotten the number. It was supposed to be for police use only. Then the thought hit him that he should have given the number to Doyle, and he made a mental note to call him tomorrow and pass it on. Might serve as a reminder to the G-man of his parting words, "if *I* happen to run across anything . . ." It couldn't hurt.

"The lady called again after he left." She handed him another slip. This one came in at 7:18 and had Holly Stryker's home number on it and the notation that she would be there the rest of the evening. "I asked her if it was important enough for me to give you a beep. She said it was. I did. You didn't answer."

Morrison looked at her a little baffled and then remembered turning off the thing on his hip when Doyle finally showed up at Miller's. "I had it off, forgot to turn it back on. She say anything else."

"Nope. Two other calls." Two more slips handed over.

He took them, said thanks and walked into PT Task Force, Limited. One of them was from the watch commander at Area Four, Lieutenant Rivera, who, it appeared, had finally gotten his desk and telephone back from the senior Grantham. The other was from Johnny Nolan and said it was nothing that couldn't wait until morning and he would check in then.

Morrison called Rivera first. "Got a couple of things for

you," the lieutenant said. "After you left, the guy from Gang
Crimes came in. You know the guy. He's from downtown.
What's his name, big guy, begins with a *T*, I think."

"W, maybe. Lloyd Ware."

"Yeah, that's him."

"I'll give him a call."

"You downtown?" Morrison said he was. "At eight
o'clock? Anyway, I gather he talked to somebody downtown."

"Maybe Norelli, he came back here after we left you. I
haven't talked to him, though."

"Well, this guy said he had information that the Westerns
got some idea about what went down last Friday night. He
said it didn't have anything to do with any other gang. Why
the kid was there and why he got shot, he doesn't know, but
he thinks the Westerns might. Says they're working on that.
But GC got one big problem, he said, the gangs don't trust
them very much. Can you imagine that? The bangers out there
have some doubts about the motives of the guys from GC.
What is this world coming to anyway? Nobody trusts nobody."

"That it?" Morrison had the receiver couched between his
cheek and his shoulder as he opened the bag and took out the
two hot dogs. They smelled pretty good, the Jack Daniels must
have given him an appetite. He unrolled one from white, waxy
paper and took a bite.

"No. Johnny Nolan got a call just as he and Nabasco were
about to check it out. One of his snitches. The two of them
went to see him. When they came back Nolan said the snitch
told them we might want to talk to some of the Lords' upper
echelon for information on the PT case. The bangers know
something but he didn't know what. Nolan said he and Nabasco would follow it up in the morning. I think he tried to
get somebody downtown, too. Well, that's all."

Morrison hung up and went out to get a cup of coffee to
wash down the dogs.

With the feast over, Morrison picked up the slip with Holly
Stryker's home telephone number and dialed it. She wanted

to meet with him, she had something for him about the "double slayings," as she called them.

Ingratiating herself, Morrison said to himself, for a future exclusive, but he listened. She said she didn't want to talk about it on the phone, could they meet somewhere? Tonight? How about the morning, he suggested, unless the murderer she was going to finger for him might escape under the cover of darkness. Make it at the restaurant around the corner from 11th and State, on Wabash, Dottie's, at eight A.M. She said she'd be there.

"How did you get the number here, by the way?"

"I've got my sources."

"Which you can't reveal?"

"Right."

"See you in the morning." He was about to hang up when she said, "How will I know you?"

"I'll be the guy with the gun. No, that won't work, everybody in there's got a gun, except maybe Dottie. I'll be at the counter. Just ask for me, I'm a regular."

It was nine-thirty when he reached Jim Harkness at home. "I just wanted to let you know I'm meeting with a member of the press in the morning. Holly Stryker. You remember, the one with *Metro News* who's bucking for a Pulitzer on PT."

"What the hell are you doing that for?"

"She says she's got something. Remember, knock on every door . . . listen to every line . . . follow up every lead?"

"What the hell could she have that we don't?"

"I don't know, that's why I'm meeting her. I think it's more she wants a contact inside, a source. We'll see. Anyway, I wanted to tell you, seeing as you're concerned about leaks. I wouldn't want you, a friend, much less anyone else downtown, to get the idea that I'm the leaker."

"I told you the other day that thought would never enter my mind."

"You also wanted to subpoena my telephone records."

"I just asked who you called. Jesus Christ."

"Not Him. But I wish I could get through to Him. We could use some divine intervention."

"The Reverend Hunter has a monopoly on that. Maybe he's shared some of his revelations with the reporter. They seem to be pretty good pals, judging from today's paper."

"Yeah, I read it."

"Where you meeting her?"

"At Dottie's, eight o'clock . . . everything out in the open, in the very shadow of Chicago Police Department central headquarters."

"Let me know if she has anything. We have our daily get-together at nine," Harkness said, referring to the superintendent's ritual morning meeting of the CPD's top brass. "Anything of interest on this one I'd be delighted to share with the superintendent."

"Don't hold your breath. Incidentally, she called me three times on the direct line before I got back here. How do you suppose she got the number?"

"The lady sure does have her wires connected, doesn't she?"

"Sources, she calls them. I got another name for it."

"I'm glad you called, Joe."

"Just covering the bases."

"Be sure to cover home plate, too. You know how we do that downtown, don't you?"

"Send you a memo."

"You keep this sharp, Joe, you might end up a deputy yourself one of these days. Copy Flanagan—who you're meeting, where, why, then a follow-up on the shit she gives you and anything else your keen mind picks up. We don't need to know what you and the lady order for breakfast."

Morrison wrote a note to Norelli about his conversation with Holly Stryker and that he was meeting her in the morning and left it on the desk for him.

Detective Steiner, a gaunt veteran waiting out the days downtown until his retirement, had replaced Officer Hennessy at the telephone outside PT Task Force, Limited. His look of boredom when Morrison emerged was in direct contrast to the Irish smile on the freckled, cherubic face he had been greeted with an hour earlier. Morrison said goodnight to Steiner, wondering at the same time if Hennessy would also wear an expression like that after a couple of decades on the job.

✤17

HOLLY STRYKER BEAT HIM TO DOTTIE'S AND WAS SITTING at the counter when Morrison walked in a little before eight. The place was crowded. Second-shifters in uniform from the First District, which occupied a good part of the main floor of police headquarters around the corner, were finishing up before rollcall. Others who earned the same kind of living but without the uniform in niches on floors above in the same building were also there. And, of course, there were some members of the laity, the regulars who worked at other jobs in the neighborhood. Dottie's did a very good business, especially around shift changes.

Holly Stryker was by no means the only female in the place and not the only good-looking one either, but she was the only one with a slender leather briefcase propped next to her leg on the floor and a reporter's notepad and ballpoint pen lying on the counter next to her coffee cup. Morrison stopped behind her and tapped lightly on the shoulder pad of her silky blouse. "Miss Stryker, I assume?"

The stools on either side of her were occupied, one of which by an overweight patrolman who was trying to blot up the last of his egg yolks with a forkful of hashed browns. He looked back at the same time she did. "Sergeant Morrison?" he nodded and the patrolman, who Morrison didn't know, said to him, "You can have this seat, sarge. I'm finished, gotta get across the street for rollcall anyway."

"Don't hurry," Morrison said, then to Holly, "we'll get a table."

They went over and stood by a table at the window until the busboy finished cleaning and setting it and then sat down.

Blocking the view of bustling Wabash Avenue was the back of a panhandler outside. Despite the warm weather he was wearing a soiled, raggedy down vest. Dangling from his neck was a square of corrugated cardboard on which was scrawled:

**VIETNAM VETERAN
VICTIM OF AGENT ORANGE
PLEASE HELP**

"Sign of the times," Morrison said, looking out the window at him.

"What a rotten war that was," Holly said, and turned back to Morrison. "Well, I'm really glad you agreed to meet me. I think it could be mutually beneficial."

The waitress arrived. "So what can I get you kids today?" She was about fifty-something and to her everyone was a kid.

"Go ahead," Morrison said.

"Just coffee and grapefruit juice."

"That all?" the waitress asked, looking down over her glasses. Holly Stryker said it was. The waitress shook her head. "Not healthy. Breakfast's the most important meal of the day. Skinny's not necessarily healthy."

"That's really all I want."

The waitress looked at Morrison. "And you? You better have something. You've been looking a little peaked lately."

"Two poached eggs, rye toast, orange juice and coffee."

"Good boy." She turned away and headed for the call-in counter in the back.

"Maggie's mother to us all. Now where were we? Oh yeah, mutual beneficial time. Before we get to that, Ms. Stryker, I'd like to know a little about you. Who you are, where you're coming from. I guess it's the detective in me . . ."

The truth was, he *did* wonder about her. Somehow she seemed out of place covering murder in the city slums. Dressed as she was, wheat-colored skirt, white shimmery blouse and blue linen blazer with matching pumps, she looked more like she should be on her way to an ad agency up on

Michigan Avenue to write about Toyotas or Big Mac specials or new horizons in the skin-cream business. She had sharp, intense blue eyes, though, like the kind he would find in someone whose work was usually decribed as in the line of duty.

She smiled. "Don't I fit your preconceived image, detective? Never mind, here's the bio. I grew up in Moline. That's one of the Quad Cities . . . on the Mississippi River." The eyes danced. "In case you aren't familiar with the world outside Chicago. I went to school at Western Illinois in Macomb and Northwestern here, apprenticed at the *Trib*, got nowhere and went to work for *Metro* two years ago when it was just getting started. I'm still employed there."

"I know, I've seen your byline."

"I'm glad. Moving right along . . . I'm part German, part English, part Italian—so far as I know. I've never delved much into genealogy. Hobbies are reading, tennis, golf, which I play quite well, and, surprise, cooking. Never been married, am heterosexual, never been arrested. Do not smoke. Drink moderately. Have never been treated for mental illness or drug addiction. So far as I know, I am free of neuroses, including penis envy. How about yourself, Detective Morrison?"

He had to smile. Holly Stryker, it seemed, was something else. "I'm a cop."

"I know, What else."

"That's my life story. They've got some other particulars in my file across the street but I doubt you'd be interested."

"You from Chicago?"

"Born and raised."

Maggie brought the coffee and juice. "Your eggs'll be up in a minute," she told Morrison, then cast a cold eye on Holly Stryker before departing.

"Ever do anything else besides police work?"

"I was a bagboy in a grocery store in high school."

She waited.

"It was pretty exciting, especially the day these masked guys came in and robbed it. Killed the manager, two of the kids stocking shelves and some customers. I think it was that incident that got me into law enforcement.'' She still waited. ''It never made the newspaper or the nightly news but I thought it was a big deal at the time. My father being the store manager.'' He smiled.

This wasn't going the way she had intended. She tried to get to it. ''I don't want to seem indelicate after what you just told me, but could we talk about what I came here for?''

''Why not? Now that we know each other.''

She opened her notebook, punched the button at the top of her ballpoint pen. ''You don't mind if I take notes, do you?''

''No, but I thought the reason for our meeting was that *you* had something to tell me.''

She did, about her newfound source, Alderman Hunter, who had taken her into his confidence. It turned out she had no light to shed on who might have murdered the alderman's young constituent, much less the mob-connected man in the trunk who died from bullets fired from the same gun.

The eggs arrived, staring back at Morrison from the little bowl like glazed owl's eyes. He buttered a piece of toast and dug in.

What Holly Stryker could tell him was that the alderman/ reverend was voicing his suspicions of a police cover-up to her. No surprise there, Morrison thought. Hunter had insinuated the night before on television that he had information wrapping the crime syndicate, police headquarters and City Hall together in some secret cabal whose purpose was to play down, sidetrack and generally avoid bringing to justice the murderer or murderers of his young constituent. It had been Hunter at the top of his game. Cover-up. Christ, they hadn't had this many detectives assigned to a single case, this much pressure coming down from the top, since a pair of CPD undercover narcs were tortured and summarily executed in a garage on the south side more than two years ago.

''So what else is new?''

''He thinks the police are protecting the Outfit in this.''

''His thinking that is not something I would consider new.''

''Are they?''

''Come on. You don't really believe his line of crap.''

"It isn't like they haven't been in bed before."

"That sounds like him talking." She said nothing. "And do you really think if there was such a thing, *I* would know about it?" She kept up the ploy of silence, just staring at him across the table, letting him do the talking. Morrison had used the same technique when he was back in Homicide—let the talker talk his way into trouble. He was a little surprised she knew the tactic, wondered if they were teaching that in journalism school these days, but he went on anyway. "Me? You think something like that would trickle down to my level?"

"You could have an inkling, things do pass down in their own way, I'm sure."

"And if I did, and I don't, what would possess me to tell you?"

"Your sense of indignation, your concern for justice. You have a reputation. I did some homework."

"Well, just to set the record straight, the only sense of anything I have at the moment is of overwork. The babblings of your alderman friend notwithstanding, there is no cover-up. That's crazy. We've got a task force of eleven detectives working full-time on this case. Not to mention the time put in by regular Tacs and uniformed cops on the street. And there are outside agencies." Timothy Doyle came to mind and his SAC and the FBI. "We're doing our best, Ms. Stryker."

"Why can't you convince Alderman Hunter of that?"

"That's not my job, I'm glad to say. My job is finding who killed Manny Peters and Rayfield Tees." As he finished off the last of his coffee Maggie magically appeared and filled it. "You want some more, honey?" she said to Holly.

"A little."

A little is what she got, and Maggie was gone. "Do you think it was, how should I say it, someone from outside the neighborhood?"

"It could be, and it could be someone from the 'hood. Look, we've had our chat. You said you had something to tell me that might help our investigation. I doubted it but on the off-chance you did I met you. I can't help you with your saga in the *Metro*. So maybe you wasted your time, too."

When the check came she grabbed it. "My treat. I invited you." Morrison let it go. "I'm just doing my job, like you're doing yours," she said.

"And I've got to get to mine." He started to stand up.

"Well, I do have one thing. It won't help you find a killer but it's something you'd like to know." He stared down at her. "My friend the alderman, as you call him, hasn't announced it yet, but he's putting together a demonstration. Thursday night he's holding another service at his church with Mrs. Tees. His associates will be hitting the street to drum up a crowd for the service . . . and the demonstration on Friday. Oh, and coincidentally, Friday night's the mayor's big event at the Hilton Towers, the one where His Honor is getting an award from the Knights of Columbus . . . it will be on television. Just thought you might want to know."

"Thanks . . . for the breakfast." He smiled.

"Think nothing of it. But on the other hand, don't forget it either." She smiled.

AT PT HEADQUARTERS NORELLI was on the telephone when Morrison walked in, picked up the other phone and dialed Jim Harkness's extension.

"Wish I could tell you we have a half-black, half-white, half-male, half-female certified lunatic in custody for the murder of the young Rayfield and Manny. No such luck."

"So?"

"The lady from the *Metro* says your nemesis is planning a demonstration to embarrass the mayor, and we, I believe, are the instrument he plans to use."

"When?"

"Friday night."

"Shit. That's the KC ceremony. The mayor is getting the sword of the Knights. A big honor. You know who else is getting it that night, same time, same place?"

"No."

"The Reverend Theodore Hesburgh, former president of Notre Dame, Pete Rozelle, former head of the National Foot-

ball League, and Teddy Kennedy, still senator from the great
state of Massachusetts.''

"Sounds like a rather disparate group."

"Disparate?"

"I've been reading lately, something to keep me busy during the long nights."

"Well, disparate or not, Joe, this is a *big* thing for the
mayor. He's going to have one major shit-fit when he hears
Hunter is planning to mess it up. You have any details?''

"No."

"Picketing the Hilton. I can see the signs already. And I
can see Hizzoner's face when I tell him.''

"Isn't that where they had the demonstrations back in
'sixty-eight, the Democratic conventions, the hippies, the—''

"Yes, across the street, Grant Park was filled with them. I
was a patrolman then. I got hit with a condom balloon filled
with piss.''

"I was in high school. I thought all you guys were pigs,
too, beating up on all those kids with flowers in their hair.''

"Well, you live and learn. Me, too. I've got to get to my
meeting, Joe. See if you guys can find out anymore about what
the reverend's got planned.''

NORELLI WAS SITTING WITH his feet propped on the desk when
Morrison hung up, a mug of coffee in one hand, a stack of
papers in his lap and one in his other hand that he was peering
down at through a pair of reading half-glasses perched on the
nub of his nose. He looked over the glasses at Morrison.
"What'd the lady have to say?"

"Nothing to help us. She did say Hunter's on the warpath,
but that's mostly Harkness's worry.''

Norelli took off his glasses. "What say we do some digging
ourselves, we got a couple of hours to kill before we have to
be at Four.'' They had scheduled a progress meeting of their
own for eleven-thirty each morning in the Area Four Violent
Crimes squad room.

"You got something particular in mind?"

"I'd like to talk to Manny Peters's roommate,'' Norelli said.

"McCabe and Wilson didn't get much more than her name. Hostile, they put down on their report. Maybe with your famed persuasive style, Joe, we can get something more from her. She sure as hell must know more than she's telling."

"It's worth a shot. Call first, be sure she's there?"

"Let's just surprise the lady. We call, she'll probably take off. By the way, I talked with Nolan this morning before he hit the street. He's working with McCabe so Nabasco and Wilson can go scare the shit out of the Latinos who were in that house. They haven't been very cooperative. Nolan and McCabe are going to try to find some Western Lords if any are up this early in the morning."

"What'd Nolan want last night? He called," Morrison said.

"Just that he placed the Tees kid in a park earlier that night. According to his snitch, the kid was hanging around Altgeld Park Friday night. That's exclusive Lord turf. He was with some of the regular bangers but the snitch didn't know if they were up to anything or not. When the snitch left about eight or eight-thirty Rayfield was still there."

"Altgeld Park. That's on Harrison, right? Near Sacramento?" Morrison said.

"A couple of blocks east of Sacramento, between Harrison and Congress. Known for its swing sets, teeter-totters . . . and drug deals."

"It's also about a block from where Rayfield got himself shot."

✛18

WHEN MORRISON AND NORELLI ARRIVED AT AREA FOUR they had Hannah Sturm, Manny Peters's roommate, in tow and deposited her in one of the interrogation rooms. "Let her stew awhile," Norelli said after closing the door and locking it from the outside.

They had tried the persuasive approach—coming across as

nice guys, wanting to nail the bastards who killed her poor
Manny. She ignored them. They tried the hard line—they
knew who Manny was, what he did for a living, that she
should be aware that the enemies he had obviously made
might consider her an enemy too. No reaction. Forging ahead:
that this was a murder case and she could find herself in deep
dark doodoo if they found out that she was withholding *any*
information that might be "germane to the investigation." She
looked off into space. They tried the harder line: because of
her lack of cooperation she was placing herself under suspicion of having been involved in the murder of the late Manny
Peters. And did she know the kind of sentence a person could
draw for murder one *or* for even being an accomplice to it?

That brought a response, but not what they were looking
for. "Oh, sure," she said, "I popped him in the head, threw
him over my shoulder, carried him downstairs and dumped his
two-hundred-pound ass in the trunk of his car." She looked
like she could conceivably do that, Morrison thought. "Did I
leave a calling card? Is that where I made my mistake? You
guys are something else."

"You could have hired someone to do it," Norelli said.

She told them to fuck off.

ALL OF WHICH WAS why she was now sitting in the interrogation room at Area Four. They hadn't brought her in handcuffed, nor had they handcuffed her to the railing bolted to
the interrogation room wall. Not that they hadn't thought of
it, her attitude and all, but they figured it best not to get carried
away, that she would doubtless be consulting an attorney as
soon as someone let her make a phone call.

Lieutenant Grantham looked up when they walked in,
glanced at the clock on the wall. "You're early," he said. It
was eleven-fifteen. "Your reservation was for eleven-thirty."

"We'll wait in the bar," Norelli said, "if you find it in-
convenient for us to loiter in here."

"You guys are always welcome. Just so long as you don't
bring any of those pompous assholes from 11th and State
along with you. Present company excluded, of course, Joe."

"Like to use one of your phones," Norelli said.

"Be my guest," Grantham told him. "Use the one on the desk over there."

A uniformed officer appeared in the doorway and said to Morrison, "That woman you put in IR three, the one looks like Jack Palance, she's makin' a helluva racket poundin' on the door down there."

"What does she want?"

"Out, I'd say."

"Tell her we'll be down in a few minutes if she behaves herself."

"Who the hell did you bring in?" Grantham asked.

"Manny Peters's ladyfriend. Want to meet her?"

"I don't think so."

"A wise choice, lieutenant. She does not like policemen."

AT ELEVEN-THIRTY ONE CORNER of the squad room at Four held all the members of the PT task force and other detectives, the only two missing being Johnny Nolan and Eddie McCabe.

With good reason. They were standing amidst a carpet of litter in a courtyard between two project buildings in Rockwell Gardens, having conversation with several Western Lords which was not easy with the noise from all the little kids running around, apparently having a good time, paying no attention to the bangers and the cops whom they knew for what they were but chose to ignore since there was no hassling or shooting going on.

It had started twenty minutes earlier when Nolan and McCabe were heading back to Four and saw two of the bangers standing in front of a liquor store on Western Avenue and decided to have a few words with them. They knew them by their street names, Slipball and Torky, and Nolan knew that Slipball also had a birth certificate that carried the name Wallace T. Jones, having had several occasions to arrest him on suspicion of murder, aggravated battery, carrying a concealed weapon. McCabe wheeled their unmarked car halfway up onto the curb next to where Slipball and Torky were standing. Torky was younger but on the rise, Nolan knew, a street commando like Slipball but as yet without the credentials.

The two looked on amused when the car bumped over the curb and squealed to a stop.

"How you ever get a license," Slipball asked as the detectives stepped out of the car, "parkin' like that? Right at loadin' zone, too." He pointed at the No Parking sign which was almost touching the front bumper of the police car.

"Wallace, Wallace," Nolan said. Slipball hated the name Wallace. "Got a new hairstyle, huh," referring to the eraser-head crop of hair sitting on top of his head.

Slipball ignored the question. "What bring you this part the 'hood?"

Prepositions were not part of Slipball's vocabulary. By choice, Nolan suspected. Nolan leaned against the No Parking sign. "Nothing one would consider out of the ordinary in this 'hood. Just a double murder."

"Little Dirt."

"Little Dirt?" McCabe didn't take it as a name.

"Friday night. Eye-sen-how-er. We talkin' same thing."

"Rayfield Tees."

"You call him what you want."

"Rayfield Tees and a white man named Manny Peters."

"Who give a fuck 'bout a white man name, what, Minny Peter, you say?"

"This one's important to us."

"Us, too. Little Dirt. He growin' with us. Gonna be one."

Nolan took over. "We already know that. We also heard that his passing was not gang-related."

"You doin' your job, officer."

"You know anything about it, anything you might want to share with us?"

"Share. Say what, Torky? You got anythin' share?" Torky did not.

"Torky doesn't talk?" McCabe said.

"Torky talk. Sometime. Not to you."

"Well, Wallace, you talk. So—"

"Whyn't you call me my right name? Wallace died

sometime back. Slipball born then. Slipball be me. Slipball talks. Wallace, he dead.''

Nolan nodded. ''Okay, Slipball, you or any of your associates got any idea who might've killed your little pal and the white man named Manny Peters?''

''Well, now that you ask.'' Slipball looked over at Torky, gave him a little juke, then back at Nolan and McCabe. ''We way ahead you, man. Solo say when you guys come snoopin' round 'bout this he wanna be told.'' Both Nolan and McCabe knew who Solo was. Who didn't in the neighborhood? Solo was *the* lord, at least in this 'hood. He called the shots, literally. His sheet in the CPD files was as long as his cash flow.

''We would be happy to chat with Solo,'' Nolan said. ''Where might we find His Excellence this time of day.''

''Everplace. Torky, go give a call.'' Torky disappeared into the liquor store.

They waited.

NOLAN AND MCCABE WALKED into the squad room just as the meeting was coming to an end. ''Did we miss anything?'' Nolan asked, his boyish smile in place as he approached the desk where Morrison and Norelli were half-sitting, half-standing. Lieutenant Chatham, standing off to the side of them, shook his head. ''Don't worry, we got something,'' McCabe said, stopping next to his watch commander. Nolan said to Morrison and Norelli, ''We been talking to a couple of Westerns. Seems they could be cooperative in this. They're real pissed because little Rayfield was not a victim of the ordinary fun and games in the neighborhood. As they told me and Eddie, he was an innocent bystander.''

''Who told you?'' Norelli asked.

''Solo, we just got done talking to him . . . in a garden area of Rockwell.''

Norelli and Morrison both looked to Lloyd Ware.

''Solo's the man with the Westerns,'' Ware said. ''has been ever since he killed Motorman Foster,'' referring to Solo's predecessor as leader of the Western Lords, ''something we could never prove but we just kind of took for granted. You know, like everybody knows Jimmy Hoffa didn't just disappear to go on a vacation. At any rate, Solo's been in charge a couple of years now. A ruthless little son of a bitch. How'd you find him? He's usually pretty elusive," he said, looking now at Nolan.

"He found us. We were talking to a couple of his commandos. They said he wanted to talk to us. They called him. You know, he's got a beeper. The guy's got a fucking beeper. Anyway, we met with him over in the Gardens."

"It's not us he really wants to talk to," McCabe said. "He acts like we're messengers." McCabe looked pissed about that.

"He told us this wasn't a gang thing," Nolan said. "I told him we already knew that. He said they knew we knew that."

"Get to the *point*, Johnny," Morrison said.

"The point is, he implied they maybe know a lot more than we do and maybe it would be to our mutual advantage to talk. 'You do my dick, I do yours,' is the way he put it. He wants to know who's in charge. I told him the mayor and the superintendent of police. He said he didn't want to talk to us anymore but we should pass his invitation along to somebody who was in a position to deal. As he was leaving he said *deal* again to make his point."

"Where can we find him?" Norelli asked.

"You can't," McCabe said, "unless you know his beeper number. He wouldn't give it to us." McCabe would have been much happier if they had just been able to slap Solo around and kick his ass into the gutter instead of watching him and his bodyguard stroll that exaggerated arrogant stroll back to the Batmobile black Corvette they arrived in and which McCabe knew cost more than he made in a year *without* the gold spoke wheelcovers.

"Solo said to set it up through Slipball. He can be found at M&R Liquors on Western Avenue over near Van Buren. It's his office, I guess."

"WHAT KIND OF DEAL you think he's got in mind?" Morrison asked Lloyd Ware afterward.

"Guess it depends on what he's got for us. Way I figure it, he wants something from us. Not that he doesn't want to avenge his little cadet. He does. That's the code. That's what keeps guys like Solo in power. But I don't think he's in a position right now to do that. I don't think he's got the resources."

"It seems to me they got resources like the FBI these days—the weapons, the organization, the money," Norelli said.

"That's not what I meant." Ware shook his head. "We know it wasn't some gang thing. If it was, Solo already would have dispatched somebody to drive by and shoot up a couple of Disciples or Cobras that did Tees. He wouldn't want any part of us for that. I don't think he knows who did it and doesn't have the resources to find out. Maybe, in this case, we do. Or so he figures. Maybe that's the deal. An alliance that might work, unholy as hell. I don't think he wants us to give him the guy if we find him, I think maybe he just wants something to show to save face. You never know with these guys. What I do know is he definitely wants something from us or he wouldn't even consider talking to you."

"So tell us some more about this Solo kid," Morrison said.

"First, he's *not* a kid. He's about thirty, thirty-two. He was with the Lords on the south side in his younger days, out in Englewood, a killing field. He rose pretty high in a very short period of time because he was first, smart, and second, a killer. Maybe I got the order wrong. He doesn't look threatening, a wiry little guy, you'd think he'd be a runner or a booster or a small-time pusher, maybe. But you look into his eyes, you'll get the message, Joe. You'll know why he runs the show out there. They're cold, snake cold."

"So how did he end up on the west side?"

"In Pontiac, which he called home for a couple of years— I believe it was a plea-bargain manslaughter charge . . . there were a bunch of them down there, Westerns, and other Lords. Anyway he won over the Westerns while he was in the joint down there, his rep, the way he operated. When he came out, the south side was pretty well sewn up for the Lords. It was easier just to move in and work the west side. Which he did. Motorman didn't have a chance, made the mistake of thinking he could control Solo. Motorman, one morning they found him in a bed in his girlfriend's apartment, dead. Of natural causes.''

Morrison and Norelli looked puzzled.

''Natural causes, you know, you get shot in the head four times, you naturally die. His girlfriend was on the floor in the bathroom, she died naturally, too. Throat cut.''

''And Solo took over,'' Morrison said.

''He did. You know how he got that name Solo? He handled everything on his own, everything that required extreme action. Goes back to his earlier days on the south side. Somebody needed to be taken out, he'd say okay, consider it done and it was done. He never asked for help or back-up, so the story goes, just went off and the next thing his buddies knew the guy they didn't like was a dead issue. Gang Crimes calls him So Low, but everybody knows Solo; means the same thing, I guess. Our future partner!''

✦ 19

WITH TEN THOUSAND IN THE BANK, FIGURATIVELY SPEAKING, and another ten out there just waiting for him, and of course his boss, Jimmy Pagnano had the urge to move fast in this no-brainer deal that had fallen into his lap.

The cash seemed clean: unmarked bills, Treasury Department paper and printing, relatively small denominations, no sequences; still it was put away to rest for a while. It would eventually circulate, once laundered. Swayze checked out, too. Jimmy had talked personally with Lenny Sasso. Lenny Sasso vouched for him, said he was sort of a flake but definitely not a plant. Pagnano knew about government entrapment, and though he did not worry about it with the obsession of an

Aldo Forte he took the trouble to be careful. Lenny Sasso's word was good, but not like a message from the pope. Still, everything seemed copasetic, which was the way he put it to Joe Alessi when he gave Joe his share of Swayze's down payment on a corpse.

Swayze's wife answered the telephone in the room at the McCormick Inn when Pagnano called late Tuesday afternoon. He recognized the twang in her voice. "Hey, fellate, it's Jimmy. Vaughn-Boy around?"

"He is not. And the name's *Felice*."

He smiled. "How'd I get that mixed up?"

"Short memory you got." She smiled too.

"Me? Never." He smiled to himself, remembering the action in the big room which wasn't so big after all, but deciding he didn't want to go any further with it. "So where is he and when'll he be back?"

"He's . . . I don't know. Makin' some calls. He's got a job, you know."

"So he told me."

"So he's out tryin' to sell desks and stuff like that. Keep up the image. Veebee says you gotta log the calls, keep the boys back at the office happy. Especially now, you know what I mean?"

"Yeah, he sure wouldn't want to lose that job now, would he?" Pagnano heard something in the background at the other end of the phone. "You alone there?"

"Why? You wanna come over?" She didn't wait for an answer. "Your memory maybe gettin' better?"

"No, I don't wanna come over. And you didn't answer my question." She could feel the anger rising, like in the restaurant when he was unhappy with Veebee.

"Yeah, well, Red's here. He's waitin' for Veebee, too. They're going out to that Deerfield place again soon as Veebee gets back."

"You pretty chummy with the redhead?" The tone of his voice mellowed a little.

"No-o. Come on, Jimmy. Gimme a little credit."

"Okay. So when's Vaughn-Boy getting back?"

"About five, he said. You want me to have him call you?"

"No. Tell him to hang around there, I'll call him. Tell him I don't want him running off to Deerfield before I talk to him. Got me?"

"Sure, I got you." She paused. "Got you good, as *I* remember it."

"Yeah, yeah. It was good. My memory's not as bad as you think. Even if it was I got the teeth marks to remind me. Saw 'em just a few minutes ago when I was taking a leak."

"You made my day, Jimmy. Afternoon, anyway. That's some poker you got."

"You announcing that to the redhead?"

"No, he's in the crapper, can't hear a thing."

"Okay, as I said, tell Vaughn-Boy to sit tight when he gets there."

She hung up and looked back across the room at Red Ryan lying on the bed flipping through the room copy of GuestHost. "Those Italian guys," she said to him, "they love it when you tell them they got great pricks. And the thing is, this guy does. I mean hung. He also thinks I'm dumb. Like I don't know the words." She glanced at the digital clock next to the telephone. "Hey, I didn't realize it was this late. We better get dressed, Veebee's gonna be back here any minute."

MORRISON AND NORELLI WERE back at 11th and State when the call from Johnny Nolan finally came. If they wanted to talk to Solo they should be at M&R Liquors at eleven o'clock. Slipball would meet them there and take them to Solo. That was five and a half hours away. Norelli went home, said he and Morrison would meet back at 11th and State at quarter to eleven.

Morrison sat there for a while after Norelli left, thinking, idly tapping a pencil on the desk, staring through the window at the sun out there to the west, its normally fierce glow at this time of year dulled by the hazy pollution and gray-soaked sky, its shape distorted. It looked, he thought, like an overripe lime, a blend of pale green and dark yellow.

Finally he reached for the phone and dialed. At the other

end he got the answering machine: "We're not able to come to the phone right now so leave a message after the beep." His oldest daughter Peggy was the emcee these days, talking a little too fast, a little too breathlessly. But it was appropriate that she handle the job. Having just entered the terrible teens a little more than a month ago, she was probably getting ninety percent of the calls anyway. In true teenage style, *totally* and *awesome* dominated her vocabulary.

"It's just your dad," he said to the machine. "Nothing important, just wanted to see how you and Sandy were doing." Sandy was not yet eleven but she was already more rebellious than her sister. "She needs something you can't give her and never did when you had the chance," he remembered his ex saying to him about six months after the divorce. That was almost two years ago but it still rang in his head. "What the hell is that supposed to mean?" he had asked. "If you don't know it wouldn't do any good my explaining it." She may have been right there, he thought. But he also suspected the divorce may have contributed to Sandy's so-called attitude problems. He still didn't know what exactly it was that he didn't do or couldn't do. Some of it he chalked up to his persistently unhappy former wife who did like to talk in enigmas and make statements that, for him, were unanswerable. He left the hotline number at 11th and State on the machine and said he would be there for the next few hours if either of his daughters wanted to call.

He dialed another number, this one with a 212 area code, New York City, the Big Apple. There were answering machines there, too. But on this one the voice was smooth and soft.

He had talked to Linda Tate a couple of times since she moved out more than a year ago. She was his refuge, lover at times, back then when he truly needed somebody—the two burnouts, marriage one, Homicide two. And she had her own need for escape. He never realized how much, how deeply he really cared for her, how much he had gotten from her, until she left. Trite but true. She couldn't hack it in modeling anymore, not even in Chicago, the old Second City, although he could not understand why, she being the most attractive woman he had ever known. So now she was giving it a shot in public relations, a job with the Marriott hotel chain. Only problem was they sent her to New York to prove herself. He felt a need to talk to her, sitting there, wondering where she might be. What was it, seven o'clock in New York? Or who was she with? He didn't leave a message on her machine.

SLIPBALL WAS WAITING FOR them just inside the door of M&R Liquors at a little after eleven, a Schlitz Malt Liquor can in hand. Others appeared to be sharing a bottle of something in a brown paper bag. Morrison and Norelli looked at the little group, then at the man behind the counter, a mural-sized collage of pint and half-pint bottles behind him, big sellers in the 'hood. The man was sitting on a wooden kitchen stool, arms crossed and resting on a medicine-ball stomach. The black suspenders that creeped over and under the belly to his beltline contrasted with his white T-shirt. He knew who they were and what they wanted but asked anyway. "Can I help you with somepin?"

"We're looking for a guy who goes by the name of Slipball," Norelli said.

The man nodding toward the group whose conversation had come to an end when the two detectives walked in. They were staring back, looking like they were waiting to have their group picture taken, although none was smiling.

"Which one of you's Slipball?" Morrison asked.

The one with the eraserhead haircut smiled at them, said, "Hi."

"And Solo?"

"You must be More-sin 'n Norawelli."

"Close."

"Close counts. Solo, he waitin'. C'mon."

They followed Slipball out of the liquor store and walked west with him on Monroe Street. He led them into a breezeway that ran along the side of one of the Rockwell Gardens high-rises. There was one lightbulb above the walkway inside a wire-mesh cage at the far end. Other lights were burned out or broken. They were replaced only on the first Tuesday of each month, by a Housing Authority directive. Slipball stopped in front of a door that led into the project building. "We wait here," he said.

A few minutes later three figures appeared at the end of the breezeway where the working bulb cast a cone of light down onto the walkway. The three took up the breadth of the breezeway as they walked toward Morrison, Norelli and Slipball. The one in the middle, a point guard striding between a pair of power forwards, they took to be Solo, having been told of his diminutive size. The erasercut added some three or four inches to his height and made Slipball's look puny by comparison.

"Come on in here," Solo said, foregoing unnecessary introductions and opening the door they were standing next to. There were lights in the corridor, illuminating graffiti-covered walls. "Welcome to the Gardens," Solo said, and in the pale yellow light looked the two detectives up and down.

"We're not going to do our talk here, I just want to look at you two first." Solo smiled, but it was the eyes that caught Morrison's attention, the ones he had been told about by Lloyd Ware. There was no life in them, no matter what expression the rest of his face took on. "You're not uncomfortable in this situation, I hope." Norelli had his back to Morrison watching Slipball and one of the bodyguards, both of whom had stayed back at the door.

"No, no, we're happy to be here," Morrison said, looking at Solo and then at the tall guy with the shaved head standing next to him. There was a ridge of bumps down the middle of the man's head and a little unevenness on each of the sides. Morrison glanced back at Slipball and the other bodyguard. "Why am I getting the impression we're in some kind of confrontation here? I thought we were here to have a friendly chat."

"We are. But it's tough to break old habits. You know that. That's why your pal there"—motioning to Norelli—"got his hand inside his jacket. Right?" Then to the two at the door: "Come on over here. Make these officers feel a little more comfortable."

When they did Norelli folded his arms in front of him and just stared at the four. It still looked like a confrontation. "So let's talk," Morrison said.

"A minute, my man. We're not doing our talking here. I believe I mentioned that. I'm talking with only *one* of you, the one's in charge. That you, I take it."

"We're both in charge."

"No. Somebody's always in charge, somebody the *one*. I know that."

"Well, in this instance you're wrong. On this case *we* are the one. Norelli's from Homicide, I'm from Organized Crime. This is a special case and we're in charge of it, both of us, even up. That's the way it is."

Solo looked from one to the other. "Okay, not saying I believe you, but what the fuck." His attention drifted back to Norelli, who held him with his own frigid eye contact. "You got a little of the blood in you," Solo said. "I can see it."

"My mother was black."

"Was? She ain't no more?"

"No."

"Oh." He paused a moment. "But she was *all* black?"

"Black as yours."

"And your old man, name Norelli, must be a greaseball. *All* white?"

"Italian . . . *all* white. And he's alive and I know who he is and where to find him and we even celebrate Father's Day together. How about you?"

Solo stiffened, let it pass. "Well, you a half-'n'-half. And so I doubt then you be in charge. So I talk with you, Moe-sin."

Morrison looked over at Norelli, who shrugged and gave him a better-you-than-me look. Morrison was sure that at the moment Norelli was tempted to forget the deal and beat the shit out of Solo. A bad idea, he decided.

"Okay," Morrison said, "where do you want to talk?"

"Follow us. Come on, Skull," and he and the phrenolo-gist's dream boy started down the corridor. Morrison followed. Just before the two elevators at the end of the hall, Solo stopped and took hold of the doorknob to one of the apartments. "In here," he said.

The room it opened into was vacant and he saw when Solo flipped the wall switch and the overhead fluorescent light flickered, a rat scurried across the floor.

"Get a lot of those little critters on the first floor. Get some upstairs, too, but not as many. Maybe they lazy. More rats down this floor than people. First floor's least desirable. Safer upstairs. Quieter, too. You know they shoot the rats down here. All kinds. They doing the city a favor, ridding the vermin, pest control."

Morrison said, "Let's cut the shit. You got something you want to talk about. So let's talk."

"Let's do."

THE CONVERSATION BACK DOWN the hallway was chitchat. Slipball asked Norelli, "Where do you live, half-'n'-half?"

"In a house."

"I mean 'hood. You live white or black?"

"None of your fucking business."

The other brother, who had accompanied Solo, slouched against the wall, looking up at the ceiling then down to the floor, occasionally revolving his head around like boxers do when they're introduced before the first bell.

"How long you been huntin' criminals, half-brother?" Slipball asked.

Norelli ignored it.

"You hom-cide, your buddy say. Like seein' dead heads, huh? Seen a lot, I bet."

Norelli just looked at him.

"Me, too." Slipball did not need answers to keep a conversation going. "Lots 'roun' here. My brothers . . . real brother, he got himself shot. Crossed over Western in the middle of the night. My cousin, he O.D.'d . . . You ever kill anybody?"

Norelli broke his silence. "You want to talk, why don't we talk about your friend Rayfield Tees?"

"Don't know nothin'. Except Little Dirt was a nice kid.

Everbody liked Little Dirt. Right, Whacko?'' Whacko, who was back to leaning up against the wall, looked at Slipball and nodded.

"We could start with who you think might have killed him."

"I told you. We don't know nothin' 'bout that thing. Anything be known, Solo know it."

The door down the hall opened suddenly and Morrison came out and, walking fast, headed in their direction. Solo and his buddy Skull also stepped out but did not follow him.

"Let's go, Franco," Morrison said, barely missing a stride and Norelli fell in beside him, then they went through the door and out into the still humid night air.

In the car, Morrison behind the wheel looked over at his partner. "Solo claims there was a witness to the shooting . . . shootings. He also has a good buddy sitting in Cook County jail who's been arraigned on counts of extortion, battery and possession of an illegal weapon and is waiting for trial. Had to do with a little intimidation of an Arab store owner in the neighborhood. Doesn't take much to guess what Solo's deal is."

"What kind of witness? He could just be pulling—"

"Uh-uh, Franco. He says he can *produce* a witness who not only saw it but saw the faces of the two guys who did the killings."

"Two? He said *two*?"

"He did. It wasn't a slip. He was giving that to us. He also said the witness to the murders saw the two guys close enough to identify them."

"And the person who saw all this is—?"

"Come on."

"He's saving that, I know. Dumb question. So what's the deal he wants for his buddy?"

"Wipe out the whole thing. But I told him that was impossible. He said that a lot was possible when the stakes were right. I said we'd have a look into the whole situation with his buddy, who incidentally is a guy called Lonesome Dennis Page. I told him we had to talk to certain people downtown

. . . in the state's attorney's office. He understood. He said the ball was in our court. He'd be waiting to hear from us. I said we would be back to him tomorrow.''

"Too bad you weren't wired.''

"Wouldn't have mattered. The way he worded things there was nothing that would hold water in court. I just gave you my translation of what he said. He's a shrewd little sonofabitch. By the way, as a parting gesture of good faith, he told me the two guys were white.''

✥20

IT WAS A SCRAMBLE IN THE MORNING BEFORE THE DAILY TEN o'clock meeting of the brass at 11th and State, but everybody got there. Morrison and Norelli had something new to report, word was. The super, his deputies and their PR man Lt. Arnie Troy were on hand, plus several others from headquarters and an administrator from the state's attorney's office.

Morrison's boss Lieutenant Goldman came into the conference room. "Understand something's up,'' he said to Morrison.

"A lead. But we're going to have to deal for it.''

Goldman was wearing a lightweight tailored tan suit. "It would be nice to wrap this one up.''

"I agree.''

"You're a good detective, Joe,'' Goldman said, taking hold of Morrison's arm just above the elbow and pulling him toward him. "But I'm your boss. And I would not mind being kept apprised of what the hell is going on.''

"Well, we got some information late last night from the gangbangers that they might be able to produce a witness. That's it. I didn't think you'd want me to call you at midnight to tell you that. I thought it could keep till this morning.''

"I don't like surprises, Joe.''

Superintendent Williams arrived then, and Morrison told them about his conversation with *the* Lord of Lords from Western Avenue, then took questions. Meanwhile, Norelli was talking with the lawyer from the state's attorney's office. Then they headed out, the brass back to their offices in the building, the man from the state's attorney's office back to his headquarters in the criminal court building at 26th and California to dig out everything they had about Lonesome Dennis Page and the charges pending against him and what they had regarding the Arab he had been harassing. So he could talk to the Felony Review Board.

Superintendent Williams, big smile on his face now, had said he would immediately contact the mayor's office to let them know of "the unfolding situation" and then bade the SA administrator godspeed in his work.

Just before leaving, Morrison got Deputy Superintendent Harkness to the side. "I didn't think it was necessary to mention this to everybody before letting you know, but Solo also told me he was asked to help round up a lot of souls for that demonstration downtown Friday night by your buddy the reverend."

"Why'd he tell you?'

"Just tossing bait, I think. He wants a deal and he wants us to know where he's bargaining from. I got the feeling we strike the right deal, his heart won't really be into turning out bodies for Friday night's festivities. I think that was the message."

"The SA already had the message before he got here. You could tell by looking at him. The Hall wants clean faces on this, and if it means letting go of a fucking murdering dope-dealing neighborhood role model, well, so be it, and you'll get a deal.'

"I hope so. I also thought you'd like to know the kinds of friends the reverend alderman keeps."

"No secret, Joe. He's pals with the Disciples, too. He plays both and gets away with it. He throws up this image of keeping the peace between the two of them. The divine arbiter. I don't disagree he's got the ears of the gangs. They listen because he does things for them in City Hall, in the council, in criminal court, on the street, everywhere. And they do things for him. They vote, and they get out the vote. The slogan is kind of like 'vote for Alderman Hunter . . . and nobody gets hurt.' It's their kind of alliance.''

MORRISON AND NORELLI WERE late getting to Area Four.

Grantham came out of the watch commander's office when he heard Morrison and Norelli. They all knew about the meeting with Solo because Morrison had called Gerherdt at one A.M. and told him about it. He asked him to get hold of the first-shifters, midnight-to-eight, who were out on the street to see if they could dig up anything about a potential witness on their own or from any of their snitches, any scratchings at all about somebody who might have been there because there was word out that one did indeed exist. The same at rollcall for the entire second shift.

Neither watch had anything to report on a witness. Gang Crimes, according to Lloyd Ware, had corroborated what Johnny Nolan's snitch told them. Rayfield Tees was in Altgeld Park with a group early Friday night. The group consisted of full-fledged Western Lords, a couple of holders like Rayfield and some groupies.

Lieutenant Chatham said that they had gotten identifications on most of the prints found on or in the car. Those on the car radio belonged to one Jaime Contagua, the man who held legal residence in the shack down the street. His were also found on the car door on the driver's side. The prints they found on the trunk matched those of Contagua's brother-in-law, who happened to be boarding in the house at the time of the crime and was still there. The prints on two of the hubcaps had not been identified yet but who cared about those . . . The palm print on the steering wheel was not totally identifiable but was pretty close to that of Señor Contagua. Although everything wasn't in yet, Chatham said, it appeared that the car had been professionally cleansed before the Mexicans arrived to strip and disembowel it and leave their prints all over it. Contagua, confronted early in the morning by Nabasco and Nolan, and faced with his incriminating fingerprints, had admitted they tried to denude the car, swearing on the soul of Our Lady of Guadalupe that they thought the car was abandoned and they were just taking advantage of the gift God left near their doorstep. They had not taken *anything*. When brother-in-law popped the trunk and saw the body they all took off, feeling that it was not sent from God after all. They also swore they had seen nothing nor heard anything earlier.

That was about it. Morrison and Norelli reminded everybody of the importance of finding out anything about the someone who may have witnessed the double murder . . . and the importance of keeping this particular aspect of the investigation as secret as possible. He did not want to leave it all up to the Solo deal, when and if it went through.

GUSSY TUSCANO WAS ON the fairway of the twelfth hole at the Greycroft Country Club when one of the locker room boys came hotrodding up in a golf cart with a message the telephone caller said was urgent enough to interrupt him on the course.

"Go see what it's all about, Cockeye," Gussy said to Mario, the bullet-hole-eyed soldier who drove Gussy's cart but was not a playing member of the foursome.

Five minutes later he was back and handed Gussy a small piece of paper with a telephone number on it. Gussy looked at it and recognized the number. "Wants you to call as soon as you get a chance," Mario said.

Gussy looked at his ball lying in a sand trap near the thirteenth hole. He had a wedge in hand, addressed the ball and swatted at it, sending a spray of sand onto the outer edge of the green but leaving the ball inches from where it had been. *"Fangulieri,"* he said, picked up the ball and tossed it up onto the green, three-putted and sat down in the passenger side of the golf cart, writing a five on his scorecard.

Still in the cart after finishing the round, Gussy totalled his score. "One-eighteen," he said to his cart chauffeur, which did not include the tosses from trap to green or rough to fairway, several mulligans and at least four putts he missed which he picked up and scored as gimmes. "What a game God invented to torture us." He handed the scorecard to the driver. "Destroy it, Cockeye. I never want to see it again."

In the locker room he spoke into the telephone with his distinctive gravelly voice. "Returning your call," was all he said.

The voice at the other end said, "The incident last Friday night. Word is there was a witness to it." And the voice told Gussy everything he knew about it.

"Keep in touch," Gussy said, and hung up. He walked over to Mario. "You get hold of Aldo Forte and Joe-sep Alessi and tell 'em I want to see 'em at the house." He looked at his watch, it was almost one-thirty. "This afternoon, no later than five. Sharp."

✦21

VAUGHN SWAYZE HAD BEEN PACING AROUND THE LOBBY OF the McCormick Inn for fifteen minutes before Jimmy Pagnano came through the revolving door. Pagnano led him toward an empty corner of the lobby. "Right on time this time, right?" Swayze said while they were walking. Pagnano ignored him. Pagnano did not bother to sit down on either the couch or the leather easy chair against the walls in the corner, just turned to face Swayze. He did not look happy.

"Everything's okay?" Swayze asked.

"Not everything."

"What's the matter? The money's all there. You counted it, right, right?"

"Right."

"Well, what's wrong?"

"I can get you the body. That's not a problem. But you can't do it the lamebrained way you said. What you get is an old body, a throwaway."

Swayze looked puzzled.

"Throwaways are real old, the kind been around for a couple of months, no identification, nobody claiming 'em. They go out to some cemetery in Homewood," referring to a suburb out south of Chicago but still in the county, "and they bury them out there in a pine box, just like in the movies. My guy at the morgue told me how it can be done."

"I'm lost here, lost."

"Why am I not surprised? Look, Vaughn-Boy, I'm going to make it simple. You don't get the body and dress it up and have it brought in by the cops. It's all done on paper. All done inside. The only thing you gotta do is get your clothes and your wallet and anything else you want that should be on you to my guy. He sees to the papers. He dresses up the throwaway for you. Your grieving wife Fellate comes in, he wheels you out, she identifies you—it would help if she could show some tears—the body is released to her. He switches the papers around and the morgue thinks the throwaway is on his way to Homewood and you got the body which you get to my undertaker and he torches it for you. You got the papers from the morgue, the papers from him, and Fellate files for your insurance dough. Simple. Okay?"

"Yeah, I guess. Her name is Felice, by the way."

"Yeah, right. You're gettin' a helluva deal for twenty grand."

"Comin' up with it is tough." He caught Pagnano's glare. "It'll happen, Jimmy, don't worry, don't worry. It's just twenty gees is twenty gees."

"You're talking about walkin'-around money, Vaughn-Boy. Look what you're going to haul off to the bank after you die." Pagnano thought that was real funny. Swayze laughed along with him but didn't see all that much humor in it.

"So go back to Detroit and wait'll you hear from me. My guy said he'd let me know soon as they got a safe throwaway. Said it might be a week or two. The sooner the better, hey, kid."

"Yeah, yeah, sooner the better."

"Go get 'em, Vaughn-Boy. And relax." Pagnano gave him a big grin and a wallop on the back.

"Yeah, well, I'm gonna stick around here for a couple more days. But I better get Felice back to Detroit, case something comes up quick with your guy."

"Good idea. How is she anyway?" Pagnano conjured the memory of himself slouched in the chair by the little desk in the big room upstairs, her naked, kneeling in front of him, doing what she did best.

"She's great, isn't she?"

"She seems like a real nice gal."

"Terrific's the word. We been married three years now and it's still honeymoon hotel. I mean, I don't want to sound like an asshole but she worships the fucking ground I walk on."

"I noticed that. Must drive her crazy sitting up in that room all alone waiting for you."

"Yeah, well"—Swayze smiled and twitched a little self-consciously—"actually she's not alone. She's with Red. He and me, we're going out to Deerfield when I finish up here. I told 'em to wait up there, knowin' how you don't like committees and all."

"Good thinking, Vaughn-Boy." Pagnano took a step toward leaving, stopped. "What's all this you and the redhead got going in Deerfield?"

"A deal. Red's deal. He worked on it while he was in prison. He needs a partner, somebody to help carry it off. Me."

"A scam."

"Yeah. Out there, they got this place, the Berto Center, you know, where the Bulls practice. We've been checking it out, surprising how easy it is to get in out there."

"So what're you going to do, steal basketballs?"

Swayze laughed nervously. "Red's got a scam he wants to pull on one of the players just signed a big contract. We been following him. Red wants to get a feel for the guy, the lay of the land, you know what I mean. Red thinks he can get close to him. Then we apply the old sting. If anybody can pull it off, it's Red. I mean we're talking big bucks here."

Pagnano shook his head. "Do me a favor . . . don't do *any-*

thing till you get your body and you pay me and you're out of my hair, okay?''

"Oh, it's gonna take a while, the Bulls thing."

Pagnano walked across the lobby toward the door, still shaking his head.

PAGNANO'S BOSS, JOE-SEP ALESSI, was also shaking his head, not in astonishment like Jimmy but in despair, while Aldo Forte looked on as they sat in Gussy Tuscano's Florida room and listened to the old man tell them of his earlier telephone call about the witness.

Aldo Forte was in the crosshairs of Gussy Tuscano's unhappy eyes. "You were out here the other day, Aldo. You tell me there's a little something extra that happened but it's okay. The young guy you brought with you, the good-looking one, his name's . . . I can't remember."

"Franconi," Aldo said. "Angelo Franconi."

Joe-sep Alessi stared at Gussy Tuscano. A lot was skittering back and forth in Joe-sep's mind at the moment.

"He tells me, too. Nothing to worry about. He was there. There was a botch, but Peters is dead and everybody walked away clean. Now this."

"I don't know. I only know what Angelo told me," Aldo said. "Angelo is not a fuck-up, Gussy. He's smart, he's stand-up. He wouldn't hide some shit like this from me."

"Better have a talk with him, Aldo."

"No question."

"You got a, what should I say, involvement, with this kid, too, huh?" Gussy said, looking over now at Alessi.

"He sees my daughter, that's all . . ."

"I heard that."

"I told you myself, Gussy."

"Oh, yeah, that's right. What is it they say, the memory's the first thing to go? No, the second." They all laughed, a little comic relief. "Which is a lot of bullshit anyway."

Gussy got up and started to pace, glanced at Mario, who was leaning against the French window that opened out onto the terrace and pool. "Cockeye," he shouted, although he was not that far away, "mix me up a gin and tonic, three hunks of lime in it. You want something?" he asked Forte and Alessi. They said they didn't. "Come on, come on. What's with the polite bullshit, uh? You want an old man to drink by himself?" He stopped pacing and even produced a little smile. Aldo said he'd have a gin and tonic, too, and Joe-sep chose a vodka on the rocks with a squeeze of lime.

"I told you I don't like this drug business. It's nothing but trouble. How many times I tell you all that?" They nodded. "Ten, twelve, who the fuck knows, a lot more than that." Gussy started pacing again. "I tell you leave it to the spics, the niggers. But I let you go because you want to do a little something on the side. And see what happens."

"We thought it was a quick, clean one-shot deal. That's all we wanted," Aldo Forte said. "Me and Joe-sep talked it over, an in-and-out thing and a couple hundred grand. I mean it was a natural . . . until that fuckface Manny Peters decided to crawl through a window and steal the stuff from us. I mean I wouldn't give you a thousand to one something like that would happen."

"But it did."

"It did. I know, you don't need to tell me. It's been a big mess ever since." Aldo looked over at Alessi, then back to Gussy Tuscano. "So what're we going to do about it now?"

"Nothing. Not yet. We gotta see if they really got a witness. Could be just a lotta cooked-up shit. But if they do we gotta be prepared." He stopped his pacing to take the drink from Mario. "Contingency plan, that's it. That's what we got to talk about this afternoon."

MORRISON AND NORELLI WERE in the small conference room in the Criminal Court Building at 26th and California listening to the assistant state attorney explain the deal that the Felony Review Board said they could live with.

"That good enough?" he asked when he finished outlining the deal.

"We'll find out, won't we?" Morrison said.

"We really went overboard for you guys on this. By the

way, the semi-automatic handgun that Lonesome Dennis was carrying was not the only gun involved. In the car there was an AK-47 automatic rifle, capable, as you know, of shooting up a city block. That's federal but we can't do anything with it because it was found in the car that he'd been in but the car wasn't his and there's nothing to connect it to him. We informed ATF about it''—referring to the Treasury Department's Bureau of Alcohol, Tobacco and Firearms—''but it's not a problem as far as you're concerned. Just thought you might want to know the kind of guy you're putting back onto the street.''

Morrison reached for the telephone on the table and dialed the number he was reading from his pocket notepad. Slipball came on the line. ''Tell Solo I got him his deal. We need to talk,'' Morrison said.

''No problem.''

''Now.''

''Just wander on by M 'n R. I be there.'' He giggled.

Morrison thought Slipball had probably been at M&R Liquors for some time. ''Solo's who I want.''

''I know that. You just come, I take you. Solo already tole me what do.''

THIS TIME SOLO ENTERTAINED Morrison in the front seat of his Corvette. ''Sporty, huh?'' he said when they got into the two-seater.

''I don't like cars made of fiberglass,'' Morrison said. ''Sorry.''

Solo started the engine. ''I'll give you a little spin 'roun' the 'hood. Maybe change your mind. Maybe you get to likin' it, buy one for yo'self when the ol' Christmas bonus come rollin' in. You probably wouldn't want a black one like this one, black and shiny like an old nigger singer's hair.'' He looked at Morrison, got no response. ''I figure for you blue, probably light blue, or maybe tan, somethin' neutral.'' They were heading west on Madison in the twilight. ''So let me hear what you got for me.''

''If your witness proves out to be a real one, flesh and blood and contributing to our investigation and not somebody you just rousted up to bullshit us so you can help your buddy get out . . . if this witness gives us something we feel—''

"Spare me the shit, Moe-sin. Okay? The witness is what you would call reliable. You gonna find that out right quick when we deal. So let's get on with it.''

"The state's attorney is willing to drop the battery and extortion charges. The only charges against Lonesome Dennis will be in regard to the weapon. Two counts, both misdemeanors. Sentence will take in time already served, what is it, two months now? He'll be released after he appears in court where the other charges will be dropped.''

"What are the two charges *not* being dropped?''

"One count of carrying a dangerous weapon in the city and one count of failing to register a firearm. Both misdemeanors.''

"Sounds all right." Solo knew his way around courtrooms and the world of jurisprudence as well as most practicing attorneys.

"Two other things. First, he will be placed on probation for a year, so tell him to behave himself because we will be watching him. Second, he, you and the rest of your people lay off the Arab. Let him run his convenience store by himself. He gets the protection Lonesome Dennis was offering him but he doesn't pay for it.''

"Now hold on, I can't be responsible for everybody tryin' to make a living on the street.''

"Don't fuck with me, Solo. It's hard enough for me doing this. Don't make it worse or you'll regret it. Trust me. We're going to tell the Arab that we don't want any flak from him. We're going to explain we really don't have a case against the defendant that will stand up in court. We're going to tell him we know that hulk named Lonesome Dennis *did* threaten him, *did* beat on him but we can't prove it in a court of law. We're sorry, but we're promising him protection and we're giving him your word that *you* and yours will abide by that.''

"Lucky man, you know, in a 'hood like this.''

Morrison took that for a yes.

They were heading back east on Lake Street under the elevated tracks. The hookers were out, taking advantage of the warm weather.

"Enjoying the sights?" Solo asked. "You guys from downtown don't get around this part of town too often, I expect."

Solo pulled in behind Morrison's car, which was parked in front of M&R Liquors. "Could I buy you a drink now we're partners?"

"Are you kidding?"

"I'm kidding."

Morrison walked over to the unmarked car from Area Four. All four hubcaps were missing. He turned back to Solo, who threw the Corvette into reverse and peeled backward about ten yards and then forward to come to a stop next to Morrison standing there in the street.

"Bad 'hood," Solo said, "but you got friends here," and then roared off down Western Avenue.

Morrison didn't know what he meant by the last remark until after he unlocked the car and got in and saw the four hubcaps stacked neatly on the passenger seat next to him.

✦22

VAUGHN SWAYZE'S DAY WAS EVEN MORE EVENTFUL AFTER meeting with Jimmy Pagnano. The only damper on it was when he got himself arrested at the end of it, hauled into the East Chicago Avenue district stationhouse along with his buddy Red Ryan, where they then spent an uncomfortable three hours.

It had started out fine. Back up in the big room in the McCormick Inn he checked out the Greyhound schedule and found a bus for Felice back to Detroit later that afternoon. He and Red dropped her off in front of the terminal just west of the city and after hugs and kisses and "Take care of yourself

Veebee'' and ''Oh, I'm gonna miss my Veebee so'' drove out
to Deerfield.

Which was when things started to go wrong. When they got
to the Berto Center it was closed up, only two cars in the
parking lot. None of the fancy Mercedes or macho Jeep Cher-
okees or Range Rovers the basketball players tended to favor.
Where were the Bulls, they asked the caretaker who they en-
countered while looking in one of the open windows. He told
them the Bulls weren't working out that afternoon, they were
downtown at the Chicago Stadium doing some kind of benefit
thing for some kids' hospital.

So they piled back into Red Ryan's car and headed the
twenty-five miles back to the city. They got there before the
ceremonies began, the ceremonies being a $250-a-ticket cock-
tail party held on the stadium hardwood court which included
a tour of the locker room where the Bulls dressed and un-
dressed and the press booth and the private VIP suites, the
proceeds going to Children's Memorial Hospital and the good
publicity to the Bulls organization. The bigwigs were all filing
in with their wives and guests along with wealthy hangers-on
and high-profile local politicians.

Swayze and Red Ryan were not dressed for the occasion,
but Red tried to talk his way into the stadium claiming they
were the fathers of two children at the hospital who had been
invited to the party by the Bulls' owner that morning. The
usher didn't buy it but didn't not buy it either, so he told them
to wait just a second and went and got two of the Bulls' security people, who definitely did not buy it because they knew
the owner was in Palm Springs, California, and had been there
at the league owners meeting for the past two days. And they
also recognized Swayze and Ryan as the two who had been
hanging around the Berto Center lately and whom they had
already begun to wonder about.

When confronted, Ryan pleaded that they were just Bulls
fans who couldn't get enough of the team and the players and
made up a story so they could get in to see them up close.
They were sorry, they wouldn't do something like this again,
they would be on their way. Goodbye.

The security men didn't buy Red's explanation and told one of the detectives from the CPD special-events unit about the two they thought were acting suspiciously. A few minutes later, when one of the security men spotted Swayze and Ryan standing outside the big cyclone-fence gate that protected the area where the players parked their cars, they were pointed out to the detective, who said he would keep an eye on them.

Which he did. And when the players began driving out of the protected parking lot, he watched the redhead and the curly-head hustle to their own car, which was parked on the street, and fell in bumper-to-bumper behind their intended mark's car. He and his partner followed the player downtown, where he gave his car to the valet parker in front of Michael Jordan's restaurant on Clark Street. Ryan and Swayze slowed down but then went on to park a block and a half away from the restaurant. The detectives parked too and followed them back to the restaurant, which had a line of would-be diners and celebrity watchers waiting out in front.

Ryan and Swayze went to the front of the line and were trying to convince the maitre d' to let them in to the bar area when the two detectives tapped them on the shoulder and led them back outside.

They drove them to the East Chicago stationhouse. They talked to them together, they talked to them separately. There was nothing to hold them on, but there was something to hassle them about. A run through the computer showed Cyril Ryan, a.k.a. Red Ryan, had recently been released from the federal prison at Terre Haute, Indiana, where he had been serving time for fraud and interstate racketeering and that he was currently on parole. Nothing came up on Vaughn Swayze.

Swayze and Ryan stuck to their story of being just a couple of fans, "hero worshippers," Red called them. The detective knew it was a crock but there wasn't anything he could do about it.

Finally the detective and his partner told them they did not know what kind of shit the two of them were up to but they had better stop pretty damn quick. They were putting their names and identifications in the computer, they were warning the security people at the Bulls about them, and the message they wanted the two of them to take away from the East Chicago Avenue district was that if they got one tiny complaint from the Bulls or any member of that organization they would have both of their asses back in tow and they would not be waltzing out after a three-hour stay. One of the detectives reminded them of the new stalking law, which was much more serious than the harassment ones they had on the books and which would not only put Ryan in violation of his parole but which could result in both of them being charged with a felony. Did they hear that? *Felony.*

Swayze and Ryan walked out of the stationhouse and decided that maybe they should rethink their plan to scam a *nouveau riche* Bulls ballplayer.

MORRISON AND NORELLI WERE in the conference room, along with Deputy Superintendent of Investigative Services Flanagan, at the Criminal Courts building a few minutes before eight o'clock in the morning. A young lawyer from the state attorney's office got there a few minutes after eight. A tall, balding man with a carefully cultivated look of unfriendliness and dressed in an expensive glen-plaid suit, conservative paisley tie and black Ferragamo slipons was next, a few steps ahead of his client—the large, round-shouldered, semiswaggering Lonesome Dennis Page, who was dressed in the dull blue jumpsuit issued to all county jail inmates.

They all sat down. They all knew it was just a formality. The defense attorney unzipped the carrying case he had under his arm when he entered the room, slid out a folder and put it on the desk in front of him. Why, nobody knew, because he didn't open it, just placed a hand on top of it and said, "My client is prepared to plead guilty to the two counts involving unlawful possession of a firearm, both misdemeanors." The defense attorney looked around the room at the faces staring back at him. "Agreed?"

"We are all in agreement," the assistant SA said, not sounding too happy about it.

Lonesome Dennis Page nodded when his attorney looked at him.

"Good." The defense attorney had a smile for all of them.

Afterward Morrison accompanied the defense attorney to a small office down the hall and listened as the man succinctly told Solo over the telephone that it was a done deal. Then Morrison took the receiver that the attorney held out to him, the smile back again.

"Got a pencil, Moe-sin?" Solo said over the phone.

Morrison had a ballpoint pen and his notepad open on the desk in front of him. "Let's have it."

"The person you will want to talk to is named Latrona Meek. She is a little girl, was Little Dirt's . . . Rayfield's . . . special. She about twelve years old, with him the night he got himself killed. She tell you all about it."

"Where do I find her?"

"In the Gardens. Where else? Try Two-six-oh-one West Monroe, apartment four-twelve. She be waitin' for you with her mama."

"And she can identify—"

"Moe-sin, I told you that. She saw the boys. The white boys. Right down to the ponytail one of them sportin'. You just go talk to her." There was a pause, then Solo added: "Pays to have a lot of eyes and ears on the street, don't it, Moe-sin?" There was another awkward pause. "Well, I do. Organ-i-zation, Moe-sin. You can just call me the Organ-i-zation Man."

"I'll keep that in mind. But just remember, Organ-i-zation Man, this girl, if she doesn't pan out, your buddy doesn't walk."

"Not to worry, Moe-sin."

Morrison cut the connection and quickly dialed the number of the watch commander's office at Area Four. When he got Lieutenant Chatham, he asked him to have Nolan and Nabasco go to the address in Rockwell Gardens that he had gotten from Solo and pick up one Latrona Meek, "twelve-year-old girl who was the alleged witness in the PT murders, and escort her and her parents or guardian directly down to their office on the third floor at 11th and State." He said to be sure to tell the two Ns, especially Nabasco, that they were to handle her very gently, not, for God's sake, to scare her in any way.

A STACK OF NOTES was waiting for Morrison and Norelli, which Norelli had gathered up and taken into their office. Morrison had stopped to talk to his boss, who to his surprise was in and on the telephone. Morrison was not a slow learner, he remembered the little protocol message delivered the morning before. When his boss Ted Goldman placed the receiver back in its cradle Morrison told him the details of their morning meeting at the courthouse, then ordered up mug shots from the files of suspected hit men who earned their livings in the Chicago area.

In PT headquarters, Norelli said to Morrison, "You sure you don't have something going with this Stryker? You got one message here and she just called again. She doesn't want to talk to me, just you."

"Yeah, we had one date. Breakfast."

"She a good cook?"

"At Dottie's, wiseass. And she told me, despite the fireworks between us, she never goes to bed with a guy on the first date. Plus I had to get over here for a meeting. She didn't say what she wanted, huh?"

"Nope. Just tell Joe it's important I talk to him, was all she said. Joe, not Detective Morrison. She said you would know what it's about."

"She did?" He didn't.

The detective manning the desk outside stuck his head in the doorway. "Nolan's on the line."

Morrison took the call. "What's going on?" It was a surprise. Nolan and Nabasco, he thought, should have been on their way with Latrona Meek and her parents in the backseat of their squad car.

"First, there was no Latrona Meek at the address you gave us. There was no one at all in that apartment. She lives there, the kid, with her mother, we found that out, but neither one was home. The manager opened it up for us."

"What about the neighbors?"

"We already talked to them. One said we ought to maybe try this guy's apartment on the seventh floor. Melinda, that's the mother's name, the neighbor said, spends a lot of time there. Sure enough, that's where we found her. With her boyfriend. We woke them up. Melinda is something else, stoned out of her head."

Morrison was shaking his head, thinking he should have known it seemed too easy to be true. "And she doesn't know where the kid is?"

"You got it."

"Hang on." Morrison cupped the mouthpiece and said to Norelli, "See if you can get Slipball and tell him we need to talk to Solo right away. The kid's not there, the mother's a junkie and says she doesn't know where in hell the kid is."

Back to Nolan: "She got any idea where the kid *might* be?"

"Joe, the lady's on Pluto. She hasn't the foggiest about anything. Plus she doesn't want to talk to us. César's got her cuffed to a bedpost up in the apartment. She's not a happy trooper. I think she was dusted by the angels last night. We found PCP in the apartment. You know what that can do."

"Where are you now?"

"Down in the security cage on the first floor."

"Look, we've got to keep this quiet as possible, you know that."

"I know that."

"At the same time we've got to find her. What about the boyfriend, he any help?"

"He said he hasn't seen the kid since the last time he was downstairs in the Meeks' apartment, which was like a few days ago."

"All right, get a description of the kid from him. If the guy gives you any beef tell Nabasco he doesn't have to be polite anymore. And see if the neighbors have any idea what she might be wearing. As soon as you get that phone it in to Chatham at Four. I'm going to call him as soon as I hang up and get everybody we can out on the street looking for her. Oh, and bring mama in."

Norelli was off the phone when Morrison finished up with Nolan. He told him Slipball was not at M&R Liquors but that they seemed to know where to find him and would relay the message. Morrison called Lieutenant Chatham and passed the word. Norelli thought it a good idea to ring up Flanagan, who no doubt had already informed the superintendent and his fellow members of the brass at 11th and State that they were bringing in an eyewitness to the PT murders, which unfortunately they were not now because they did not know where she was.

✦23

SOLO SOUNDED GROGGY WHEN HE GOT AROUND TO TELEphoning Morrison and Norelli. He was not a daytime person. Nor, as usual, did he want to talk to Norelli, who answered the phone and passed it over to Morrison.

"Slipball tells me you got a problem of the urgent kind. So tell me about it, Moe-sin."

Morrison told him.

"Shee-it."

"So you got any idea where we might find this little girl?"

"No, I don't know where she might be. I just woke up, man. It's not outa the ordinary for kids like Latrona not to be at home, you know. The 'hood's one big playground all hours of the day or night."

"So where in the playground might she be playing?"

"You know, I knew it." Solo said in soliloquy, "I shoulda just kept her with me. That's what I shoulda done. That hophead of hers couldn't look after her own tits they weren't attached to her. I thought maybe I spooked the kid. I guess I did."

"I don't know what you're talking about."

"That's right, you don't. Last night, don't recall the exact time but sometime after we made our deal, I went over and talked with Latrona and her mama. Told 'em what was happening. Told 'em the girl should help the Man out. In this particular situation anyway. That *I* wanted her to. That *Solo* wanted it that way.''

"I take it you know the mama . . . Melinda.''

" 'Course I do. I know everybody in the Gardens. How you think I know Latrona was there with Rayfield? I got my eyes and ears out everywhere. You didn't know that, Moe-sin? You better spend more time out in the 'hoods.''

Solo explained that he did know the mama. They had, in fact, been very good friends. The lady was one luscious little piece until she turned to drugs. She was not even worth looking out for anymore, what she did to herself the last couple of years, he said. Where did she get the drugs to do it, Morrison wanted to ask but didn't.

Solo said the girl Latrona was scared when he talked to her the night before. She was scared of the guys who killed her friend Rayfield. She was scared of the police, too. She didn't want to talk to anybody. But he was convinced she would after he talked to her. He was wrong, she got spooked and took off. The way he figured it. And the mama, nothing spooked her anymore except the thought she might not be able to get her hands on something to smoke or snort or stuff in a needle and stick in her arm or leg.

The kid probably did not go very far, Solo said. No one went too far out of the 'hood, especially a kid, a scared kid. He would get the word out that *he* wanted her. The eyes and the ears would find her. He did not want his deal for Lonesome Dennis to fall through.

Morrison clicked off and immediately redialed, getting Lieutenant Chatham on the first ring. "Nothing on the girl, I take it?''

"Jeez, I just talked to you five minutes ago. We're good over here but—''

"Okay. When somebody does find her I want them to be careful, gentle. She's scared, she's running and she doesn't think she's going to get anything but trouble from us. The

minute she's found, find a cozy spot for her there with maybe
a motherly policewoman for company, give her an ice cream
cone, everybody smile and nobody say anything to her except
that we're great guys and she's got nothing to be afraid of.
Norelli and I'll do the talking when we get there. Please pass
that word along, lieutenant.''

"Sure. By the way, Nolan's already phoned in a description
of her. He said he and Nabasco are going to go through the
apartment to see if they can find a photo, then they're bringing
the mommy downtown.''

WITH ALDO FORTE IN the Amalfi Club were Angelo, Marty
Sicari, Danny Isso and Carmen DiSavio, whom Joe Alessi had
sent over at Aldo's request. They were not playing cards. For
the moment they were not even talking after Aldo's revelation
about the witness. Finally Aldo broke the silence. "So where
is this Pack kid? Where is the little prick?''

Everybody at the table squirmed but none had an answer.

Carmen said, ''I told you when I checked out of the hotel
Monday morning I went to the room first. It was in order, just
the way the maid must've left it on Sunday. So they had to
have left before she cleaned it during the day Sunday. I even
messed the bed up, threw some towels around the bathroom,
opened up a bar of soap, made it look like somebody slept
there the night before.''

Forte looked over at Angelo. "What can I say, Aldo? I gave
'em the tickets, dropped 'em at the hotel. They knew they
were supposed to be on the first flights they could get out of
Chicago. Especially after what else went down.'' He shrugged.
"The last I saw was of them walking into the hotel. I can't
figure it.''

Aldo shoved his chair back. "C'mon with me, Angelo, I
gotta call Gussy. Maybe he'll want to talk to you again. There
is going to be shit to pay. The rest of you stay put. I gotta
figure this out.''

Angelo followed Aldo to the door. "We'll go over to that
McDonald's on Ogden and call.'' Then he shook his head.
"No, wait a minute, we can't. That's where I made a couple

calls yesterday. We'll go to the Walgreen's up on Ashland. No, that's too far to walk.'' He turned back to the group at the table in the corner and called out, ''C'mon Danny, we're gonna need a ride. Get the car.''

When they got to Walgreen's and the pay phones near the check-out counters Aldo decided he did not like it. Too many people coming in the automatic doors one way and too many going out the other, passing right by the telephones. Plus the guy talking on one of the phones seemed to be looking at them as they walked up, then was a little too obvious in his attempt to ignore them. ''We'll go down the street, find another phone,'' he told them. So the three, walking abreast, looked in shop windows until they came to a laundromat about a block south with a pay phone hanging on the wall near the door. Two women were at the far end talking to each other, another was sitting in a plastic chair with chrome legs, reading a magazine. This would be fine, Aldo said, and they went in. Aldo dumped a handful of coins on the steel ledge beneath the telephone and then picked out a quarter, a dime and a nickel for the toll call to Oak Brook.

Mario answered the phone on this particular line, as he always did, and went to fetch his boss. Gussy's private line was the only telephone Aldo Forte trusted because for one, he was told to trust it by Gussy, and for another, he knew Gussy had it regularly vacuumed by a guy who used to work telephone electronics for the U.S. Marshal's office. ''We got a little problem,'' Aldo said. Despite his guarded trust of Gussy's telephone line, Aldo still never used names talking on it. ''That situation we conversed about yesterday, one of the boys, I find out, never made it to his vacation destination.'' No response. ''You there?''

''I'm here. You're telling me you don't know where he is?''

''Not at the moment. We're trying. I thought you ought to know.'' Aldo cleared his throat. ''We'll find him but in the meantime—''

''You come out here. What you tell me *is* a problem. There is maybe an even bigger problem. You bring that young fellow along with you, the one you brought the other day." Gussy didn't deal in names either.

WHEN THEY PULLED INTO the circular driveway in front of Gussy Tuscano's house there were five cars parked, none of them belonging to the Tuscano family. Which made Aldo even edgier. He didn't recognize any one of them. "You come in with us, Danny," which was not the norm, Danny usually being left with the car on occasions like this. But Aldo had this feeling, maybe it was the tone of Gussy's voice on the telephone, maybe it was just that he didn't really know what to expect, things going the way they were. Danny was armed, dedicated—*take the bullet*. Would he? "Shame to have you sittin' out here if there's a party going on inside."

Gussy was out beyond the expanse of grass behind the swimming pool playing bocce ball on the court he had installed under his personal direction the first week he moved into the mansion. It was a swath of fine clay, precisely leveled, six feet wide and seventy-two feet long, where Gussy and five of his buddies, none under sixty-five, were currently studying the lay of the balls on the court. One of the players had his ball close to the *pallino*, the smaller goal ball, seemingly protected with another ball. This was not bowling. It was a game of finesse, strategy and boldness. As Gussy liked to say: The Romans played it—Nero, the fairy, he played the violin. Caesar, the conqueror, he played bocce ball. The bocce ball sets Gussy stored in the pool house came in velvet-lined cases of fine Italian leather. He had ordered them from the Abercrombie & Fitch of Rome, a tony specialty shop named Guido's on the Via Veneto. For what he had paid for those and the court he had laid at the back of his property he could have had an Alfa Romeo two-seater.

Sitting under the shade of an umbrella table by the pool was Joe-sep Alessi, in his hand an oversized old-fashioned glass filled with vodka on ice. Angelo Franconi was there too. He looked at the three of them. "Sit down, we got enough for a game of bridge." He nodded in the direction of the bocce ball game. "We gotta wait till the game's over."

As Aldo, Angelo and Danny looked out toward the game, they saw Gussy measuring his options, then looking at his companions in play, from one to the other. Ball in hand, he concentrated now on the *pallino* but he didn't roll. Instead he softly lofted a daring aerial shot. The ball arced in what seemed like slow motion over his opponent's supposedly protected ball, landed gently and rolled to within four inches of the *pallino*. ''A bravora,'' one of the old men shouted, his arm raised in the air, ''*a bravora*,'' and the others nodded.

Gussy looked jubilant. Even from that distance they could see it.

''You brought an army,'' Joe-sep said to Aldo.

Aldo shrugged. ''I didn't see your car out there.''

''Got a new one. You see a Sedan DeVille, silver? That's it, just picked it up this morning.''

Aldo nodded, looked out toward Gussy. ''He said there is a problem.''

''I know.''

''What is it?''

''That I don't know.''

''I've got one. I told Gussy on the phone. One of the fuck-ups from Camden never showed in New Orleans.'' Alessi gave him a look of sudden concern. Aldo acknowledged it. ''I know. The smart-ass one, the one Carmen said was a first-class asshole. Danny Pack's his name.''

''Where is he?''

''Who the fuck knows? His buddy's down in Lauderdale, just where he's supposed to be. But who knows where the punk is?'' Aldo went on to explain that Dick Alan, a former colleague of theirs who was now semiretired down in Fort Lauderdale, had checked that out for Aldo and even made contact with Roy Echols by telephone. He was going to talk to him again and see if Echols knew where his partner might be. Earlier, at Aldo's request, another connection in New Orleans had checked on Pack, who was supposed to be at the Sheraton down there waiting for the word to go home. But he wasn't there and there was no record of him ever registering at the hotel, at least as of nine o'clock that morning.

Alessi nodded. "You're right, Aldo, we got ourselves a problem."

When the men finished their bocce-ball game, they all seemed to be talking at once as they approached the pool. No one was more effusive than Gussy as he said goodbye to them. The smile was still on his face as he walked over to the umbrella table. But it faded as he dragged over a chair and sat with them.

"I see you're all taken care of," he said looking at the drinks in front of them. Emma had come out while Gussy was rolling his bocce ball and brought an antipasto plate as well as two bowls of nuts.

"How'd you do?" Joe-sep asked.

"I won. Whatta you think."

"They didn't let you, did they?" Alessi was one of the few who could stick it to Gussy.

"You kidding? Those guys? They'd kill to win."

"No little hedge here, little nudge there? All on the up and up?"

"Whatta you say? You tell me, whatta you saying, Joe-sep?" Gussy knew he was being put on by his old friend, and for just a moment the smile came back.

"Well, I play golf with you, Gussy, so I just thought I'd ask." Everybody laughed.

Unlike at golf, Gussy would never cheat in a bocce-ball game. Never. To Gussy, there were only two of the eleven commandments that were inviolable, the fourth and the last one: Honor thy father and mother, and Thou shalt not cheat at bocce ball. The other nine could be stretched or broken, that was human nature, but never the fourth or the eleventh.

"Joe-sep, you hold your tongue. You talk like that, keep it up, I have Cockeye cut it out and stuff it up your ass." All laughed again. "Where the hell is Cockeye?" Gussy shook his head. "What the hell, it isn't him I want anyway. It's Emma. I need a drink."

"We were talking about the problem I told you about," Aldo said. "Joe-sep hadn't heard about it."

Gussy looked back, intent now. "I want you to tell me the

whole thing now, again." He looked over at Angelo. "How're you, sonny boy?"

"Fine, Mr. Tuscano."

"Good. I got some questions for you too. But later." He looked back at Aldo. "We don't need nobody else here for this conversation."

"Go back to the car, Danny," Aldo said.

"And, kid," Gussy said to Danny Isso, "when you go into the house, tell Emma to come out here before I die of thirst. And tell her to put some music on."

Aldo Forte repeated the story he had just told to Alessi. When he finished, Gussy just nodded. Then "Vesti la giubba," the clown's lament from *I Pagliacci*, came over the speakers and the rapturous and powerful voice of Placido Domingo caused Gussy to hold up his hand and stop conversation. He sat there, listening, his eyes turned to the sky, his mind in the music. When the aria ended he said, "On with the costume," then held his arms out to his guests, "that's what Vesti la giubba means, on with the costume . . . the show must go on." He seemed genuinely moved. When an all-male chorus singing "Funiculì, Funiculà" boomed out next, Gussy came back to reality and turned to Angelo: "Now you," he said, "you tell me again, Angelo, just what happened that night. Every detail. Don't forget nothing. Don't skip *nothing*."

Angelo was nervous. It was apparent in his voice, and the way his fingers kept stroking his thumbs as he talked. But he told the whole story again, this time even including the fact that he had yelled out in surprise when he saw the kid, which caused the two gunmen up under the expressway to turn and see the kid.

Gussy interrupted him. "Did you go up there, where the kid was?"

"No," Angelo said. "They did . . . I stayed outside the car, then they came running down to the car."

"Okay, then what?"

Angelo told him about taking them back to the hotel, getting rid of the guns and the shovel, calling Aldo, dropping off the car.

"So you say we got a problem," Gussy said to Aldo when Angelo finished. "Let me tell you how big a problem we got." His eyes moved from Aldo to Angelo to Joe-sep and back to Aldo. "We heard it was possible they got a witness to this. Right?"

"That's what you told us," Alessi said. "But Angelo, he don't see how they could."

"Well, Angelo maybe needs glasses. Because they do have a witness. I got another phone call earlier today. They got one. Little girl . . . girlfriend of the nigger kid. She seen them, Aldo. She seen the two of them, Joe-sep. She seen them, sonny boy. I don't know where she was, but they tell me she seen two guys shoot Manny Peters and then shoot the kid. She saw them real close, is the way I hear it."

Nobody said anything and Gussy just let the silence hang.

Finally he broke it. "So close, she said one of the guys had a ponytail haircut. Did one of those guys wear a *ponytail*?"

Whatever color had been in Aldo's and Angelo's faces faded. Gussy was staring at both of them. So was Joe-sep Alessi.

"Yeah," Aldo said, "one of 'em did. The Pack kid."

"The one that's supposed to be in New Orleans but isn't?"

"That's the one . . ."

"You see now how big a problem we got?"

✛24

"YOU HAVEN'T GOTTEN MUCH BETTER AT RETURNING PHONE calls," the voice on the phone said to Morrison, who was ready to pack it in for the day.

"I've had a busy day. Contrary to popular belief, Ms. Stryker, we all don't spend all our days ripping off fruitstands. So how can I help you?"

"I'm going to Alderman Hunter's meeting, it starts at seven.

It's going to be a whiz-banger, I'm told. He's supposed to announce something his investigation has come up with which, in his words, is 'shattering and alarming.' You want to come along with me?''

''No.''

''It would be nice to have some personal police protection, little female person like me.'' No response. ''It's going to be over by eight sharp, I'm told, so everybody can get out on the street and start collecting bodies for the rally tomorrow night. You remember that, don't you?''

''We're all looking forward to it here.''

''Okay, look, I've got to file my story by ten tomorrow morning. He's got something to say tonight that's going to upset a lot of people. I think I know what most of it is. And I've come up with something else on my own that's sort of on the alarming side. I really would like to talk to you about it.''

''Look, I'm just an investigator on this case. I'm not involved in the politics and racial issues and all that kind of stuff.''

''It's more than that. Believe me.''

No response.

''So you don't want to go to the service, will you at least meet me afterwards, eight-thirty, say, someplace? You name it.''

''All right.''

''Where?''

''Some place north on my way home.''

''How about Little Mo's, it's on Armitage and . . . let's see . . .''

''I know where it is,'' he said. ''It's a cop hangout. Sports fans and cops, all your world-class crazies.''

THE PLANE HAD FINISHED its climb and the seat belt sign had just been turned off when the flight attendant asked them if they would like another drink. They had had one on the ground while the other passengers were boarding and the plane was preparing for takeoff.

Jimmy Pagnano asked what kind of red wine they had. She said she would have to check. She came back with a bottle of California cabernet sauvignon. He looked at the label. "Stag's Leap, sounds like a dirty movie to me." She forced a smile.

"I don't know anything about American wines. You got any Italian wines?"

"No, I'm sorry. We have another kind of red wine, it's French, a burgundy."

"I don't want any of that French crap. This'll do. You want some wine, Angelo, or you want another of that stuff you were drinking?"

"Rum and tonic. But no, I'll have some wine with you."

"Good. So bring us two glasses and leave the bottle." The attendant smiled and went back to the little galley to open the wine and get a couple of wine goblets.

"Treat you right, first class," Pagnano said.

"Nice. Expensive, though. I never flew first class before."

"It's great, everything's free, big seats, better booze, better food, and you don't have to wait half the flight to get something like the rest of the herd back there. Only way I fly."

"Well, you can afford it."

"What's this afford shit? Look, Angelo, it's not something you worry about. I know it's better, I know it's the way I wanna go. I don't know if it costs any more. You know why I don't know?" Angelo didn't answer. "Come on, you know why."

"No."

"I don't know, Angelo, because I *never* ask. When I call up to get tickets I say I want two tickets to Miami or Vegas or whatever the hell I'm going, first class. The travel agent says we got these flights on these airlines and I pick one and that's it. She tells me what the tickets cost, a grand or whatever, and I say fine. You don't ask what the assholes back there are payin', so you don't know you're payin' any more. Simple. Right?"

The flight attendant returned with the wine wrapped in a white towel and poured them each a glass. "Would you rather

I just kept the bottle up there so it doesn't get in your way?''

"No, no," Pagnano said, snatching it from her. "You can keep the napkin, though," and handed it to her. He turned quickly back to Angelo. "Somebody said it, I don't know who it was, but it's like if you gotta ask the price you can't afford it. Guy's right, whoever he was."

"Yeah, well, I gotta ask these days."

"Yeah, yeah, I understand, Angelo. But one of these days you won't. You keep doin' the right things, everything's gonna be first class. Joe-sep, he likes you, I know. Seems your boss Aldo does, too. So just hang in, kid."

"I know. Don't get me wrong, Jimmy. I'm doin' okay. Aldo is taking good care of me. Joe-sep does some things for me, too, because of Anita, I know, but he still does. But I'm not what you'd call rolling in it."

"Give it time, kid. Do what you're told. Earn the trust, that's the biggest thing. You're doin' okay. Wine's not bad, eh?''

Pagnano poured some more into each glass. "I know where you're comin' from. We all came up the same way. Put in the time, pay your dues, watch your ass and know who's butterin' your bread. And above all, respect, you give respect where you're supposed to. And that's all. Simple." Pagnano took a swig of the wine, licked his upper lip. "What time we get in down there, you remember?''

"Eleven-fifteen, Florida time."

"Yeah, lose an hour. Had to go to Palm Beach, no more flights this late to Lauderdale. But Dick Alan got somebody pickin' us up. You'll like him, he's a stand-up guy, been around a long time, older than Joe-sep and Aldo but you wouldn't know it to look at him.''

MORRISON AND HOLLY STRYKER had the house special hamburger, with cottage fries and cole slaw. When he asked how she found out about the place she said Jimmy Nolan had taken her there. When he looked at her a little too long she added it was after their ridealong. She hadn't had time to stay for the hamburger that day, though.

They talked about Reverend Hunter's call to arms, that nothing was being done because young Rayfield Tees was black and was killed in a black neighborhood. It happened every day. Murder, rape, assault shrugged off by the police because of who the victims were and where they were from. But what he had uncovered was that this was not just an ordinary killing. It was a killing carried out by members of organized crime, a mob hit—white criminals who made their living at the expense of law-abiding citizens. And that was why the police were dragging their heels on it. They didn't *want* to catch the killers . . . because the politically connected members of organized crime did not want the police to find the killers. There was collusion between the two "mendacious bodies," as he called them, and Hunter claimed he had proof it was a cover-up. He got a great response, Holly Stryker said. The people who left the Avalon Tabernacle Church, she said, were true believers.

"I'll tell Jim Harkness about it," Morrison said. "That's his area, the lucky guy."

She told him then what she had heard and was hoping to put together for her story. That the police had a witness. Which caught his immediate attention. The police had a witness who they were keeping under close cover. Why?

He looked across the table at her with a long-practiced sincerity that even an experienced reporter wouldn't be likely to question and told her that he could state "categorically" they did not "at the present time" have a witness nor had they talked to anyone "purporting to be a witness to the crime in question."

"But if there was a witness, hypothetically speaking, if you had one or were looking for one you'd heard about, you might not share that with the press, correct?"

"If it wasn't in the best interests of the investigation, right, we wouldn't. Where did you hear this witness angle?"

"A source."

"Same source gave you our hotline number?"

"We don't reveal sources, we do our best to protect them. Just like you guys do."

Neither of them ate more than half of the half-pound hamburgers. When the waitress loomed over them with checkpad in hand, Holly Stryker ordered a decaf and Morrison said he'd have another Jack Daniels on the rocks, even decaf kept him awake at night. She paid the check and asked the waitress if somebody could call a cab for her.

"You didn't drive?" Morrison asked.

"In that neighborhood," she said, referring to the location of the Avalon Tabernacle Church, "are you kidding? I cabbed it."

"How'd you get over here?"

"A member of the reverend's ministry gave me a lift."

Morrison said he would be happy to drop her off on his way home. . . .

Which was how he ended up in her one-bedroom apartment in Wrigleyville at ten o'clock that night.

She didn't have any Jack Daniels but she did have a bottle of Jameson's some guy had brought over last St. Patrick's Day. It was still about four-fifths full.

She picked up the story she had started for the next day's *Metro* from the table next to her word processor and showed it to him. It was about half-finished, she said. She would flesh it out in the morning. He read it, questioned the credibility of a statement from an "informed source," and thought to himself it was, on the whole, relatively innocuous. But then there was nothing as yet about Alderman Hunter's discoveries and theories and secret information, not to mention her own "rumor" of a mysterious witness. He wondered what the second half of the article would be about. . . .

When the level of the Jameson's bottle had reached midway, he and the glass he was drinking from were no longer near it. The glass, with a few ice cubes now reduced to the size of dice, was on the bedside table in her bedroom with the bed in which he was lying and breathing into Holly Stryker's ear. She held him close to her, her own breathing coming slowly but her hands still moving up and down and around his back in soft strokes. The only noise besides their breathing was the hum of the window air-conditioner. Despite it, there was perspiration oiling both of their faces. "Wow," she finally said. "I'd hate to imagine what you're like if you drank the stuff that keeps you awake."

He considered saying *I hope it was as good for you as it was for me*, but he couldn't bring himself to do it. Instead he just reached across her to the table and grabbed the drink. Some of the cold condensation on the glass dribbled onto her bare stomach and breasts and she screeched.

"Sorry about that," he said. There was a faint remembrance of the Jameson's in the water from the melted ice cubes. He put the glass down. "I don't smoke after, just drink."

She pulled him down onto her and held him there, wrapping her arms around him again, rubbing his back, his buttocks, running a finger down the crease between them. "You don't put as much into postplay as you do foreplay."

"I'm a little out of practice these days."

She rolled off him, lying now on her side, her face only inches from his. "One would never know it."

He was thinking about saying maybe it was time he got on home, they both had a busy day tomorrow. But before he could, she was out of bed and had snatched up his glass from the table and headed for the door. "You want just ice or some water on top?"

"Just ice," he said before thinking better of it. But she was gone from the room and back again before he even had his shorts on.

He was sitting on the edge of the bed when she handed it to him. She sat next to him, put her head on his shoulder. They just sat that way for a while. He took a sip of the Jameson's, which had regained its robust taste. She lifted her head from his shoulder and said, "There's one thing I didn't tell you that Hunter told me. But now, I mean, after this, I think I ought to."

The tone of her voice was softy, shy almost. It wasn't all that real, Morrison thought. "So?"

"Hunter said to me after his service that he had it on good authority that the man who killed Manny Peters and the boy was a cop."

"You've got to be kidding."

"No, wait a minute, Joe. He wasn't saying it was done by the police, not an accident or a mistake or anything like that. He said there was no question this was an execution carried out by members of organized crime for whatever reason. The person they hired to do it, that he said he had information about, was an off-duty cop. That's why there's such a big cover-up. That the police know it, City Hall knows it, the top echelon where it's a lot easier for them to cover it up than take the heat."

Morrison looked at her. Shook his head. "Cops aren't the best paid guys in the world. A lot of them get second jobs. It's okay departmentalwise, too, off-duty jobs. Some guys work security at a plant or a rock concert. Those guys in the yellow jackets you see at the Bear games and the Bull games, security, they're all off-duty cops. Other guys work as bartenders or handymen. Some guys just can't make the mortgage, make all the ends meet without a little outside job. They *don't*, however, hire out as hit men, for chrissake."

"It's not as if a cop hasn't worked the other side of the law before."

"I don't know where the reverend gets his information. Maybe Disneyland, Oz, or more likely the back of his twisted mind, but he's putting out information that nobody else has."

"He said he might drop it tomorrow night."

"Did he tell the rest of the press this?"

"Not that I know of. It just came up when we were talking. He knows we've gone after this story a lot harder than any of the other dailies."

"A little secret between the two of you?"

"I wouldn't put it like that, Joe. He just said, off the record—"

"Did he tell you not to print it?"

"Well, no, but—"

"Tells you something, doesn't it?" Morrison stood up and began putting his shirt on.

"I don't know just what you mean."

"He's *using* you. Lets you and your newspaper provide the

lead for his story. It always sounds a little more authentic if it's in the newspapers or on the tube first.''

''I don't think he's doing that.'' The tone was soft and shy again. She looked down at her bare legs, tapped her feet gently on the carpet, looked back up at him as he buckled his pants. ''Try to understand where I'm coming from, Joe. He tells me that. Okay, I don't have anything to corroborate it, but I don't have anything that says I should disbelieve it.''

He started to say something but she added, ''Please, Joe, let me finish. I'm just trying to get at the truth. I hear from another source that there's a witness. I hear it's all hush-hush. Why? Why shouldn't I be skeptical? That's where you can help me. Personally I don't for a minute believe *you're* protecting a cop in this, or the people above you are—''

''Holly, one thing, if it was a cop, he wouldn't be protected. That's crazy. There would be no way we could get away with something like that. Do you realize how big this investigation is right now, how many people are involved?''

''I do. And I know you could dispel the whole idea if you did come up with a witness. Just tell me, is what I heard right or wrong? Is there a witness or isn't there?''

He looked at her for a few long moments before saying, ''You know, you are a very good-looking young lady.'' He stuffed his tie into the side pocket of his suitcoat. ''You are no doubt a dedicated reporter. But you're not yet very good at getting information out of somebody like me, in spite of your talents in bed.''

''You sonofabitch.''

''I'm a sonofabitch? Holly, as they say in show business, know your audience.''

''You really *are* a sonofabitch.''

''Oh? I'm not the one trying to use somebody. You're pissed because I didn't pay the price.''

''You're going to regret this. I'm the one,'' she said looking down at her nakedness, ''who's been used.''

''Well, if you believe that, Holly, call the cops. Press charges. Theft of services, that's a crime.''

She grabbed up the small lamp on the bed table and threw

it at him, but it was plugged in and the plug stayed in the socket and so it went only as far as the cord would let it and fell onto the bed.

Joe Morrison was out the door.

✤25

DICK ALAN WAS A STAND-UP GUY, ALL RIGHT. HE WAS THERE at the Palm Beach airport himself to meet Jimmy Pagnano and Angelo Franconi. Looking like Florida personified: white pants, light multicolored madras short-sleeve shirt not tucked in, no socks, white patent leather loafers accented by thin gold chains across the vamps, sunglasses even though it was eleven-thirty at night. He was sixty-four years old but with his leathery tan skin and thick, brilliantly white hair and a body that still tapered he did not look at all past his prime.

They would stay at his house that night, he told them as they walked out to his white Lincoln Town Car with the spoked wheelcovers and the white leather interior. But first they would make a stop at the establishment in which he was a silent partner over in West Palm. It was called the South Coast Palace and bore the subtitle ''A Gentleman's Club,'' which was the term for a topless bar where the dancers sometimes gave the clientele a glimpse of the pubes. It made it all the more special that way, coming when one didn't expect it. But the Palace was a class operation, Dick Alan explained to them, not like the joints back around Rush Street in Chicago or out in Cicero, like the Surf and Turf, he added to get Pagnano's goat, with all the hustlers and B-girls. The girls here, as they would see, Dick said, were more than a step above. The club was semi-private, which meant it had certified dues-paying members, the regulars. It was also open, of course, to their guests and to those who could drop the name of a member or maybe even the name of a guest of a member or anyone for that matter who just looked like someone with money and did not appear to be crazy enough to provoke a confrontation with one of the club's hosts, guys in white trousers and flowered Florida sportshirts and the orange blazers who would have been known as bouncers in the strip joints of Chicago and Cicero.

THE NEXT MORNING ANGELO awoke with a horrendous hangover. Probably all the red wine, Jimmy Pagnano said. Lots of sulfides in the red, Pagnano said, but he looked no different than he had when they got on the plane in Chicago. They had gone through two bottles of the cabernet on the plane and then five or six drinks at Alan's gentleman's club, finalized with a before-bedtime hit at Alan's house. The late August heat and humidity had not helped.

Pagnano and Angelo were sitting on the aft deck of Alan's yacht, a thirty-six-footer with two separate sleeping quarters, a bathroom with a shower, and a galley. There was an eating area with a table and chairs and buffet on the deck before one got to the stairs leading below. The two of them were sitting in deep-sea fishing chairs anchored to the deck at the stern. Angelo had a big plastic tumbler filled with orange juice. He hoped the vitamin C from it and the extra-strength Tylenol and the Alka-Seltzer he took would cure his self-inflicted wounds. Pagnano had a plastic mug of coffee. All the insulated plastic drinkware had an anchor emblem on it with the words *Good Times* beneath, which also was the name of Alan's boat.

The boat was moored to a dock in the canal behind Alan's house. The house, like most others on the canals between the Intracoastal waterway and the Atlantic Ocean in Fort Lauderdale, was white with a rust-colored Spanish tile roof, was large and expensive. There was a swimming pool and patio between the main house and the dock. Dick Alan lived well with his companion of the past six years, a young woman he introduced to them as Loretta, who appeared to be approaching thirty and who, according to Pagnano, once worked in a place Alan had another interest in just outside Lake Tahoe on the Nevada side.

Alan came out from the sliding doors to the patio and

walked out to the dock. "So you got everything you need, boys?"

"Everything's fine except my head," Angelo said.

"The kid's not quite in the big leagues yet," Pagnano said.

Alan smiled. "You boys have a good time at the Palace last night?" He didn't wait for an answer. "How'd you like the goodnight kiss?"

It made Angelo Franconi wince, remembering. Alan prided himself in being a good host, which was why he told two of his best girls to give his guests "goodnight kisses." With Angelo, the kiss didn't take, despite all the practiced efforts of the redhead who he vaguely remembered said she was from Plano, Texas, where she had been a homecoming queen. The booze had Novocained him, he conceded. It occurred to him, in the room in the back of the Palace alone with her . . . what if this got back to Joe-sep Alessi, how would he take it, his daughter's boyfriend being with a whore from Texas, even if she was one with class from a club owned by a Joe-sep associate, the classy Dick Alan? The thought combined with the booze defeated the ex-homecoming queen's considerable talents. Actually Angelo would much rather have been back in Chicago with Anita Alessi, even if they were only sitting and talking and kidding around. He really did think of her a lot, just about all the time in fact in spite of the distractions in his life.

"So what's the agenda?" Alan yelled down to them. After he had picked them up at the airport he had told them he'd talked to Roy Echols again on the telephone. He was at the Yankee Clipper, a nice hotel on the far south end of the Lauderdale beach, just where he was supposed to be, but he had no idea where his partner was if he was not in New Orleans.

"I think Angelo has a little talk with Roy Echols today," Jimmy Pagnano said, "and then we see what we see."

"Okay, you guys just let me know what you want."

"We're all appreciative of your help, Dick," Pagnano said. "I speak for Joe-sep and Aldo as well as the both of us here."

"Hey, what are friends for?" Alan held his arms out.

"Beautiful day. Stay like this, things work out, maybe we take the boat out and do some fishing later."

Angelo used the house phone in the Yankee Clipper, but Roy Echols was not in his room. He wandered around the lobby, walked out by the swimming pool and along the deck chairs that faced the ocean. No Roy. Angelo took off the thongs he had gotten at Dick Alan's and the salmon-colored T-shirt that bore the imprint of WENDT'S at the top and GYM at the bottom, the words serving as the ceiling and floor for a boxing ring with a figure face-down in crucifix posture on the canvas. His blue running shorts could pass for bathing trunks, he decided, and he walked down to the water's edge. It was a calm ocean, just a gentle lap slapping at the shore. The water was warm as he strolled ankle-deep about a hundred yards each way. No Roy on the beach or in the water. By the time he was back by the pool he had worked up a good sweat, the previous night's indulgences purged by the Florida sun. He put the T-shirt and thongs back on and walked into the lobby. The air-conditioning felt wonderful. He tried Echols's room again, still no answer. In the gift shop he bought a People magazine, walked over to the bar, which ran along a wall on the far side of the lobby. Nobody was at the bar but several of the tables around it were occupied. He sat down on a stool and ordered a screwdriver served in a tall, tulip-shaped glass, the rim of which was draped with a slice of Florida orange.

Behind the long bar, above the shelves of liquor bottles, were large windows that looked onto the pool. The effect made Angelo feel like he was in an aquarium. Occasionally a kid would swim up to one of the windows and look in, his or her face distorted underwater as it came against the glass like in a mirror in an amusement-park funhouse.

"Got yourself a human aquarium here," Angelo said to the bartender. "Never saw anything like it. Up in Chicago they got a thing at the zoo where you can walk down a ramp and look underneath at the seals swimming around." He was thinking of the time a couple of months back when he and Anita had gone to Lincoln Park Zoo. Zoos were not among Angelo's ordinary haunts, but it had been fun, as Anita had promised, and he remembered the seals who would swim up to the windows there just like the kids here. That was also the day they first went to bed, after the zoo, after a sandwich in a little outdoor cafe on Clark Street, back at his apartment. It had been awkward, she was a virgin, but it had also been beautiful. That was his word for it, and he'd told her so.

"Doesn't bother you, all those people looking over your shoulder all day long, huh?"

"They can't see in. You can see them, they can't see you," the bartender said.

"They know all that? You can see them?"

"Not all of them." The bartender was a big man, in his early to mid-sixties. He leaned his elbows on the bar and his face toward Angelo and spoke quietly, as if he were setting up a conspiracy. "Couple weeks ago we had a guy in there"—he nodded toward the last window to Angelo's right—"the deep end. The guy's got his feet on the ledge there and's holdin' on with one arm, and there's two little girls playing around in the middle of the pool. Nine or ten, maybe. They were the only ones in the pool, it was kinda rainy, surprised anybody was in it at all. But there he was, hangin' on and facin' down toward the kids. You can't see his head because it's above water but that's the way his body was facin'. And it's about six o'clock and the joint is jammed, cocktail hour. And this guy's wearing red-and-white checkerboard trunks, looks like a tablecloth, with a big pot belly hanging over it, and he's got one hand inside, workin' away."

"Jesus," Angelo said, shaking his head in disgust.

"I know. There had to be thirty, forty people in here. Suddenly one guy says, 'Look at that!' and everybody starts to look up and see the guy poundin' away, and then you hear the titters and laughing or gasping, some of the women anyway. Finally he quits and hoists himself out of the water. Can you imagine that guy showin' up at the pool the next day or on the beach in those trunks? Takes all kinds, right?"

"Give me another one of these," Angelo said, pushing the empty glass across the bar, "but no vodka this time." He wanted to push the image of the pervert out of his mind.

"You box?" the bartender asked when he put the fresh drink in front of Angelo. He'd noted the logo on Angelo's T-shirt.

"Used to. When I came to Chicago I did for a while. Haven't in a couple of years."

"What were you?"

"Light heavyweight."

"Tough class."

"Tell me about it. I wasn't all that good, which is a reason to get out of it. I did win most of my fights but I wasn't a pro. If I was I would have gotten trimmed pretty good. How about you?"

"Yeah, long time ago. I was a welterweight then, if you can believe it. Back during the time of Robinson, Sugar Ray, he was champ. There was *nobody* like him. I don't think any-body since coulda beat him. Kid Galivan, he was great, too. Johnny Bratton another, I think he was from Chicago. Honey Boy, they called him. Those guys were great. Don't get me wrong, I never boxed in that league but I used to follow it all the time, like my buddies did the Red Sox. I had a few small-time pro bouts in Massachusetts, where I was from, then a couple down in New York where I really got my ass kicked. That was it for me. I don't even watch it anymore. It's all hype for TV these days. A sideshow." Two men sat down at the end of the bar and he went off to tend them.

When he came back Angelo asked, "This the only bar in the hotel?"

"Yeah. Except for the one outside for the beach and the pool."

"I must've missed it."

"When you go out the main door to the pool, it's to your left, down a ways."

Angelo left a ten on the bar, picked up his People magazine and went upstairs and outside and over to the square bar with the thatched roof over it—and there was Roy, lobster-red, drinking a pina colada with a woman who looked to be in her mid-forties and who should not have been wearing even a semi-bikini.

Roy was startled when he looked up from looking down the cleavage of his friend and saw Angelo standing there.

"How we doin', old buddy?" Angelo asked. Roy was searching for something to say, surprised as he was. "Tried your room a couple of times but got no answer." Angelo put his hand on Roy's bare shoulder. "We're buddies," he said to the woman. "I just got in town."

"Yeah, how you doin'?" Roy said. "This is Vivian." He didn't attempt to introduce Angelo because for one thing he didn't know Angelo's name.

She smiled up at Angelo. "Sulzberger, Vivian Sulzberger."

"Nice to meet you." Then back to Roy: "Say, I gotta talk to you." He looked over at the woman. "I'm sorry to interrupt like this."

" 'Course," Roy said, standing up from the barstool.

"Nice talking to you, Billy," Vivian said to Roy. "Maybe I'll see you around the beach later."

"Hope so," Roy said.

The two walked back into the hotel.

"Pardon me if I seem a little surprised," Roy said when they were back inside the building.

"Life, they say, is full of surprises . . . Billy," Angelo said.

"What're you doin' down here anyway?"

"You think it's hot down here, this is the North Pole compared to Chicago. There is a lot of heat, as you can imagine. Better I'm down here than up there, that's the consensus. I was told to come down here. Let's go somewhere else. We gotta talk."

In Roy Echols's room Angelo said, "Look, we got a problem." A nervous look in response. "Not with you, it's your buddy. Danny Pack. He never showed up in New Orleans."

"I know. This guy's called me about it, says he's my contact down here."

"Dick Alan?"

"That's him."

"Well, he is your contact. He's the guy who's gonna give you the second half of your fee."

"I didn't say anything to him because I didn't know who

he was. He just gave me his name and dropped Aldo Forte's.''

"Well, trust me, Dick is the man," Angelo told him.

"Okay, so . . .''

"So you got any idea where your buddy is?''

"I didn't know he didn't get to New Orleans.'' Angelo looked at him skeptically. "I didn't, honest to Christ. Look, after you dropped us back at the hotel we went up to the room, had a couple of drinks while I called the airlines. I got myself a Delta flight to Lauderdale, first one, eight in the morning. I got Danny on one to New Orleans on American for eight-forty-five. We caught a couple of hours of shut-eye and then left.'' Roy gave him a what-else-can-I-tell-you look.

Angelo gave him a you-can-tell-me-this look. "So where is he if he isn't in New Orleans?''

"I don't know. Maybe he just ain't where he's supposed to be in New Orleans. I mean maybe he's in a different hotel there.''

"Why would he do that, Roy? He knows he's supposed to be contacted there. How can he be contacted if he isn't where he's supposed to be? That doesn't make sense.''

"Danny doesn't always make a lot of sense. He's got this thing, you know, he doesn't always do what he's told to do. He's a very independent guy, you know, does what he damn well pleases, doesn't always think of the consequences, you know what I mean? But Danny's good people, believe me. You don't have to worry about him.''

"Well, they are worrying about him in Chicago, I guarantee you. I'm telling you there's big-time pressure up there. Everybody's looking everywhere. Aldo is very nervous and very unhappy. If this could ever get traced to him . . .''

"Hey, never.''

"Sure, but where is Danny Pack?'' Roy shrugged, Angelo let out a sigh. "The other thing, you are not getting the rest of your money until we find Danny Pack and are sure he is safely out of sight. I brought the money down here for you and for him, but it's with Dick Alan now and that's where it stays until Pack is accounted for. So Aldo says.''

"The only thing I can think is maybe he stayed in Chicago.

I wouldn't put it past him. We left the hotel room together but I went on to the airport. He didn't go with me. American is a different terminal, anyway.'' Roy looked worried.

"Why would he have stayed in Chicago?''

"Well, I know he don't like to fly. And he had this old girlfriend there that he talked to. You know Danny used to live in Chicago.''

"I didn't.''

"Well, like I said, he talked to her. And I know he called her again in the morning before we left the hotel room. I came out of the shower and he was talking to her. But honest to God, I didn't hear what he was saying.''

"You know who she is?''

Roy looked even more worried now.

"This is not something we can screw around with,'' Angelo said. "I'm sure you understand me.''

Roy understood. "Her name's Winnie. I remember that only 'cause he told me it was short for Winona, which I thought was a real fruitcake name. Winona Wendell, Winnie Wendell. She used to be married, but since Danny last saw her she dumped the guy, he said. She was working at a supermarket, Cub Foods. I remember that because of the Cubs. I remember he said it wasn't too far from the ballpark on a street I think he called Clydeburn. I don't know Chicago but that's what the street sounded like.''

"Clybourn,'' Angelo said.

"Yeah, that's it.''

"You got any way to get hold of him. Some number? Somebody else who might know where he is?''

"He lives by himself. Got some girlfriends in Philly, Camden, but nothing regular. I can give you his number in Camden. We can call him from here if you want. You can call Jersey Cartage, see if anybody there's heard from him. You got the number there, right?''

"I don't. Somebody in Chicago probably does, but give it to me anyway.''

Roy wrote the numbers down on the notepad by the telephone and handed them to Angelo, who picked up the phone.

* * *

AFTER THE 11:30 MEETING at Four Morrison pulled Johnny Nolan aside. "Got two things to tell you, Johnny," he said. "First, quit thinking with your dick. And second, you so much as say good morning to that young woman from the *Metro* named Holly Stryker again and I'm turning your ass into Internal Affairs. And I understand driving a taxicab these days not only doesn't pay too well but it's got shit benefits and it's not too safe either."

"What're you talking about?"

"You know what I'm talking about. A lot of us have been wondering where she's been getting information that nobody else in the press is getting. And I was wondering how she got our hotline number downtown. Now I know. So *that's* why I'm telling you."

"She was just a ridealong, Joe. If I said something—"

"She also rode along to Little Mo's. Let's just drop it, okay? You been warned."

How did Morrison know about Little Mo's? Nolan was thinking. He felt the wall pressing against his back right there even though he was standing in the middle of the room. "I didn't mean any harm, Joe. I just—"

"I know you didn't. That's why I told you the first thing. Use your head instead from now on, okay?"

"Okay."

"When did you tell her we had a witness?" Morrison asked. Not *Did* you tell her, but *When?*

"Well, I guess it was yesterday afternoon. I mean, I didn't really tell her we had a witness. I said there was talk that somebody might have seen the shooting. That's all."

"That she construed as a witness. Which I would construe as a witness. Which *anybody* would construe as a witness. Does she know the name of this potential witness?"

"Hell, no. That I wouldn't never—"

"I shouldn't have to tell you this but I will anyway. That little girl out there, right now she hasn't got any protection. If the wrong people find out who she is she could be reunited with her boyfriend real quick."

"Come on, Joe, I'm not a moron."

"I didn't say you were. Just remember what I said about one word to Holly Stryker and the joys of driving a cab for a living."

OVER THE PHONE ANGELO told Jimmy Pagnano the information he had gotten from Roy Echols. Pagnano said he would relay it to Chicago. When he hung up, Angelo told Echols that Dick Alan thought it would be a good idea if they all stuck together until this thing got straightened out. "He said we should all stay at his place." Angelo said he would wait while Roy packed up and checked out and then drive him over there.

✛26

MORRISON GOT HOME AROUND SEVEN ON FRIDAY NIGHT. HE had a small apartment up on the far north side. After his divorce went through he sublet it from his former partner in Organized Crime, Norb Castor, who was living out his life in a wheelchair on full disability—seventy-five percent of his top salary—down in Florida.

It was furnished sparingly. Morrison had bought some of Castor's old furniture, and some stuff from the house where he had lived with his wife and two daughters. His wife had sold the house, which she got in the divorce settlement, and moved into a townhouse in Des Plaines, a suburb out near O'Hare Airport. Other than being new and relatively maintenance-free, he could not understand why she would go out there with the jets roaring in and out at all hours of the day and night. But then, he hadn't understood her at all the last five years of their marriage anyway.

He had the television on, watching the six o'clock news. On the table was a copy of the afternoon *Metro* that he had picked up earlier and read at 11th and State. Holly Stryker's article was on the front page again. It had been occupying a space there on the bottom righthand side all week. It only faintly resembled the article he had seen the night before. Must have had a busy morning rewriting, he thought. She really had nothing new to add, but the emphasis had changed to the discoveries of Alderman Lorenz Hunter and those the press and media (he didn't know of any other than herself and her newspaper) were also unearthing, none of which the Chicago police would comment on or, as she put it, "seemed aware of."

The article implied Machiavellian schemes and subterfuges from City Hall, perhaps the hint of a police scandal and scramblings to cover it up, the odors of political influence trying to derail suggestions of possible organized crime involvement in the murders, and, far from least, allusions to a mysterious witness whose existence, the article stressed, authorities would neither confirm nor deny. It sounded to Morrison like the article deserved a dual byline under its headline:

RUMORS RAMPANT BUT NO PROGRESS IN WEST SIDE

DOUBLE MURDER,

by Holly Stryker and Lorenz Hunter

On the tube the anchorman was talking about the alderman's march on the Hilton Hotel and Towers scheduled to get under way shortly on Michigan Avenue. Their minicams were already there, showing the police barricades erected in front of the hotel and the reporters trying to find somebody to interview, settling for a police sergeant who was curt and a spokeswoman for the hotel who seemed thrilled about the star-studded banquet they were hosting that night—every citizen had his or her right to exercise their Constitutional rights, didn't they, she said when asked about the planned demonstration that was beginning to take shape outside. There was a hastily erected speaker's stand on the grass of Grant Park across the street, which the minicam was now focusing on.

Why don't you show the '68 riots, Morrison said to the screen. The police billy-clubbing demonstrators and the tear gas and throwing the demonstrators into the squadrols. And then, as though reading his mind, the station did. After the stock footage the anchorman said: "Stay tuned for further developments at the Hilton Hotel and Towers on magnificent Michigan Avenue. We will be there live to report the events as they happen."

Morrison thought his pal Jim Harkness must be having a lovely time down there. He got himself a beer and picked up the telephone. This time he did not get an answering machine at the New York number, just the soft familiar voice he listened to in his mind on a regular basis.

Linda Tate did not sound all that surprised to hear from him. He called from time to time and she did sometimes, too, but they hadn't talked during the last two months. He was surprised when she answered the phone. "Thought you might be out of town for the weekend," he said to her. "Thought most New Yorkers left town on summer weekends."

Linda said she had just gotten back from a week on Cape Cod. She and a friend had rented a place the week before in Falmouth, which sounded like Foul Mouth the way she pronounced it, showing she had not entirely lost her midwestern roots in the year or so she had been in New York. She didn't say whether the friend was male or female and he didn't ask.

He told her a little about the case he was working on, then quickly said it wasn't why he had called. He just wanted to talk to her. There was the usual You-got-any-plans-to-visit-Chicago from him and When-are-you-coming-to-New York for her. They missed each other.

She had seen the revival of *Guys and Dolls* a couple of weeks ago, she told him, and thought of him every time the detective showed up on stage to hassle Nathan Detroit and Nicely Nicely Johnson and Harry the Horse. She told him the roadshow version was probably coming to Chicago pretty soon and he should see it. He said why didn't she come along with it. She said why didn't he come to New York, she wouldn't mind seeing it again. He said he might just do that one of these days. A break would be good, he was working seven days a week these days. He was going in tomorrow, Saturday. What was she doing? She didn't feel like doing anything tomorrow, she said, maybe read a book.

Talk . . . talk . . .

He felt pretty good after he hung up. Wishing, like AT&T said, he could reach out and touch someone, but unfortunately Indiana, Michigan, Ohio, Pennsylvania and New Jersey were in the way.

He redialed and this time did get an answering machine. He left word for either of his kids to call him at home anytime before eleven.

DICK ALAN PLAYED HOST for dinner. Just the guys: he, Jimmy Pagnano, Angelo, Echols and Tommy Fleischer, who captained the *Good Times* and served as guide when Alan decided he wanted to go out fishing. Loretta was nowhere to be seen, she could have been out somewhere or salted herself away in one of the many rooms of the house.

It was a catered affair. Alan had made the arrangements himself with Caprio's over on the Intracoastal, one of the best seafood restaurants in the area, and Plato Mercourious, the owner, had sent over an elaborate dinner built around baked Florida grouper with a rich silken sauce and the redolence of fresh basil. Two young Cubans in pleated white shirts and thin black bowties brought in the dinner, set it up and served it, then hurried back to Plato's place on the Intracoastal.

Alan told them stories of his own fishing exploits in the Atlantic, down in the Caribbean, around the horn in the Gulf. There were stuffed-fish trophies on the walls of the recreation room of the house with a big framed board of photographs of Alan with other fishing mates posing by their catches. His boat, he told them, had the best of sonar and fish-tracking equipment, and Tommy Fleischer could find a school of mackerel in the Dead Sea if he had to.

After dinner Alan held forth on tarpon fishing, the challenge of which they were going to experience a little later. Tarpon and shark you fished for at night, he explained. That's when they feed. Sharks were a pain, more for the show, so you could go home and say you caught Jaws. Get your picture taken with the monster with its mouth open showing all the jagged teeth. But they were lugs, the sharks. Throw out a load of chum and garbage and dangle a line in the slop and then just lug one in. Tarpon, now there was one of the great big-game sport fish.

"Come on, I'll show you one." He took the three visitors down a hall to his bedroom in the back. Tommy did not join them, stayed out on the patio with a can of Dr. Pepper and a pack of Camels, which he chain-smoked. On one wall hung an enormous fish with large silver-dollar-size scales which must have weighed more than a hundred pounds when it had its own innards instead of a taxidermist's stuffing. "Now that's a tarpon," Alan said. "Caught it over on the other side, in the Gulf, outside Charlotte Bay just off Boca Grande. One of the best tarpon fishing waters in the world. Brought her in in nineteen eighty-six. I chartered a boat over there. Took two hours to get that sucker on board. Broke water at least five times. One of the most beautiful sights ever, a tarpon leaping out of the water, twisting, thrashing, trying to chuck the hook. Only thing as good is a marlin, a blue, but that's another game." The three just stared at the fish on the wall. "So what do you think of the fish?" Alan said. All three said something that struck a note of awe, which pleased the host, as was expected of them.

"WE'LL FISH TILL TWO," Alan said as the boat headed out to open water. It was nine o'clock and the four were on the rear deck, Tommy Fleischer up front in the pilothouse. It was a still night, the ocean placid like it had been during the afternoon when Angelo went wading up and down the beach behind the Yankee Clipper. It was difficult to hear above the roar of the boat's engine, which was under full throttle. "It should take us about an hour to get where we're going," Alan shouted, his hand cupped to one side of his mouth. "Tommy wants to try the tarpon grounds up north, out from the bay at Jupiter. So relax and enjoy the ride." He started for the front of the boat, then turned and yelled back to them. "Figure out how you want to fish. There's only two chairs and we only run two lines at a time. So it's going to be turns." With that he turned and disappeared down the steps to the cabin below.

When Tommy cut the motor there was nothing but gently rolling water and a black sky freckled by stars. A gibbous moon painted a river of light on the ocean. The boat moved at a speed just above idling. Alan had taken over while Tommy was in the back with the others baiting the hooks and setting the lines. Tommy was explaining to them that they would be trolling but at times he would be turning the boat and showed them how to avoid crossing or tangling their lines when he did. He told what to do if they got a hit. "Just sit back and be ready for the fight of your life," he said before going back up to the pilothouse.

Alan came back to join them. "You decide on who's going to fish first?" They hadn't. He went back to one of the teakwood cabinets that lined the walls and took out a deck of cards. The three drew cards, and Pagnano and Echols were high with a queen of hearts and a nine of spades; Angelo had the three of spades. The system, Alan explained, was that after a half hour in the chairs Pagnano and Echols would give them up and he and Angelo would take over. Half an hour later they would switch again, keeping it up that way until two in the morning unless they wanted to quit earlier.

Jimmy and Roy took their chairs like a couple of school kids told to sit down by their teacher, and Alan got the rods from their stanchions on the back of the boat and handed one to each of them. "You're in business." He looked at his watch. "Ten-thirty we switch. Good luck." He went to the back of the boat, standing there between the two lines trolling out into the ocean waters, and looked at the sea spread out behind them, the moon's glimmering light dancing on the water. "A beautiful night," he said. "Calm water, clear sky, that means the fish are relaxed, good fishing weather." Then he turned to the two in the chairs. "You guys want a beer or a pop?" They both opted for beer.

He looked at Angelo standing behind them. "Come on with me, kid," Alan said to Angelo. "I'll show you where the stuff is below. Let you earn your keep while you're on this cruise.''

Angelo emerged from the stairwell a minute or so later, but he wasn't carrying beer. In one hand he held a wooden, dowell-like handle to which was skewered a two-foot length of picture-hanging wire entwined into a braid almost a quarter-inch in diameter. The handle fastened to the other end dangled down next to Angelo's ankle. As he moved toward the boat's stern, he gave it a flip and caught the other handle in his free hand.

Roy Echols was sitting there staring out at his line wondering just what the hell he would do if a big fish hit on it. Jerk the rod back, start reeling quick, that's what the Tommy guy had said. Roy was holding the rod in his left hand with a grip tighter than he needed, an amateur's expectant grip; he touched the reel handle with his right hand, held it, cranked it just a little. It moved easily and gave off a little whirr. Wouldn't it be something if he caught a fish like the one hanging on Alan's bedroom wall—Roy Echols from Camden, New Jersey, deep-sea fisherman, sportsman, maybe they'd hang it on the wall at Jersey Cartage—

There wasn't even a moment for Roy to identify what the silver-gray thing was that flashed suddenly down through his line of vision. All he felt was a jolt of pain as the loop of wire was wrenched tight around his neck and the panic that exploded inside him as the air to his lungs was instantly cut off.

The fishing rod he was holding flew from his hand and clattered on the deck and his hands flew up trying to get a grip on the wire to pull it loose to stop the strangling. But it was impossible to get his fingers under the wire even by clawing through his own skin, which he was doing in that terrifying moment, the blood from the scratches joining that from the circle of blood seeping from under the braided wire as it pressed through the skin of Roy Echols's neck. In the shock of what was happening Roy could see nothing in front of him other than a pulsating wall of darting black-and-white particles. He could hear no sound, no scream coming from his throat although he could feel the scream deep in his chest as it tried to burst upward and out.

Behind him Angelo held the wire tight, the muscles in his forearms rippling and his arms trembling against the pressure, his knuckles white from the deathhold grip he had on the handles. His eyes were frozen with the intensity of what he was doing, riveted on the sunburned bald spot on the back of Roy Echols's head.

A moment after Roy's fishing rod had hit the deck, Jimmy Pagnano had dropped his rod and jumped up, grabbing the fish-cleaning knife with its six-inch razor-sharp blade that had been conveniently left on a counter behind them. He went back around in front of Echols, watched Echols thrash about. Echols's hands were still up at his throat but now were clawing only weakly at his neck. A glaze was beginning to form over his eyes when Pagnano began working with the knife. In seconds Roy Echols's chest looked like a big bloodshot eye— thin, red rivulets of blood broadening, oozing, then flowing. Pagnano was breathing heavily as he flailed away. In his fury he even slashed at the thighs and the shins of the legs that were jerking like a puppet's. The viciousness and the surprise of Pagnano's attack had startled Angelo but he forced himself not to loosen his grip as he stared at Jimmy Pagnano's mad dance instead of the bald spot on the back of Roy Echols's head.

At the top of the steps to the cabin Dick Alan stood with his hands on the brass newel posts and watched the scene unfolding at the stern of his boat.

When Pagnano finished, he stood there panting, sweat pouring down his face, blood all over him. He let the knife drop to the deck of the boat. Angelo slowly released his grip. One end of the garrot fell away. Roy Echols's lifeless body collapsed down in the fishing chair.

Alan got out of a cabinet two large-size scuba-diving weight belts and handed them to Pagnano. It served to bring Jimmy back from whatever world he had lapsed into.

Pagnano now threw one of the belts to Angelo. "Put it around his waist tight as you can get it." He wrapped the other one around Echols's chest just under the armpits and secured it. He grabbed Echols by one arm and pulled the body out of the chair. "Come on," he said to Angelo, "give me a hand." Angelo took hold of the other arm and they dragged Echols to the back of the boat and pitched him into the ocean. They watched the body hit the water with a slapping sound and then slip beneath it, a small, dark slick coming to the surface and spreading out slowly and then just floating there on the moonlit ocean.

Tommy appeared with a hose in his hand and began washing down the deck and the chair where the late Roy Echols had been sitting. Pagnano looked at Angelo just standing there, looking somehow lost. "Little messy," Pagnano said, both of them now splattered with Echols's blood.

"Why?" Angelo finally said, still in a kind of daze.

"Why what?"

Angelo gave a little slow slashing gesture with one hand.

"Why'd I cut him?" Angelo nodded. "Make him chum. Remember, Angelo, remember Dick Alan, he said the sharks feed at night. And remember this body *is never to be found*. That's why I cut him. This body is never gonna be found. Chum for the sharks."

Pagnano grabbed the hose from Tommy and sprayed it on Angelo, washing the blood away. "Baptism," he said, smiling now at Angelo and then handing him the hose. Pagnano pointed a finger at his own bloody chest. Angelo aimed the hose at him. "With me, it's Confirmation," Pagnano said, his smile broadening.

✛27

BY 11:30 MONDAY MORNING MEETING TIME AT AREA FOUR, Latrona Meek was still missing. So were Solo and Slipball. Latrona's mother Melinda was back home in Rockwell Gardens, unhappy not so much because her daughter was nowhere to be found but more because a cop was parked on her doorstep, which impeded her day-to-night life—unable to buy or use stuff gotten from the westside candy merchants or turn a trick for walking-around money which was impossible when you were virtually under house arrest. Not officially, but Melinda Meek had been told while down at 11th and State just before they let her go Saturday morning that if she budged from the entrance to her apartment building before her daughter turned up they would have her in Cook County Jail on counts of child neglect, abandonment and abuse. And if that was not enough to keep her home, a round-the-clock police escort would.

THERE WERE SIMILAR PROBLEMS at the Amalfi Club. Aldo Forte's people were having no success trying to find some people too. Angelo got there just before noon.

"So how was Florida?" Aldo said when Angelo pulled up a chair between the two older men Aldo was sitting with.

"Hot, fishy smell to it. Dick Alan's quite a guy."

"One of a kind," Aldo said. "You should have his money. And another thing, he's never spent a single night in the can. Not a one. They been trying to lay something on Dick Alan for years. The feds, the tax guys, the screws in Florida, the screws back up here, everybody. Dick Alan is always a step ahead. Something to keep in mind, Angelo."

"He lives well," Angelo said quietly.

"Always has. When he was up here he was like a fashion plate. Always the fancy handkerchiefs popping outa his coat pocket, silk suits, crocodile shoes, went to the best joints, had the best-looking broads. Dick Alan always had style. You go to his club?"

Angelo felt a twinge in his stomach. "Couple of nights . . . except Friday."

"Get yourselves lost for a little while," Aldo said to the other two men. After they left he said, "Have a little pleasure along with business down there, huh?"

Angelo gave him a required, knowing smile. "Why not?"

"Like you said, Dick Alan's some guy." Angelo, Aldo thought, seemed a little fidgety. "You did good, Angelo."

Angelo just looked at him.

"Down there. You got it done good."

Angelo nodded. "Oh, yeah . . . it worked out . . ."

"First time's somethin' else," Aldo said. "A lot of guys are dumb, bring the shit on themselves, this guy was one of them. What was it Yogi Berra said, what's gotta be done, gotta be done. Something like that. So you did. Jimmy said you did fine."

"When'd you talk to Jimmy? We just got in this morning, only two hours ago."

"Joe-sep told me. I talked to him last night. Jimmy'd already talked to him."

"What'd he tell you?"

"Just about your night out fishing. Joe-sep thought that was pretty funny."

"Funny?"

"Yeah, he said nobody goes fishing for fucking tarpon the end of the summer." Aldo laughed out loud. "Springtime you fish for tarpon. Joe-sep thought that was a riot."

"None of us knew that." Angelo tried a smile.

"Jimmy did. Said he had trouble keeping a straight face through the whole thing."

"Jimmy's something else."

"Jimmy lives for that kind of stuff, really loves it. And you?"

"I can't say I loved it, Aldo." He looked him straight in the eye. "I didn't, but I did it."

Aldo brought the chair back down onto all four legs with a thump and leaned across the table to Angelo. "You remember what I said about steps?" Angelo nodded. "You took a big one. A *necessary* one."

"I know." He still held the hard-eye contact.

Aldo straightened up, a smile forming. "Let's take a walk."

Outside, walking toward Grand Avenue, Aldo said, "You are getting close, kid. But don't get too anxious. Just relax, like in that song, 'Que Sera,' the one Doris Day sang, what will be, will be. You want to be made. 'Course you do. I understand." Angelo nodded slowly. "Joe-sep Alessi, he's pleased with you too, kid. That's good. That's another big step." He paused for a moment. "That's one you gotta be specially careful you don't screw up."

Angelo said, "I know."

"Now on something else, this Pack punk. Nobody's heard diddley about him in Camden so it don't seem he went back there. Still nothing in New Orleans. Word's out around here, lots of people looking for him but nothin' yet."

"What about his old girlfriend?"

"She ain't in the telephone book. There's a lot of Wendell's but no Winona or Winnie or W, the way the broads like it listed these days. There's no Cub Foods on Clybourn. Gussy's got somebody downtown running a police scan on her for us. See if that comes up with anything. Carmen is out there day and night since Pagnano passed the word from down in Florida. Carmen sees this as a mission. He did *not* like the guy from the start, said so right off. Maybe we shoulda listened. Anyway, Carmen seriously wants to find him, the circumstances being what they are right now. Carmen's not Pagnano, but in this situation he *is* another Pagnano. Carmen's got a short fuse. Pack lit it."

"You got anything else for me this afternoon?"

"No. Take it easy, Angelo. Go home and get a rest. You had a tough weekend."

"Yeah." Angelo got up and went over to the telephone in the corner. He dialed a number. When Anita Alessi came on the phone he said, "Hi. I'm back." She sounded happy. "Hey, look," he said, "I gotta talk to you."

"Is something wrong?"

"No, it's just . . ."

"You sound sort of funny."

"It's just I wanna be with you. I really need to be." There was an awkward silence. "Really, Anita."

"Okay. Your place?"

"I'm leaving now. I'll be home in fifteen minutes."

"I can't make it that quick," she said in almost a whisper. "But I wish I could."

He hung up, waved to Aldo Forte and headed for the door.

*   *   *

EDDIE MCCABE AND FRANK Wilson were in the watch commander's office Monday afternoon shooting the bull with a couple of other detectives before they headed back out onto the street. Wilson was explaining that he thought he had finally discovered the answer to the riddle of life. "Your parents ruin the first half of it, and your kids ruin the second half. It used to be they'd say she's sweet sixteen and never been kissed. Now it's she's sweet sixteen and thank God she tested negative for the HIV virus." He was on another downhill roll that day.

McCabe turned the conversation to the denizens that lurked about the streets day and night out there on the west side, which was about as uplifting. "You heard about the guy they brought in here last night?" Wilson had because McCabe had told him about it first thing that morning when he arrived at Four for rollcall. The others hadn't. "Guy's from the south side. Looks like your ordinary drughead. Twenty-four. Dreadlocks. Smart-mouthed them 'cause they threw him up against a wall and patted him down. Never mind he was thirty feet from a drughouse at four-thirty in the morning hanging out there with another guy who had eyes looked like fried eggs. Know what they found on him?"

"Money," Frank Wilson said.

"That's right. Almost ten grand, nine thousand eight hundred and eighty dollars and change." McCabe slammed his fist down on Lieutenant Grantham's desk. The lieutenant was not behind it because he was down the hall "having the need to tap a kidney," as he was wont to say and do at least twelve times a shift. Wilson kept telling him he probably had a prostate problem, there was a lot of that prostate stuff going around among guys over forty.

"And here's the kicker," McCabe said, "along with the ten Gs he got two welfare checks in his pocket, one made out to him and one to a woman who happens to be his girlfriend and the mother of four kids, which is why her check was a lot larger. He was waiting for the currency exchange to open, he told the guys who collared him so he could cash the checks. Can you *believe* that? They brought him in because he had

such a mouth. But you can't hold a guy just 'cause he's carrying a fortune in his pants pocket. Too bad there isn't a crime
against stupidity, that kind of money in this neighborhood that
hour—''

The telephone rang. McCabe, the closest, picked it up.
''Area Four Violent Crimes, Detective McCabe speaking.''

''Hi.''

After a pause McCabe said, ''Hi. What can I do for you?''

''Moe-sin or that other guy Norawelli there?''

''They're not here right now.'' The voice sounded familiar.
''Can I help you?''

''No. Tell one them call Slipball.''

''Oh, Slipball. Wallace. I know you. I was the officer with
Johnny Nolan the other day when we talked to you in front
of that liquor store on Western Avenue. Remember, Wallace?''

''The one can't drive? Sure. Drive sidewalks.''

''Right, Wallace. That's me. So what can we do for you?''

''It's Slipball. I told you, Moe-sin or Norawelli.''

''And I told you they aren't here.''

''Moe-sin, he give me a number in case Solo wants talk.
So Solo wants talk but I lost the number. So maybe you give
me, huh?''

''Sure, Wallace,'' McCabe said, and read the hotline number slowly. ''You got it this time? You writing it down?''

''You an *asshole*, Cabe. Just like your buddy, Nolan.''

As McCabe and Wilson were on their way out, Nolan and
Nabasco were on their way in. Wilson had stopped to look at
the *Daily Bulletin* on the front desk, McCabe was passing the
time talking to Officer Polenski. When he saw Nolan and Nabasco approaching he said, ''Here comes the Moth with his
faithful sidekick César, Mexican for Tonto.''

''The moth?''

''That's my new nickname for Nolan.'' McCabe fished in
his sportcoat pocket and came up with the shred of a newspaper clipping. ''The *Tribune* runs these little lists every day.
You ever seen 'em?'' He held the scrap of paper in front of
Polenski. She hadn't. ''You know, human interest, trivia.

Lists. Like Letterman's Top Ten, but this stuff's serious. This one's great, it's about the sense of smell. Says a bloodhound can smell fingerprints *six weeks* old. Another one, a polar bear can smell a dead seal *twelve miles* away. How's that for usin' the old schnoz?''

Nolan and Nabasco stopped at the desk, said hello.

"We were just talking about you," McCabe said.

"Yeah," Officer Polenski said. "McCabe was comparing you to a moth."

"Says here the male moth can smell a female moth *seven miles* away," McCabe said. "So I thought that might be a good name for you, the Moth."

"Seven miles, that's not very far." Nolan gave them a wide grin. "Right, César?"

César took up the *Daily Bulletin* Wilson was putting back down on the desk. "Anything in here to restore your faith in humanity?" he asked Wilson.

"Yeah, yesterday a guy overdosed on heroin at 26th and California," referring to Cook County Jail. "I didn't know they kept the commissary open on Sundays over there."

Nolan looked over at Polenski. "Moths, for chrissake. They eat wool, don't they?" Officer Polenski nodded. "Real pain in the ass, the little buggers, keepin' 'em away from your clothes. Or pain in the nose, I should say. You ever smelled moth balls, Polenski?"

" 'Course I have."

"How'd you get the little legs apart?" Nolan thought *that* was the zinger of the day.

Polenski rolled her eyes and gave him an oh-you-asshole look.

Wilson said, "That's twenty years old, Johnny."

"Not to Polenski."

Wilson turned to Nabasco. "Anything going on out there we should know about?"

"Nope."

"The girl, the Meek kid?"

"Not a thing."

"There's one more," McCabe said. "You know a tsetse fly

can smell a cow's breath miles away, it says. It doesn't say how many, just many."

"Come on, Eddie," Wilson said.

As they started toward the stairs McCabe turned back. "Hey, Donna, can you think of anything worse than smelling—"

"Absolutely nothing," she said before he could finish the question.

✛28

SOLO HAD TWO PIECES OF INFORMATION FOR JOE MORRISON. First, nobody in the Westerns or the projects knew where Latrona Meek was. Second, he was unable to talk with the one person who might be able to tell him where she might be because there was a big man in a blue uniform babysitting Melinda Meek ever since she came back to Rockwell Gardens.

"I hear she's getting edgy," Morrison said. "Coming down. Been a couple of days now . . . home alone. We're hoping the more uncomfortable she gets the more she might want to tell us something about her daughter's whereabouts. So far all she says is 'I don't know.' "

"The problem is, you goin' about it the wrong way, Moesin. I speak her language, you don't, never will. Let's get it done, man. Let's quit the shit. We both want the kid, you for your reason, me for mine. I don't know if mama knows anything worth anything, but I like to find that out for myself. I know how to do it."

"So let's hear it."

"Okay, here's what we do. You get me by the Man. Me, be alone with the lady—you know I know the lady, I bring her some candy, make her happy and she talks to me. And maybe we find the kid before something happens to her."

"Can't you talk to her without feeding her dope."

''Moe-sin, she's an addict. That's all she thinks about. Trust me, I know what I'm doing.''

I know you do, Morrison said, talking to himself. *You are also putting me in the middle of something that could turn around and bust my* cojones.

''So Moe-sin? You still there?''

''Yeah. Okay. It'll take a little while. I've gotta go through a channel on this to protect my privates. You can understand that, I'm sure, Solo.''

''My man, I most certainly can.''

''I will get you into her apartment without the cop being there with you. *I* do *not* know you are bringing her a present of any kind. As far as anybody's concerned, if this should ever come up, nobody knows where she got it. She had something stashed. This was the first time she could get at it. Whatever. You didn't bring it. You tried to talk her out of using it but you couldn't. Okay?''

''Hey, you beginning to think clearly, man. Little help, you could be one of us.''

''Just tell the cop your name, Solo, and he'll let you in. And be alone, okay?''

''I'm never alone. I bring Skull along. He can keep the officer company outside the apartment while Melinda and I chitchat. It's the way it's gotta be.''

''Okay, but for chrissake be . . . discreet.''

''That's *me*—discreet on the street.''

''Call me at this number as soon as you finish talking to her. I don't want any crap, I'm bending a lot on this.''

''We will keep you informed.''

''And if I'm not here leave a number where I can reach you.''

''Unlisted. Sorry. But you know, Moe-sin, you can always reach me through Slipball, and by this time you must know where he can be found.'' And Solo hung up.

''You agree with what I'm doing?'' Morrison said to Norelli, who had been listening to the conversation on the other phone in the office.

''Officially, no.''

"We gotta be together on this."

"Unofficially, yes. All we know is he's going in to try to talk to the lady for us. Right?" Norelli shrugged. Morrison picked up the phone again and began dialing.

AT FOUR-THIRTY THE HOTLINE rang. Morrison signaled to Norelli and they both picked up the phones. "Morrison here."

"Say, this hotline really does work," the voice at the other end said.

Morrison recognized it and gave Norelli a signal to hang up. "Timothy Doyle, professional Irishman and federal inspector. To what do I owe this honor?"

"How about a drink? It's your turn."

"It's only four-thirty, and besides I'm waiting for an important call. Why? You got something for me?"

"This is a drink you will want to have, Joe."

"Could you come over here instead? I've really got to wait for a call, it's important."

"This is between you and me. I can't come over there. Believe me, Joe, you need this drink, and it won't take long."

"Okay, same place as last time?"

"That's fine."

DOYLE WAS SITTING AT a table in the corner when Morrison got to Miller's Pub—the Federal Building was six blocks closer to it than 11th and State. There was a Jack Daniels on the rocks waiting for him. "Thoughtful of you," Morrison said as he sat down. Doyle's was a Beefeater martini with a pair of jumbo olives resting at the bottom.

"This has got to be quick, Joe, I got to be back by five-thirty for a meeting. You got yourself a witness to the Manny Peters murder, I hear."

"How'd you hear? You tapping *our* phones too these days?"

"No, but don't give us any ideas."

"When did you hear this?"

"Last week."

"That's when *we* found it. Let me clear one thing up, we

don't *have* a witness. We've been told there is one but we've not located that person alleged to be a witness and as we speak that person is still MIA.''

"I know."

"You do? How? As I recall, your SAC couldn't care less about our problems and the murders of insignificant people.''

"That's still true.''

"So how did you find out last week?''

"They've been talking about it.''

"They being the Outfit?''

No answer.

"You'd think by this time they'd be a little more cautious.''

"They are, Joe. But sometimes we're a step ahead of them, sometimes they're a step ahead. We got the gizmos and gadgets but they get around them and then we come up with something else . . . it just keeps going. At the moment, though, we're a step ahead.''

"I gather.''

"Your witness, her name's Latrona Meek. Right?'' Doyle did not wait for an answer. "She lives in the Rockwell Gardens housing project on Monroe Street. A kid about twelve.''

Morrison was genuinely surprised. "Where the hell did you hear this?''

"Don't worry so much about where we got the information, Joe. Worry about where *they* got it. Because they *got* it. And that's how we got it. You got a leaky operation over at 11th and State, Joe.'' Morrison was thinking of Johnny Nolan and Holly Stryker and Alderman Hunter and the springholes they were wet with. Now he thought maybe he was on the *Titanic*. "Just like you, Joe, they're looking for her, too. Seriously looking.''

Morrison drained the Jack Daniels. "When did you find this out?''

"Today, Joe. You better find her before they do.''

"They'd kill her. A twelve-year-old kid . . .''

"It doesn't mean anything to them. The only thing that matters is that she could bring them down. Dominoes, Joe, and the direction they could start falling is uphill. We, or you for that matter, turn one guy and he gives us somebody a step up. It's been happening to them too much lately. That's how they took down Gotti in New York, and we did Gus Alex here. The old code isn't so sacred anymore." Doyle looked at his watch, held up two fingers to the bartender. "Let me tell you what I know—and what I think you should do."

Morrison took out his notebook and a pen.

"Remember, Joe, this is off the record. My name can't come up. The SAC still wants no part of it . . . even after I told him the kid's life might be at stake. I'm over here today on my own, Joe."

"I understand."

"Joe, I trust you, I know you. But promise me *nobody* else over there gets to know you got from me what I'm giving you. There's more at stake here besides the kid. Trust me on that."

Morrison nodded and they waited as the waitress set the fresh drinks down in front of them.

"Manny Peters was eliminated because he stole some stuff, drugs, from *them*. Stupid. He got the consequence. It was to be a lesson. Not that anybody mixed with the Outfit should need a lesson after all the ones that've been given before, but apparently they still do. Anyway, this kid, the Tees kid, just happened to be there at the time of the consequence. He wasn't involved. Just a wrong-place, wrong-time thing. And they dropped him, too. If they'd known the girl was there, she'd be right up there playing a harp along with her boyfriend." Doyle finished the very last drop of his martini.

"The guys who did the hit on Peters came from out of town and, from what I understand, are back out of town. It's kind of a tradition with them—you want a body found, you bring somebody in from the outside; you don't want it found, you use your own people. Right now the two who fucked it up are dead meat."

"You know who they are?"

"No. Just that they were in and out of town. From what I hear they haven't been dispatched yet but it's for sure on the agenda."

"You wouldn't want to share with me how you're getting all this information?"

"I can't. But here's what I think you have to do. First, needless to say, is find the girl and get her stashed away. Second, get the mayor to use some of his influence in Washington to put some pressure on *us* to help. He's suffering the heat—I read the papers—so get the word to him to get the word to Washington to cooperate formally. The SAC, I don't have to say, will do whatever the Bureau recommends. Now's the time. You can make the argument that this time we should all be in this together because maybe the fish will be big enough to satisfy the tastes of my SAC and Washington. If we can get to those two hitters before *they* get to them and we can turn just one of them . . . who knows who we might bring down? Right now, from what I know, I think it could be a *capo* or two." He shook a finger at Morrison for emphasis. "Get the girl, for her own sake, for the sake of all of us."

"You think there's a chance they might have already found her? That's why we can't find her?"

"Not as of three o'clock this afternoon." He looked at his watch again. "Joe, I got to go." He started to get up.

"Go ahead, it's my turn anyway."

Doyle leaned over the table toward Morrison. "Be careful who you talk to over there about this. *They* got a lead-out wire somewhere."

"I've got to talk to somebody."

"I know, just be sure of him, whoever it is."

"Paranoia is already setting in. I can feel it." He pointed to his head.

Doyle straightened up. "Let's talk as soon as you get anything, either on the girl or on the political arm-bending front."

Morrison paid the check and grabbed a cab back to 11th and State. He was in a hurry.

✦29

NORELLI WAS GONE FOR THE DAY WHEN MORRISON GOT BACK to 11th and State. But he had left a note: *Dep Sup Flanagan requests our presence at the 10:00 staff meeting tomorrow.* There was another handwritten note next to it: *See me first thing in the morning or call if you aren't going to be in the office.* It was signed *Ted.* Morrison wondered what the hell that was about.

There had been no call from Solo or Slipball or anybody who might be taken for either one of them according to the detective sitting by the telephone outside PT headquarters. Morrison called Area Four to be sure whoever was babysitting Melinda Meek on the third shift knew that Solo might be dropping by to talk with her. The babysitter had been informed of the situation, he was told. On his way out Morrison gave the telephone detective his card with his home phone number on it and told him to give the number to Solo or anybody phoning for Solo and tell him to call whatever the hour.

THE BLINKING LIGHT OF his answering machine was on by the time he got up to Rogers Park and his apartment. Morrison tapped the button on the answering machine. It was his daughter Peggy returning his call. Her crackly voice said that she and Sandy said hello and asked when they were going to see him again and said don't bother to call after seven because both of them were going to be out and mom wasn't going to be there either. How many days ago was it he talked to their answering machine? It was tough for two human beings to converse directly these days, he thought. It was also just after seven. That was the only message on the machine.

He had some bourbon and there was some beer in the refrigerator. He poured himself a shot and popped a can of Old

227

Style Light. It had been a long time since he had had a boilermaker, shot and a beer, breakfast of champions. He was drinking too much these days, he thought, and drinking alone. Not good. These days he was alone most of the time he was not on the job.

Everybody was not alone. Jim Harkness was at the head table of the semiannual banquet of the Chicago chapter of the Bar Association at the Four Seasons Hotel downtown, where he was slated as one of the after-dinner speakers. Morrison knew that because he had tried to get in touch with him when he got back to 11th and State after talking with Doyle.

His kids were out fooling around somewhere in the last dog nights of summer before school started next week. His ex was out with somebody but he didn't care with whom or where they were or what they might be doing . . . didn't even want to think about that.

He didn't know where Solo was but he knew he wasn't alone—didn't Solo say he never went anywhere alone? He hoped he was with Melinda Meek finding out something useful.

Franco Norelli was at home, no doubt watching television with his kids. Was Timothy Doyle's meeting over? Probably. Probably home helping his calendar-art kids pack up to go back to college.

ALSO NOT ALONE WAS Jimmy Pagnano, who was holding court with four of his buddies at a corner booth in the cocktail lounge at D'Amico's . . . Aldo Forte was playing pinochle at his table in the Amalfi Club . . . Joe-sep Alessi was finishing dinner with his wife and wondering what it was that was so important his daughter Anita was missing the family dinner. She had called, she always did, so he wouldn't worry about her, even though she was twenty-five years old now. She said she would be home by nine. Maybe he would hold off on dessert and have some with his little girl when she got home.

At the moment Anita Alessi was not only not alone but was very content lying naked under a sheet, wrapped in the arms of Angelo Franconi. It was the second time they had made love that day. The first was only moments after she arrived at his apartment that afternoon—hot, anxious, frantic, as if they had only minutes left in their lives. And when all the passion was over, the warmth and petting in the aftermath, and then the kidding around and the wrestling and the tickling and delicious silliness. After that she called home and told them not to wait dinner. Angelo called and ordered a pizza and they got dressed and ate the pizza as soon as it was delivered and drank a bottle of chianti. Then out of their clothes and back to bed, this time the lovemaking slower, sweeter, without the desperateness.

DANNY PACK WAS WITH his girlfriend, too, in her apartment on Clybourn Avenue. And they had shared a pizza for dinner, too, a frozen Tombstone cheese-and-sausage that she had brought home with her after punching out at five at the Cub Foods Supermarket on Elston Avenue.

IT WAS A LITTLE after midnight, the red digital lights on his clock radio told Morrison when he managed to focus on them. The phone was ringing. The telephone was on a table in the living room and he weaved his way to it in the dark, flicking on a lamp just before picking up the receiver.

"Thought you might be out for the night. Was just about to hang up, took so long."

"I was asleep." Morrison recognized Solo's voice.

"Already? You not a night person, huh, Moe-sin?"

"Not when I work all day."

"Oh, yeah, some of you guys got to do that. I forgot."

"Let's cut the shit, Solo. You talked to the kid's mother, I take it."

"Did. She as happy as a bird on the wing, for the moment anyway."

"And?"

"She think the kid could be over at her cousin's. Her cousin got kids 'roun' Latrona's age. She run over there before, Melinda says, when she want some space. She run some other places too but those were usually in the project, the Gardens.

Melinda, she has never been too good keepin' track of her child. And Latrona, 'cording to her mama, ain't no real home-body. Well, we know she didn't run anywhere in the Gardens this time. So you got to try the cousin. I can't. I got a problem there. The cousin, she lives in Horner. That's waaay outa my territory. That's Disciple land.''

Horner was the Henry Horner Homes, another Chicago Housing Authority high-rise project, which the Area Four cops called the Henry Horror Homes. It was not far away geographically from the Rockwell Gardens, only about a mile or so northeast, a mere ten-minute round-trip for a drive-by shooting. A branch of the Gangster Disciples, who on a day-to-day basis got along worse with the Westerns than the Huns did with the Visigoths, ruled the Henry Horror Homes project. The only time Solo's Westerns would have any inclination to visit it would be on an assault or retaliatory basis, not a conversational or fact-finding one.

Morrison was not familiar with the geography or the demographics or the current states of war and peace in the world of west side gangdom, but he understood what Solo was saying.

"We will not be inquiring over there. But feel free."

"You got a name for me over there, make my life a little easier?"

"Nadina Jones. And an address and an apartment number. You think you're dealing with amateurs?"

"Spell the name."

Solo did and Morrison wrote it down along with the address of Melinda Meek's cousin.

"Now Melinda says she got no knowledge of her kid bein' over there but it's the only place she can think of. Nadina's got three kids of her own and she's one of them good samaritans far as kids go. Worth a try. Good huntin', Moe-sin.''

"Thanks."

"Oh, and one other thing. Word I found out today is there's somebody besides you and me been making inquiries after Latrona. Been talkin' after her 'roun' the Gardens.''

"I already heard that myself.''

"That's not good, Moe-sin. How you think they found out about her, her name and all?"

"I wish I knew."

"Well, let me know you need any more help in your police work. We always here to help."

Morrison could see in his mind's eye the white fence of teeth in a smile below the cold eyes. "Help, yeah. You are always a big help to us."

"Lonesome Dennis, he lookin' forward to not bein' lonesome no more. He missing the 'hood. So hurry your asses."

Morrison slammed down the receiver and sat there staring at the telephone for a moment. Well, he was not going over there alone. He may not have been an expert on gangs but he did know neighborhoods and he knew the Henry Horror Homes did not get their nickname without good reason.

He thought of Norelli sleeping next to his beautiful wife. Norelli was his partner in this. Then he thought of his conversation with Tim Doyle that afternoon and hesitated. Finally he dialed Norelli's home number. Norelli, startled from his sleep, sounded decent under the circumstances and said he would meet Morrison at Area Four headquarters in an hour.

"WHAT'RE YOU GUYS DOING here at this hour?" Sergeant Gerherdt said when Morrison and Norelli walked in together. They had coincidentally pulled into the parking lot at the same time.

"We're going to make a house call," Morrison said. "Over in the Horner Homes."

"Wear a vest. And a SWAT helmet. Wish we had an armored vehicle you could sign out." Morrison and Norelli were the only two who did not call him Bilko and that had more or less endeared them to Gerherdt.

"An ordinary unmarked car will do but we would like a backup," Morrison said.

"I'll call one in while you're getting the car. Tell 'em to meet you out front." Gerherdt looked at his assignment chart. "How about Thompson and Hudson?"

"Don't know 'em."

"They're okay, been together a long time, think alike, from the same mold. You won't have any trouble recognizing them, they're both big guys, about six-three."

As THEY STOOD AROUND the two cars out front on Harrison Street, Morrison explained to Thompson and Hudson they were looking for a little girl about twelve years old who was scared and on the run and who they thought might be currently making her home in an apartment on the fifth floor of one of the Henry Horner Homes on Lake Street. He gave them the address.

"Ever been in that particular building?" Norelli asked.

"We been in every one of them. More often than we want to," Hudson said. "We're the players on the Violent Crimes ballclub, and Horner's one of the city's stadiums for such events. It ain't fair they always got home-field advantage, but that's the way it is."

"So what's the building like?"

"Four entrances," Hudson told Norelli. "The building's like a cereal box, entrance from each side in the middle and at each end. Stairwell at each end—there's eight floors—and two elevators in the middle. A security cage but the guy in it is too afraid to come out of it. Even if one of the elevators works, take the stairs. About a month ago two R.O.'s took one of the elevators in the building just west of there responding to a call and it stalled. Word got around the building fast there were a couple of cops stuck in it and they started throwing bricks down the shaft on top of it and a couple of garbage cans. Then somebody started shootin' down at it right around the time we got our cars over there."

"The girl's not exactly armed and dangerous," Morrison told the Tac officers. "We just wanted you guys along in case she's around and tries to slip out while we're upstairs. And, oh yeah, we are scared to death to go into the building alone."

The two smiled. "Well, at least you got street smarts," Thompson said.

Morrison described the girl, then told them to cover the four sets of doors on the first floor.

When they pulled up in front of the building it was almost four in the morning. It could have been four in the afternoon with all the activity going on outside the project buildings. "Maybe we should've asked for a couple more back-ups," Norelli said.

There were kids playing around the building and in the Horner Tots Playpark, as a scarred and lopsided sign identified it, among the broken equipment and swingless swingsets and sandless sandboxes. Little kids, eight, nine, ten years old. There were older kids loitering around in small groups. There were adults who did not look like park supervisors. Morrison suggested they take a walk around outside the buildings first, see if there was a little girl that resembled Latrona Meek messing around out there.

Hudson pointed up to one of the many open windows of the building. "Kid fell out of one of those about a week ago. Two-year-old. Seven stories straight down. Hit the concrete walk. There was another one last summer. I guess over here there's some good things you can say about Chicago's winters—at least they keep the windows closed."

To Morrison, looking up where Hudson had been pointing, the building looked like a patchwork quilt—some windows opened, some boarded up with plywood, some with sheets or blankets or other fabrics pinned over them, others with black scorch marks framing them from some past fire.

There was no one to be found who might be taken for Latrona Meek. Morrison asked a couple of the older kids if they knew her, and maybe seen her around the last few days. None had. He had little chance of getting a straight answer. He knew that but he had to ask anyway.

So they went into the building and he and Norelli started the climb to the fifth floor. They rapped at the door marked 512. Then pounded. There was a rustling inside and then a male voice wanting to know who the hell it was and what they wanted at this hour.

"Police," Norelli said. "Detectives Norelli and Morrison. We want to talk to Nadina Jones."

It was Nadina Jones's husband, Arthur. Solo had not told

them Melinda Meek's cousin was a married woman. The man looked at their identification through the crack in the chained door, although he didn't really need to; two white guys out there in ties at four o'clock in the morning in the Horner projects, they were not selling interior decorating services or collecting for the United Way.

By the time Arthur, who was wearing only a pair of jockey shorts on this hot night, let them in, Nadina was standing there behind him looking very uneasy about the whole situation. There were not three kids in the apartment, there were four. Latrona Meek was not among them. Three of them were Nadina's children and the fourth a friend of theirs.

They talked for a few minutes. Arthur was out of work at the moment. And Nadina worked days at a Church's Fried Chicken store over on Western Avenue. The apartment was picked up, a few things from the kids were strewn around but that was about all. It looked clean, like someone took real care of it. The two older kids, maybe fifteen and thirteen, had wandered into the living room to see what was going on. The other two stayed in the bedroom but were looking out from the doorway with a mixture of curiosity and fear in their eyes.

The Joneses seemed cooperative but they weren't giving anything up regarding Latrona Meek. Morrison tried to convince them they were only out to find Latrona for her own good. He explained the whole situation, what had happened and how the girl fit in. She was in deep trouble, not with the police. They said she probably didn't know how much danger she was in, that she probably was just afraid both of the people she saw kill her boyfriend and of the police that she knew wanted to talk to her.

Nadina gave in and told them the girl had been there for several days. She thought she had run away from Rockwell because of something Melinda was doing or did to her. Latrona was a very close-mouthed little girl, Nadina Jones told them, but Nadina knew what Melinda Meek was like these days so she let Latrona stay without a lot of questions. But after a while Latrona was being hassled downstairs because word had gotten round she hung with the Westerns before she came over to Horner. Now she was afraid of the bangers in Horner and so she took off again.

Nadina said the girl had talked about going south. One of Latrona's girlfriends, somebody from Rockwell, had moved out to 71st Street and Stony Island with her mother not long ago, Latrona had told her, and the girl had mentioned maybe going out there. See if she could stay with her friend. Nadina, however, did not know the girl's name.

Morrison gave Nadina Jones his card after scribbling his home telephone number on it as well. "If she comes back here, for her sake, *keep* her here and call me right away. Don't call anybody else, not even Latrona's mother. Just call *me*." He got her to promise she would. Arthur said he would, too.

"You by any chance have a picture of her?" Norelli asked as they were about to leave.

Nadina did. "Took one last year with Olantha," and she nodded to the girl who was standing with her brother over in the corner of the room. "When we had that picnic. Latrona come along with us. Go get those pictures, Olantha. They in the bureau drawer, top one."

Olantha disappeared into the bedroom and emerged a few seconds later with a packet of photos, from which Nadina extracted one of Latrona with Olantha. Two young girls barefoot, in shorts and T-shirts, standing on the grass in a park, arms around each other, smiling at the camera. Olantha's hair was shorter then but she was easily recognizable. Morrison pointed to the other girl in the picture, a few inches shorter than Olantha, whose T-shirt carried the message *Born to Dance*. "That's Latrona?"

"That's her. Looks older now, more sort of tired, you know what I mean? She weren't into the things then she is now. It shows on her nowadays. Latrona's a wild one but she still is a good child. You look at her there, in the picture, you can see her goodness there. She was happy then, she loved the picnic. But she got to runnin' with the wrong crowd. And that mother of hers, she ain't no mother at all." She stopped short of saying her cousin was a doper and a hooker. "Latrona's got good in her, she just don't have no roots."

ON THE STAIRWAY GOING down Morrison said to Norelli, "Damn good, Franco . . . the picture. I must've lost it. It didn't even enter my mind to ask. A few years ago I would have without even thinking about it."

"I almost forgot myself."

Morrison looked at the little girl with the tantalizing smile in the photograph, a smile surely erased now as she moved through the streets of the worst parts of the city, hiding, afraid, as Nadina Jones said without any roots to hold her down, nothing to give her some protection from what was out there. And he thought, *This girl living off the streets, she's the same age as my own Peggy.*

✤30

IT WAS SEVEN-THIRTY THE NEXT MORNING. MORRISON closed the door to Deputy Superintendent Harkness's office and sat across the desk from him. He told him about the cousin in the Horner Homes and what had come out of their four A.M. visit there. That Latrona Meek had moved from one jungle to another and now another. And he gave him everything that was said in his meeting with Timothy Doyle except Doyle's name. Harkness did not ask, he had spent enough time on the street earlier in his career to know the code, that if Morrison had felt he could tell him he would have.

Harkness leaned back in his chair, his fingers interlocked and the hands resting on his trim stomach. "So we have a major leak that drips into the ears of organized crime." He did not sound too surprised. "Who do you think it is?"

"I was hoping maybe you could help there, Jim."

Harkness did not move or change expression. "You think it's me, Joe? That why you came to see me first?"

"No, hell no." Morrison looked surprised. "Just the opposite. I decided you're the only one I can trust.''

Harkness leaned forward across the desk, fixing Morrison with his eyes. ''We're talking about a serious breach here. We're going to have to take some serious steps. And I will. Anything else?''

''We got a picture of the girl last night. Color shot of her at a picnic taken about a year ago. I already have it at the lab for blow-ups. I'll bring them to the meeting at ten. I figure we run it in the *Daily Bulletin* as a missing child who may possess information about a felony. No more than that. I think quietly we finagle some special attention from the commander out in Englewood. That's where we think the kid might be now. We don't have to reveal what we want her for. At this point the second-to-last thing in this world I want is for the press to get hold of this and connect her to the PT case and start spreading the word. The first-to-last, and I don't have to tell you, is to give *them* something that might help *them* find her.''

''I can take care of that upstairs. I just announce we've gained information that we have a legitimate worry about leaks to the Outfit. Word to that effect should make everybody watch their asses . . . and shut their mouths. What else?''

''Can we get the FBI to open up to us on this officially? They know a lot more about the case than they're telling us. I know that for a fact. The asshole SAC over there won't do a thing for us . . . unless he's told to. Can we bring down some pressure on him from Washington? You've got the mayor's ear better than anybody around here, better than anybody *I* know, anyway. Can you get the mayor to go to bat for us in DC, see if he can get them to issue an order or at least pass the word for the Bureau office here to help us in this?''

''I'll do what I can.''

Morrison stood up. ''How come they want Norelli and me at the ten o'clock meet?''

Harkness shrugged. ''Flanagan wants to pick your brains. Rub you up and down a little. The blowtorch is passing hands, Joe. The Hall feels it so they grab it and aim it at the super, who turns it on Flanagan and he on . . . I bet you can guess. Hunter is making life very uncomfortable for the mayor. The longer this goes, the worse it is for him. And nobody likes to see the mayor squirm more than Alderman Hunter.''

"So maybe it will help us with the mayor, going to bat for us in Washington.''

"Maybe.''

Morrison got up. "You know, Jim, I swear I'm getting more paranoid every day. I got a note to be in my boss's office first thing. I don't know what Goldman wants. I don't even know if I trust him. I never knew him before he took over O.C. He's smooth, so smooth I think he lives inside Jiffy Lube. I don't know, what do you think of him?''

"He's been around, Joe. Lots of connections. Never heard anything bad about him.'' He saw that Morrison did not look convinced. "Come on, Joe, a little oil isn't an Exxon spill.''

"You know, last night I almost didn't call my partner because I didn't know whether I could trust *him*.'' Morrison shook his head.

"How long you been downtown now?''

"About two years, a little more.''

"Wait'll you been here six or seven. See you upstairs at ten, Joe.''

IT WAS A QUARTER to nine when Morrison walked down the hall to Ted Goldman's office.

"What happened to you?'' Goldman asked, eyeing him the same way Harkness had. "You going to behave like that on a weeknight, you should at least go home and shower and change before coming to work.''

"Where I was shacked up was over on the west side with Franco Norelli following up a lead on the whereabouts of La-trona Meek. After that I spent an hour or more over at Four, where I managed to dig up an electric razor but nothing from Giorgio Armani. Sorry about that.''

Goldman, without a hair out of place, looked and smelled like he had stepped out of the shower just minutes earlier and into a sprinkling of eau de cologne strong enough to kill wasps on contact. The suitcoat on the hanger behind the door to his office might have carried an Armani label. "And did you find her?" Goldman asked.

"No. She's still missing."

"Nothing at all on her *yet*? A police department big as ours can't find a twelve-year-old girl?"

"She's been seen, so we know she's around somewhere. That's all I can tell you," which, of course, wasn't true. "But we got a lot of people looking."

"Where?"

"Around the Henry Horner Homes. She's scared, from what I heard. Scared of us. And it's not us she should be scared of."

"You think she's still over there?"

Morrison felt like a boxer bobbing to avoid left jabs. "Don't know. We're going to give it a daytime canvas. Already started, I think, out of Four." He had asked Sergeant Gerherdt to relay to Chatham when he took over the watch command that they would like some eyes roving around Horner in case the little girl might decide to come back to her cousin's home. "I'll keep you posted. Is that what you wanted to see me about?"

"Well, for one thing, yes. I also wanted to remind you that I don't want to hear things from somebody else that as head of O.C. I should already know about."

"I've been keeping you informed. There just hasn't been a whole helluva lot to pass on."

"The Horner Homes?"

"I heard about that at one in the morning. Norelli and I went out there and were there till four-thirty. I could've called you at home but I didn't think you would have appreciated that."

"Right about that." Goldman fiddled with the knot of his seventy-five-dollar silk tie. "You're going to be at the staff meeting, you and Norelli, I hear."

Bet you heard it just before you left me that note last night, Morrison thought. "We've been asked, yeah."

"Why?"

"I don't know. I just got a note saying our presence was

requested. Way I figure, they want an update from the horse's mouth.''

"I'm going, too.''

"You are?'' Goldman, Morrison knew, was not normally invited for the daily ten o'clocker.

"I'm going because I told Flanagan I had some ideas about the PT case I wanted to kick around with them and would like to get some feedback.''

"Maybe that's why they invited us, Norelli and me.''

Goldman seemed uneasy for the moment. "Maybe.'' It did not sound sincere.

Morrison figured that Goldman had come up with those ideas *after* learning that he and Norelli were slated to attend.

"Oh, and, by the way''—keep the man informed, Morrison was thinking, better no surprises, wasn't that what Goldman had said, and as long as they were going to be at the meeting anyway—"before I forget, we did accomplish something on our sunrise mission this morning. We got a picture of the kid.''

"You did?''

"Yeah, from a cousin of the mother. You'll see it at the meeting. They're making prints of it right now.'' Morrison half-smiled at his boss. "Now all we gotta do is find her. Right?''

"That would not be a bad idea.''

"I better go straighten up a little. Wouldn't want the brass to think I was rutting around all night.''

"Never hurts to look good, Joe.''

JIMMY PAGNANO HAD A lot of things on his mind that day, too, but one of them was not Vaughn Swayze. That is, not until he got the call from his friend at the morgue. He put aside the other worries that had been laid on him by Joe-sep Alessi . . . things like where the hell was that punk Danny Pack and where the hell was the little shine kid who could finger Pack . . . and dialed the Detroit number Swayze had given him. He got Swayze's wife.

"Veebee's out sellin' his little socks off,'' she told him. "I think he's in Livonia today or maybe Ypsilanti. I can't keep it all straight, where he goes, you know?''

"Well, tell Veebee I heard we can probably get for him what he wants next week. After Monday, which is Labor Day, they're due to do a little housecleaning over there. Tell him.''

"You mean they got the—''

"Fellate, shut up. Just listen.''

"*Felice.*''

"Shut up, is what I said. Felice, Fellate, whatever. Tell him he's gotta be over here Tuesday. I'll explain all the details to him then. Got that?''

"Sure, I got it.'' Her tone of voice changed. "You want me to come along, too, Jimmy?''

"Not this time. You gotta stay home till you're called, then you come over to the big city.''

"Oh, too bad.''

Pagnano envisioned her sitting over there on the edge of the bed sucking on the fire-red-polished nail of her index finger. "Tell Vaughn-Boy not to forget to bring a change of clothes and a sackful of money.''

SOLO WAS GETTING TO be a regular magpie these days, Morrison thought when the gangleader called in the afternoon. Maybe Slipball got himself killed or was in such a drug-induced stupor he couldn't make Solo's conversation arrangements anymore. Solo, that bitter little man he had met for the first time in the Gardens not too many nights ago, seemed almost cordial.

He wanted to know what had happened with Melinda Meek's cousin, and Morrison told him. Solo said that on the south side, unlike at the Horner Homes, he could help. It was his old stomping grounds, he said, which Morrison took literally. He still had contacts out there, even some active business associates. He would see what was happening in the Englewood 'hood, he said. That was it. *Good hunting* had become his signature sign-off to Morrison these days, like they were a couple of male-bonded buddies.

"He's being pretty damn cooperative," Morrison said to Norelli later.

"Don't think there's any benevolence in it, Joe. The guy's a user. There's only one thing he wants out of this. If that Lonesome character wasn't facing the next three or four years in the penitentiary he wouldn't be lifting a little toe to help us."

"If he's such a cold bastard, and I don't say he isn't, why do you think he's so concerned about Lonesome Dennis's future?"

"They're real close, Joe. Lonesome could give us Solo on a first-degree murder charge if he wanted. But he'd go to the chair himself before he'd do that—anyway, that's the way they see it in GC. Lonesome's a kind of guy Solo wants around him, not sitting in some cell block down in Menard or Pontiac organizing buggery parties."

"Strange, the beds we get into."

"Yeah. Next time it'll be some wiseguy giving us a gang-banger for a favor of his own."

✛31

DANNY PACK WAS ENJOYING HIMSELF IN CHICAGO. FLUSH with money, hanging out with old pal Winnie Wendell, who had dumped her husband the earthmover operator a year ago and now had her own apartment under her maiden name of Kokonitz, and finding a couple of cronies still around, one of whom turned out to be a ready source of quality cocaine which he and Winnie Kokonitz sucked up their noses when she wasn't working over at Cub Foods or they weren't out cabareting. He was going through money like crazy but he was having a fine time doing it. And he still had another five grand coming as soon as Roy collected it. Which was what possessed him to start making telephone calls.

First he called Roy down in Lauderdale to find out what was going on, but they said at the Yankee Clipper he had already checked out. So he tried the hotel *he* was supposed to be at in New Orleans to see if Roy might have left a message for him there. But Roy hadn't. He knew he should have told Roy where he could be reached in Chicago but at the time he didn't want to hear all the hassling he would get from Roy if he told him he was going to hang around for a while and renew old acquaintances. Roy did everything by the book, in Danny's opinion. Roy had no free spirit in him, that was his problem.

So Danny called their boss in Camden, Connie Damoro, the owner of Jersey Cartage, Aldo Forte's buddy from way back. No, Roy had not come back home. No, he did not know where Roy was. What he did know was that Danny was supposed to be in New Orleans and was not. Where might he be?

"How'd you know I wasn't there if you didn't talk to Roy?"

"They told me from Chicago," Connie said. "They called. They wanted to be sure you were long gone from there, and when they checked the hotel you were supposed to be at, you was not there. That did not make them happy."

"Fuck 'em. We did our job. Didn't leave no loose ends. What difference does it make where I am?"

"Whatta you mean no loose ends? You killed a little kid."

"Couldn't help that, he was there. What else could I do? Anyway, he wasn't that little a kid."

"There is major heat over there. They're bustin' ass to find whoever did this. You aware of that?"

Danny wasn't. He did not read newspapers except for the sports section or watch the tube except for a ballgame, although since he'd been hanging around Winnie Kokonitz's place during the day he'd gotten to watching the talk shows, the ones with themes like wives whose husbands liked to wear lingerie and people who had sex with their parents when they were kids.

"That makes my friend Aldo very nervous, more so than

normal, and that is really fucking major nervous,'' Connie said, feeling pretty nervous himself.

"Tell him to relax. There's no problem. They're a bunch of assholes here anyway. You shoulda seen the guy was our contact. Fat little shit who thought he was Joe Pesci or somebody. Carmen the tough guy, tried to boss everybody around. I didn't like the tub-ass from the start.''

"You know, Danny, some people gotta get a life, you gotta get a head. You got a real attitude problem.''

"That's what they used to tell me in school. I been workin' on it a long time.'' Danny thought that was funny. "Anyway, I wanna find Roy, see if he got the rest of the money from the assholes.''

"Well, I'll ask him if I talk to him. So where can he get hold of you if he calls in?''

Danny was thinking. "You don't think he woulda run out with my dough, do you?''

"Sure, Danny, for five grand he's gonna chuck everything and take off for Tahiti and live in splendor with all the native girls. Jeez, don't you trust anybody?''

"No.''

"You are not winning your fight with the attitude thing, Danny. So how does he get hold of you?''

Danny gave him Winona Kokonitz's telephone number.

In Chicago, Aldo Forte relayed the number to Carmen. It had taken Aldo a few hours to get news of the number due to the convoluted way he conducted his incoming and outgoing telephone activities. But it did not take Carmen more than a few minutes and one telephone call to translate the number into an address.

It was after sundown when he and a pal, Frank Mapes, arrived at 2733 North Clybourn. It was a small entrance stuck between two stores that led to the two apartments above them. The names on the two abutting mail boxes were W. Kokonitz, handprinted in red ink, and Norm & Vera Buckman with the address on a little return-address label the Tuberculosis Society sends each Christmas along with a solicitation letter. Carmen figured the *W* was Winnie. When he rang the bell he got no answer: four more times, the same.

He and his pal Frank went across the street to the Qwik-Stop convenience store, which had a pay phone, and called the number. No answer again. So they went back outside and sat in their car parked across from 2733. There was a light in the apartment to the left of the entranceway but the one to the right was dark. The light in the apartment to the left went out at exactly 11:30, just the time Jay Leno and David Letterman were saying good night to their audiences. They sat there all night but nobody came in or went out the doorway marked 2733.

At seven-thirty a man emerged, looking to be in his fifties, and walked to the bus stop at the corner. "Must be Norm whatever-his-name-is," Carmen said to his pal. They waited until Norm boarded the Chicago Transit Authority 151 bus, and then Carmen said he was going over and see if Vera whatever-her-name was home and maybe if she knew where W. Kokonitz might be.

Five minutes later Carmen was back. Vera was home, very nice, he said. She even went over and knocked on her neighbor's door for him after he told Vera he had an important message for Ms. Kokonitz about a relative of hers who suddenly had taken ill. Ms. Kokonitz was not home and, yes, she was known to Vera as Winnie. She was probably at work, Vera told him. She worked different shifts over at the Cub Foods store, the one on Elston Avenue between Diversey and Fullerton. . . .

When Carmen asked for Winnie Kokonitz at the service desk in Cub Foods, the girl who ordinarily cashed checks or gave aisle directions or took complaints said she thought Winnie wasn't due in until nine but would check for him. The manager came to the desk and told him Winnie was not going to be in at all that day, she was taking some time off and wouldn't be back until the Tuesday after Labor Day.

Carmen asked the manager if by any chance he might know where Winnie Kokonitz could be reached at the moment because he was with an insurance company and had some important business to discuss with her. The manager said he was not allowed to give out that information even if he had it, which he didn't. But one of Winnie's fellow check-out clerks, who overheard part of the conversation, said Winnie told her she was going out of town with her new boyfriend for the long weekend, was leaving right after work yesterday, in fact. She didn't know where they were going, though.

NORELLI AND MORRISON WERE going to be in town and on call, but there was not much they could do unless something broke. Norelli had gone home in the middle of the afternoon on Friday and Morrison was just getting ready to leave when the phone rang in PT headquarters. He answered it.

"Well, this is a first, answering your own phone."

He recognized the voice and wondered what she wanted. "Somehow I didn't expect it to be you."

"Life is full of surprises, isn't it?" Holly Stryker said.

"You could say that."

"*I* certainly could."

A pause. "So as they say, to what do I owe the honor of this call?"

"You go to movies much?"

"No, not much. Why?"

"You ever see *Sleeping with the Enemy*?"

"That what you called about?" Morrison tried not to sound as uneasy as he felt.

"No. Just want you to know I don't harbor grudges."

"That's nice."

"And that I thought I would pass something along to you and see if you might care to comment on it. Pure business."

Another pause. Finally Morrison said, "Am I supposed to guess what it is?"

"Alderman Hunter is calling for a grand-jury investigation. Into the handling of the investigation of the murder of Rayfield Tees."

"A grand jury?" Morrison was surprised.

"That's what he told me."

"He hasn't any grounds."

"He apparently thinks he has. He's going with it on the six o'clock news tonight."

"It's just more bullshit political flak."

"He's serious. He and his attorneys are filing on Tuesday."

"What's his angle?"

"He knows who your mysterious witness is."

Morrison felt the chicken salad sandwich he had for lunch do a somersault in his stomach.

"And why you're all keeping it such a secret," she said.

"And why is that?"

"Because, according to his sources, the witness is a cop."

"A cop?"

"The cop who earlier was rumored to have carried out the hit. Would you care to comment on that?"

"Jesus Christ," Morrison said, sounding indignant but with a smile on his face. "He really knows . . . Jesus. How did he find out?"

"Sources. Like everybody else, he's got his."

"That son of a bitch. And we tried so hard—" He cut himself off, like shutting off an indiscretion.

"You want to elaborate?"

"I can't, I've nothing to say . . ."

"Is there anything else? You sure?"

"Yeah, well . . ."

"Say it."

"Wow."

"You really are one real son of a bitch. I can't believe you—"

He hung up, the smile on his face broadening.

✦32

VAUGHN SWAYZE WAS SO EXCITED DRIVING OVER TO CHI-cago Tuesday morning he had to make pit stops in Ann Arbor, Kalamazoo and Portage, that last in Indiana, turning it into the longest one-way trip from Detroit to Chicago since the Windy City was added to his sales territory. He drove straight to the bungalow Little Red was renting on the northwest side only to discover that the redhead did not have a telephone there. So he dropped off the briefcase containing the ten thousand dollars for safekeeping—Chicago, like Detroit, he figured, was not the kind of city you should wander around in with all the cash in the world that you were able to beg, steal or borrow in a duffle bag—and shot the bull with Little Red before going out in search of a telephone to make contact with Jimmy Pagnano.

MORRISON AND TIMOTHY DOYLE were lunching *al fresco* at a little table whose dirty white umbrella carried the label Vienna Hot Dogs, behind a storefront that billed itself as Mort's Sandwich Shop, on Wells Street just south of the Board of Trade. It was one of those places for people in a hurry, more a carry-out joint although inside you could sit on a high stool at a counter or lean over one of the stand-up tables between it and where you put in your order for a sandwich and a soda pop or coffee. And for the summer crowd there were small tables wedged into the areaway outside between it and the building next door. Morrison was trying to eat an Italian beef sandwich without getting the watery gravy all over his shirt and tie; Timothy Doyle, whose idea it was to meet there, was having less trouble with a double hamburger, although occasionally an eely grilled onion would slither out when he took a bite and fall into the paper plate he was hunched over.

After they got their food from inside and sat down, Doyle asked if there was any word of the girl. Morrison said there was nothing as of noon, the end of their daily get-together over at Four. She was now referred to as Where's Waldo among those on the task force.

A hovering bee was interested in Doyle's hamburger. He waved at it with his burger but it persisted, following the moving burger as if attached by an invisible wire. Finally he put the hamburger down and swatted at the bee with both hands, which finally drove it to another table. That out of the way, he said to Morrison, "Clout is a wonderful thing to have. You guys sure have a lot of it."

"We do? I mean right, we do." He looked with sudden interest across the table. "Something happen I should know about, Tim?"

"Well, you got us into this with you. Fax from Washington was on the SAC's desk when he came in at eight this morning. You not only got clout, Joe, you got rapid-transit clout. That's something we rarely experience here."

Nice going, Jim Harkness, Morrison thought. "Well, I'm glad to see the mayor's still got some. He should, he's a Democrat and the President's a Democrat and Illinois is a swing state and the mayor carried it for him despite all those downstate Republicans. I'd hate to think the system was breaking down."

"We've been talking about this most of the morning, the SAC and me. And we've been talking to Washington, too. We've decided that by giving you our full cooperation we might also be able to serve our own interests. That's the way the SAC put it in his return memo to the Hoover Building in DC. We'll go over it, you and me, in detail tonight. You don't mind working a little overtime, do you, Joe?"

"That's what I've been doing the past couple of weeks."

"I want you to meet me around nine." Before Morrison could ask why Doyle wanted to meet at that hour, Doyle said, "I've got my reasons. Just trust me on that, okay?"

Morrison shrugged. "Your place or mine?"

"Don't know where yet. I've got things to work out this

afternoon. It won't be either your place or mine, though, I can tell you that much. I'll let you know where later today."

Doyle picked up his waxy cup and sucked on the straw until a grating gurgle from the bottom of it told him only chipped ice remained of his 7-Up.

"You mentioned *your* interests . . . in that memo," Morrison said.

"We've got some."

Morrison waited. Doyle said nothing. "But you're not going to tell me what they are."

"I don't know why you need to know—but on the other hand it probably doesn't really matter. You want to catch the guys who killed Manny Peters and the kid. You want to clear the case, clean the streets of a couple of killers. Great. And you'll get everybody off the mayor's back and the CPD's back. And your bosses will be happy and the mayor can get back to the important things in his life like his reelection campaign. Well, I hope we can help you put away the bad guys. But that's not our real concern . . . we think we've got a shot at bringing down a *capo*, maybe two, along with them. That's our major interest."

"What time you think you'll know about tonight?"

"Can't say. Which is why I've got to get moving. For now, Joe, this is just between us. No partner, no boss, no brass, *nobody* over at 11th and State. Not until we get things sorted out tonight." He reached over and took hold of Morrison's arm.

"Okay. But tomorrow—"

"Tomorrow's tomorrow. Talk to you later."

"HALSEY HAWKINS IS THE name," Jimmy Pagnano said, his hand on Swayze's shoulder as they stood under the canopy in front of D'Amico's Ristorante. "You just ask for him. He's got a flattop, a big guy, looks sorta like Dick the Bruiser, the wrestler. Remember him?"

Swayze shook his head. "I'm not big into sports."

"Never heard of Dick the Bruiser? Don't like sports? I thought you were big on the Bulls, you and the redhead guy, those trips out to Deerfield to watch them practice.''

"Oh, that. A different game. I mean I don't care a hoot about basketball.'' Care a hoot, Pagnano said to himself, my seventy-year-old aunt, she used to say that, didn't care a *hoot* for Kennedy, didn't care a *hoot* about California the one time she went there. Where is this fucking guy from anyway? "We were workin' something there. I told you about it.''

"I remember.''

"But that's all over, heat got to us on that one. Little Red and me decided to drop it.''

"Lucky for the Bulls.'' Pagnano gave him a quick smile. "Not having to go head-to-head with you two.''

"Yeah . . . So I just go over there, the morgue, ask for him—''

Pagnano held up his hand. "Here is *exactly* what you do. You go over there tonight after ten o'clock. He works the ten-to-six shift. You go in the back side, the west side of the building, same place they bring in the stiffs. There's like a loading dock with a door next to it. That hour of the night the front entrance is locked—so nobody can escape.'' Pagnano thought that was funny. "You go through the door and there's a desk or counter and there'll be somebody behind it, probably Halsey, but who knows?''

"Probably not a lot of people around that hour anyway, huh?''

Pagnano gave Swayze a condescending look. "People don't necessarily die during regular working hours. Especially those who end up in the morgue. Fact is, three o'clock in the afternoon's probably down time, three o'clock in the morning's sometimes rush hour. So you just ask for him—*Halsey Hawkins.*''

"Got it.'' Swayze repeated the name phonetically. "Hall-zee Haw-kinz.'' He was sweating, dabbing at his forehead with a handkerchief. "Hot out here. Hot.''

"And be sure you got your belongings, your whole outfit . . . underwear, shirt, suit, tie, shoes, You got your ring, your watch, your wallet, your change, your keys, everything you'd have on you if you did get yourself killed. Understand?''

"Got it."

"And you got it in a big brown paper bag, like they give you at a grocery store."

Swayze gave him a blank look.

"The size of it . . . the brown bag . . . bigger than a lunch bag . . . never mind. Just have the stuff. He'll take you off somewhere. He'll ask you some questions for the forms that gotta be filled in. He'll take the stuff from you and he'll explain the procedure you just follow. Okay?"

"So when do I get the body?"

"Hang on. He'll tell you that. Probably not for a couple of days. He's gotta set the thing up. But it'll be before next week because that's when they clear out the John Does lying around over there."

"When's Felice come over, you know, to make the identification?"

"Who knows? Maybe she won't have to. According to Halsey it maybe can all be done on paper. He just screws around with the paperwork and suddenly you're a dead man with the papers to prove it and they show you been identified and your body's been released to a funeral home where it's roasted, only it'll be John Doe who's roasted." Pagnano smiled at him again. "But don't worry, Vaughn-Boy, your little lady'll get the ashes and the urn."

"Good, good," Swayze said, wiping the perspiration from his forehead with his now soggy white hankie.

"Look," Pagnano said, "I got to get going, got other things to tend to. You let me know how tonight works out." He slapped Swayze on the back. "And don't forget it's C.O.D. Halsey's gonna tell you exactly how to make the final . . . installment." Pagnano signaled to the parking attendant, who had been perched on a stool by the door to D'Amico's, from which he now leaped as if he had just been goosed and raced off into the parking lot.

Pagnano handed the kid who had pulled his Cadillac Eldorado up to the curb a five and as he was getting into the car shouted, "Have a nice night, Vaughn-Boy. You'll like it there, it's very *cool* inside." His laughter disappeared with him into the car. Swayze had parked a block and a half down the street so he didn't have to lay anything on the car hiker, money for the moment being as tight as it was.

CARMEN WAS GETTING MORE pissed with each passing half-hour. He had been sitting in front of 2733 North Clybourn all afternoon. He and his pal Frank had tried the telephone and the doorbell first thing in the morning, first thing being seven A.M, but got no response. That was all right, he thought, the ponytail and his girlfriend had stayed over for one more night wherever it was they went for the holiday and were coming back in the morning. He often did that himself after pontoon-boating the weekend away around Lake Koshkonong in Wisconsin.

But she was supposed to be back at work. Nine o'clock. Unless maybe she was working a later shift, the Vera woman said she worked different shifts over there. So when nobody showed up at 2733 by nine-thirty they went over to Cub Foods. Carmen went in. There was a different girl behind the service counter. And, no, she said, Winnie Kokonitz was not there. And, yes, she was supposed to be there. That's all the girl knew. The manager Carmen had talked to before the weekend answered the page on the loudspeaker that echoed through the vast spaces of the almost-empty supermarket. Winnie was late, he said, when he got to the customer service counter. Which was not unlike her. Something must have come up. The manager asked Carmen if there was a message he wanted to leave or a name and number where she could reach him. Carmen said no but thanks.

So they went back to 2733.

At three P.M. Carmen went to the Qwik-Stop and called Cub Foods, asked for Winnie Kokonitz. Still not there.

"If I wanted to spend my life on a fucking stake-out I'd a been a cop," Carmen said after he was back in the passenger seat of the car.

"I know, it's a pain," his pal Frank said. "But what else we gonna do?"

"Nothing." Carmen shifted uncomfortably, wishing they

were in a bigger car. The Honda Accord was inconspicuous enough but not really built with Carmen's shape in mind. "Where the hell is the little jizzbag anyway?"

"You don't like this guy."

"I didn't like the little fucker to begin with. Ever since I saw the punk in a ponytail and dressed like a spic. First I thought he was fruit. With the girlfriend and all, maybe I was wrong there. But then I saw right off he's a fuck-up . . . world class. Then I got a job I'm going to really like. And then I can't find the little fucker." He whacked the dashboard with his fist. "Everybody in this city is missing. The ponytail, the kid. The kid don't have a ponytail and she's a *girl*."

"They'll turn up."

Carmen reached down and fiddled with the radio, the Cubs postgame show over now, trying to find some music that might calm him down but getting an Hispanic station instead that brought back to mind with detail Danny Pack standing there in the hotel room with the white suit and the gold buttons and the black shirt with the funny collar. He swore again and switched off the radio. "You know about the kid, not the one we're going to whack, the other one, the girl, with all the connections we got in this city, you'd think we'd have found her by now. I mean, it's been days," he said, trying to think of something besides Danny Pack. "Things are changing, you know. Couple years ago, we'd a had her in half a day. There isn't the respect out there like there used to be." Carmen shook his head in dismay and disgust.

DID THEY LIKE TO play games or was it they just wanted to make it unpleasant for him because he got the mayor to call in a favor in Washington, Morrison wondered as he drove out of the city on the Edens Expressway. He had not even gotten the afternoon call Tim Doyle had promised until seven that night, just about the time he was thinking of packing it in.

Even then Doyle was brief, just gave him the name of a motel, the room number, and nine o'clock.

It wasn't even in Cook County. It was in Lake County, the town of Highwood, halfway to the Wisconsin border. A good hour's drive with all the roads torn up and lanes blocked off during the pave-and-patch construction season. It was still summer-warm and there was not much of a breeze, but the air streaming into his open window felt good and there were a lot of stars visible in the sky out here away from the smog and glare of the city lights.

The motel was an old one and not even a quarter of the parking spaces were occupied outside the room when Morrison pulled in just before nine. Probably was on its last legs, he thought, now that Fort Sheridan, the sprawling army base just down the road, was closing down. Morrison remembered when the fort was Fifth Army Headquarters and a thriving place before all the Defense Department cutbacks. When he was in Homicide some five years ago he had been in a group of four sent up there to conduct a kind of seminar for the military-police unit assigned to the post on murder investigations. He thought it was kind of strange and a waste of time going to all that trouble when he found out there had been only one homicide on the base in the previous forty years and that was when some G.I. went on a rampage after returning from a tour of duty in the Korean War.

He found room 115 on the ground floor of the two-level motel. The curtains were closed but he could see there was a light on inside. He gave a quick rap on the door. A moment later Doyle opened it a crack. He gave Morrison a big smile and opened the door all the way. "Right on time, Joe."

Doyle's tie was pulled down and his collar open, sleeves rolled up to his elbows, his curly blond hair tousled. Looked like he had had a tough day at the office, a long one, Morrison thought as he stepped inside. Could have passed for a frazzled accountant couple of days before April 15th if he wasn't wearing a shoulder holster.

The other man sitting at the small round table in the corner of the room near the window looked fresher in a polo shirt and no shoulder holster. There were cream-colored file folders and a small state-of-the-art tape recorder on the table.

"Nice night for a drive, Joe," Doyle said. "Get you out of the city for a change." He turned to the other man, who was beginning to stand up. "Meet Joe Morrison," he said to the man.

"Hi," the man said, and extended a hand. "Angelo Franconi . . . nice to meet you."

✦33

THEY TALKED UNTIL MIDNIGHT. ANGELO FRANCONI WAS NOT an agent of the FBI, Doyle explained, but what was known as an infiltrator. He had come out from New York after things got a little too warm for him there and, while still in his mid-twenties, had decided on a career change—as Doyle put it. Since his arrival and after the appropriate introductions, he had been slowly but steadily working his way up in the Aldo Forte street crew. Lately the rise had been accelerating at a velocity that had surprised the few in the Bureau who knew about him.

Angelo Franconi cleared up a number of things for Morrison. He confirmed that the hit on Manny Peters was designed as punishment and as a message to anyone who might entertain thoughts of stealing from the crews. It was ordered by Aldo Forte after Manny had lifted a narcotics package worth a couple hundred thousand dollars that was scheduled to become the joint property of Forte and Joe Alessi. The two hit men had been brought in from out of town, somewhere out east, Angelo did not know exactly where. They screwed up by killing the boy who just happened to be on the scene. It was an awkward situation from a public-relations standpoint and uncomfortable because of the heat, but at first the thinking was it would blow over. This had all been discussed with Gussy Tuscano himself. Angelo said he had been there at the time.

But then the word about a witness, the girl, made its way directly to Gussy "and all kinds of shit hit the fan," as Angelo put it. "Gussy has a source at police headquarters for that kind of information. I've no idea who it is and I don't think Aldo Forte does either. Gussy told us a witness could finger the guys, and that one of the guys could maybe be turned and finger Aldo, and who knows where it might work its way to, who might end up taking a fall? Aldo got the message loud and clear. The two guys from out of town were dead men as soon as Gussy got the word about the witness. So is the witness . . ." Doyle was nodding in corroboration as Angelo talked.

"Only thing is," Angelo added, "they can't find one of the guys. Both were supposed to be in and out of town, do the job and disappear."

"One of the guys?" Morrison said.

Angelo looked uneasy for the first time. "Yeah, one. The other I hear has already been taken care of. Out of town somewhere."

"You got a name on him?"

Franconi shook his head. "Maybe I can find out. But the other one, the guy they're looking for, his name's Danny Pack. They think he's back in Chicago. Shouldn't be, but apparently is and everybody is hunting for him, as you can imagine."

"Not a real smart guy," Doyle said.

"The job doesn't call for college credentials," Angelo said. "And from what I gather this guy's not one to do much thinking before he acts. He's the one that shot the kid and screwed up the whole thing from the beginning . . . at least that's the way I hear it."

"How much do they know about the girl," Morrison asked.

"This one?" Angelo said, pulling a Xerox of the front page of the CPD *Daily Bulletin* with the picture of Latrona Meek in the lower righthand corner and the notation that she was a missing child and the enigmatic reference to the fact that she might have information "related to a felony under current investigation."

"Goddamn," Morrison said, "how'd they—"

"They know as much as you guys do," Angelo said. "I told you Gussy's got a source. Soon as this came off the press he had a copy in his hand and the word that this was *the* witness. A half-hour later Gussy's guy, Cockeye he calls him, drops off a copy of it to Aldo Forte at the Amalfi Club. Now everybody's got a copy.''

"Swell guys you got working with you downtown," Doyle said. "Twelve-year-old girl's carrying a death sentence around with her and one of CPD's finest is I.D.'ing her for the executioner.''

"You know," Angelo said, "the girl could get a pass on this if they find Pack first and then lose him forever. According to Aldo, the girl's nothing to him if both hit men no longer exist.''

"Which is why *we*," Doyle said, "would like to find Danny Pack alive. And why *we* would like the CPD to find the girl before they do.''

"They aren't about to wait around," Angelo said. "They find her, she's dead.''

"They got any leads to her whereabouts that maybe we don't?" Morrison asked.

"Not that I know of. They been all over the west side. They know you got somebody watching the building where she lives and they're stuck to her mother. Like you, I'd say right now they're mostly watching and waiting." Angelo took the copy of the *Daily Bulletin* back from Morrison and put it with the papers on the table. "Look, if I hear anything you'll be the first to know, but by the time I hear it, it'll probably be too late.''

"From here on, Joe," Doyle said, "you and Angelo will work direct on this. You both keep me informed but you don't need a middleman if things start happening.''

They worked out arrangements so Morrison could contact Angelo directly and vice versa. "I guess we've got to have some kind of code name for you," Morrison said.

"How about Angel?" Franconi said. "That's what my girlfriend calls me.''

"A little close to Angelo, don't you think?" Morrison said. Doyle said, "Gabriel.''

Franconi grinned. "As in the guy who blows the horn up

there,'' his eyes going up to the ceiling, ''or as in Peter Gabriel, the guy who sings?''

''Whichever you want,'' Morrison said.

The grin on Franconi's face faded. ''You know, I'm very close to becoming made. I don't want this to screw it up. I mean, I want to help you out, Joe, and I sure don't want to see a little girl get killed, but I don't want to blow my cover over this. I hope that is not on the agenda,'' this hope aimed at Doyle.

''It is not,'' Doyle said. ''Washington wants to see who we can bring down on this. We want to see how high we can go. We're talking Forte and maybe Alessi.''

Angelo seemed uneasy again. ''I don't think Alessi's vulnerable . . . Forte can be tied to it, he made the arrangements. The hitters can finger him, I think. But Alessi, I don't think that's a good possibility—''

''He's not in it now?'' Morrison said. ''Looking for this Pack guy, the girl?''

''Well, he is and he isn't.''

Franconi seemed uncomfortable, Morrison thought, and wondered . . .

''It's in Aldo Forte's ballpark. Gussy Tuscano made that clear to everybody. Alessi, he's on the fringe. Everybody's on the fringe, every crew in the city, 'cause Gussy wants this thing taken care of.''

Doyle looked at Morrison, seeing his curiosity about Franconi's reactions to the mention of Alessi, and decided they'd better get it out on the table. ''Angelo's a little squeamish on the subject of Alessi, Joe . . . he's got a girlfriend . . .''

''You keep her out of this,'' Angelo said. ''What's she got to do with it?''

Doyle looked back to Morrison. ''She's Joe Alessi's daughter.''

''Jesus,'' Morrison said, ''when you infiltrate you really infiltrate.''

''She's a *totally* different matter. Let's just drop it, okay?''

Morrison, looking at Franconi, decided it was best not to pursue it at the moment.

"Alessi may be a longshot," Doyle said to Morrison, "but," turning to Angelo, "one we can't overlook either."

"Look, I'm not trying to protect Alessi, for chrissake. I mean I want to bring down Gussy Tuscano. You know that, Tim. We been talking about that for what—a year or more now?" To Morrison: "I get made, I can maybe bring Tuscano and the rest of his people with him. I been working for this all along, I've had to do some stuff . . . I'm in this to bring down somebody big. I just got to be made, and I'm almost *there* . . ." Franconi's intensity was apparent in his voice. "And all of a sudden we're talking about bringing down *the* two guys who can get me made. I'm getting a bad reading here."

Doyle said, "Relax, Angelo. We don't have to bring them down right away. There's no statute of limitations on murder. Morrison can clear his case, we can save the girl and we can use this later when we need a bombshell, when the time is right. We know your feelings, so just take it easy."

"Do you know they never got a guy *made* before," Angelo said to Morrison, "in the history of the whole FBI. I am this far," he held his thumb and index finger about an inch apart, "from being the first. They got at guys and got 'em to break the code, testify. After the fact. But they never got a guy inside, while things were happening. Well, we're almost *there*."

"We're getting a little off the track here," Doyle said. "Let's concentrate on our next step, see where it takes us. What's vital is that you two be in touch. Now let's call it a night."

On the ride back to Chicago, Morrison felt a kind of awe for Angelo Franconi, thinking about the double life this young man had chosen for himself. He knew damn well he himself could never have managed it.

BACK HOME, MORRISON CHECKED in with the hotline downtown, hoping there was a message from Solo. There wasn't. There wasn't even a full shot of bourbon left in the bottle in the kitchen cabinet. Must have finished it off the other night, didn't remember, though. There was still a bottle of schnapps and he poured himself a glass, about five ounces, no ice. The first sip traveled all the way down and settled like lava at the bottom of his stomach. He hadn't had schnapps in a long time; he thought of the nights when he was still living at home near the end, waiting for the divorce papers, sleeping alone, and the bottle he used to keep there in the closet of his bedroom, replacing it every Monday or so. Bad times. Bad thoughts of them. It was Linda, the expatriate living in New York, who got him off schnapps, got him off taking a shot of it before bed. He took another swig and looked at his watch. About two-thirty in New York. He pictured Linda lying on her side, blond hair splayed out against the pillow, mouth closed with a little smile that moved up the side of it. And a leg sticking out from under the sheet, her beautiful curved calf, slender foot, terrific ankles. He wondered what she was dreaming about at that moment. Him? He'd sleep on that.

✦34

MORRISON WAS LATE GETTING IN THE NEXT MORNING, HELD captive by his own thoughts in a coffeeshop in Rogers Park, where he sat at the counter reading a newspaper. There was nothing in the paper about the case. Alderman Hunter had not followed through on his threat to file with the grand jury yesterday which was no big surprise. He had thundered on Friday night, accused and judged and damned. Well, the reverend got his face on camera and his name in the paper over the weekend, which was what he wanted anyway.

Thinking of Hunter reminded him that Holly Stryker had not had anything in the Saturday *Metro* or Tuesday's paper either. Which struck him as a little strange after the way she was talking Friday night. Well, it was nice to flip through the pages and see that most of the violence, at least of the moment, was relegated to Sarajevo or Mogadishu or Miami. Chicago, at least this particular morning, had apparently nothing much to worry about other than a threatened schoolteacher strike and the mayor's new plan to bring riverboat gambling to the banks of the Chicago River.

He kept going over what Angelo Franconi had told them the night before and found himself full of questions which he began writing down in his pocket notebook. In the morning's clear light, there were a lot of things that begged for answers. He tried at least to work the questions together into some order over a third cup of coffee and get them on paper before driving down to 11th and State.

CARMEN WAS LATE GETTING going that morning, too, having hung around Clybourn until midnight, when he and his pal finally packed it in. He tried Winnie Kokonitz's telephone number as soon as he woke up just before eight. No answer. He was beginning to wonder if Danny Pack had found out they were looking for him and had run, taking the supermarket bimbo along with him.

VAUGHN SWAYZE WAS SNORING contentedly, his chest heaving as he lay on the small bed in the back bedroom of the bungalow Red Ryan was renting. His meeting with Halsey Hawkins at the morgue was all he could have hoped for. A body would soon be forthcoming, a piece of cake was the way Hawkins put it. In a week he and his devoted wife would be on their way to realizing the big-time stake he'd been dreaming about for years. All he had to do now was wait and establish residence at a motel here and make a lot of calls on customers this week so his being in Chicago would look legitimate.

So after the good news from Halsey Hawkins, he and Little Red had hit the town, actually it was just one nightclub down on Rush Street, a pricey place featuring a trio and a beautiful blonde billed as a "chanteuse" and a comedian who got his laughs from profanity and insults. They blew a bundle and put it on Little Red's Visa card because there was still some air in it, whereas the four cards Swayze had in his wallet were already over the credit limits. They didn't get back to the bungalow until after four A.M.

ANGELO ARRIVED AT THE Amalfi Club at ten and got the message not to stray from the premises because Aldo Forte wanted to talk as soon as he returned from making some business calls from his pay phones of the day.

MORRISON WAS IN TED Goldman's office just before lunch when the uniformed policewoman stuck her head in the door and told him he had a call on the hotline.

"Isn't Norelli down there?"

"He is, but the man said he only wanted to talk to you."

"He have a name?"

"Don't know, Norelli just sent me down here to get you."

"Okay." Morrison got up, thinking of Solo, and walked quickly back down the hall.

But it wasn't Solo.

"Gabriel," the voice on the other end of the line said. "I think we should talk."

"Right, you got a place in mind?"

"I'm coming downtown. Meeting my girl for lunch. How about you pick me up, say, two-thirty in front of Buckingham Fountain, west side of it, on Columbus Drive?"

"I'll be there."

"You got something that doesn't look like a police car, marked or unmarked they all look the same except to maybe Mother Teresa."

"I'll use my own car. It's a Chevy Cavalier, dark green, two-door."

"I'll be looking for it. See you about two-thirty."

ANGELO "GABRIEL" FRANCONI DID not look like an undercover nor did he look like a tourist as he got up from where he was sitting on the rim of the huge fountain reading a newspaper when Morrison drove up. He had the walk of an athlete, a little bounce to it, a certain cocksureness, Morrison thought. He was wearing aviator sunglasses and another polo shirt that showed the taper of his body and the muscular arms with black hair tightly curled like that on his head. Now Angelo dropped the newspaper in a wire trash can at the curb and got in next to Morrison. "Nice day," he said as he closed the car door on the warm bath of sunlight outside. "Summer doesn't want to quit."

Morrison shifted into drive and headed north through Grant Park. "Yeah, good day to be outside."

Morrison took a right on Monroe Street and drove over to Lake Shore Drive.

"I wanted to talk to you about last night," Angelo said. "I wanted to clear up a couple of things. I also got a couple new slants for you this morning." Angelo once again seemed a little uneasy, Morrison thought. "So you want to just drive around or should we go sit down somewhere?"

"Whatever you want." Morrison was on Lake Shore Drive now heading south, then reversed himself. "Actually, I'd rather we stopped. We can park in the lot at Meigs Field," Morrison said, referring to the private airport on a plot of landfill in the lake south and east of downtown. "Shouldn't run into anybody over there."

When they got to Meigs, Morrison cut the engine and took out notebook and pen. The lot was nearly empty, not a place where people left their cars. The private airport's clientele usually arrived in limousines or taxis or left by them. There were only a few puddle-jumping commercial flights in and out daily, but the airport was still busy with corporate planes and the private toys of the privileged taking advantage of the field's five-minute round trip to downtown Chicago.

Angelo looked out across Burnham Harbor with its yachts and sailboats moored between the airstrip and the city. In Chicago they called every marina a harbor. Beyond the boats and across the Drive, Soldier Field stood out like an anachronism—the bank of classic columns at the top of each long wall giving it the look of an uneroded Parthenon. The Bears still played their football games there, but it was a far cry from the soup-bowl modern stadiums fashioned more after the Roman Coliseum so that people could look down on the action and yet feel a proximity to it like they did when the lions ate up the Christians or the gladiators beat each other to death. Soldier Field was more like an amphitheater, a long oval where Ben Hur might have driven his chariot around its track, which is why it was less than revered by professional football fans. It did have one claim to fame, besides the Bears, as every tour guide was quick to point out; Soldier Field was the site of the famous Dempsey-Tunney heavyweight title fight in 1927, the ''long count,'' the one where the referee gave Tunney about fifteen seconds to get back on his feet and enable him to retain by decision the championship belt he had won from Dempsey the year before. When Morrison first heard the story all he could think was that it sounded like something that would happen in Chicago.

''You a Bear fan?'' Angelo asked, still looking out at the stadium.

''Isn't everybody? Bears and Bulls, the only things that hold this city together. Aren't you?''

''I was never much on allegiances, you know, to sports teams. Where I grew up, you didn't follow them all that much.''

''I thought you were from New York.''

''I am. But by where, I didn't mean the city. I meant where in it. In the homes, was in a couple of them. I didn't have any family. I was in foster homes, but by the time I was old enough to get into sports I was in public homes. I boxed and played the other sports but never followed the teams. Everybody was mostly into survival and getting whatever you could without getting hurt or caught.'' He shrugged. ''You don't want my life story.'' And added silently, *Neither do I*.

Angelo turned in his seat so he faced Morrison. ''So let's talk business. First, let me repeat, this whole thing was not my idea or my choice. I think maybe I got that across last night.''

''It wasn't a decision they'd let you make.''

''Yeah, well, it wasn't.'' Angelo fiddled with his sunglasses. ''I don't mean I don't want to help you in this. This whole thing with the little kid bothers the hell out of me. I can see them all knocking each other off, who gives a shit.'' He got a noncommittal look back from Morrison. "But a kid, that's something else."

Morrison waited.

"Well, like I say, one thing's one thing. A kid who just happens to be a problem is another. Look, I left a sitdown this morning where they were talking about *how* they were going to knock off the kid when they find her. Just one of your ordinary morning coffee klatches, right? One guy says, just break her neck and throw her off a building over there where she lives or maybe out a window. Happens all the time. Kids aren't careful over there. They're stupid, he says. Kids do that kind of shit to each other in that neighborhood. She'll just be another statistic. Another guy says, hey, why not just give her a wham-bang of crack and O.D. her. That won't raise an eyebrow anywhere over there. Everyday occurrence. No, Aldo says, she got to disappear forever. That's the best way. Back and forth they kick it around, like they were talking about getting rid of some pet turtle or a bellied-up goldfish."

"Which is why we've got to find her first."

"Let me tell you one thing, Joe, even if you do, they're still coming after her. As long as that Danny Pack is still out there. They're scared of him. He can nail Aldo to this. The way wiseguys these days have been falling off the bandwagon to save their own asses, Aldo's got reason to sweat. Aldo said it again this morning . . . the kid can nail Pack, Pack can nail him, so things being as they are, the kid has got to go. And . . ." Angelo pointed at the notepad . . . "you might want to write this down for future reference, Aldo says Gussy Tuscano told him that Gussy *would* know where you had her hid if you got to her first."

A Lear jet roared overhead taking off, drowning out what Morrison was starting to say. When it was past and climbing into the pastel blue sky above Chicago, he repeated himself. "Maybe we could be real lucky and find this Pack guy first."

"Or we . . . maybe I should say they . . . could find him. That would solve the problem too," Angelo said. "Which brings me to another thing I learned this morning. They got a line on a girl Pack supposedly is holed up with here in Chicago. How they got it I don't know. Who the girl is, I don't know either. But Aldo thinks they're close. There's a guy named Carmen DiSavio ... ever hear of him?" Angelo spelled the last name.

Morrison hadn't.

"He's muscle, just a street soldier. But Carmie was the go-between for Pack and the other guy they brought in to kill Peters. I don't have to tell you, more than anybody he'd like to see Pack permanently gone."

"You know this Carmie pretty well?"

"He's part of a different crew. He does his thing, I do mine, sometimes we run into each other on something but not often. We are not buddies, if that's what you mean. But I know Carmie's on Pack's case, night and day, the way I hear it."

This time it was a twin-engine Cessna. It didn't make as much noise as the Lear but they both stopped to watch it lift off and dip its wing as it angled out over the lake.

"You see, Carmie don't like this guy. Not just because he fucked up and jeopardized a lot of important people. From the start he didn't like the guy. He told people that, didn't trust the guy, said he was bad news, he had a gut feeling about it. Well, seems he was right. So all this has been nagging at him and now Carmie doesn't just dislike the kid, now he hates him. And when Carmie hates, believe me, he hates."

"Carmie's not the only guy looking, though."

"Hell, no, everybody's out there with their eyes and ears open, pokin' around. Me included ... supposedly, anyway. But with Carmie it's a mission now. If he finds Pack, the guy's gonna wish he'd had a nice clean execution." A sharp image of what happened to Roy Echols flooded in to his mind, including his own part in it ... a part there was no way to avoid, he told himself, and keep his cover ... "You heard of Jimmy Pagnano, haven't you?"

Morrison nodded. "Hard not to have, in this business. He's with Alessi."

"That's him. Joe-sep's top dog. He's a real psycho." As opposed to Angelo Franconi ...

Morrison was writing in his notebook. "You have some idea where we might find Carmie today?"

"No, I heard he lives by himself somewhere over in Little Italy. I can try to find out, see where he hangs out. I don't know myself. It's not all that easy. I can't walk up to Aldo and ask him. Aldo is paranoid as it is. I think he still worries about his mother turning him in . . . and she's been dead five years. Maybe Doyle's got something in that computer of theirs. Seems to have something on everybody else."

"What crew's he with?"

Angelo hesitated. "Alessi's . . ."

Morrison looked at him, changed the subject. "I take it you still don't have anything on where Pack was from?"

"No, nothing. Just out east."

"Doyle's running a check on known hit men from out east . . . New York, Boston, Philly, Baltimore. I talked with him this morning on the phone, I guess I forgot to mention that."

"He have anything more to say on my feelings about being brought into this?" Angelo asked.

"No. He just said you were all wrapped up in getting made by the Outfit, that's all." Doyle had said "obsessed," but Morrison decided to put it another way.

"Well, I am. And I'm just a step away. Aldo Forte's real pleased with me these days, told me as much this morning. With all the other things he's worrying about and besides his general nutsiness, I think it's significant he said something like that to me."

"And nothing more on the other guy?"

Angelo turned and looked out the front windshield toward McCormick Place, which from where they were parked looked like an aircraft carrier in dry dock. "No, nothing there either."

"You think you could find out a name on him?"

Angelo turned back to face Morrison, composed now. "Look, the way to get along with Aldo Forte is not to ask questions. Not give him *anything* that might strike the littlest note of suspicion in his head. I never *ask* anything. I just listen. And I do what he tells me. Which is why, I think, he's pleased with me." Angelo shook his head. "No way I'm asking anything. If I can pick something up some other way, you got it. That's all I can promise. I know the people I'm dealing with here. Believe me . . .''

"This Pagnano, what were you doing on an airplane with him?" Joe asked abruptly.

"Oh, that . . . we were doing a job together. Picking up something for Aldo and Alessi.''

"Drugs?"

"No, no. We don't get involved in that. This thing with Peters, that was, what do you call it, uncharacteristic. We were picking up some money.''

"Two of you?"

"It was a lot of money. It was for Aldo and Joe-sep so we both went. Nobody trusts nobody in this business.''

"What was the money for?"

"I don't know. Remember . . . I don't ask questions . . . try to do what I'm told.'' Angelo looked at Morrison. "What do you care what the money was for? It hasn't got anything to do with what *we're* into, you and me.''

"Just curious.'' Morrison gave him a little smile. "Pagnano is always of interest, his reputation and all.''

Franconi nodded, looked down toward McCormick Place again. "Looks like airplanes should be taking off from the roof of that. We got a lot to do with things going on over there, McCormick Place. Gonna come out one of these days. With all the stuff being shipped in and out of there for the conventions, lot of expensive stuff to grab. Heists all the time. But that's another story.''

"You got a lot of other stories, I bet.'' Morrison was smiling again.

"That's what Timmy Doyle likes about me.'' Franconi smiled right back.

"I heard a story about McCormick once,'' Morrison said. "Not exactly McCormick but off it.'' He pointed out to the lake on the east side of the huge convention hall. "When Daley was alive,'' he said, referring to Richard J., Chicago's multi-term mayor for most of the nineteen-fifties, sixties and seventies, who was more monarch than mayor, "he used to go fishing out there, about fifty maybe a hundred yards off it. He'd go like twice a year, once in the spring and once in the fall, and he'd always catch at least a ten-pound Coho salmon. Once, as I remember it, he got something like a twenty-pound Chinook. It was always in the paper, him holding it up, big smile on that jowly face of his. And after each time he went fishing he would say the same thing. 'Is dis a great city or what? Where else in America can da average guy on da doorstep of his city catch a fish like dis.' Rumor was that every time he went out, so did the fire department's scuba unit and some guy in a wetsuit would be down there under the boat attaching a fish they got from one of the charter boats to Hizzoner's line. When he reeled it in his cronies would tell him what a fish, what a fish. The mayor never noticed it was dead when he landed it. Or pretended not to. Knowing Chicago, it's probably true.''

Angelo did not know much about the late mayor, having come to Chicago after the Boss, as Daley was known to politician and citizen alike, had passed on. Angelo told Morrison what it was like growing up in New York City without a family, a home of his own. How he first got in trouble. What it was like in a juvenile home. Getting out and ending up a runner for some New York guys who were associated with one of the families. He was eighteen at the time. He made some money, got himself into some more trouble, went to Riker's Island, got out, made a little more money, but was never happy. He wanted to do something legitimate but never seemed able to find anything. Then he got in bigger trouble and was going to go away for heavy-duty time. He was twenty-four. That's when he met up with the FBI. That's when they talked to him. And that's when he thought he might be able to do something straight after all. He served a year, to establish credentials, as they put it, got out and was relocated to Chicago. And here he was.

Morrison asked him about his girlfriend, the daughter of Joe Alessi. And Angelo forgot to be cautious, said he was crazy about her. Didn't know how it happened, never expected it to happen. *Knew* it was something that could be disastrous for him. He had always managed to control things—when he was in the homes or on the street or in the organization—but then something like this girl comes along and . . . well, he'd never felt this way about anyone. He'd never had any parents, relatives, not even a close friend. And then there's Anita Alessi. Don't worry, he told Morrison, he'd work it out . . . He apologized for blabbing this way, not like him, but he figured Morrison was somebody he could trust and he badly needed that.

Morrison dropped him off at the entrance to the Grant Park underground garage not far from Buckingham Fountain, where Angelo told him he had parked his car.

Angelo Franconi struck Morrison as a man with a lot on his mind.

✥35

THE 11:30 A.M. MEETING AT FOUR WAS SPECIAL. NOT BE-cause there was any sensational breakthrough or sudden new lead. It was more that those coming in from the street for the meeting had made their way through a hundred pickets stomping back and forth in front of the main entrance of Four on Harrison Street, chanting slogans, shouting demands. The placards they carried had been handcrafted at the Avalon Tabernacle Church after the Wednesday night special service that the Reverend Hunter had presided over.

Most of the task force members just shoved their way through making disparaging comments to the marchers or grumbling out loud. Eddie McCabe was the only one who stopped. He stood there on the curb writing down the messages from the placards in his notebook because he thought they were worthy enough for keepsakes. He wrote a little commentary of his own after each, figuring he would categorize them all later.

Who Killd Rayfield Tees???
(illiterate)

Keep Em Separate
Church & State
Police & Mafia
(anti-police)

White Men's Justice
Don't Go
(racist)

Pig Killers
(Do they really think we kill pigs?)

Martin Luther King
Malcolm X
Emmett Till
Rayfield Tees
(Oh, c'mon)

We Want Justice
Not Pig Shit
(Seem to have a hang-up with pigs)

Just Anuther
Cop Cover Up
(Why nut?)

He logged a total of sixteen different statements before one of the marchers asked if he was from the press. "No, I'm a poet," McCabe said. "Last year I was a shepherd, but I got laid off." The man gave him a dirty look and shuffled on.

After pushing his way past the crowd in front of Four, as he was opening the door, Morrison heard his first name called and turned to take in Holly Stryker moving quickly toward him. They stepped inside after Norelli.

"You're here early," Morrison said, nodding toward the round clock on the wall whose hands showed it was not quite eleven-thirty. "Your buddy isn't due till noon from what I hear."

"I'm just looking around. And he's not my *buddy*."

"Since when?" Morrison turned abruptly to his partner.

"You know Ms. Stryker? Holly Stryker of the *Metro*? Well, this is *she*." Then to her: "And this is Detective Norelli. And we're both in a hurry."

"Have you looked at the *Metro* lately?"

"Yeah, I see you're off the front page."

"We haven't carried anything on the Peters/Tees murders other than the bits coming out of downtown."

"I've noticed that."

"You know why?"

"No."

"Because I thought about what you said last Friday night, and I talked to Hunter, and I didn't get many answers to what I was asking. And the answers I got didn't get, well, they were the answers." She looked at him as though surprised by what she'd said, and wondering if he understood what she meant.

Morrison stared at her. "You're beginning to sound like a Homicide detective."

She allowed a smile at that. "I talked to my editor, told him what I thought. That whole thing about a cop as the witness or having something to do with the murders . . . that was just a Hunter ploy. You told me that. And I believe you, or at least think you're a helluva lot more believable than Hunter." She looked away from him for a moment, out through the glass doors at the placard-wavers, and then back. "He even said, what gets their attention is what counts, what gets things done, and sometimes the means do justify the end. I'd forgotten what a lousy excuse that is . . . maybe because we use it in my business too . . . I just wanted to tell you." She forced a smile. "No hard feelings, then?"

"No."

"C'mon, Joe," Norelli said, "we gotta get upstairs."

"I think I was wrong about her," Morrison said as they double-timed it up the stairs. "She's not so bad."

Norelli gave him a look. "She's better looking than Mike Royko."

Morrison laughed at the mention of the famous Chicago *Tribune* columnist. "Got more hair, that's for sure. But what I meant is I think she maybe found the right street to walk down, to get where she wants to go. You know what I mean?''

Norelli did.

THEY WERE ABOUT HALFWAY through their meeting in the squadroom upstairs at Four when the detective came out of the watch commander's office and told Morrison he had a call. Morrison followed him back into Grantham's office and picked up the phone.

"Say, detective, you a hard man to find.''

"Solo?'' Morrison said.

"Right, and I'm a busy man. Spendin' far too much time tryin' to track you down, not to mention doin' police work for you. If it wasn't for Lonesome I wouldn't be investing a quarter in you. But business is business.''

"So what can I do for you?''

"Hang on.''

Morrison heard some muffled words Solo was saying away from the phone. He couldn't make them out with Solo apparently holding his hand over the mouthpiece at the other end. Another voice came on then, a soft one, speaking slowly. "You bin lookin' for me, I bin told.''

"And who are you?''

There was a pause and he could hear Solo say, "Go ahead, tell the man.''

"Latrona. Latrona Meek.''

Then Solo was back on the line. "Kind of makes your day, don't it?''

"Where are you?''

"Someplace . . . someplace safe. You get over and see Slipball, you know where to find him, and he bring you to us.''

"We're on our way.''

"Hey, hold on. You didn't say it.''

"Say what?''

"We do good work.'' There was an awkward pause. "Hey, Moe-sin, you couldn't find her. The wiseguys couldn't find her. But Solo could . . . so go ahead, tell me.''

"I'll nominate you for a Citizen's Merit Badge.''

"That's better. Respect's an important thing.''

Morrison hurried back out into the squadroom, whispered something to Norelli and headed over to Jim Harkness and Lieutenant Grantham.

"I need the deputy's ear," Morrison said.

Grantham gave him an uneasy look, but before he could remind Morrison of the protocol of rank Harkness clapped the lieutenant on the shoulder. "I've got to get back downstairs anyway. His Eminence should have arrived by now. It was good talking to you, Lou. Look me up next time you get downtown." He took Morrison by the arm. "Now what can I do for you?"

"We got the girl, Jim. Latrona Meek."

Harkness stopped, looked back at where Grantham had been standing but was no more. "When?"

"Just now. We don't have her. The Western Lords do. Solo, remember him?" Harkness did. "He found her and he's holding her. Norelli and I are going to pick her up."

"Anybody else know about this?"

"No, I just got off the phone with Solo. *And* her."

"Where are you bringing her?"

"Downtown. Where I'm going to sit with her until we know everything she knows . . . even things she doesn't know she knows."

"As soon as you've got her down there we'll issue some sort of statement." Harkness smiled.

Norelli joined them. Harkness said, "Nice when things start happening. I still get that old feeling, just like when I was on the street. It almost beats sex." He started toward the stairs and they fell in step. "I've got to go confront His Eminence. Going to be easier than I thought a few minutes ago."

✤36

LATRONA MEEK OUTWARDLY WAS A DOCILE GIRL. HER EYES were large and a soft brown, plaintive-looking, especially with the tearing on her lower lids. Her watery eyes and the tremble in her hands, uncharacteristic of a twelve year old, were not going to go away until she stopped using the drugs the late Rayfield Tees had introduced her to.

She left with Morrison and Norelli, reluctantly but quietly, and only after Solo told her she had to go and that she had to cooperate with them. There was something about her that reminded Morrison of the pictures of prisoners found alive in the death camps after World War II. She wasn't wearing broad-striped pajamas, rather grime-stained olive green shorts and a dirty wrinkled blouse that once was a light tan, but the feeling was still there. Her knees and elbows were scuffed and dirty, her fingernails chewed down to the quick, her nose runny.

According to Solo, he got word of her whereabouts about four that morning. Contrary to popular belief, she was not haunting the Englewood area. She had gone there, true enough, looking for her friend Selantha Tatum. But after a couple of nights on the street, hanging out in an abandoned building that served that area of the 'hood as a drug house, halfway house and neighborhood contraband storehouse, she learned by chance Selantha and her aunt had moved on to Woodlawn, about four miles away, where the aunt had a cousin. So she went there, found them and bunked in with Selantha and the aunt in the cousin's two-room tenement until one of Solo's old pals in Woodlawn discovered she was in the 'hood and passed on the word.

They brought her into a conference room on the sixth floor at 11th and State, down the hall from the offices of Jim Harkness and the other deputy superintendents. It was much less austere than the rooms they normally questioned a witness in. The walls were a soft cream color with framed photographs of past police superintendents and colorful prints of the more picturesque parts of the city. There was a large built-in book-case that made up a wall and housed rows of black binders and sets of legal tomes. Latrona sat in the highback leather chair at the head of a long mahogany table, dwarfed in it, and holding tight onto its oak arms as if she might suddenly go tumbling out of it.

Morrison and Norelli were treating her with all the defer-ence the police would show a lost and frightened and innocent child, even though they knew Latrona, however lost and frightened, was not exactly innocent. There was an uneasy quiet in the room, a kind of truce. Latrona, after all, had not been raised to love cops. A few minutes after she sat down, Jim Harkness came in with a black woman cop dressed in ordinary street clothes that he introduced simply as Miss Reyn-olds. They sat down on either side of Latrona at the conference table and talked while Morrison and Norelli stood by the door, looking on.

Morrison had sent another cop out to get Latrona a ham-burger, fries and a strawberry milkshake at Dottie's. She had said she wasn't hungry but she looked to him like she hadn't had much of anything to eat in some time. So figuring she was as timid under the circumstances as she was distrustful, he ordered the food anyway. When he added a milkshake to the order he gave to the cop, it got her attention and she asked for strawberry.

After the food came she at first picked at it but then wolfed down the shake. When she had finished, Morrison and Norelli sat down with Harkness and Ms. Reynolds, better known as Alex, for Alexandra . . . a smooth smart woman who worked out of a special unit at 11th and State, which handled special cases, from rape crisis counseling to hostage situations to cops contemplating suicide. Harkness's quiet tone when he talked to Latrona got her to relax a little. But it was Alex Reynolds, with her penetrating eyes and a street toughness that the girl could sense, together with a certain big-sister air, whom the girl seemed to be looking to when anything was asked of her. And it was Alex Reynolds who got Latrona Meek talking about the night her nightmare began . . .

Latrona told them she and her boyfriend had gone over there under the expressway to be alone, they'd been there before, it was their own place where nobody bothered them. She didn't offer what they were doing there that night or the other times and no one asked. Everything was going fine, she said, and then the cars came. "And one of the men, he went diggin',", she said. "And he got some suitcase from where he diggin' and he throw it in the car on the other side of the street. And they shoot the other man . . . and goddamn them, they shoot Rayfield. Right there in front of me." She sounded almost dead herself when she said it. "He say somethin' when he fell but I didn't hear what it was. Oh God, he make a noise like he's throwin' up and his body jumps once and then . . ." Her watery, enigmatic eyes stayed on the female detective. "They come up to look at him, two of 'em. I was behind the pole and they don't see me. I knew they kill me if they did. One said somethin' to the other and then they run back to the other man and they all get in the car and drive off. I wait and I go over to Rayfield and just look at him there, bleedin'. I know he was dead. I run then before they come back and do me . . ."

Morrison leaned over on the table. "How many men were there altogether, Latrona?"

"Three. The two and the other one by the car, the car they drive away in."

"Did you *see* the third man?"

"No, he was by the car the whole time."

Latrona then described the two men she did see. The one with the ponytail she especially remembered because he was the one with the gun, the one who shot Rayfield. She said she thought she would recognize both of them if she saw them again.

They told her they were going to have her look at a lot of pictures. Morrison, Norelli and Harkness left her with Alex Reynolds and moved out into the corridor. They talked there for a minute, then Harkness went back to his office to start making arrangements for where they could safely stash Latrona Meek. And to inform the superintendent. Norelli went to get mug shots of known local hitmen and hoodlums, and Morrison left to call Timothy Doyle at the FBI regional office.

Alex Reynolds took Latrona downstairs to the women's locker room for a shower, sent a uniformed cop to dig up some clean clothes and called for a doctor to come over and examine her. By the time she was back in the conference room on the fifth floor, the stains and odors of the street were gone, at least outwardly, and if she smiled she might even have once again looked like the little girl in the picture at the picnic.

Latrona looked at photos for most of the afternoon, patiently waiting as each was put before her, and shook her head or said uh-uh, as each was turned over onto an ever-increasing pile. She did not hesitate on any one of them, which prompted Norelli at one point to ask if she really was sure that she could recognize the faces of the killers. She looked at him without a flinch from those watery eyes and said, "I know the man when I see him. Both men." She pointed at the stack of photos facing down on the table. "They not in there."

Tim Doyle arrived around four o'clock with another satchel full of mugshots. He met briefly with Morrison in PT headquarters and then they took the photos up to the conference room on the sixth floor and gave them to Norelli.

Harkness was briefing Arnie Troy, the departmental PR lieutenant, on what he could reveal at the press conference they had called, which was scheduled for four-thirty downstairs in the press room, when Morrison and Doyle appeared at his office door. The press and the media had already been informed by telephone that there was a major development in the case. "Build the story this way," Harkness had said. "Build it and they will come," was Troy's comment. "And how is Timothy Doyle of the estimable Federal Bureau of Investigation today?" Troy said as the two men shook hands. He looked back at Harkness. "I didn't know we'd brought the feds in on this. I take it that is something you don't want shared with those assembled downstairs."

"That's a safe assumption," Harkness said.

"Fine." Troy hesitated a moment. "Is there any chance it might be brought up by them? The press?"

Harkness looked at Doyle and Morrison. "No. If by some chance it does, just say we're using every available source to find the men responsible for these two murders. Which is the truth."

"Well, everybody who's anybody around here knows we have the girl by now," Harkness said when he and Doyle and Morrison were in the office alone. "It gets out . . . so I suppose the bad guys know too. Either of you heard anything about that yet?"

"No," Doyle said. "I haven't heard from our man. But then it was left that he and Joe deal direct on this." Doyle looked over at Morrison.

"I haven't heard from him either, today."

"Make contact," Harkness said. "See what they know . . . if they got any plans we should know about." Harkness leaned back in his swivel chair, hands resting on his trim stomach, fingers tapping against their mates. "Personally I don't think they'll try anything with the girl now that she's in the public eye." He looked at his watch. "At least she will be in ten minutes. No way to stop it, not these days with the people's sacred right to know."

Doyle agreed, but added, "They also know she could start one of those domino games they hate so much. They just might take their chances taking her out and trying to weather the flak rather than risk going down because of what she can start."

Harkness looked at Morrison. "I got bad feelings about this too," Morrison said. "Especially after talking to our friend Gabriel. I get from him they'll do anything to protect their own asses in this. They're scared of the guy they hired, who unfortunately is still around."

"Okay, I'm not going to argue the point. But it won't matter if we do our job and keep her hidden. I would hope we're at least capable of that . . . We've got several possibilities. I know a couple of homes we could put her in, retired brass, friends, very clean. Stash her in one of them and put an around-the-clock guard with her. Or you familiar with Maryville?'' They both nodded, aware of the large Roman Catholic orphanage out in the far northwestern suburbs. ''I know the priest who runs the place. We've been involved in functions together, fundraisers, dinners, things like that. He's a helluva guy. We could slip her in there and she'd never be noticed, they come and go all the time. I know he'd do me the favor. And we could put an undercover or two there to keep an eye on her.''

Doyle hesitated, then said, ''No offense, but we know things said around here have a way of getting to the wrong parties. I think we could put her into the Witness Protection Program—''

''That's federal,'' Morrison said.

''So is organized crime, Joe. Granted the crime in question is local, not federal. But it does have every appearance of involving organized crime, and that at least makes it of federal interest. Trust me, I can get her into it. I've already talked about it with my SAC in the event this thing came up. It would, of course, just be temporary, but we could keep her out of harm's way better than anyone else for the time being.''

''I've got no problem with that,'' Harkness said.

''The deal is, though, nobody around here knows where she is once we get her. Not the superintendent, not either of you, *nobody*.''

''That won't work,'' Morrison said.

''Yes it will, Joe. You need her to be somewhere, we'll produce her. You want to talk to her, we'll make arrangements. You, Joe, Jim here, a prosecutor from the State's Attorney's office but nobody else. The rules in these things are very strict. It's why we haven't lost anybody since the program began back in the sixties.''

''Under the circumstances, it does make sense to me,'' Harkness said. ''But I'll have to get a formal okay from the super.''

''Can you do that now? I mean in the next hour or so.'' Harkness nodded. ''Okay, here's what I suggest. We keep her around here. She's still going through photos. Get her some dinner. You stay with her, Joe.''

"I'll have Alex stick around, too," Harkness said to Morrison. "Give you both some company."

"What about my partner in this?" Morrison asked.

"Sure, have him stick around," Doyle said. "But in our deal it's just you and Jim here. From the time we take her, we deal only with you two."

"Okay. Doesn't make for the best partner relationship but—"

"I can get this going right away," Doyle said. "But I think it best we keep her holed up in that conference room and take her out later tonight. A couple of marshals will come over and take her off your hands. They're real good at this kind of thing. I'll be with them. I don't know what time yet but I'll let you know in advance, Joe."

Harkness's private line rang and he picked up the phone. "I'll take it," he said to his secretary on the other end. A moment later he said, "What's up?" into the mouthpiece. No more than ten seconds elapsed when he said, "Very good" and hung up.

He leaned across the desk toward Morrison and Doyle. "The witness program sounds like a *very* good idea for Ms. Meek," he said. "That was Norelli. Latrona Meek is now a full-fledged witness. She just nailed one of the photos Tim brought over."

✦37

MORRISON AND ANGELO WERE WALKING ALONG THE ESPLA-nade named Solidarity Drive that stretched into Lake Michigan from the Field Museum of Natural History and the Shedd Aquarium on Lake Shore Drive two blocks out to the Adler Planetarium. It was a beautiful slice of land, a parkway of grass and trees and statues running between the two one-way streets that looped around the planetarium at the eastern tip. They were on the north side of the esplanade, the more picturesque, looking out as it did across the water to the greenery of Grant Park with the backdrop of Chicago's lakefront skyline. A steep lawn sloped down to a long concrete boardwalk and seawall that ran the length of the slender peninsula. People were fishing, some staring absently out at their bobbers hoping a school of lake perch might field-trip by, while others cast out and reeled in searching for a hungry, indiscriminate Coho or perhaps the king, the Chinook. Fishing was the only activity in the area at eight in the morning except for an occasional car or taxicab plying the road. It would be alive with people in a few hours when all the museums that populated the area opened.

"Word about the Meek girl we got from the six o'clock news," Angelo was saying. "Don't know about Tuscano, but he didn't get hold of Aldo until after we heard the news, and I don't know whether he got it from his source or the same way we did."

"A little nervous over at the Amalfi?"

"Aldo goes from seeing himself carted off to prison to wailing about Pack and why isn't he dead yet. He took me off into a corner of the club last night as I was leaving and said, 'You know, Angelo, you're one of the only ones I can trust around here anymore. You understand we gotta kill that kid,' like I hadn't gotten the message already. 'I don't like it,' he says, 'but sometimes that's the way things got to be. It's gotta be done by someone I can truly trust. Stay close, Angelo,' he tells me. Joe, I get the strong feeling if he finds out where she is he's gonna want *me* to whack her."

"You think you get made without doing the real down and dirty?"

Angelo looked over at Morrison but didn't say anything.

Joe didn't press. This whole thing was down and dirty and there were no black-and-whites. Not for the likes of Angelo Franconi, that was for sure. And not really for Joe Morrison either.

They had reached the bulb of land at the end of the espla-

nade where the domed planetarium sat like some giant mole.
People were standing around at the foot of the broad set of
steps that led up to the entrance. "Let's go sit by the water,"
Angelo said. "Take in the view."

As they walked down the grassy slope to the breakwater
wall, Angelo pointed at the skyline. "Look at that, this can
really be a beautiful town."

"This side of it, yeah. I see it more a city of contrasts, but
then, that's the way I guess I see everything. It probably comes
with being on the force too long."

"Too long? You? How old're you anyway, not even forty,
I bet."

"Close. Time on the job is relative. I wouldn't have said
that when I was your age and that's only ten, twelve years
ago." They reached the bottom of the hill and sat on the shelf
of granite blocks that ran along and above the boardwalk.

"This whole thing's getting to me," Angelo said, looking
out across the water. "I talked to my girl last night. Tried to,
anyway."

"She feel the same way about you as you do about her?"

"Yeah, I think."

"Your life isn't complicated enough?"

He ran his fingers through his curled black hair. "It's tough
enough walking the line between two lives. Then I met her
. . . of all people. I couldn't just fall for some nice-looking
ordinary girl . . . *I* gotta fall a ton for Joe Alessi's daughter."
He looked over at Morrison. "It's the last thing in the world
I would have wanted. Hey, it started out as a lark . . . I met
her when Aldo brought me over to Joe-sep's about six months
ago. She's beautiful, and I, you know, started flirting, nothing
serious. I mean, I never figured we'd even go out, her being
who she was and all, and then she asked me to go to this party
with her, and I asked her to go somewhere with me . . . and
well, we just hit it off. Really did. We kept seeing each other.
Her old man knew about it. I made sure of that and he, you
know, sanctioned it. And I don't know exactly when it happened but something did, something sudden and it was like
something I never knew before. Sounds corny but it's true.

The same for her. It just *happened*. And now I'm in so deep I don't know where the hell I'm going.''

"You talk this over with Doyle?"

"No, not really. Not much. He knows I'm going out with her. He gave me the speech. It's not good, it's trouble. But I don't think he knows how I really feel.'' Angelo looked over at Morrison. "I don't know why I'm laying all this shit on you. I can't with Doyle. I don't feel anything in common with him. He's, you know, FBI, big college grad, house in the suburbs, kids in fancy colleges. We don't have a whole helluva lot in common.''

"I can see why he isn't real happy about your love life. It could be sort of inhibiting—''

Angelo shook his head. "It's something I gotta work out myself. I tried talking to Anita last night. I kind of asked what she'd think about just getting out of here, Chicago, and starting a whole new kind of life. Me and her, someplace else, alone.''

"I don't think that would be too easy, Angelo.''

"I know. She thought I was crazy, she adores her old man, she's his princess, and she knows it. She doesn't know what he and Aldo and the rest of them do when they're not sitting around the kitchen table or out on the patio. I mean, she maybe knows a little of it, but she doesn't know the worst, or refuses to think about it. If you told her or I told her, she wouldn't believe it. She's a girl from the old school . . . the man's business is his business, it's not part of family life. Joe . . . you're a good guy to listen to all this. Be an even better guy and don't tell any of it to Doyle. Let me work it out . . . although I haven't got the faintest fucking idea how I'm ever going to do it, with him, with Anita, with myself . . . well, you got other things on your mind, otherwise you wouldn't have made contact. So what can I do for you?"

"Anything on Pack?" Morrison said.

"Still no word. I was right, though, Carmie DiSavio is all over it. From what I hear, he keeps telling Aldo he's close, he's got a line on the guy. Nobody sees him around. He's a man on a mission, the way I hear it.''

"What does the name Roy Echols mean to you?"

Angelo was startled, tried not to show it. "I know the name."

"He Danny Pack's buddy?"

"Yeah, how'd you know?"

"The girl identified him. His picture was in with the out-of-towners Doyle brought. How'd *you* know?"

"How'd I know what?"

"That he's Danny Pack's running mate."

There was a kind of . . . what, Morrison asked himself . . . anger, defensiveness . . . in Angelo's eyes. "Look, I haven't been totally candid with you about everything. Maybe I better straighten out some things."

"Might be a good idea."

"Like I told you, he's gone, this Echols guy." Angelo looked out at the water with its rolling swells. For the moment it looked like the ocean to him and he shuddered inside. "His name didn't matter, I figured."

"That doesn't figure at all, Angelo."

"Look, what difference does it make, since he's gone? Pack is alive, that's who you want. I knew the two of them came in town to do a job. I learned that the night they did it. I didn't know their names at the time. I didn't know where they were from. I still don't, just that they were from out of town." Angelo looked at Morrison. "By the way, where were they from?"

"The Philadelphia area. Camden. Echols anyway, that's all we know at the moment," Morrison said. "Doyle's running a federal tracer on Pack and we're having a local one run on him through the Camden and Philly PDs. So how did you come to hear about it that night?"

"I learned about it at a party with Anita that Joe-sep was throwing for his brother. At the time, I looked on it as business as usual. The Peters guy . . . well, you don't rip off the family. Basic."

"How come you never told Doyle?"

"I told you, it was business as usual. Nothing he or the Bureau would be interested in. Mob kills mobster, big deal.

Yes, it was a murder, but them killing each other off, you know . . . who really cares?''

"The guy getting knocked off, probably," Morrison said. "His family if he's got one."

"Come on, Joe, you know what I mean."

Morrison did, he'd heard it plenty of times before from Chicago's finest. "Did Alessi tell you about it that night?"

"No. It was Aldo. He called me while I was at the party."

"Did he tell you who the third guy was . . . besides Echols and Pack?"

"Third guy?" Angelo felt his throat tighten.

"The girl told us there was a third man there. The two of them went off in a car with him after they killed Peters and the boy. You have any idea who that guy might be?"

"Yeah."

"Who?"

Angelo made the decision, looking out at the lake again. "Me."

"*You?* And you said you didn't know who these guys were or where they were from?" Morrison could not keep the incredulity out of his voice.

"I didn't, I honest-to-God didn't. It's part of the whole need-to-know thing. Aldo told me I didn't *want* to know. All I needed to know, he said, was that I was to be the follow-up. I was supposed to be there to get the dope and bring it back and get the two of them the hell out of there after they whacked Peters. Which is what I did. I *had* to do that much. I took them back out to the airport—the hotel across the street from it, to be exact—and I dumped the coke where I was told to. And I went home and I went to bed and I didn't sleep one second the rest of the night."

"I still don't understand why you didn't tell Tim Doyle this."

"I didn't tell him," Angelo said, talking to the lake before turning suddenly to Morrison, "I didn't tell him because *I didn't want him to know.*" There was a panic in Angelo's eyes. "The kid. You know how the kid got killed? *I* got him killed." Angelo looked away and then dropped his face into his hands. Morrison waited. Finally Angelo looked back up. "After they finished and started back toward the car, I flicked on the headlights. And there was the kid standing up there behind them. He was standing there like a fucking deer caught in the headlights, frozen. I lost it, jumped out of the car. Panic, goddamn me, I yelled. They turned and saw the kid and he started to run . . . and Pack shot him. After that everything seemed like it was in slow motion. I kept thinking, my God, he shot the kid. My God, my God, was all I could think, and they were up there by him and then they were turning down toward me but it seemed like a damn movie slowed down, like it wasn't *real*, everything out of, you know, sync. And I kept thinking why did I yell and they kept coming down to the car and I was saying to myself why the fuck did I not keep my mouth shut and then they were there at the car, getting in and we just took off and . . ."

Morrison started to say something but had no words.

"So you see," Angelo went on more calmly now, "I already got dirty hands. I got people's trust and I got dirty hands and I got a kid killed. And I got a girl I just want to be with and I don't want to hurt her. And I got everything I been working for the past two years about to happen. And at the same time it's all coming apart." Angelo picked up a chip of granite that had come loose from the block they were sitting on and sailed it out into the lake. "I gotta get back. Aldo said stay close." He got up and started up the hill. Morrison watched him go, not wanting to feel sorry for him but unable not to.

When Morrison talked briefly with Doyle later that morning he said, "You know, that Gabriel, he's a grenade with a loose pin. You know that when you gave him to me?"

Doyle nodded. "I guess love can do that to a guy."

✦38

CARMEN HAD GIVEN UP HIS ROUND-THE-CLOCK SURVEIL-lance of 2733 Clybourn but kept dialing the telephone number of W. Kokonitz of that address as an hourly routine. He had learned from the manager of the supermarket that Winnie Kokonitz had called in and asked for more vacation time and was not expected back now until the following Monday.

The day before he had thought about breaking into the apartment to see if there was anything inside that might give him a clue about where the lovebirds had gone. He was working alone now and had gone upstairs to check out the lock system on the apartment door, but then Vera next door came out and asked if she could help. She remembered Carmie and asked after Winnie's ailing relative. It was enough to deter Carmie from any breaking and entering.

Finally Aldo Forte got hold of him. "Be at the McDonald's on Ohio Street, the big one, Ohio and LaSalle, one hour."

AND HE WAS ALREADY at a table at McDonald's, an Egg McMuffin half-eaten and a large paper cup of well-creamed coffee in front of him when one of Aldo's emissaries, a gofer everybody called the Deuce, walked in. Carmie saw him first but just sat there waiting until Deuce spotted him.

"Aldo heard from New Jersey," the gofer said as he sat down. "Pack called again last night lookin' for Echols and his five grand. Seems Pack's been gamblin' at one of them Indian reservation places in Wisconsin, somethin' dooflamboo, up in the North Woods." Carmie, a sometime Wisconsite, figured the Deuce was talking about the legalized gambling casinos on Indian lands that had just opened up in the last year or so at Lac du Flambeau.

"He still there?" Carmie was thinking what a perfect place

to deal with Danny Pack, up there in God's country with all the woods and lakes around, take him out where there was nothing but deer and chipmunks and ducks to watch it go down.

"No. Supposed to be tapped out. That's why he wanted the money he got coming. Supposed to be on his way back here with his girlfriend today. That's what he told 'em in Jersey. That's what Aldo told me to tell you. Tell you he's comin' back with the broad, that's what Aldo said."

"That's good news, Deuce." Carmie took the rest of his Egg McMuffin in one bite and his cheeks rolled like seaswells around his face as he chewed.

"Aldo said you need any help I was to hang around or you should get hold of anybody else you might need. Said he figures the guy should get back sometime this afternoon, being maybe a six-hour drive. That's what Aldo said."

"You go back and see Aldo. Tell him to consider it a done deal. I don't need anybody. Tell him the next time he sees me I'm gonna have for him a ponytail mounted on a plaque to hang on the wall at the Amalfi."

"I don't think that would be the best. Aldo said to tell you to make sure this guy is disappeared, like forever. I don't think he's gonna want—"

Carmie stood up. "Hey, I was only kidding. Behave yourself, Deucie. I got business. Try the Egg McMuffin, it ain't too bad."

In his car Carmie said aloud, "Like they say in Green Bay, the Pack is back. On his way, anyway."

CARMIE WAS WRONG. DANNY Pack was already back, lying at that very moment butt-to-butt with Winona Kokonitz, who like Danny was out cold in her flat above the store on Clybourn. After Danny won a little more than a thousand back on the craps table at the Tepee Casino in Lac du Flambeau and Winnie was four hundred ahead for the night on the slots and it nearing two A.M., the weeknight witching hour, he decided they ought to head back to Chicago. They drove through the rest of the night and were in bed at Winnie's before nine.

Danny Pack slept like a rock for three hours, then was up, pacing the apartment, nervous. It had started yesterday afternoon when he called and could not find Roy Echols. Not in Florida, not in Camden, nobody knew where he was, although they didn't say that, they just said that he wasn't around at the moment. Now Winnie tells him that Vera next door came over and woke her up and told her some guy had been by a couple of times looking for her, something about a relative being sick, but she didn't have any relative who would have any idea where she lived, she said, except for her ex, and he didn't have a friend in the world, much less someone who'd be coming around to tell her he was sick. Danny Pack was having that feeling, the one you got in prison when you just *knew* something bad was going to happen, maybe something brewing from inside, maybe from the powers that be. You were there long enough, you got a feeling, a sixth sense. That was what he was feeling now. That's why he was scrambling around the apartment, jitter-walking.

MORRISON AND DOYLE WERE on the phone, Morrison telling Doyle he had the report from the police in Camden, who had checked out Roy Echols and said he had not been seen in town for several weeks. Nobody knew where he was, where he went, nothing. Danny Pack, they were able to provide a profile. He had a sheet, nothing federal, but he was associated with the same cartage company Echols was, allegedly Outfit-owned. He, too, had not been seen around town for approximately the same length of time as Echols. They faxed mug shots of Pack, which Morrison had on the desk in front of him.

"In the mugs he doesn't have a ponytail," Morrison said. "According to Camden he doesn't have the rep Echols does in Outfit circles but he's obviously connected."

"You going to run an APB on him?"

"I'm going to talk to Harkness about it as soon as I get off the phone with you. I think we'll probably just run it in the Daily Bulletin in the morning. It'll get back to Tuscano, but that doesn't matter. They already contracted him out. We can't

do anything about them. I just don't want publicity that might
alert him and make him run.''

"Yeah, well, good luck.''

"By the way, Gabriel told me this morning he knows the
two guys from Camden. Met them.''

"You're kidding.''

"You think I'd kid about that?''

"No. But he never said anything about that, even the night
out in Highwood.''

"He didn't think it was anything you'd need to know, the
federales not being interested in little murders on a local level.
Also, I think he didn't want you to know he drove the back-
up car that night for them and then dropped them out at
O'Hare.''

"Jesus, Mary and Giuseppe.''

"Something he had to do. You wanna be made, you got to
do certain things. It's a tough call. That's his attitude. But he's
also feeling guilty about it, the kid getting killed. It's really
ragging on him.''

"How come he tells *you* all this stuff and not me?''

"Maybe because he feels I come from the same side of the
tracks. He *knows* you don't. Anyway, I thought you might
want to know.''

"Real thoughtful of you. Let me know if he confides to you
anything else he doesn't want to tell me.''

ANGELO WAS STAYING IN his apartment, not the Amalfi, the
reason being he was with Anita Alessi. Aldo Forte knew where
he was. Angelo had told him . . . not whom he was with, there
were limits.

Anita was sitting curled up in the corner of the couch, her
legs tucked under her, wearing a pale pink slip with a bit of
lace running across the rim of the bodice and around the bottom hem. Her panties and bra, the same color and with the
same lace trimming, lay next to a pair of pantyhose at the foot
of the bed on the other side of the room. Her dress was draped
over the chest of drawers next to the bed. Angelo was on the
phone talking some business. She was not listening, deep in

her own thoughts, thinking about how she wanted to put things to Angelo when he got off the phone.

They had made love after she arrived, in fact they were in bed five minutes after she walked through the door. But somehow it hadn't seemed right. Angelo seemed to be going through the motions. She knew the difference. When the phone rang Angelo had bolted from the bed like somebody stuck him with a cattle prod. While he stood there talking stark naked she got up from the bed and shimmied into the slip, which was the closest thing handy. She still didn't feel comfortable being naked out of bed. He lovingly kidded her about that, said it was because she was still an innocent little girl in the body of a goddess and hadn't come to terms with it. That was one of the things that made her so special, he would quickly say. But today something was wrong, she was woman enough to feel that.

When he hung up Angelo gave her a quick smile and disappeared into the bathroom. A moment later he was back, wearing a white terrycloth bathrobe. He did a little bob and weave for her, throwing out a couple of quick left jabs into the air and then a roundhouse right cross so sloppy it would have gotten him nailed if he was in the ring, and then plopped down on the couch next to her, looping his right arm around her shoulder.

She looked at him, eyes questioning. "What's the matter, Angelo?"

"What do you mean?"

"Something seems to be eating you. Can't you let me in on it?"

"Nothing. I don't know what you're talking about. Everything's fine."

"That's bull, Angelo."

"What? Come on. What brought all this on?"

"Don't bullshit me."

He looked at her. "I got a lot on my mind, honey. Some problems. That's all."

"About us?" She looked wary, like she was going to hear something she didn't want to hear.

He put the left-jab fist under her chin, raising her head a little, and bent over and gave her a kiss.

"You see, one of my problems is I am so goddamn in love with you I don't know what to do with myself."

She smiled. That was not something she didn't want to hear. "Well, that doesn't seem like a problem."

She kissed him back. Inside he felt he was sliding down a dark tunnel with oily black walls with nothing to grab onto and no bottom to stop his descent and saying mostly to himself, "Oh God, oh God . . ." as her tongue explored the cavern of his mouth.

WINNIE KOKONITZ WAS NOT kissing her boyfriend but he too was distant with worries of his own. He had called the cartage company once but his boss Connie Damoro was not in. Paula, the girl who did everything around there except load trucks and was the niece of Damoro, said he'd be calling in and she'd let him know he called. She didn't know anything about Roy Echols. Was she supposed to? "He's outa town like you. He don't check in either." Danny said he heard yesterday that Roy was back. She didn't know anything about that. If he was, he hadn't been around. But that was nothing new.

Winnie said she was going to the store, what little was in the refrigerator had turned bad while they were gone and they were out of beer. Danny gave her a fifty and told her to get a bottle of vodka too, good stuff, like Smirnoff or one of those ones from Russia or Poland, not the rotgut cheap stuff.

There were a couple of other calls Danny figured he would make, try to find out if *anybody* had heard something about Roy. Roy's girlfriend worked somewhere in Philly, a hairdresser, but he couldn't remember the name of the place. He thought maybe it was Sylvia's or Silkie's, something like that. All he knew, it was on the north side of town. Maybe he'd have some luck with the operator.

CARMIE WAS EXPECTING TO see somebody arrive, not go out, as he sat in the uncomfortable Honda across Clybourn Street and down a ways from 2733 when the woman came out the door and walked directly to the Chevy Camaro the color of a maraschino cherry that was parked at the curb in front of 2733. He had only been there about ten minutes. Well, look at that, Carmie said to himself. Could they be back already?

She was no spring chicken, Carmie thought, but she wasn't too bad. She looked like she was mid-thirties. She wore skin-tight shorts, a loose-fitting T-shirt and sandals. Her hair was long and curly, dark for the first inch or so out from the scalp then a kind of flat, hay-colored blonde. A little old for Danny, maybe, but then again he wasn't no prize.

She could be a friend of the woman who lived next door, though. He watched as she maneuvered back and forth to get out of the tight parking place. If it's *her*, Carmie thought, she'll be coming back. Then he got a bright idea, pulled himself out of the car and hustled over to the Qwik-Stop.

DANNY PACK HAD JUST hung up the telephone, having gotten nowhere with the operator in Philadelphia. There wasn't anything listed under Sylvia's or Silkie's and if he did not have anything more specific she could not help him, the operator sing-songed. He swore at her, or at the telephone, or at himself for not remembering the name, Roy had mentioned it enough times.

The phone rang. Maybe it was Connie Damoro. It wasn't, it was some asshole for Winnie wanting to sell her insurance, the Loop Insurance Company, the guy said. He told him to fuck off.

Carmie wondered if all insurance agents had to put up with that kind of crap. But Carmie didn't care, in fact he had a big smile on his face as he walked out of the Qwik-Stop.

♣39

CARMIE WAS RIGHT. ABOUT AN HOUR LATER THE MARA-schino cherry Camaro pulled up in front of 2733 and the woman got out, gathered up two brown bags of groceries and went upstairs.

Dining in tonight, Carmie thought. Musta hit a bum streak up in Wisconsin. Can't afford to take the girlie out to dinner.

Winnie with the two heavy bags and her purse dangling from the crook of one elbow jabbed at the upstairs door with the other elbow. The sound was loud enough but nobody answered it. Finally she put one of the bags down and dug out her key. Danny Pack was lying on the couch, the phone in his ear. He glanced at her when she came in mumbling and then directed his full attention back to the telephone.

She carried the groceries into the little kitchen. She was just about through putting them away when he stepped up behind her. "Big help you are," she said.

"You could see I was on the phone. What am I supposed to do, drop everything 'cause you got a coupla bags of groceries? Am I a bagboy?" He looked upset but gave her a half-playful swat on the butt. "You get the vodka?"

"Yeah, I got the vodka. It's in the refrigerator."

He poured himself a half-glass filled with ice. "Something strange's going down," he said. "*Nobody* knows where the hell Roy is. I talked to a couple of guys. They don't know. Damoro tells me yesterday that Roy's around but nobody else knows about it and Damoro isn't there today. I don't like it."

She gave him a look. "You into something I don't maybe know about? Some shit?"

"Whatta you mean?"

"You and that guy Roy. You keep talkin' about him."

"He owes me money."

"I *know* he owes you money. Besides the way you're act-ing, I'm gettin' other funny feelings, too. You know I go over to work to get this stuff and everybody asks me where I been. Some guy's been over there looking for me, my boss tells me, and calling, something about insurance, this guy's with an in-surance company and says I got money coming and they're trying to find me. And like I told you, Vera said somebody was by here about a relative of mine. I'm no rocket scientist, Danny, but these things aren't adding up right. I got nobody who's gonna leave me diddley-shit. And I'm thinking maybe it's you this guy's looking for, not me. Could that be, Danny boy?"

CARMIE DID NOT WANT to go in and take Pack now—he would have to kill the girlfriend too, and that could get messy, especially with that nosy next-door neighbor. He wasn't going to stay in there forever. Better to wait. Hope he came out alone. If not, he figured then he'd have to go in. Carmie was talking out loud now. "She made a stupid choice in the first place ever hooking up with an asshole like him."

UPSTAIRS WINNIE TURNED ON the television to catch the six o'clock news. Danny was sipping on his second vodka and eating pretzels and wondering what the hell was going on, where the hell Roy was, why the hell Connie Damoro never called back. He wasn't listening to the news, not really watch-ing it either, until suddenly all his questions were answered in one freeze-frame on the screen. It took a second to register, but there he was, clear as the old Liberty Bell in Philly, Roy, looking stone cold, staring back at him from the tube.

The words were coming through: "As reported earlier to-day, the police are still searching for the man identified by a witness as Roy Echols of Camden, New Jersey, a suspect in the August twenty-sixth slaying of Thurman Peters and Ray-field Tees on Chicago's west side . . ."

"Jesus God, that's *Roy*," Danny Pack shouted.

Winona Kokonitz turned from the TV to Danny. "What?"

"That's Roy, the guy I'm looking for."

The broadcaster went on: "Police are also seeking another man alleged to have been seen with Echols but who also remains unidentified . . ."

Roy's picture dissolved from the screen in favor of the male/female broadcast team seated behind the anchor desk. She was saying something about contacting authorities if any listener had information about Echols's whereabouts. But Danny had already tuned it out.

"How did all this happen?" Danny was saying. "Witness! What witness? There *wasn't* any witness." Danny grabbed the phone and started to dial Connie Damoro's number in Camden again. Then he thought better of it. "Holy shit, I got to get out of here."

"You *killed* somebody?" Winnie said. "You were with him, you were the guy with Roy, weren't you?"

"Look—"

"Oh, my God. Danny."

"Look, look, I'm out of here. According to the TV they don't even know who it is that's the friend of Roy's. Far as you're concerned, *I was never here.* Anybody comes by, you haven't seen me in three years." He looked closely at her. "You don't have a problem with that, do you?"

"Of course not, Danny. I don't want nothing to happen to you. The guy who was here, the guy who came by my work looking for me. You think he was a cop?"

Danny looked at her like she was a child. "If *he* was a cop *I'd* be all over the tube now. And so would you."

He started to throw some of his clothes into the overnight bag he'd brought with him when he and Roy had flown into town, it now seemed months ago. He grabbed the six plastic packets of coke they still had left from the end table drawer, put two of them on the table. "For you to remember me by," he said, giving her that boyish smile, the one that always got to her, and stuck the other four in his pants pocket.

"Where're you going?" she asked.

"I don't know. I still got a ticket to New Orleans that's good. I don't know whether I better use that or not now. I gotta get away and think. Think this thing out." He zipped the bag shut and headed for the door.

He headed down Clybourn at a good clip, his eyes scanning the street for a taxicab as he went. At the stoplight at Fullerton he spotted one unloading a girl with an oversized bag slung over one shoulder and a leather briefcase in hand. He almost knocked her over jumping into it.

The cab took him out to Mannheim Road near O'Hare Airport, where he had the driver pull in to one of the second-rate motels along the strip there. He checked in at the desk up front and was walking to his room at the other end, overnight bag in one hand and room key in the other, when a man approached him from the parking lot side. It was dark out now and he couldn't see the face at first but he recognized the shape and the voice. "You got your geography all screwed up, kid," Carmie said. "This ain't New Orleans."

"I was just thinking about going there," Danny Pack said and let the bag drop from his hand to the ground. "You must be a mindreader. Even got a one-way ticket," pointing at the overnight bag next to him, "in there." In the other hand, he maneuvered the room key so he grasped the diamond-shaped hard plastic room tag in his fist, the key itself sticking out from between his index and middle fingers.

"Well, you're going to have to postpone your trip for a little while. Somebody wants to have a little talk with you first," Carmie said. He was standing there with both hands in the pockets of the tan windbreaker he was wearing. He looked pleased as a lottery winner.

Danny, moving quicker than Carmie expected, lashed out and his fist smashed into Carmie's face, the key protruding from between his fingers tearing a ragged gash along Carmie's cheek. The power of the punch knocked Carmie into a parked car, then onto his ass. As he hit the asphalt the gun Carmie had his hand on inside the windbreaker pocket went off, the bullet leaving a smoking hole in it, ricocheting off the ground and then pinging off the metal door to room 112. Danny took a quick step forward, bringing his right foot back for the kick.

Carmie, sitting there, dazed, legs spread out in a vee in front of him, still managed to get the gun out of his pocket, raised it and pulled the trigger.

The bullet hit Danny Pack square in the chest, the impact knocking him back against the motel wall, which held him there for a moment. The next shot hit in the vicinity of the first. Danny Pack toppled forward away from the wall and off the narrow sidewalk, falling face down on the black surface of the parking lot.

Carmie dragged himself up, holding his bloody cheek in one hand and the gun in the other. He was unsteady on his feet, like a drunk, but he made it to where Pack was lying. He nudged his toe under Danny Pack's chest and got him over on his back. He then pumped four more bullets into his chest.

There was noise from the balcony above, where several doors had opened and the guests had come out to see what was happening. And then screaming when they saw the carnage in the parking lot below. The man who had checked Danny Pack in at the front desk stepped out, looked and ran back inside.

Carmie staggered to the Honda Accord, got himself in and roared off, leaving strips of smoking rubber on the pavement and a shrieking squeal hanging in the night air.

✢40

MORRISON WAS WORKING THE NEW YORK *TIMES* CROSSWORD puzzle, the one syndicated on Sunday in the Chicago *Sun-Times,* thereby saving himself the $2.50 difference in the newspaper price, when the telephone interrupted.

"You're gonna want to meet me," was all the voice at the other end said.

"I am?" Morrison recognized Angelo Franconi's voice.

"Two o'clock, same place as yesterday, where we were sitting."

And the connection was broken.

CHICAGO'S FAMOUS WINDS HAD kicked up in the twenty-four hours since they had last sat down in the shadow of the Adler Planetarium, winds bringing with them a cloud cover and chill to the air. The lake was slashed with whitecaps moving toward the breakwaters and beaches that stretched to the north. The water was swelling up along the seawall around the planetarium and flowing over onto the concrete boardwalk. Franconi was sitting on the grass up from the shelf where they had been yesterday, gazing out at the tumultuous lake when Morrison spotted him and started the descent down the green slope.

"No boats today," Angelo said as Morrison sat down next to him. There were also no fishermen along the walkway that stretched back to the mainland and was methodically washed with a rush of water and then drained as the lake swells rose and fell. There was no one else sitting on the grass and only a few people amid the winds swirling along the parkway above as they made their way between the aquarium and the planetarium.

"Small craft warnings, I heard it on the radio driving down here," Morrison said. "But then I wasn't planning on taking the ChrisCraft out today anyway. So what's up?"

"They got Danny Pack last night."

Morrison was clearly surprised and showed it. "They did."

"That's the word. I just heard about it at the Amalfi this morning. When I walked in there Aldo called me over. He was calmer than I've seen him in days. He nodded and even tried to smile, which is not like him. 'I got some news,' he said, then took me outside. He doesn't even talk in the Amalfi anymore. We have to go out and stand in the alley next door. There he tells me, 'They got the punk last night,' the way he put it.

" 'Pack?' I said. He gave me a nine-millimeter look that could kill. You don't use names around Aldo, even out in the alley. He nodded, though.

"I told him I thought that was great, like I was congratulating him on his kid getting married or something. There were people walking around out there, Sunday morning. That made him a little nervous. He said let's go back inside, he'd fill me in later but for now he just wanted me to know I shouldn't worry about the punk anymore. But then as we're walking back toward the door he said, 'It wasn't clean, Angelo,' and he looked worried again.

"I asked him what he meant and then *he* used a name. 'Carmie fucked it up.' He was obviously upset again.

" 'How did he do that?' I asked. He said he didn't know. Period. We went back inside and he went to his table. That was all he had for me. I hung around for about an hour, then I had to go, I was invited to the Alessis' for brunch. It was Anita's idea but Joe-sep went along with it. He even invited me himself when I was over there last night picking her up. Joe-sep's got a specialty, he makes these scrambled eggs with Italian sausage and green peppers and oregano and I don't know what else. It's a tradition, according to Anita, Joe-sep's Sunday brunch. And it's an honor for me, she says, because it's normally just family."

"You call him dad?"

"Not funny."

"You're right, it isn't funny."

"Something else . . . just before I was leaving the Amalfi, Carmie came in. The whole side of his face was one big bandage, looked like a softball was wrapped onto the side of his head with a bunch of gauze and tape. I asked him what the hell happened. He said he cut himself shaving. Real funny. He did not look like a happy soldier.

"When I went to say goodbye to Aldo he said, 'Look at that asswipe,' meaning Carmie. He also said Carmie got twenty-eight stitches in the emergency room at Mount Sinai Hospital last night. He didn't sound too pleased. Whatever went down, I think Carmie managed to rise to the top of Aldo's shit-list."

"You have any thoughts on what the messy part was? You said Aldo said it wasn't clean."

"I didn't get any feel for it from Aldo. But Joe Alessi, he knew about it last night. Before we sat down for the eggs and were standing around drinking Harvey Wallbangers, another

Joe-sep specialty, he started talking about it. I think he already had the details but he didn't give them to me. He did say Carmie didn't do it according to the way they—meaning himself and Aldo and, I guess, Gussy Tuscano—wanted it done. He said it would probably turn out okay but it should have been better, cleaner. Then the others came around and we didn't talk about it anymore."

Morrison shook his head. "I wish we could find out something *first* once in a while. I mean, a gang finds the Meek kid for us. The Outfit finds Pack first. You think there's a chance we might ever find *anybody* first?"

"I doubt it," Angelo said.

"Where's Pack's body?"

"That I don't know. Hey, maybe you can find it first . . . a first." Angelo stood up. "I've got to get back. Aldo said he wanted to see me again later this afternoon, don't know about what. I'll do what I can and call later when I can get away."

"Try me at the number downtown first. I think I'll go over there for a while. Otherwise I'll be home."

They started up the hill together. "Well, at least little Latrona's off the hook now."

"Seems so. Guess you won't have to knock her off."

"Not funny, Joe." *Not funny at all,* he added to himself. "By the way, they were pissed they couldn't find out where you guys put the girl. Tuscano especially. He couldn't believe his source couldn't come up with it. That's according to Aldo."

"I'm glad we did something right."

"I'd still keep her under wraps, Joe. Never know what they'll do. One thing I've learned, they can be very unpredictable. It's one reason they survive."

"I hear you," Morrison said as they reached the sidewalk at the top of the slope and started walking down. There were not many cars in the parking slots that circled the planetarium for a Sunday afternoon, Morrison noticed, but then, the summer was over and the tourists' kids were back in school and the lousy weather on top of it . . .

"You know, this is the first time, I think, they haven't been able to get something out of your headquarters that they really wanted," Angelo was saying. "At least in the last year or two. I think your leak, their contact, is pretty high-level."

"I think you're probably right."

"When I think about the girl, she was as good as dead if they knew where to find her. Can you imagine that?"

"Sure I can. Don't forget, I've been exposed to their kind of shit a long time myself." Morrison stopped at his car parked on Solidarity Drive. "Where'd you park?"

"Down by the aquarium."

"Want a ride?"

"No, thanks, the walk'll do me good."

Morrison looked at Franconi. "What would you have done if they gave you the job of taking the girl out?"

Angelo was startled. "I wouldn't have done it . . ."

"But *what* would you have done?"

"They wouldn't have given me the contract—"

"You seemed to think they might the other day."

"Well, that was just thinking about the worst possible scenario. I have to do that, comes with the territory."

"I'm sure. But what if they *did* give it to you? What if Aldo Forte said you do the job you'll be a full-fledged made guy?"

Angelo was clearly not liking the drift of the exchange. "I told you, I wouldn't have done it. I'd get to you or Doyle so you could stop it before it could happen. I'd figure out something . . ."

Morrison finally let up.

"I've got to admit, Angelo, I don't envy you your job. What a way to make a living."

"You got a tough job, too. Somebody could shoot you too. Right?" Angelo did not wait for an answer. "Or either one of us could be the shooter . . . given a situation. Right?"

And suddenly, the dream Angelo had had a few nights ago and that he could not shake came back to him, complete with its bitter aftertaste. It had been so vivid that night, him staring down at the red, bulging, pulsating baseball-sized boil as he pulled the garrot tighter and tighter, being drawn toward the redness, his own head coming down on it, watching, mesmerized, as its color faded into a moist, membranous pink, taking on the shape of a pair of soft lips, speaking unintelligible words in a hushed whisper, moving closer to hear them, until his face was almost on top of them, and feeling himself slipping and being swallowed by them—which was when, thank God, he had come awake and gotten out of bed, his heart like a pneumatic hammer inside his chest.

"True," Joe Morrison was saying.

"What?"

"I was answering your question. Given a situation . . ."

"Oh, yeah." Angelo started to say something, hesitated, then went on. "You ever kill anybody, Joe? On the job?"

"No."

"You ever think about it?"

"Of course. You ever met a cop who didn't?"

"Right, yeah. Well, I guess you're lucky."

"I tried to a couple of times," Morrison said, reaching down to unlock the car door.

"How do you mean?"

"I mean I shot a couple of guys, and when I did I guess I was trying to kill them. I know I didn't want them up and shooting me. But none of them died. I guess I wasn't a very good shot."

"How'd you feel afterwards, after shooting the guy?"

Morrison gave him a look. "I just did what I had to do . . . under the circumstances."

"Yeah, did what you had to do. Yeah, that makes sense."

"Be sure you keep in touch," Morrison said as Angelo walked off.

✜41

"I WAKE YOU UP?" FRANCONI SAID WHEN MORRISON AN-swered the telephone. It was a few minutes before midnight.

"As a matter of fact."

"Sorry. Aldo took some of us out. This is the first chance I got."

"No problem."

"You find a body belonging to a guy named Pack yet?"

"No. We don't even know where to look. You know where it is?"

"I do."

"Where?"

"Right under your noses."

"What do you mean?"

"The morgue."

"What?"

"C'mon, you know the place. The little hotel you guys got for wayward bodies. They wanted to get rid of the body so nobody would ever find it. Carmie tried to make the grab at a motel out near O'Hare, did a dumbass thing, tried to do it alone, but the guy put up a helluva fight from what I heard. That's what happened to the side of Carmie's head. The kid almost got away, but Carmie shot him in the parking lot and there was a helluva lot of commotion but he managed to get the hell out of there. Needless to say, he didn't have time to bring along the body."

Morrison was trying to remember reports he had read when he went downtown that afternoon. There were two homicides but neither one fitted with this. "I didn't see anything in our reports—"

"The motel was in Franklin Park, on Mannheim Road. It wouldn't make the Chicago reports. Check the county. It was

Franklin Park cops that brought it in. Plus, from what Aldo told me, there was no identification on the body, just a plane ticket to New Orleans in his suitcase and that was in a phony name." A pause. "That was the plane ticket I gave him that night."

"Who'd Aldo get all this from?"

"I don't know exactly, but it came from somebody at the morgue. They got sources everywhere, Joe. Anyway, he's a John Doe over there, the way I hear it. Look, I can't stay on this pay phone. I'm in a gas station. You take it from here."

MORRISON AND NORELLI WERE in the Medical Examiner's office at the morgue on Harrison Street waiting for Tim Doyle to bring in Latrona Meek from wherever it was they were keeping her. There had been an autopsy set for eight that morning on the body of John Doe, brought in at 10:03 P.M. September 10th. It was evident that the cause of death was from multiple gunshot wounds, but homicides always mandated autopsies. Morrison had gotten hold of the acting chief M.E. the night before and had the autopsy postponed and then made arrangements for the girl to take a look and see if she could identify the body. It was a special case, Morrison told the M.E., with the girl being in the federal witness program, and so they did not want to go through ordinary channels on this.

Doyle arrived a little after nine. The M.E. asked where the witness was and Doyle told him outside with a pair of U.S. marshals; he would bring her in when everything was set up. The M.E. picked up the telephone on his desk and dialed, read off a number and told whoever it was on the other end of the line to ring him back when the body was ready for viewing.

"How's the girl holding up?" Morrison asked Doyle.

"Seems to be doing okay. She didn't have much to say on the ride over. I asked her if she wanted to see her mother while we're in town here. She said she didn't care. You still got a guard on her mother?"

"No."

"So it's a good thing the kid doesn't care," Norelli said.

"We probably couldn't find the mother without several days' notice."

"Why are you guys always so negative?" Doyle asked.

They didn't answer that.

It took some ten minutes before the M.E. got the word everything was ready for them, and Doyle went out to get Latrona Meek. They brought her into the viewing room, a rectangular, unfurnished space with yellow walls, one of which included a large picture window. A cream-colored shade was pulled down. It was, ironically enough, not so different from the nursery area of a hospital where one could look through a similar pane of glass at a newborn baby. The room had a heavy, artificial, fruity aroma that came from air fresheners.

"Shall I do the honors?" the M.E. said. He was a tall, pleasant-looking man with wavy gray hair and large plastic-rimmed glasses, in his mid-sixties. He was wearing a pale blue doctor's robe over his street clothes. Two marshals stayed back by the door.

The M.E. took the girl by the arm. "Would you step over here by the window, please? It's Latrona, isn't it?" She nodded and let herself be guided up to the window. "Latrona Meek, that's a pretty name, sounds like a singer." A trace of a smile appeared on her face and quickly disappeared. "Now, Latrona, they're going to raise the shade here and you will see the man you are being asked to identify." He had her stationed just to the left of the center of the window and pointed down directly in front of her. "All you will see is the man's face, from the shoulders up. Just take your time."

He tapped on the window with a knuckle and a moment later the shade slid upward electronically. There was the shape of a human body giving form to the white sheet draped over it. The head, still covered by the sheet, was where the M.E. had pointed. Behind the gurney, where the body was lying, was a young black man in a pale green jumpsuit and a rimless cap of the same color and a pair of semi-transparent disposable plastic gloves. He was looking out at the M.E., who nodded back to him.

The attendant reached across the body and took an edge of the white sheet in each hand and gently peeled it back to reveal the head of the corpse, folding it neatly at shoulder level and then stepping back.

Latrona Meek's eyes went wide and she let out a gasp, then turned quickly to the M.E. and to the others.

Morrison said, "What the hell—"

Everyone looked bewildered, nobody more so than the M.E. Because they were looking down at a head that looked like it might have been contrived in the special-effects department for a horror movie. It was ashen gray and fleshless, the cheeks sucked in like sinkholes, a few long straggly hairs striking out from the otherwise bald head, the neck a withered, collapsed pole the texture of lizard skin.

"This is the wrong body," the M.E. said, shaken and gesturing sharply to the young man inside to cover it back up.

Timothy Doyle leaned down to Latrona Meek. "They made a mistake here, honey. This isn't the person you're supposed to look at." He led her back away from the window.

"I don't know what happened," the M.E. was saying, "but I'll get it straightened out." He started for the door, then turned to Morrison. "Why don't you take the girl back to my office. She can wait there."

Doyle and the two marshals headed for the stairs leading back up to the M.E.'s office, and Morrison and Norelli followed the M.E. down the corridor to a door that led into the cooler and then into the viewing room. The attendant was just starting to roll the gurney back out when the three of them descended on him. He could tell something was wrong by looking through the window, but because he could not hear anything he did not know just what the problem was.

There was shouting from the M.E., who had stripped the sheet off the corpse, and bewildered looks from the young man piloting the gurney and other attendants who had come over to see what the commotion was about. Finally a supervisor arrived with a brown manila folder. "Here it is," he said. He held the toe tag of the cadaver with his thumb and index finger and waved the folder in his other hand. "Same number." He moved up the body to where the arms were crossed on the chest, picked up one of the scrawny arms with the plastic wristband and turned it toward the M.E. and Morrison and Norelli. "Same number here, too. That's the number you asked for." He dropped the wrist and the skin-and-bone arm bounced on the steel gurney, then slid off and swayed back and forth. The supervisor opened the folder. "John Doe," he said, "logged in night before last."

The M.E., who had been so reserved in the viewing room with the little girl, snatched the folder from him, looked at it, then back at the supervisor and the young gurney driver standing next to him. "I don't care what the damned number is. Does this thing look like a man in his mid-to-late twenties, one hundred eighty-six pounds, six-foot-one, blond hair in a ponytail with a time of death thirty-six hours ago?" He pointed at the corpse on the gurney. "This one's been dead for months."

"Well, it's obviously a mistake," the supervisor finally said, stating the obvious. "Got the wrong papers with the wrong cadaver. We'll get the right one for you." He smiled weakly. "It's gotta be here somewhere." Nobody smiled back.

On the way back to the M.E.'s office, where they were all going to wait, Morrison asked Norelli, "You think *they* might've gotten the body out of here?"

Norelli thought for a moment, shook his head. "Too flagrant," he said. "A homicide, too risky. But then . . . you never know with these guys."

✦42

DOYLE WAS READING THE FRANKLIN PARK POLICE REPORT when the Medical Examiner, Morrison and Norelli came into the office.

"Anything interesting?" Morrison asked as he sat down on the couch next to Doyle.

"The kid from Camden had a sense of humor. A Philly fan. He registered at the motel as Lenny Dykstra."

"I bet he didn't die laughing."

"No wallet, no identification," Doyle said, ignoring the humor. "An open-end one-way airplane ticket to New Orleans in the name of Joseph Martin. Four packets of cocaine. Two thousand six hundred dollars and forty-six cents in cash. A sheet of paper with telephone numbers on it. Four in Chicago, each with a first name alongside it . . . Sammy, Ron, Phil, Winnie. Another with a Fort Lauderdale area code that checks out to the Yankee Clipper, a hotel there. Another to New Orleans, the Sheraton Hotel there. Clothes in the suitcase. That's it. Franklin Park thinks it's a drug deal gone sour, the coke, the cash, adds up to it." Doyle looked at Morrison and Norelli. "But we know different."

"And as we speak our people are on the street checking out the listees of those telephone numbers and the motel where Lenny Dykstra chose to stay," Morrison said, "with photos of Carmen DiSavio in hand. Fingerprints were lifted from John Doe on arrival and run through AFIS, which turned up nothing. Sent routinely on to Washington yesterday. I called Camden this morning and asked them to fax a set of Pack's prints directly to AFIS. We should have something on that later in the day."

Doyle nodded toward Latrona Meek, who was sitting in the Medical Examiner's chair behind his desk and doodling on a piece of paper. "The kid's doing pretty damn well, considering."

"Considering," Morrison said, "she saw her boyfriend murdered in front of her and she's been living on the streets for a couple of weeks and she's scared somebody's going to kill her and she's having a little bout with drug withdrawal and we top it off with a surprise horror show—"

Doyle said to the girl, "Is there anything you need, hon?" She didn't respond. "Latrona?" She looked up. "Anything we can get for you?" She shook her head and went back to doodling.

"Send somebody out for a strawberry shake. She likes those," Morrison said. Latrona actually smiled.

VAUGHN SWAYZE WAS NERVOUS as he punched at the touchtone telephone in the lobby of the Holiday Inn. He had change spread out on a metal shelf beneath the phone. He needed it because twice now he had gotten a wrong number by hitting the wrong button, he was so jittery. Finally he got through to Vernon's.

Jimmy Pagnano was not there.

"You got another number I can reach him, this is important, really important."

"No. Gimme a number where you're at and I'll give it to him if he comes in."

"This is really urgent urgent. Can't you—"

"I'll tell him that if he comes in."

"I'll call back every fifteen minutes. You think he'll be in, right?"

"I don't *know* whether he'll be in. Just give me a fucking number."

"I can't, I'm outside at a pay phone. I'll keep calling back. Be sure'n tell him. Be sure. Tell him."

Probably it was too early, but he tried D'Amico's. Pagnano wasn't there either.

Swayze swept up the coins and walked back to the lobby, where Little Red was sitting reading a newspaper someone had left behind. "Not there. I'll keep trying."

Three calls and forty minutes later he got Jimmy Pagnano at Vernon's. "What's so urgent, you little wiener?"

"I got a problem, Jimmy. A problem. I got the body last night. I got it. You got the money, didn't you?" There was only silence from the other end. "Jimmy, hey, Jimmy, you there?"

"I don't know what you're talking about."

"Jimmy, we got the body and I took it in to the funeral guy this morning and he takes one look at it and won't touch it. It's got six fucking bullet holes in the chest, Jimmy, bullet holes, in the chest. And he says it's a fresh corpse and he don't want nothing to do with a murder. It was supposed to be a throwaway I was getting."

"Sounds like maybe you do got a problem. You got a phone I can reach you."

"No. Little Red, he doesn't have a phone. So I'm outside."

"Call me back in an hour."

"Sure, you'll get it straightened out, huh, Jimmy . . . straightened out?"

A pause. "So if the funeral home don't have the body . . . you aren't driving around with it or anything?"

"No, hey, *Jimmy.* Gimme some credit, huh, credit. I got it back at Red's. In that bungalow he's renting, he got a freezer in the basement. All taken care of. Gimme a little credit."

MORRISON AND NORELLI RAPPED on the door to the first floor apartment in the two-flat in Uptown, the one with the name *H. Hawkins* on the letterbox. A woman answered, looking out the crack in the door, the chain on.

"Halsey Hawkins here?" Norelli asked. He held his badge and I.D. up to the opening.

"He's asleep. He works nights."

"We know that. Wake him up."

She did not have to. The noise at the door had awakened him.

"Whatcha want?" he asked from somewhere behind her.

"We want to talk to you, Halsey . . . about last night. Now

open the door or we're going to have to haul your sorry ass downtown and book you.''

Halsey Hawkins opened the door.

"You were on duty last night at the Medical Examiner's office," Morrison said once they were inside.

"Yes, sir, my shift, eleven to seven . . .''

"Five bodies were checked out of there last night. Four went to potter's field in Homewood, one to the Melman Funeral Home. Your name was on all five releases.''

Hawkins worked at a nervous grin. "Housecleaning, hundred-and-twenty-day wonders. Do it every four months.''

"Those aren't the ones we're here about. The one that went to the funeral home . . .''

"Oh, that one.''

"Yeah, that one. Seems there's no such place as the Melman Funeral Home anywhere in Cook County, much less the address that was on the release form you signed.''

"Well, they had papers. Everything looked okay to me.''

"We know, we saw the papers. A woman identified the body last night as her husband, a Vaughn Swayze of Detroit, Michigan, cause of death, heart attack, record of autopsy signed illegibly. You signed the identification papers.''

"Sure, she came in and said she heard her husband was there. I checked and we had the man. Just followed procedure. We showed her the body and she I.D.'d it. Signed for it. She made a call and later the funeral home showed up, two guys, and they took the body, signed for it.''

The telephone rang and the woman picked it up and handed it to Halsey Hawkins. He said he would call the person back and listened to what sounded like a harangue at the other end, which the detectives could hear but could not make out the words. When Halsey said he was talking with the police, the call came to an abrupt end.

"We don't believe the body that was delivered to Melman, whoever that might be, was the body of Vaughn Swayze.''

"Why not?'' Hawkins looked genuinely confused.

"Because there's another body over there that's missing. A

John Doe, a homicide. Came in the night before last with multiple bullet wounds."

"What's that got to do—"

"We think the body you gave to the Melman people was the John Doe that just came in. It's nowhere in the morgue."

He looked scared now. "I just signed the papers, looked at 'em and signed 'em. I didn't see the body go out."

"Who did?"

"Well, we got guys who do that. I gave 'em an order sheet and they went back and got the body, took it out on the dock and then the two men from the funeral home took it."

"We're running a trace on this Vaughn Swayze. Do you think maybe there was a little mix-up last night? Maybe somebody wanted that other corpse, the John Doe, and you were accommodating them? You want to tell us what really went on last night, Halsey?"

"I told you everything I know. Jeez, gimme a break. It sounds like maybe a mistake was made—"

"One was. And a body we are interested in is missing, a homicide victim. You got *any* idea how deep a pile of shit you could be in if you are a part of this?"

"Me?"

"*You*. Obstruction of a first-degree murder investigation is a starter, aiding and abetting in the perpetration of a homicide can put someone in the joint for a very long time. We intend, as they say, to throw the book at you if we find out you are implicated in this and are not telling us."

Morrison handed him his card. "You get any ideas before we come back with more, you might want to give me a call."

When they left, Halsey Hawkins was so anxious to use the telephone, he almost fell over the coffee table.

WHEN SWAYZE WAS ABLE to get through to Jimmy Pagnano at the end of the day, Pagnano said, "You were right, Vaughn-Boy, you got a *big* problem. You got the wrong goddamn body. They got the numbers mixed up over there and they gave you the wrong one. You got a body the police want. You got a body we don't want the police to get. *You got me in the middle of it.*"

"Hang on, Jimmy, hang on. We can work this thing out. Hey, no big deal. I just take the body back to Halsey, to Halsey, and we run a switcheroo. He gets back the wrong one and I get the right one. Simple."

"No, it ain't simple, Vaughn-Boy. *I* want the body you got. The deal is off."

"No, it can't be. Jimmy, I paid the money, both payments. Every penny I could drum up you got. I just gotta get the right body. Hey, just let me handle it, Jimmy—"

"The deal is off. Now tell me where that fucking body is, where that little redhead lives before I come find you and make it so little Fellate's gonna have to go back down and identify you for real this time."

"I'll be back in touch," Swayze said, "back in touch," and hung up.

His face was as pale as the winter moon when he walked over to Little Red, who was sitting in the same place in the lobby of the Holiday Inn as he had been that morning.

"I gotta think this out," he said. He started to wipe away the perspiration that had begun to show on his forehead. "We got ourselves a problem, Little Red. I gotta figure something out."

IN THE LITTLE OFFICE off the kitchen at Vernon's, Jimmy Pagnano threw the telephone onto the floor, setting off an electronic squeaking from the receiver, before he kicked it across the room. "He hung up on me. The little fucker hung up on me." Pagnano was more astonished than angry.

✦43

"I REALLY THOUGHT YOU HAD A WRAP ON THIS ONE," DOYLE said, sitting across the table from Morrison in the cocktail lounge of the Hilton Towers, where Doyle had suggested they meet rather than the drier confines of 11th and State or the Federal Building.

"So did I. The little girl safe and sound again?" Morrison asked.

"Tucked away. Best home she's had in this life. She's still scared to death, but I think she may be getting to like life away from the projects."

"Shame she's going to have to go back."

"Maybe we can do something about that," Doyle said.

"She's got a mother there, and mother is not about to give her up and watch the welfare disappear. Biological mother's got all the rights these days anyway, fitness has nothing to do with it. Happens all the time. Department of Family Services sends abused kids, tortured kids, back all the time. It's the way the system works. Latrona's a victim of it."

"Great system. Well, as I said, I thought this was over and done with this morning. Kid nails the hitter from Camden for you. You got yourself a murderer, if a departed one. Case closed."

Morrison said, "It would have been nice if we'd had a corpse for her to identify. The fingerprints, incidentally, checked out with the ones from Camden." Morrison gave Doyle a slightly patronizing smile. "We're still waiting for a check report from the FBI, even though Washington had the request a day earlier."

"We're a little more complex an operation than the Camden PD, Joe. Well, too bad . . . I was hoping we could maybe bring down Forte with the corpse. Take him down for a murder. I'd settle for that. Not like Gabriel, who wants to bring down the whole Outfit, Tuscano on down, by himself.'' Doyle shook his head. "The guy's getting out of control. The thing with this girlfriend. He's begging for trouble.''

Morrison's beeper went off. "The hotline. I better see what's up. Order me another Jack Daniels.''

Morrison was gone almost ten minutes. "Still no body,'' he said as he sat down. A little grin began to form around the corners of his mouth. "Norelli says Eddie McCabe, one of the detectives out of Four, talked to the two workers who brought the body out last night. They said they thought something was a little out of the ordinary. It was the first time, they said, they ever loaded a stiff into a Chevy van. When they mentioned that to the guys from the funeral home, they said their hearse was in the shop. The guy from the morgue said that probably explained why the Chevy van had a bumper sticker that said *Alamo*.''

"They've got balls, you've got to give them credit for that,'' Doyle said, sipping on his martini.

"The Outfit?'' Morrison shook his head. "Even if they don't know we know who the John Doe is, which I think was the case, at least at the time the body disappeared, I don't buy they would come in like that. All the trouble of papers and such crap? And a rented van? You ever hear of them *renting* a vehicle they were going to use in a crime? I think they would have just glommed the body and been gone. Let's try and sort it out. Who would know, after all, who got the body or how they got it, except for their connection, and he's not about to say anything about it.''

"I take it you haven't talked to Gabriel today.''

"No. Hope to tonight. I left a message on his answering machine.'' Doyle did a double-take. "Our own little code,'' Morrison said. "Don't worry.''

"The mob can do some stupid things, but on this I guess you're right.''

"Besides, there really is a Vaughn Swayze. Wilson, Mc-Cabe's partner, checked him out and, like the papers at the morgue say, he's from Detroit. Nobody's at the address there but the apartment's under his name and according to what Wilson could find out, he lives there with a wife, no kids, and works for a company called Carmichael Office Furniture. They confirmed all that, and his boss said Swayze was supposed to have been in Chicago on business last week. He thought he'd have been back in Detroit by now, for the weekend. They're running a make on him in Detroit, and I just told them to run one in Chicago, just in case. Who knows? Leave no stone unturned, no door unknocked upon. Just like they teach in the Academy.''

"Anything else?"

"Johnny Nolan and his partner," Morrison said, "have been tracking the leads on Pack. He was shacked up with his girlfriend here in Chicago. The Winnie on the list, she's Winona Kokonitz. She wasn't home but her neighbor was and the lady I.D.'d Pack, had seen him around the last week or two with Kokonitz. And get this, she took one look at the picture of Carmen DiSavio and said she knew him too. He's been around a couple of times asking about Kokonitz. Seems she and Pack had been out of town for the last few days and while they were gone this 'nice heavy-set man who had some bad news for her' had come by several times.

"The Kokonitz woman worked at a supermarket, the neighbor told them, so Nolan and Nabasco went over there. She was uncooperative until they told her Pack had been killed. Then she fainted. When she came to she admitted they'd been together, had gone off to Wisconsin to some casino. She swears she didn't know he was in any trouble until the day they got back, and then he left and that was the last she ever saw of him. She never saw Carmen DiSavio before, she said when they showed her his picture, but her boss and one of the other check-out women recognized him. Seems he was there too looking for her. They said he claimed to be with some insurance company.''

"You going after him?"

"Quietly. Franco and a couple others are going out looking for him now. If they don't come up with anything we'll issue an APB tomorrow.''

"Well without the *corpus* you don't have the *corpus de-licti*." Doyle shook his head. "Even with it, what've you got? What're you going to charge Carmen DiSavio with, a per-verted interest in Ms. Coconuts, or whatever her name is?"

"Give us a little time. Maybe somebody at the motel saw him. There's blood and flesh on the motel-room key Pack had, and according to the incoming morgue report there was blood on the hand of his body, which we unfortunately do not have, and on the clothes of the victim, which we do have. They were still at the morgue and they've been sent to the crime lab. I think we can probably get Ms. Coconuts, Ms. Kokonitz, to identify them. Maybe Gabriel will come up with something else we can use."

"Maybe." Doyle looked for the waitress. "One more . . . Gabriel's running out of time. He's slipping from the asset to the liability side of the ledger. That's why I was hoping we could bring down Forte. It would be a waste of a great effort if after all this he can only bring down someone like DiSavio, and I don't know if he can even do that. He's got himself so involved with the girl and this thing about being made . . . I don't know, maybe he'll work it out. He's good. Hope so, anyway."

Morrison's beeper went off.

"*This* is the city that never sleeps," Doyle said.

The beep was from Franco Norelli. "Guess what, Joe? The computer check we ran on Swayze just came back. Positive."

"Here? Chicago?"

"You got it. Popped up right away. Seems he and a guy by the name of Cyril Ryan were hauled in for making pests of themselves around the Chicago Bulls. Team security thought there was something funny and passed the word and the first district checked it out and thought they were tailing one of the players. Don't know the reason but when they found out this Ryan guy, a.k.a. Red Riding Hood according to his sheet, is out on parole, just out, in fact, they brought him in and hassled him around a little. And guess what Cyril was in for? A scam. He's got an arm-long record. He's a con man."

"Any Outfit ties?"

"None that I see here. I got his address from the parole office and caught Nolan and Nabasco before they checked out at Four. They're on the way to see the guy. He's living out on the northwest side. I told Nolan to let either one of us know if anything comes up. Red Riding Hood. Can you beat it?"

✦44

"YOU CALLED, I GOT THE MESSAGE," ANGELO WAS SAYING to Morrison, having unexpectedly shown up on Morrison's doorstep in Rogers Park.

Morrison had made them drinks, bourbon for himself, a diet Pepsi for Angelo. "Well, it's a surprise, but nice to see you . . . You guys by any chance have a body we're looking for?"

"Pack? No, they're looking all over for it too. It's a kind of fiasco."

"There isn't someone named Swayze working for you, paying back a favor, something?"

"No, but I know who you're talking about. That's where the fiasco comes in. This guy Swayze's got the body. Forte's going crazy. Ditto Alessi. The story goes like this . . . this guy Swazye wants a body from the morgue nobody wants, a homeless, anybody who just died and nobody claims. It seems he wants to pull an insurance scam. That's the word. Somehow he gets in touch with Jimmy Pagnano. You know, we talked about him. Well, Jimmy set up this thing with a guy he's got over at the morgue and gets it arranged. Piece of cake. Pagnano's morgue guys brought up an old body that was supposedly headed for the dump out in Homewood, the place they bury the unclaimed, and set it aside for pick-up. He's supposed to give it to Swayze or whoever's picking it up for him."

"The guy at the morgue named Halsey Hawkins?"

Angelo looked at him. "Yeah . . . you know this story already?"

"No, go on. Hawkins is the guy who had his name on papers over there."

"Well, in the meantime Pack's body's brought in. Somebody in the back fucks up and gets the identifications mixed up. When Swayze shows up they go fetch the body for him and off he goes with it. Only it's *Pack's* body he's got, not the unknown soldier."

"And you guys don't know where Swayze is? Pagnano doesn't?"

"No. And he's very upset. Alessi is all over his ass about it. It brings Alessi in on this. Pagnano's his numero uno, everybody knows that ... you guys, Doyle, everybody. It's at least very embarrassing for Pagnano. And he's one guy you don't want to embarrass or offend."

"Doesn't Swayze know he's got the wrong body?"

"Yeah, Pagnano's talked to him, but the guy's in hiding or something. They figure maybe he's trying to peddle it to some funeral home on his own. A real asshole entrepreneur. You know, a quick shot, log it in with the papers and the undertaker turns around and roasts it. Give the ashes to the insurance company, figuratively speaking, and collect on the policy, like he originally planned as his endgame."

"Who's going to take a body with a chest tattooed with bullet holes and a set of papers that says the guy died of a coronary? I saw the papers, the morgue copies," Morrison said.

"Somebody, maybe. Pagnano had some undertaker all set to take a four-month-old corpse of an old man as a guy in his thirties who supposedly collapsed a couple of days earlier. This undertaker didn't want any part of a homicide, which shows that despite a larcenous heart he's also got some brains. But who knows what somebody else might do out there, the price being right."

"Swayze have any idea *whose* body he's got?"

"From what I hear, not the foggiest. I don't think he knows much of anything except he's got a body that's not easy to peddle. Anyway, Swayze sure doesn't know he's such a popular guy, so many people looking for him." Franconi tried for a smile but with all that was roiling inside it didn't come off . . .

"What about Carmen DiSavio?"

"He's under the covers. He knows he's in some shit, knows he fucked up doing the hit. The main thing is Pack's dead, that's what he told Joe-sep, who along with some others don't necessarily agree or see themselves off the hook."

"We're looking for Carmen. Do they know that?"

"Not just on what I told you, I hope." The surprise turned to concern. "That could be traced back to me, Joe."

"We got witnesses who peg him stalking Pack's girlfriend, we got people at the motel who think they might be able to identify him, we got stuff from the scene. Don't worry, we got enough on our own to warrant looking for him."

"I hope so. The paranoia's rising over there. To give you an idea, the contract on the kid, the little girl, it's still on . . . they got word you guys had her at the morgue this morning. They had somebody get over there to follow her, find out where you guys are keeping her. It was too late, everybody was gone, but they're still looking."

"How the hell did they find out we had her there?" Morrison asked, already suspecting the answer was from a leak to the Outfit.

"Don't know. I do know it wasn't until *after* she was there that they found out. You figure it. Right now, the point is, you give 'em a chance, they're going to take her out. She's still a witness, even to dead men, the way they see it now. And one of 'em is available . . . even if a corpse . . . to be connected to them."

Morrison nodded. "Back to DiSavio."

"They might whack Carmie . . . Aldo talked to me about it this afternoon." Angelo's face was tight.

"And the job might be yours?"

"He said if they decide to do it they'd like it to be Jimmy Pagnano and me." Angelo's knuckles were white, fists clenched. He forced himself to go on. "The last step, Aldo called it. Said he and Joe-sep had talked about it, Pagnano and

I carry this off, I got their backing with Tuscano. I'll be made . . .''

Morrison suspected this was the real reason Angelo had shown up at his apartment. "You thinking about doing it?"

Angelo sidestepped. He was sweating now. "Pagnano would do it. He enjoys it."

"You'd be there, same thing legally."

"The man's a killer, an animal." He was, of course, talking mostly to himself. Roy Echols on the boat came back to him . . . but at least then he hadn't had time to think about it.

Morrison got up, took a step toward the kitchen where the bourbon was, then stopped. "You really want to get made so you'd kill somebody for it?"

Angelo said nothing.

"You want another Pepsi?"

"No . . . look, Joe, you said it the other night, sometimes you gotta do what you gotta do."

"Bullshit, and apples and oranges."

Angelo stared down at the carpet. "Joe, my whole fucking life's falling apart. All I want is to go off with Anita and get away from this shit, both sides of it." He looked up at Morrison. "Yours and theirs."

"Have you told Doyle this?"

"He wouldn't understand. I don't know where the hell to go. I got into this, I admit, to be somebody, maybe be a fucking hero, bring down those bigshot shits. *Me*. All I had to do was get myself made. And then Anita comes along. I asked her again today . . . about going away, the two of us. You know what she says to me? She said all she wanted was to marry me. Be with me the rest of my life. But we couldn't run away. Why would I even think of something like that? She doesn't understand. She still worships her old man, loves her family. I told you, she doesn't want to know the truth so she doesn't."

Morrison, with nothing useful to say, kept quiet.

"I got things pulling me apart, Joe."

"I know . . ."

"You don't know." Angelo was really sweating now. "You don't know, Joe."

"Start looking for the trapdoors, Angelo. You once told me you always had one."

"I've been thinking about them." Nothing more specific. Then: "Soon as they find out you're looking for Carmie, that end is going to come to a head. Can you call it off or maybe postpone it. You'll be signing his death warrant, you know."

"Too late, probably. We're doing it on the quiet but there's enough word going around that I'd be surprised if it didn't get back already. But I'll make a call as soon as we're through."

Angelo got up. "I better get out of here. Aldo wants me to hang close all the time."

"We should talk again first thing in the morning," Morrison said. "Where can you be, say, maybe eight, eight-thirty?"

"How about the planetarium, where we met the last couple of times? I like it there, close to the water . . . If something comes up and I can't make it I'll change my answering machine message to I can't *answer* the phone, but if you'll leave a message. Right now it's I can't *come to* the phone. I'll then get back to you when I can and we'll set up a new time."

"You got something to help you sleep?" Morrison said. "I mean, don't drink much—"

"A head-butt with a Mack truck is about all that would work tonight," Angelo said as they started to walk toward the door. "The last week or so I been getting used to getting by on maybe an hour or two of sleep. I hate to wake up alone, I'm fucking scared to go to sleep."

"I've been there. That's why I got out of Homicide. I'm still there, some nights."

"Well, at least we've got something in common," Angelo said, then stopped at the door. "Say, Joe, you know when I asked you the other day if you ever killed anybody, how come you didn't ask me, you know, if I ever killed anybody? Didn't it come to mind?"

"Maybe it did. Maybe I didn't want to hear the answer."

✥45

"SAY, WE GOT A REAL FOUL-UP ON OUR HANDS," VAUGHN Swayze was saying into the telephone that hung on the outside wall of a Shell gas station about six blocks from Little Red's bungalow. He had the index finger of his other hand jammed into his ear to cut out the noise of the traffic from the street.

"You're telling me."

"Halsey, you gave me a body that looks like Swiss cheese."

"You got the wrong body, pal."

"I *know* that."

"Pagnano is very pissed. Where you got the body?"

"Never mind. I got it, that's all." Swayze did not want to tell him he had it at that very moment moldering away in the back of the rented van despite the two twenty-pound bags of chipped ice it was nestled with under a painter's dropcloth he had appropriated from Little Red's basement. After Little Red had heard about the encounter with the reluctant undertaker that morning and that the body belonged to a murder victim, he told Swayze to get it the hell out of his freezer. Little Red would not listen to reason, which miffed Swayze, but he packed it up and took it with him. Little Red told him not to come back until he had gotten rid of the corpse, not to come within a mile of his place if he still had it. Little Red had his priorities all screwed up, to Swayze's way of thinking, but there wasn't a lot he could do about it. It was the redhead's house, after all. Still, he didn't think that was any of Halsey Hawkins's business.

"You didn't *do* anything with it yet, did you? Pagnano's—"

"How the hell can I do anything with it, Halsey? Nobody's gonna touch it after they take one look at it. I mean nobody who's gonna do with it what I want 'em to do. Anyway, I figure we can work it out, you and me, make everybody happy. Here's what I think. You listening . . . listening?''

"I'm all ears."

."We just do a little switcheroo."

"*Wait a minute*. Jimmy Pagnano wants this body you got. You understand that?"

"Yeah, yeah. I already talked to him. He's just upset 'cause it got a little fucked up. You know how he is. Flies off the handle. Believe me, *I* know. He's a very emotional guy, very emotional. But I can handle him, in my own way. You see, I'm a thinking guy, Halsey. I got angles, always got angles. Jimmy Pagnano, I let him rave, you let him rave, but I got the answer here if you'll just listen to me—"

"I *been* listening. But you haven't. Pagnano wants the body. I'm telling you--"

"Screw Pagnano." Nervous laughter. "Don't tell him I said that. Look, he can have the body if you want to give it to him. I don't care. All I want is the body I was supposed to get, the one I paid twenty big ones for. Look, that's every centavo I got in the world and some of it I already owe on. My life's ridin' on this, my life. My death, maybe I should say. You know, the insurance . . . so the way I see it, you and I just work our own little deal. I get this body back to you and you give me the one I was supposed to get. And everybody'll be happy. Pretty simple . . . simple, right?''

"Wrong. A lot of people're looking for the one you got."

"Well, they'll *get* it. All you gotta do, Halsey—do I have to spell it out?—is get this body back, stick it in some out-of-the-way corner over there and suddenly discover it. Oh, my, the poor stiff got misplaced, but now here he is. I, Halsey Hawkins, found it. You'll be a hero.''

Silence at the other end of the phone.

"Look, Halsey, you got a problem with this? It's a no-brainer. But if you're worried I'll go the deal one better. I'll sweeten the pot. You got your money, right? Whatever your take was from what I gave you for Jimmy. So you're ridin', not walkin' . . . ridin'. So look, you can ride a little better.

Here's what I'll do, I'll sweeten it by a grand, another grand for you personally. How's that? I give you my marker when we make the switcheroo and soon as Felice gets the dough, soon as she cashes the insurance checks, the very first thousand right off the top goes to you, in cash.''

"Well . . . I'll see what I can do. When do you want to make this switcheroo, as you call it?''

"Soon as I can.'' Swayze thought of the corpse lying about twenty feet away in the van, seeing the people gassing up their cars and walking back and forth past it as they went inside to pay. "Soon, soon, soon.''

"I don't go on till eleven. Don't know what things are gonna be like over there till I get there. Say I give you a call after I get there?''

"I don't have a phone. I mean I'm outside. I mean I won't be at a phone, won't be at one.'' *That fucking Little Red, he's the only asshole in the city doesn't have a phone.* "Why don't I just call you after you get there?''

"Suit yourself, but give me some time to get things in order, you know what I mean?''

"Yeah, absolutely, Halsey. I'll call. You give me the word and I'll have this clunker with the air holes on your doorstep in ten minutes.''

"Not on *my* doorstep. We make the switch somewhere else. I'll use one of our vehicles. I do not, repeat, do *not* want that stupid van at our dock again. Let me check out a place to meet, make the exchange.'' There was a pause. "Just relax. I'll work it out.''

"Hey, hey. We got ourselves a deal, Halsey.'' *What you gotta do to get a simple job done*, Swayze said to himself as he hung up, then looked at his watch and figured he had better go back to that liquor store and get a couple more bags of ice.

HALSEY KNEW THE NUMBER without looking it up. "He's going to bring the body back,'' he said when Jimmy Pagnano came on the line. "I told him I'd tell him where I'd pick it up later. You still want it, right?''

"That we do.''

"Tell me what you want."

"Halsey, my man, do not worry. Tell him you will pick up the body from him, let's see . . . okay, off the expressway between Sixteenth and Eighteenth, on Canal."

"And what do I do with the body, Danny Pack, better known as John Doe?"

"Halsey, you don't *do* anything. You just call him, tell him where to be tonight. Then, like the good man you are, just go back to work like, you know, we never had this conversation. One body's lost forever. Those things happen. You know you guys over there do a great job, but what the hell, once in a while you lose one. Right?"

"Right. Understood. You'll want to know the time."

"You know the number. Leave a message."

NOLAN AND NABASCO RAPPED on the front door, the button to the chime or whatever sounding device was missing, just an empty hole where it was supposed to have been on the side of the doorway underneath the nameplate frame, which was empty as well.

There were lights on inside but no one was answering their knocks. There was no van either, not parked in front or in the small driveway along the side of the little house. The one-car garage at the rear was empty, Nabasco had checked that out before they both had climbed the concrete stairs to the entry porch.

The last knocking, more a fist-pounding, still did not elicit a response. But they could hear someone approaching the door from the inside and saw a squared-off inset of a face in the small window in the door looking out at them.

"Mr. Ryan," Nolan said loud enough to be heard through the heavy wood door. "Police, we want to talk to you." He held up his I.D. and badge to the little square pane of glass. The face disappeared, the door opened.

"What's up, fellas?" With the shock of red hair and the diminutive stature, Nolan and Nabasco could see where the Little Red came from, even though they were wrong about its origin.

"Little Red Riding Hood's what they call you," Nolan said. "Downstate, at Pontiac, around town, too. That's what it says on your rap sheet." Point made, Nolan introduced himself and Nabasco. "Mind if we come in? Got a few things we'd like to ask you."

Inside they could hear the blare of a television coming from a room in the back. Little Red seemed relaxed—and had the look of someone who had been down this road before. "What's on your mind? I been reporting in regular. There been no problems."

"Who said there were?" Nabasco asked.

"Nobody. But I figure you got a reason for dropping by in the middle of the night."

"Ten o'clock's not exactly the middle of the night," Nabasco said.

"We want to ask you about a pal of yours. Vaughn Swayze," Nolan put in, his tone more benign than Nabasco's.

Little Red gave him a quizzical look and retreated into himself.

"Come on, Ryan," Nabasco said. "Vaughn Swayze was with you when you were making a nuisance of yourself around the Bulls. So much so they ended up having you dragged in. I believe it was the East Chicago Avenue district where the two of you were entertained. You both got a warning and sent home. Your parole officer got a notification of it, too."

"Oh yeah, that. Well, sure I know Swayze—"

"Is there somebody back there?" Nabasco asked, pointing to the doorway that led into the room where the television was on and where there were some other noises that did not seem to be coming from the tube.

"Yeah." Little Red gave them a conspiratorial smile. "A lady friend. She's not feeling too well. So if you don't mind, can we just get this over? Let me know, guys, what is it I can do for you. I haven't seen Vaughn in some time, week or so, anyway."

"Would you mind asking her to step out here?"

"I told you she's not feeling well. Her period . . . you know. Come on, give her a break, will you. She doesn't know about, you know, some of my past. Just tell me what you want and I'll help you if I can—"

"You going to ask her to step out or am I gonna have to go back there," Nabasco asked.

Little Red shrugged. "Okay, okay . . . Hon, can you come out here a minute?"

She appeared in the doorway. She was barefoot, painted toenails, clinging skirt that stopped mid-thigh, a gold halter, and a pair of huge hoop earrings. She looked pretty great, Nabasco thought, but also uneasy.

The detectives introduced themselves. She said, "Nice to meet you." Smiled back at them, holding it as the silence wore on.

"And you are—" Nolan finally asked.

She looked at Little Red, who held her eyes with his for just a moment and then turned away from her. Then she transferred her attention to Nolan. "Felice," she said. They waited. "Felice Swayze."

Nolan and Nabasco conferred for a moment, then Nolan turned back to her. "We are going to have to ask you both some questions . . . alone." He clapped Nabasco on the shoulder. "Why don't you talk with Mr. Ryan back there," motioning toward the room with the television. "I'll talk with Mrs. Swayze."

Nabasco gave Ryan a move-it-asshole look, said, "Come on" and pushed Little Red toward the back room.

"Why don't we just sit down over here, Mrs. Swayze?" Nolan nodded toward the two plastic-covered loveseats at right angles to each other in the corner of the room.

"Whatever." But she did not immediately move. Taking her time, she sauntered across the room and dropped gracefully into the corner of one of the loveseats, lifting one leg while in the process affording Nolan the vision of a triangular patch of white nylon under the skirt. She lifted this leg over the other. She did not look to Nolan like a woman in deep mourning. He sat down in the corner of the adjoining loveseat.

"You heard about my husband, I take it," she said, averting her eyes from him.

"Yes, Mrs. Swayze. That's why we're here."
"You can call me Felice."

TWENTY-FIVE MINUTES LATER ALL four were in the unmarked
Plymouth heading back to Area Four headquarters, the two
detectives not buying the story that a mutual friend of the
bereaved widow and the good friend of the departed had taken
the body of Vaughn Swayze in order to arrange for its return
to Detroit, especially after neither one knew exactly how or
where these arrangements were being made and that in their
separate conversations with the two detectives the two had
given different names of the mutual friend. Now they were
sitting in the backseat, in silence, Ryan looking like he was
brooding about going back to the place with tall walls with
razor-wire on them from whence he had come a few weeks
earlier, and Felice looking out the window at the dazzle of
lights and activity in the streets outside that flew by at a diz-
zying rate. Nabasco was behind the wheel, driving down a
network of city streets to get back to the expressway as if both
passengers in the back were suffering from severed arteries.

✛46

MORRISON AND DOYLE WATCHED FROM THE CAR PARKED IN
the circular drive that girded the planetarium, drinking coffee
from oversized Styrofoam cups.

On this sunny, nearly windless morning the fishermen were
back along the seawall. It was quiet at the end of the landfill
by the planetarium, the tranquility interrupted only by an occasional auto horn off in the distance or the clank of a bail
bucket scraping on the concrete or the shout of one fisherman
to another or the roar of an incoming small plane descending
to Meigs Field just to the south of them. A few people strolled
along the broad walkway behind the fishermen, looking at the

sailboats and fishing boats whose owners were out early to take advantage of one of the last of the summery weekends. A cold front, in fact, was predicted to move in that very evening. But on this Friday morning, with the warm sun and blue skies, for the two men sitting there, car windows rolled down, momentarily taken over by the gently heaving lake, the tensions and pace of the city seemed of another world.

Breaking into the scene was a figure jogging down the concrete swath behind the fishermen, small and anonymous at first back by the aquarium, but as he neared them they recognized him. Running shorts and Reeboks, a gray T-shirt darkened with sweat around the collar and under the armpits, a Walkman clipped to the shorts and the earphones in place. Angelo was panting when he came to a stop where the seawall walkway ended at the hub on which the planetarium sat. He stood there jogging in place and looking around, then pulled the earphones down so they hung around his neck.

Morrison and Doyle got out of the car and started down the grassy slope to Angelo. He did not appear surprised to see Doyle with Morrison. Angelo's face was bathed in sweat. "Three miles," he said, glancing at his wristwatch when they got to him, "in twenty minutes, not bad. Don't know a thing more than when I last talked to you," he said to Morrison, "except that Aldo wants me at the Amalfi at ten. The gofer who called said be sure not to be late. Must be important . . . I've never been even close to being late. It's Aldo's way of sending a message. You didn't maybe find Danny Pack's body since we last talked, did you?"

"No. It's still among the missing."

"Likely to stay that way, I'd bet." Angelo looked at Doyle. "What brings you out on this beautiful day? Checking up on me?" There was no smile on Angelo's face when he said it.

"Joe and I've been talking—"

"About Carmie?" They both nodded. "No surprise." He looked at Doyle. "A real predicament."

"I'd say so."

"Yeah," Angelo wiped sweat from his face with the bottom of his T-shirt.

Morrison said, "You got to get out, Angelo. While you can still walk away."

"What if . . . what if I can finagle my way out of the Carmie thing . . . keep away from that play."

"You really think that's possible?" Morrison said. "At this point, after what Forte said to you, after what you told me last night? You think he's going to give you some sort of leave of absence after what he's said?"

Angelo looked from one to the other. "I guess not."

"And it's not just that," Doyle said. "You've compromised yourself."

"Anita?" He didn't need an answer. He looked up at the sky and swiveled his head from side to side, as if the motion would make the pieces fall into place. When he looked back at them there was almost a pulse in his eyes. "I'm compromised with *you*. How do you think I am with myself?"

"We know, we understand, that's why we want you to get out," Morrison told him. "The way you are now, you're a bad accident waiting to happen. And you know who comes out on the shit end of a bad accident with them."

Angelo shook his head. "Two, almost three years. I'm almost there. One more step, like Aldo says. Just a matter of steps."

"You got a life ahead of you, you're young—"

"Yeah, sure. Thanks." He looked over at Doyle.

"It's not all going down the drain, Angelo. If this Carmie works out the way we think it will—"

"An APB went out on Carmen DiSavio just before the second shift this morning, about seven A.M.," Morrison said.

Doyle nodded. "We think you can maybe bring down Aldo Forte, even Jimmy Pagnano. That would be a real nice bag."

"And how do I do that? Just because Aldo talked to me—"

"He's going to talk to you again if he wants you involved in taking down DiSavio." Doyle glanced at Morrison, then back to Angelo. "We'd like you to go wired."

"Hey, sure, why not. I've done everything else." But he didn't look like he sounded. And why should he, Morrison thought. ''Maybe I can even get him to say something compromising about Gussy Tuscano. Angelo the hero . . .''

"Yeah, well, we can get you rigged up in ten minutes," Doyle said. "If you got some clothes, that is.''

"Back in my car. It's in the museum parking lot, the other side of the drive.''

"You want to meet us?"

"No, thanks. I've had enough for one day. I'll take a ride."

Doyle said, "We got a safe place not too far from here. We'll have you rigged in time for your ten o'clock meeting."

"A weasel with a wire," Angelo muttered as they walked up the hill to Doyle's car.

"Think of it as another trapdoor," Morrison said.

JOHNNY NOLAN HAD FRUSTRATIONS of his own.

Over at Four, Johnny Nolan, with the help of Sergeant Gerherdt, had finally gotten Felice Swayze to admit what they already knew, that Vaughn Swayze was not dead. She told them it was Vaughn's little scheme, wanted everyone to think he was dead, get them off his back over in Detroit where he owed money and start a new life. There was the little thing about the two insurance policies, too, Nolan mentioned. That might be a nice stake for anybody just starting out in a new life.

Little Red gave up the game pretty fast too. He got the impression he stood to lose a lot. But it was not his scam, he claimed. He was just a friend of the family. He knew about it but tried to talk Vaughn out of it, told him it would never work but Vaughn wouldn't listen.

Nabasco brought to his attention that a morgue attendant described one of the funeral-parlor people who picked up Swayze's body as a short man with red hair, one he felt certain he could identify if need be. They would just have to have a line-up downstairs.

Little Red vowed his full cooperation.

The only problem was that neither Felice Swayze nor Red Ryan had any idea where Swayze was at the moment with the body that was supposed to be his but instead was Danny

Pack's. He had gone off to see if he could find an undertaker to take it off his hands or to see if he could switch it back with the guy at the morgue and get the original throwaway in order to carry off the original scam.

Nolan and Nabasco took what they had to the assistant state's attorney, figuring they at least had a nice little side case wrapped up. The ASA explained to them that no matter what happened, whether they got the original body back or not, the three—Swayze, his wife and his buddy—were facing nothing more than a misdemeanor theft charge. A human body was worth about forty-eight dollars for parts these days, he said, which figure amounted to nothing more than a misdemeanor. For a felony, the item had to be worth three hundred dollars. Since they had not filed false claims for insurance monies, there was no fraud, no attempted grand felony theft. In fact, they were out on their own recognizance. Maybe they could hold Ryan on a minor parole violation, but did they really want to, the ASA asked. Go to all that trouble? For what?

Nolan went back to the interrogation room where Felice Swayze was sitting, looking very tired and disheveled from her ordeal. She had been crying, which made a mess of her makeup, and there was no way to fix that, her purse having been impounded.

Nolan came back to the room and slammed the door behind him. He sat down across from her. "I went out on a limb. I struck a deal for you. They went for it." She looked at him appealingly. "We got this thing reduced to a misdemeanor. That's nothing. So just get hold of your husband somehow and tell him to return the body. Doesn't matter if he just leaves it somewhere and calls and tells us where it is. We're not going after him or you. Ryan, he might have a problem, breaking parole. They'll have to make a judgment call on that one. Out of my hands." He smiled at her.

"I can leave now?"

Nolan got up. "Yes. But I'm going to need an address where we can reach you."

"I'll be at Red's place, where you found us."

Nolan handed her his card. "Don't leave town without letting me know. And tell your husband when he shows up, the party's over. We want the body, we need it. He should call me or try this other number." He took the card back and scribbled the hotline number on the back of it.

She stood up then. "My God, I'm a *disaster*." She was wiping at the streaked eye shadow and mottled makeup.

"You're far from a disaster," he said looking at her long tan legs, then up to her halter.

"You're real sweet."

He opened the door for her. "Here, I'll walk you back out front. You can pick up your belongings."

"I really appreciate this. Officer Nolan, isn't it?"

"Right, Johnny Nolan. You can forget the officer." He gave her a smile again as she moved past him out into the corridor.

✤47

"YOU MADE IT," ALDO FORTE SAID WHEN ANGELO WALKED into the Amalfi, where the *capo* was sitting in his corner with cronies. A deck of cards was on the table but no one was playing, they were drinking coffee and talking. Aldo sounded sarcastic, as if Angelo were late instead of ten minutes early.

"You think I wouldn't? I ever not come when called?" Angelo had on his ingratiating smile, perfected over the last couple of years. Aldo, he thought uneasily, looked gloomier, more on edge than usual.

"Get out of here," Aldo said to the others, stressing it with a sweep of his arm. "I gotta talk to my boy here. Sit down, Angelo."

"What's up?" Angelo asked after dropping into one of the vacated chairs.

"Things are happening."

Angelo was distinctly uncomfortable wearing the little microphone no larger than the size of a dime and no thicker than a pair of them, and was acutely aware of it as he was of Aldo Forte sitting across the table from him. "Don't worry, you'll get used to it," the technician had said when he was putting it in place. "Won't even know it's there." Angelo remembered how he had felt when the tech was installing it, applying some super-stickum to the front of his scrotum with one hand while Angelo had to hold his penis up. Staring up at the ceiling, he had avoided the eyes of Doyle and Morrison.

The technician said not to worry, that Angelo could just peel it off like a piece of Velcro when he was done with it. Thinking where it was, the image of Velcro being pulled apart didn't sound too good. Where they were putting it was the safest place, the technician had told him. Never find it in the closest of pat-downs, probably even survive a strip search unless somebody lifted up his dick. And there were no wires. Thanks to modern technology it was activated by a signal, like the remote control on a television but more complex. The tiny activator was secured to the back of his wristwatch and looked like nothing more than a small blister the same gold color as the watch; all he had to do was press the watch to his wrist twice in quick succession and the recording would start—twice, not once. That was to avoid inadvertently starting it by bumping his wrist into something. Once started, the microdisc in his private parts could not be shut off and would record for up to four hours. They had tried the starting procedure a couple of times.

Which is what Angelo now did as he lazed back on two legs of the chair, his hands crossed and resting on his stomach. "Things seem to be happening a lot around here lately."

"To our misfortune, unfortunately." Sometimes Aldo had a way with words, Angelo was thinking. "But hopefully things are going to work out soon. That is the hope of everybody concerned."

"So what is it I can do for you?" That was the way you put it, talking to Aldo, the way he liked to hear it: *What can I do for you*, not *What do you want*.

Aldo held up both hands in front of him as if he were stopping traffic. "Later. We got a date." Aldo looked at his watch. "Get yourself some coffee. I'll let you know."

FIFTEEN MINUTES LATER THEY were in the back of Aldo's car, with Danny Isso behind the wheel, and heading west on Grand Avenue.

"Where are we going?" Angelo would not normally have asked such a question but under the circumstances he thought he would give it a try.

Aldo looked over at him quickly but did not say anything at first, then: "You got plans, kid? You can't enjoy a nice leisurely drive in the city?" Aldo was also fishing in his sport-coat pockets until he came up with a small yellow Post-It pad that he had taken to carrying lately, and then a pen from his inside coat pocket. He scribbled on the pad, peeled off the sheet and stuck it on the back of the seat in front of Angelo. Angelo read the shaky script: *We dont talk in the car. You know better.*

After reading it Angelo quickly nodded. "Sorry."

Aldo reached over and stripped the yellow sheet from the seat, crumpled it and stuffed it into his side pocket. "So how's the girlfriend?"

"Fine . . ."

"Hot and heavy's the way I hear it." Aldo had a smile now.

"Well, in a good way." It was not a topic Angelo wanted to pursue.

"A man needs one good woman," Aldo said, "and a dozen ba-a-a-d ones." He broke into laughter.

They had turned south on Ashland Avenue, heading, Angelo figured, to Little Italy around Twenty-fourth Street. As they passed Lake Street Angelo could see out to the west the red brick high-rises of the Henry Horner Homes. Just beyond and to the south were the Rockwell Gardens, which he could not see, but he thought abruptly of the little girl who was hiding somewhere far from there. Latrona. Twelve years old and a price on her head. There were other kids in the street who should have been in school. Hanging out. She'd probably be one of them if she was still in the neighborhood. She'd be *lucky* if she got back to this . . .

Angelo had figured right. The car came to a stop in front of a small family restaurant on Oakley near Twenty-fifth Street. The sign on the door said *Lunch 11:30-2:30—Dinner 5:00-9:00*. It was not quite eleven, but the front door was unlocked and Aldo led the way inside. Danny Isso stayed with the car, although it was as safe here as it would be in the VIP parking area of CIA headquarters.

The place was empty, the tables set with white tablecloths and little vases with artificial flowers and wicker baskets holding long thin Italian breadsticks in waxed-paper wrappers. Not even a bus-boy or a waitress was stirring. Aldo led the way back to a little corridor. There were three doors, the one on the left marked *Men*, on the right *Women* and straight back *Private*, which Aldo opened.

It was not to an office. It led into a private dining room with a round table that could seat eight, outfitted like the ones up front.

Sitting at the table were Joe Alessi and Jimmy Pagnano.

They stood up when Aldo and Angelo came in. Aldo and Alessi engaged in the customary embrace. Pagnano held out a hand to Angelo, which he shook. "How's it goin', kid? Been behaving yourself?"

"Always," Angelo said.

"That was good times down in Florida. Gotta do that again sometimes, catch us some tarpon next time." Angelo tried to join him in the good humor, but all he could think of was what was Joe-sep doing there.

Alessi smiled at Angelo. "How's my boy?"

"Fine."

"You don't look so hot."

Angelo shrugged. "I went jogging this morning. Maybe I overdid it."

"Keep in shape, that's a good thing. Don't overdo it, though. Don't be one of them health nuts. I don't want you takin' my Anita to one of them vegetable places or fern bars or juice bars or whatever they call them. Only the best, Angelo. Remember that." Alessi turned to Forte. "I gotta keep teachin' the kid. Get him dressed right, into the right places, get him to order the right things. I don't want my daughter goin' with a mope." He turned to Angelo, big smile. "But you aren't a mope, Angelo, you're an all-right guy."

Angelo didn't think he should say anything. Something was coming.

"Anita said she'd like to see you later. We was talking about you this morning. I told her I was seein' you and maybe you could come back when we finish up. That'd make her happy."

"Sure." He looked at Aldo.

"No problem," Aldo said.

"So let's get this business over with." Joe-sep yelled, and a short, skinny young man appeared. "Get these gentlemen a drink and then be sure nobody bothers us, until I tell you."

Aldo Forte said he would have a scotch on the rocks. Angelo looked over at Pagnano. "What's that you're drinking?"

"A crock of vodka . . . anchovy olives."

"Give me one of those," Angelo said.

Aldo got to the point. They knew the police were looking for Carmie. They did not know how much the police had on Carmie killing Danny Pack. But if it was enough for them to be looking for him, it was enough for them *not* to be able to find him. So the decision had been made, the imprimatur stamped on it. Joe-sep nodded his agreement through Aldo's narration. Why Aldo could talk here and not in his own car or in his own club or on any telephone you didn't have to drop a quarter in first was not clear to Angelo. It was like Gussy Tuscano's. Some places in Aldo's world were safe. All others weren't. It was where he *felt* safe.

Aldo then said words that Angelo wished had never come from Aldo's mouth and traveled their path to Angelo's private parts. "Carmie is Joe's man. He's been with the Alessi group for . . . how long, Joe-sep? Eight, ten years?"

"I brought him along at least that long," Joe-sep said, shaking his head.

Shut up, Angelo was intoning to himself . . . *don't say any-*

thing more, Joe-sep . . . Angelo knocked over the glass of water that the skinny kid had brought with the drink. It spilled
across the table and everybody jumped back like it was acid.

"Sorry," Angelo said. He tried to look embarrassed.

"No big deal," Joe-sep said. "It's just water. You spill the
vodka, that's serious." Everybody laughed.

As a diversion it did not work. Joe-sep went on to describe
in detail how Carmen DiSavio was to leave this life that evening, giving proper credit to Jimmy Pagnano as the architect
of the plan, which was painstakingly simple and brutal. Jimmy
would run the show.

As HE RODE BACK out to Elmwood Park with Joe Alessi, Angelo was battling a mix of feelings. He had not expected Anita's father to be around, to be talking, to be captured on
Angelo's little crotch-corder. In his head it was just to be Aldo
going down, maybe Pagnano later. Not Joe-sep. *Not* Anita's
father.

He thought about losing the tape. The little disc . . . right
now it felt like a white hot brand on the thin wrinkled skin of
his scrotum.

And what about his part in this? He needed to be here as a
final test . . . one more time and he'd be made . . .

ANITA WAS THERE WAITING for him. "Told you I'd bring him
back," Joe-sep said as they walked into the family room,
where she was watching television.

God . . . she looked more beautiful than ever, Angelo
thought. She gave her father a peck on the cheek and him a
kiss on the mouth. "I'm goin' back out," Joe-sep said. "Behave yourselves."

On the patio Anita said, "I just wanted to see you." She
looked out toward the flowerbeds that surrounded the yard.
"Oh, and I told daddy this morning that I was in love with
you." A coy smile. "And I told him you were the best fuck
I ever had."

He didn't smile back. "If you did, you'd be whispering it
to me in my casket."

"Well, I did skip that part. But I did tell him I loved you. I told him I never felt this way about anybody before. And that was the truth."

Angelo said nothing.

"What's the matter, Angelo?"

"Nothing."

"I mean, you love me, like you said . . ."

He nodded.

"So what's the matter, darling?"

"I guess I don't know how to handle good news."

✦48

DOYLE AND MORRISON WERE AT THE APARTMENT ALONG with the technicians when Angelo arrived, stuck his hand in the side pocket of his windbreaker and came out with a round device in his palm. "Which one of you wants this?" He looked from Doyle to Morrison. "It's all there."

The technician said he would take it and, holding it like an emerald, walked off to another room.

Angelo sat down and stroked his eyes with his thumb and index finger. "Carmie goes tonight. It's all on the tape." He looked up at them. "If it worked, that is."

"And you?" Morrison asked.

"I'm invited to the party. Representing my boss, who needless to say has other plans for the evening. Jimmy Pagnano, he put together the arrangements at the request of his boss."

"Alessi?" Morrison said.

"Yeah, you guys are getting a bonus in this thing. He was at the meet. Just the four of us in the backroom of a spaghetti house in Little Italy." Angelo shook his head as if he still didn't believe it had happened. "And he talked a lot."

The technician stepped back into the room. "Clear as a

bell," he said, smiling at Angelo. "Coming through loud and clear. Good job."

Angelo looked away from him, then back at Morrison and Doyle. "So you get Joe Alessi thrown in . . ."

The technician said, "I fast-forwarded to the middle. Couple of different voices coming in, but sharp and true. And to the end. Good there, too. Some girl, soft voice. Sounds like she likes you, old buddy."

God, he'd even recorded Anita . . . "Look, just go play the goddamn thing."

The technician quickly did and they listened, Angelo identifying the voices.

> ALESSI: Here's how it's going down. Carmie this morning was given word that the heat is still on but things are under way to get it taken care of, he shouldn't worry. He should keep under the covers for a few more days. Carmie is parked out in Forest Park at a buddy's place.
>
> PAGNANO: I told Joe-sep, Aldo, we can take him down at that Prime House Meat Market tonight . . . turn Carmie into a carcass of his own . . . (laughter).
>
> ALESSI: I talked to Carmie this morning, told him while there's still some heat it'd be a good idea maybe if he got himself out of state for a few days, go up to his place in Wisconsin and wait it out there. Hey, I said, he could help out the family at the same time. You know . . . there's a cash delivery being made at the Prime Meat tonight, half of it for Aldo and half for me. We want to see that cash out of circulation for a few days, too. I told Carmie that him and Angelo here will make the pick-up at the Prime tonight. He's to get my share and Angelo will get yours, Aldo. Then he's to take mine with him and stash it in Wisconsin until I tell him it's safe to come back . . .

"I'm supposed to pick Carmie up tonight," Angelo said. "They'll tell me where later but it's supposed to be around ten, I know that much. We go over to the Prime, where of course there is no money . . . just Pagnano, and we whack him there. And nobody ever sees Carmen DiSavio again. That's the script.''

"Where is this Prime House?'' Morrison said.

"Little Italy, I told you about it before. Where Pagnano suggested they make sausage out of Danny Pack's body when they get it.''

"They have anything to say about Pack?''

"It didn't come up. And because it didn't I got the feeling maybe it's not a problem anymore. Maybe he's already a chain of Polish sausage links.''

"So where exactly is this meat market, which I am making a note never to patronize?'' Morrison asked.

"It's on Blue Island just north of Twenty-third Street.''

"You've been there before?''

Angelo looked hard at Morrison. "I've been there. I know the layout of the place, if that's what you mean.''

"You figuring on intercepting DiSavio there?'' Doyle asked Morrison.

"Wait,'' Angelo said. "You guys always want to call the shots. At least let this one be mine. I got a plan . . .''

"Which is?'' Morrison said.

"Look, this is it for me, I want to be damn sure something comes out of it. I don't want all this to go down the chutes because you guys end up without enough legal shit to send these guys away, something gets fucked up in the system. It's happened, you know.'' He took a deep breath. "You can't do it without me, comes down to that. Carmie's an unknown commodity, who knows if you can turn him? You grab him, save his ass, he listens to the tape, maybe he doesn't buy it. Face it, Carmie's been with Alessi for a long time. He feels he's one of the trusted. You don't have him, you don't have a case . . . because you can't send these guys away for *talking* about knocking somebody off. Right?''

Angelo did not wait for an answer. "But I've got a plan that can't miss. You can take *everybody* down if there's an actual attempt on his life. And if there is a real convincing attempt, and Carmie sees all the marbles on the table, you got a whole lot better chance of convincing him his career in the Outfit is over.''

Doyle looked skeptical. "I don't—"

"Let me finish. You don't do *any* intercepting. You let *me* deliver him." He gestured toward the door to the room in the apartment, where the technician had gone. "Get that guy out here."

Doyle walked to the door and called to the technician.

"He can, I'm sure, rig me with something you can pick up outside the Prime House. You can hear what's going on inside. Soon as it's made clear to Carmie what's going to happen to him, I stop it. I say something, some word, a signal, whatever, and you guys come in. I can stop Pagnano. I'll have a gun. I can do it.''

"Very iffy," Morrison said.

"Everything I been doing for the past two years has been very iffy."

"What if you can't stop Pagnano?"

"Carmie gets killed, you get him for murder one, not attempted murder.''

"What about you?" Doyle said.

"I can take care of myself." Did he believe it? "I stayed a step ahead this far. One more time . . . just let me handle it.'' He paused, then said to Doyle: "You owe me that much.''

Doyle looked at Morrison. "It'll all be in your hands, Joe. This is local. The Bureau can't be associated with it.''

"I know. We'll just have to try to do our local best.''

"I didn't mean it that way, Joe.''

"Okay, okay. We're all a little edgy." Except Angelo, who seemed to be off in his own world.

Doyle turned to the technician. "Fix him up so we can hear him loud and clear at least a block away.''

Morrison then went to the telephone, pulling his spiral notebook out of the back pocket of his pants and opening it to what he wanted. After four seemingly interminable rings he said, "Franco, we got a break. Meet me at Four, say forty-five minutes from now. I'll explain when I get there. Do me a favor, find out who's working the third shift. We're going to need some bodies. Soon as I hang up I'm calling Harkness, get some more help from downtown.''

He found Harkness's number and dialed it.

When he got back to the others, the technician was saying, "This time it won't be so . . . private." He had a smug smile. "We just attach it to your chest." He jabbed a finger at the center of his own.

"Takes all the fun out of it for you," Angelo said. "Too bad." He turned to Morrison: "What say we make this real simple . . . you have somebody watching each end of the alley that leads to the loading dock in back of the Prime House. That's where we'll come in. There's a door next to it. Inside there's another door to your right that goes into the store itself, which is what you *don't* want. There's a flight of stairs to the left, maybe ten, twelve, and a corridor. Down toward the end of the hall there's a set of big double doors, swinging doors. Inside is the processing room, you know, the chop house, the grinders and the coolers. That's where Pagnano's going to be, where I'll be bringing Carmie. So when you see us pull up in the car . . . I'll park it right at the loading dock . . . and go in, you get ready to move in. You wait and when you hear me say whatever the buzzword is, you move in. And I give you Pagnano, your early Christmas present.''

Morrison got up to leave Angelo to his wiring. As he started out Angelo grabbed him by the arm. "I won't be seeing you again before this goes down.''

"No." They walked to the door. "You got balls, Angelo. Like I told you before, I wouldn't want to be in your place.''

"You're right, you wouldn't want to be.''

✦49

THEY STAKED OUT BOTH ENDS OF THE ALLEY. MORRISON AND Norelli and McCabe and Wilson were in the back of a yellow Ryder rented truck that was not owned by Ryder but by the CPD, especially rigged for surveillance, its interior outfitted with communications equipment. It was parked on Twenty-third Street near the northern mouth of the alley closest to the loading dock of the Prime House Meat Market. At the south end of the alley four other detectives were in the back of a van that bore the bold lettering

WOLNER'S ROOFING SERVICE
Serving Chicagoland Since 1958

on both sides and was replete with folded-up extension ladders on the roof and a scrawl of gang graffiti spray-painted on the rear doors for urban special effects.

A block away, on Twenty-fifth Street, another car was parked with a young couple in it, talking, laughing, listening to the radio tuned to a soft rock station, apparently having a good time, waiting for the call over the other radio to move in and station themselves on Blue Island across the street from the front entrance to the Prime House Meat Market. The borrowed technician . . . no name . . . from the FBI and a CPD communications man were with Morrison and the others in the truck.

They heard the crackly transmission from Angelo's wire five minutes before they saw the car turn off Blue Island onto Twenty-third Street. It kept getting clearer, until by the time the car finally made the turn it sounded as if Angelo and Carmie were in the back of the truck with them.

Carmie was talking about his place up in Wisconsin. Angelo

348

was telling him he preferred someplace warmer, if he ever got enough money it would be in Florida or Arizona, he said, someplace where he could get away from the Chicago winters. Carmie was telling him about snowmobiling when Morrison and Norelli, looking out the slots in the side of the Ryder truck, saw them get out of the car and start up the few steps to the door next to the loading dock. They watched as the two figures went in, and then Morrison turned to the others. "Okay, get ready." To the CPD technician at the radio: "Tell the others they're inside."

Frank Wilson, sitting near the back of the truck, had his hand on one of the two handles protruding from the shaft of the strange-looking, uniquely balanced battering ram, its weighted blunt head resting on the floor. The drug-busters called it the "porker," an invention mothered by Narcotics necessity that enabled one man to bust open just about any door with no more than two or three thrusts. Angelo had said he would leave the door unlocked, but if it was awkward he might not be able to and they should come prepared. It was an industrial door, he had told them, but one that opened inward and therefore they should be able to break through without too much trouble.

Carmie was carrying on about how pissy some of the farmers could be up there if you cut across their land on your snowmobile . . . as if their snow were some kind of private crop, or their cows were going to get run over or something. Suddenly they heard him say, "Jimmy, hey, Jimmy, what're you doing here?"

Morrison motioned upward with his hand at Eddie McCabe, and McCabe slid up the back door to the trunk, the grating noise of steel rollers in their tracks making more noise than they would have liked. Wilson grabbed hold of the second handle of the ram with his other hand.

The signal they had agreed on was Angelo's saying: "Carmie, you are a real asshole." Angelo figured in Carmie's case it would be an easy fit. They then would move quickly as he would make his move inside.

"Well, you never know where I'm gonna pop up, Carmie. That's part of my charm."

"Yeah, well, charm's always been one of your big qualities . . ." Carmie's voice, followed by a staccato laugh. "It's kinda dark out in case you're plannin' to play a little baseball." Carmie's voice again. It would have made more sense to the people in the truck if they could have seen the Louisville Slugger lying on the butcher's chopping block next to Pagnano. "The money here?"

"What money, Carmie?"

"The money Joe-sep wanted me to hold for him. You didn't know about that?"

"There's no money, Carmie."

"Whatta you talkin' about—"

"There's a problem." Angelo's voice.

"Hey, Jimmy, what the fuck's goin' on?" A scuffling sound. "Who the fuck you shovin', Angelo?"

"You fucked up, Carmie." Pagnano's voice. "Fucked up real bad."

"Hey, wait a minute, Jimmy, no—"

A splat and then a scream and sounds of scuffling again and a weaker "Jimmy," followed by another splat and another, duller scream.

Morrison and Norelli looked at each other in panic. Where was *Angelo's* voice, they both were thinking. Where was "Carmie, you are a real asshole"?

Instead it was Pagnano again. "Here, Angelo, do your stuff, finish him. Beat his head in. Pretend you're José Canseco." There was merriment in Pagnano's voice. There was also groaning the recorder was picking up in the background. Then suddenly—"Hey, what're you doing, Angelo? Watch where you're swinging that thing, what the Christ . . . Angelo, you fucking nuts—" The sound of another splat, not as pronounced as the other. "Why you miserable asshole . . ." Pagnano's voice, panicky now, fading on the tape as if he was backing away. "You crazy . . . I'll kill you . . ."

"Let's go," Morrison said. They piled out of the truck. The

radio operator was flipping switches, telling those in the other vehicles to get moving.

They heard the shot just as they got to the four concrete steps leading up to the door, muffled but there was no question what it was. Back in the truck the report of the shot almost burst the eardrums of the technicians listening to the tape.

The second shot came as Morrison threw open the door. Angelo had left it unlocked, like he said he would. Wilson pitched the battering ram off to the side. Morrison and Norelli were in the front, taking a quick look in before exposing themselves. But there was nothing down the dark corridor except the light coming through the two panes of glass on the swinging doors near the end of it, and a mix of noises coming from inside. They moved quickly down the stairs toward the beams of light.

Morrison shouted "Police," and it echoed loudly down the empty hall. Suddenly the two doors came open and a figure was in the hallway. From the room, light poured out and then shuttered dark and bright like on an old silent movie screen as the doors swung back and forth. Norelli called out "*Freeze, police.*" But the figure turned toward them, raising his hand. The fluttering light reflected off the gun in his hand as the other hand came up, grabbed and aimed it. Knees were bent, in a crouch, the figure statue-still.

Morrison and Norelli, in front, dropped to the floor, McCabe and Wilson behind them were still standing as the corridor erupted in gunfire. The figure went backward, crashing to the floor.

Morrison was the first to reach the body, lying motionless, head tilted at a slight angle, eyes staring up at the wall, the gun still clutched in the right hand. Norelli kicked open one of the swinging doors and lurched inside. Carmie was sitting on the floor propped up against a cooler door, a huge yellowish welt on the front of his baldish head, blood coming from it down his face and onto his clothes, another welt on his forearm, which was draped across his stomach bent at an odd angle. He was conscious but dazed and groaning. In the back of the room next to the large butcher-block table, Jimmy Pagnano was on the floor, legs clutched to his chest. Blood was coming from both knees.

Morrison was on one knee beside the body in the hall. "Jesus, God, Angelo . . ." Angelo did not hear his words.

The other detectives were inside the building now too. Norelli told one of them to radio for ambulances. Morrison was still on one knee, shaking his head, as if he could deny what had happened.

THE BODIES WERE TAKEN away, Carmen DiSavio and Jimmy Pagnano to Cook County Hospital. Angelo Franconi, pronounced dead by the MD from the Medical Examiner's office, to the morgue. Morrison and Norelli had reported to the field lieutenant. Jim Harkness had been called and was on hand; so was Deputy Superintendent Flanagan; so was Morrison's boss Ted Goldman. Outside were mobile news units from television stations and beat reporters from the newspapers. Morrison had managed to find a telephone upstairs and called Tim Doyle to tell him what had happened.

Harkness had never seen Morrison like this . . . ashen, clearly shaken. "Let me tend to a couple of things," he said, "and then I'm getting you out of here." Morrison did not argue. Norelli said he would write up the report for them and talk to whomever from 11th and State that might be poking around with bothersome questions.

Morrison stayed behind the yellow crime-scene tapes that now festooned the entire area. Flimsy as they were, they still provided a fortress of protection from the media. He was standing by himself there when he caught sight of Holly Stryker out among the newspeople. She was looking at him but not trying to get his attention.

He walked over and ducked under the strand of yellow tape. She saw the same pallor in his face that Harkness had noted. "Haven't seen a lot of you on the front pages lately," he said.

"I told you, I don't write for the alderman anymore."

"I know." He put his hand on her shoulder and bent closer to her, and as he did he caught the scent of her, of what she was wearing, and thought of that night in her apartment. He said quietly, "The story's over, the other one, the one you stopped writing about. But I owe you one. Here's your one-up on the competition. The guy who got shot tonight . . . he was one of us, not one of them." She looked very surprised. "It'll all come out . . . but you heard it here first, as they say in the *Inquirer*."

She started to say something but he put up a silencing finger. "Nose around, you'll get the story," and ducked back under the crime-scene tape.

Harkness had returned now and they left together. On the way he told Morrison the news that he had just learned they had picked up Aldo Forte at the Amalfi Club and Joe Alessi at his home. Rousted them, was the old-fashioned way Harkness put it. Both of them were being escorted to 11th and State, might already be there. Lot of lawyers would be stirring around this night and over the weekend, Harkness said.

Morrison asked about the girl, Joe Alessi's daughter, the girl Angelo loved. Harkness said he didn't know anything about that except there was a scene at the Alessi house when the old man was led out in cuffs. The girl was in for a terrible surprise, much bigger than watching her daddy being arrested and whisked off into the night, he said, and shook his head.

Morrison already knew that.

When they got to the parking lot at Area Four, where Morrison had left his car, Harkness offered to take him home or wherever Morrison wanted to go, but Morrison said no thanks, he just wanted to be alone, and drove off by himself.

When he got home he called Doyle again and told him he would go down to the morgue the first thing in the morning and take care of the identification and the papers regarding Angelo. There was nobody else to notify, no relatives, but there were the formalities, always the damn formalities. He said he would like to get it over with early before they opened the place. When he hung up, he drained off a glass of straight Jack Daniels and set his clock radio for four hours later. For no good reason he was thinking there were not going to be a lot of strawberry shakes in Latrona Meek's future just before he fell into a deep, exhausted sleep.

✦50

ON SATURDAY MORNING, EARLY, IT TOOK ABOUT A HALF-hour to drive the twelve miles from Rogers Park on the north side to the morgue on the city's west side. There was none of the glut of weekday traffic with its starts and stops and lane-jumpers and horn-blasters on Lake Shore Drive.

Morrison had the window rolled down and did not mind the damp, chilly wind blowing in off Lake Michigan. Autumn had arrived, the summer having switched itself off like a lamp a few days earlier, the way the seasons inevitably seemed to change in Chicago.

It was still too early in the morning for the soccer players or softball teams or picnickers to take over the green sprawl of parks on either side of the drive, although not for the joggers and health-walkers and bicyclists who made their way along the perimeter paths undeterred by the dim overcast day and the weatherman's threats of a thunderstorm. Morrison barely noticed them, even the robotic power-walkers, fists jabbing away at invisible midsections as they strode, just as he barely noticed the two-foot waves breaking off the gunmetal lake to his left or the palisades of high-rises on the right.

His car radio, by habit, was tuned to an all-sports station. People calling in were from the southside steelworkers' school of classic Chicagoese . . . *thes* coming out *das* and *of* lost to an elided *a*, as in "He's fulla . . ." Most sentences ended in *ya know*.

The host chattered, "Keep them calls comin' in, sports fans." Punctuated by "This is Nick from Bensenville, how's it goin' out there, Nick?" or "We got Petey on the line calling from his car phone here in Chi-town. What's on your mind, Petey?" And when Nick or Petey finished, "So long, buddy" or "Thanks for the call, buddy." Everybody was this man's buddy.

Not me, Morrison thought as he reached the downtown area and left the Drive to the accompaniment of Wally from Berwyn raging about fishhooks in the pockets of the Bears' owners and other miseries and indignities the organization was forcing Wally to endure this football season. Enough. Morrison flicked off the radio and skirted the eastern and southern rims of the Loop, catching the westbound Eisenhower Expressway for the last leg of his morning journey.

Finally he pulled around to the parking area next to the loading dock on the west side of the morgue, avoiding the main entrance and public waiting room on the other side. Inside he flashed his badge and I.D. card at the attendant behind the counter in the area separated by picture windows from the "admitting room," which actually handled both arrivals and departures. He continued to the end of the counter, turned and followed the hall down to the office where the CPD detectives assigned to the morgue spent most of their time.

During his days in Homicide Morrison would have known them by their first names and they would have greeted him with "Hey, Joe, how's it going" or "What's happenin' out there," but the two on duty this morning were new faces to him. He told them who he was and what he wanted.

"You want us to gussy it up and bring it to the viewing room?" the older of the two detectives asked. *Gussy it up* meaning to take it out of its black plastic bodywrap and cover it with a nice clean white sheet.

It—Morrison's insides squirmed with the sound of the word. Last night Angelo—alive, talking, thinking, feeling—now a cold rigid carcass lying on a shelf of steel . . . an *it*.

"The viewing room?" the detective repeated. "Want us to bring it there for you?"

"No, I'll just do it back there," motioning toward the corridor that led to the admitting room and the entrance to the cooler. "It's a formality . . ."

"Whatever you say."

The cool air and the odor hit them the moment the detective

opened the huge refrigerator door to the cavernous warehouse. Inside the eeriness descended, brought on by a silence punctuated by a metallic or muffled echoing from somewhere in its vastness and, of course, the awareness that stocked on these warehouse shelves were human bodies wrapped in glossy plastic sheets.

"Busy last night," the detective said to Morrison, "four homicides, one suicide, two traffic, five who-knows-what yet. September's a busy month, nothing like August, though, and being a Friday night and all. 'Course you know that."

"Yes."

The morgue detective handed one of the workers a casenumber slip and the man disappeared down the aisle closest to them. "Should be handy," the detective said, "coming in last night." Morrison said nothing and the two of them just stood there in awkward silence. A minute or so later the worker returned pushing a stainless-steel gurney that left a rattling echo in its wake and stopped it in front of them. He took hold of the top end of the black plastic sheet and yanked it back, which made a kind of crackling sound, revealing a head and upper torso. Enough for Morrison to make the identification, but he continued to stare down at the terribly still face.

The detective finally said, "This it?"

"Oh," Morrison said. "Yeah." He turned and the detective followed him out of the cooler and back to the counter off the admitting room.

Morrison forced himself to take care of the rest of the formalities. When he finished he moved outside and noticed the patches of fresh puddles in the parking lot and the lingering smell of rain in the air that told him it had stormed during the brief time he was inside . . . one of those quick Chicago squalls that lashed the city and disappeared. He was looking down at the rainwashed pavement, walking back toward his car, and so did not at first see Tim Doyle open the door and get out of the car next to his.

There was still a faint sprinkle in the air and the rush of

rain had left some abnormally cold winds swirling about. "Get everything taken care of?"

Morrison looked up quickly, then relaxed, seeing who it was. "Done," he said. "You didn't have to come down."

"I wanted to. Joe . . . it's tough . . . some things just don't turn out right. I know how I feel, I can guess how much worse it is for you."

"He never fired a shot, Tim."

"I know. I've seen the reports."

"He just stood there, like he was going to, but he never did. He never had any intention to."

Doyle handed Morrison a white envelope. "After you left yesterday Angelo said to be on the safe side he ought to give a deposition on his involvement in the case . . . what he knew, the wires, the whole thing. Then he wrote something and said I should give it to you if something happened to him."

Morrison shook his head. "Jesus, Tim . . . I killed him. I didn't know it was him, if I thought anything, which I don't know whether I did or not at the time because it all happened so fast, I thought it was Pagnano. But I still killed him. . . ."

"You don't know that, Joe. Four guys were shooting. You might not even have hit him."

Morrison looked down at the glistening wet blacktop and then back at Doyle. "I know it. I can't explain it but somehow I know . . ." He slit the envelope with his finger and read the note inside. Just like Angelo, it got right to the point:

Joe,

> *You were right, you would not want to be in my place. You didn't want to ask me the question, but I'm answering it anyway.*

> *I did kill somebody. I killed Roy Echols down in Florida.*

> *I tried to justify it to myself but I found out you can't.*

> *And you know. I was responsible for that young black kid's death when they killed Manny Peters. Never mind how or why. I was.*

> *Maybe you think it's out of place, me giving advice*

to a cop like you, but here it is. Always have a trapdoor, Joe.

Your friend,
Angelo

Morrison looked up at Doyle, kicked at the slippery pavement. "His girlfriend ought to know what Angelo really felt, who he *was*. How much he cared about her . . ."

Doyle nodded, but didn't need to add that to reveal the Bureau's operation was out of the question.

"Well, I'm going to pick up my kids; it's my weekend with them. Then I think I'm going to take some time off. I might go out to New York."

"Why New York?"

"I want to see *Guys and Dolls*. I hear I'm the spitting image of the cop in it."

They turned then as they heard a car pull into the lot and come to a squealing halt a few yards behind them.

Johnny Nolan got out and hurried around to the other side to open the door. A pair of legs in black nylons and three-inch heels swiveled out of the passenger side. The woman they belonged to was wearing a silky black dress cut above the knees, a pair of spaghetti straps holding it up. Nolan called out, "Hi, Joe," and led her over to them.

"This is Mrs. Swayze," he said. "You know, Mrs. Vaughn Swayze." To her: "Joe Morrison, detective." Doyle nodded and said, "Tim Doyle."

She looked . . . frightened? Sad? Nervous? It was hard to tell, but she managed a little smile. "Nice to meet you," she said.

"She has to go in and take a look," Nolan said. "We . . . found a body late last night that, well, that might be her husband." He looked at her and Doyle. "Could you excuse Joe and me for a second?"

Nolan and Morrison took a few steps away from them, and Nolan said, "They found him in a van, rented from Alamo . . . ring a bell? . . . over on Canal Street just east of the

Ryan Expressway. Empty area, railroad tracks and a couple of abandoned factories." Nolan shook his head. "Been there awhile. He was a mess, slashed up and down. Somebody was either berserk or really hated the guy. One of the goriest I ever saw. There were I.D.'s in the van belonging to Swayze. She don't know it yet, but I figure this is just a formality. You down here for the thing last night?"

"Yeah, the thing last night."

"You know, the goofy thing, this Swayze guy, he would've walked away from this whole thing. All we had against him was a petty misdemeanor. He could've gone back to Detroit like nothing happened. Nobody would've come after him. And nobody knows where the hell the body he got is." Nolan shook his head. "Crazy, isn't it?"

"Yeah, crazy . . . You better get her in there before she catches pneumonia, standing around here dressed like that."

Morrison said goodbye to Doyle and walked behind Nolan and Mrs. Swayze back toward the doorway to the admitting room of the morgue. He could not help hearing the conversation, Nolan saying, "As I said in the car, Felice, this won't take too long. I know it's a very unpleasant thing and I just want you to know if there is anything, anything at all I can do to make it easier, you just say the word . . ."

"Thank you, officer."

"Right, but forget the officer stuff. Johnny's just fine."

"Johnny," she said, and nodded. "Okay." Felice Swayze paused for a moment to reach down and pull up the strap to one of her slingback pumps. "I'm very nervous about this . . . Johnny."

"I surely can understand that, Felice. You know, afterwards . . . this is going to be a very disconcerting experience one way or the other . . . well, maybe I could take you somewhere and get you something to relax you a little. I'm off. My shift's over, I mean. This is all on my own time. I think it might help. Up to you, of course."

"Why, that's real thoughtful of you," she said. "That might be very nice. I appreciate it."

Morrison reached the wire-mesh trashbasket just outside the

door and stopped there. He heard Nolan saying as he held the door for Felice Swayze, ''I know this place up on the north side, it's called Little Mo's, it opens real early on weekends . . .''

Morrison tore the note from Angelo Franconi into little pieces and watched them flutter into the garbage can. His last words were nobody else's business. He wanted to go. Right or wrong, that's the way he wanted it.

As he was walking back toward his car, he found himself trying to remember the words to the title song of *Guys and Dolls*.